Karel Jonás

Bohemian Made Easy

A practical Bohemian course for English-speaking people

Karel Jonás

Bohemian Made Easy
A practical Bohemian course for English-speaking people

ISBN/EAN: 9783337390402

Printed in Europe, USA, Canada, Australia, Japan

Cover: Foto ©Andreas Hilbeck / pixelio.de

More available books at **www.hansebooks.com**

BOHEMIAN MADE EASY.

A PRACTICAL BOHEMIAN COURSE

for English-speaking people.

By CHARLES JONAS,

late U. S. Consul at Prague, author of the first Dictionary of the

Bohemian and English languages.

RACINE, WIS. 1890.

TO THE HONORABLE

GROVER CLEVELAND,

EX-PRESIDENT OF THE UNITED STATES,

THIS LITTLE WORK IS DEDICATED,

AS A SLIGHT TOKEN OF PROFOUND

RESPECT AND ADMIRATION,

BY THE

AUTHOR.

Why this book has been written.

The answer to such a question is simple: because there is a demand for it. And whenever there is a demand, the supply is sure to come.

Not a year passes, but numbers apply to divers booksellers and publishers for some handy book to give them a practical knowledge of the Bohemian language or to serve as a proper introduction to a study thereof.

Who are the applicants? They are business men, clerks, salesmen and travelers, druggists and physicians, ministers, teachers and lawyers. They live and follow their vocations in localities where a large fraction of the population speaks the Bohemian language; they perceive the advantage which a knowledge of Bohemian, or even a slight acquaintance with that tongue, would give them; and consequently they look for a guide.

Such a guide this little work is designed to furnish. I may say that within six or eight years past I have myself read hundreds of applications for such a guide from different parts of our country and I repeatedly promised to write a book of this kind as soon as my other occupations permitted. Now I have redeemed that pledge. It has been done, to be sure, only in an imperfect manner; there are defects and shortcomings, which in a pioneer work of this kind cannot be avoided. But I applied myself to the task with the honest intention, materially to assist the beginner in his attempt to gain such a knowledge of the Bohemian language, as would be of help to him in his intercourse with people speaking that language, or in his desire to read Bohemian literature ; and I cherish the hope, that this present result of my labor will prove really helpful to those who will make use of it for that purpose. —

"Is Bohemian a hard language to learn ?" This inquiry I have heard more than once.

I think no language is easy to learn, if a person wants to have a perfect command of it ; and Bohemian presents about a fair average of the difficulties, which a student of languages encounters. But there is no great difficulty in acquiring a superficial knowledge of any living European tongue, a knowledge sufficient for ordinary intercourse in every day life, if a person has the will and perseverance to learn it and a fair opportunity to use what he learns. Beginners who will take up this little book with an earnest purpose, will soon find out that Bohemian comes well under this general rule.

Some years ago I made the acquaintance of a business man in a small city of Wisconsin, with whom I conversed both in English and Bohemian and whom I noticed to use both languages in his general conversation with others apparently with the same ease and fluency. It was not until some time after our first meeting, that I learned the gentleman in question was not a Bohemian by birth, but a native American of German descent. Had I been told that he was a born Bohemian, I certainly would have believed it, from the way he handled the language. On our next meeting I asked him how he succeeded in mastering the Bohemian language so perfectly; and he said : "My instructor was the Bohemian. newspaper. I commenced by reading communications written by farmers in an easy, colloquial style and asking explanations as to meaning and pronunciation. In this I persevered, my stock of words and phrases grew rapidly, and I was soon enabled to understand and to make a rapid progress in conversation. Later on I had recourse to the dictionary."

This tends to show what may be done by patient application and perseverance and it may serve as an encouragement to beginners. Of course, the number of persons of other nationalities who have acquired a sufficient practical knowledge of Bohemian to employ it in ordinary intercourse and business, is very large; and I mention it simply to show, that there is no insuperable difficulty in the way, as some persons perhaps might imagine.

And with this little introduction I wish the beginner God speed !

The Bohemian language.

The Slavonic family of nations, numbering rather more than one hundred and ten millions, is composed of two great divisions :

1. The eastern division, comprising the Russians, Bulgarians and Serbo-Croats, under which latter head may also be classed the Slovenes;

2. the western division, comprising the Poles, Bohemians and the remnant of the Wends in Germany.

The Bohemian language is closely related to the other branches of the Slavonic tongue. It needs only a few weeks' study, for a person having a full command of Bohemian, to obtain a fair practical knowledge of any other Slavonic idiom. Especially is the relationship between Bohemian and Polish so close, that they might almost be considered dialects of one and the same language.

The Bohemian language is spoken in Bohemia, Moravia, part of Austrian and Prussian Silesia, and also in Upper Hungary. The Slovak idiom spoken in the last named country is simply an earlier form of Bohemian, which latter the Slovaks of Hungary used for centuries as their literary or "biblical" language; only within the last fifty years have they begun to employ their proper dialect largely in literature. But still, the language is virtually the same, Bohemians and Slovaks needing no interpreters to understand one another, and no dictionaries mutually to read their publications. As a matter of fact, the two idioms are much nearer than high German and low German.

The Bohemians in the United States.

About the year 1848 Bohemian emigration to the United States commenced. Its volume has never been so large as that of the Irish or German emigration, but it has been steady and it will naturally go on for many years to come. In all probability, it will continue as long as European emigration to this side of the Atlantic ocean in general, and it may in the near future assume larger proportions than in the past.

The census of 1870 found 42,000 persons of Bohemian birth settled in the United States. In the year 1880 there were, according to the census taken in that year, over 85,000. But it must be remembered that many of those classified in the census tables as born in Austria, are of Bohemian nationality, especially such as emigrated from the provinces of Moravia and Silesia, and not from Bohemia proper. Quite a number, also, were by mistake entered under the general heading of "Germany", as to the country of their nativity.

It is safe to say that the number of persons born in Europe, whose mother tongue was Bohemian, at the time of the official enumeration of 1880 exceeded one hundred thousand.   At this writing they number nearly 200,000, and together with the first generation born in this country of Bohemian parents and speaking the language, in all probability somewhere near 500,000.

Within the last ten or fifteen years quite a heavy stream of immigration has set in from Hungary.   At first mostly employed in Eastern mines and factories, these immigrants have in recent years been spreading west and settling on lands.   These Hungarians are mostly Slovaks.

The number of Slovaks in the United States at this time probably equals about one third that of the Bohemians proper; hence the present number of persons in the United States speaking the Bohemian language in both its dialects may be computed at six hundred thousand.

The Bohemians have their homes chiefly in the following states: New York, Pennsylvania, Maryland, Ohio, Illinois, Michigan, Wisconsin, Iowa, Minnesota, Nebraska, Kansas, S. Dakota, Missouri and Texas.

In the first five states and also in Missouri they live chiefly in the cities, following different trades and working in factories.   In the other states they are mainly farmers, as a rule very industrious and thrifty.   Many of them are of course engaged in business of all kinds and in the professions.   In their manners and customs and ways of thought the Bohemians strongly resemble the Germans, particularly the South Germans, with whom they have been in close contact in the old world for over a thousand years.   They are industrious and saving, sociable and hospitable; their favorite beverage at social gatherings and entertainments is beer, and "Bohemian beer" of different make has in recent years become quite popular in this country of ours.   Immoderate indulgence in their favorite drink may doubtless sometimes be observed among them as among others, especially in the large cities;

but as a rule, they are sober, law-abiding and extremely good-natured.

In religion, Roman Catholicism predominates among the Bohemians and they have a large number of churches, priests and parish schools in the United States. The Protestants also have numerous places of worship. Large numbers of the Bohemians, however, keep apart from all churches and religious denominations. They are liberals, free-thinkers and agnostics of different shades of opinion, enjoying the inestimable privilege of every American citizen to follow his convictions and enjoy a full personal freedom, so long as he respects the laws and the equal freedom of his fellow-citizens.

The first Bohemian newspaper on this side of the Atlantic was issued thirty years ago at Racine, Wisconsin, the first number appearing on New Year's day 1860. Now there are about twenty five or thirty newspapers in that language published in the United States, both daily and weekly, besides several in the Slovak dialect. Most of them have a good patronage and some have in fact a surprisingly large circulation. Other publications are also quite numerous. The Bohemians, and particularly the farmers, are fond of reading, eager for information, and above all they seek political knowledge, taking the liveliest interest in whatever concerns the government, public institutions and laws of their adopted country. During the civil war the Bohemians, although at that time quite generally classified as Germans, furnished a considerable contingent of the defenders of the Union and in Chicago a monument will soon be reared by the Bohemians in memory of those of their nationality, who cheerfully took up arms and gave their lives for the unity and freedom of this great country.*)

---

*) The following is a quotation from an extensive article on the Bohemians in St. Louis, Mo., which appeared in the GLOBE-DEMOCRAT of February 16, 1890: "In the territory lying between Seventh and Fourteenth streets on the east and west, and Geyer and Russell avenues on the north and south, there is a population of 25,000 souls, all speaking the language of Bohemia, schooling their children in the ancient tongue, keeping up an acquaintance with a rich and varied literature that dates

back to the ninth century, and for the most part worshiping in the Roman Catholic Church, of which Bohemia has been a stanch adherent since the ninth century. A thrifty set are these Bohemians, good citizens in all that the term implies, prompt tax-payers, fully alive to the requirements of civilization; mingling freely in business intercourse with their cousins from other lands, they yet preserve the social customs of their native land, and take an overweening pride in the preservation of its language and its literature. The Bohemian met up town in business life would be casually mistaken for a German, but a tour through their section of the city impresses one with their startling individuality.... In conversation with S. (one of their leading men) I was struck by the ease and purity of his English diction. This is a marked peculiarity of most of the Bohemians. From their own harsh and difficult language they switch off into English which betrays but little trace of foreign accent." —

The statement about the Bohemians having been steadfast adherents of the Church of Rome may be considered as a serious l a p s u s c a l a m i, because it is not borne out by history. The Bohemians were in fact a protestant nation from the burning at the stake of their famous reformers John Huss and Jerome of Prague (in the years 1415 and 1416) until the period of the Thirty Years' war, which took its start in Bohemia. Concerning the allusion to the character of the Bohemian language it may be stated as a well known experience, that nearly every language appears "harsh and difficult" to a person who is perfectly ignorant of the same and very rarely hears it spoken. Time and again have I heard, on the European continent, the English language characterized as "harsh and difficult", whereas in fact, English is a language not only full of melody as well as power, but probably the easiest of all European tongues to learn.

PART I.

SECTION 1.

General observations.

In the Bohemian language Roman characters are used in writing and printing.

In order to read Bohemian it is first necessary to be well acquainted with the sounds, represented by the different letters of the Bohemian alphabet.

In attempting to read English while giving the letters the customary Bohemian sounds, we should find most English words difficult to pronounce and a large proportion of them simply unpronounceable.

The same is true if we attempt to read Bohemian while giving the letters their English sounds.

This explains why English-speaking persons, entirely ignorant of any language but their own and supposing that the letters of the alphabet always retain their English sounds, find so many "jawbreakers" in trying to pronounce Bohemian or other foreign words. Foreign persons, ignorant of English, find themselves "in the same boat", when trying to pronounce English words, and their difficulty is even much greater on account of the complicated character of English orthography.

SECTION 2.

The Bohemian alphabet.

The alphabet of the Bohemian language consists of 26 letters, the same as the English, if accented letters, being simply a modification of the original sounds, are not counted; but, counting all the accented letters separately, we find 41 letters in the Bohemian alphabet.

The following table gives the complete alphabet of the Bohemian language, with the English equivalents as near as possible. Capital letters, of course, correspond with the small letters, accented or unaccented.

THE ALPHABET.

a	has	the	sound	of	*o*	in *done.*
á	"	"	"	"	*a*	in *arm.*
b	"	"	"	"	*b.*	
c	"	"	"	"	*ts.*	
č	"	"	"	"	*ch*	in *child.*
d	"	"	"	"	*d;*	it takes the sound of ď when followed by the soft vowels ě, i or í.
ď	"	"	"	"	*di*	in the French word *diable.* This mellow sound of *d*, imperfectly rendered by *dy*, is ordinarily heard in the English expressions *would you, could you,* when rapidly uttered, so that the terminal *d* and initial *y* are fused into one sound.
e	"	"	"	"	*e*	in *end.*
é	"	"	"	"	*e*	in *ere,* or *ai* in *air.*
ě	"	"	"	"	*ea*	in *beatitude,* or *ye* in *yes;* when it occurs directly after d, n, t, these letters take the soft sound of ď, ñ, ť, and ě sounds like e. The syllable **je,** *ye,* is an equivalent for ě.
f	"	"	"	"	*f.*	
g	"	"	"	"	*g*	in *great;* it occurs only in foreign words.
h	"	"	"	"	*h*	in *ham.*
ch	"	"	"	"	*ch*	in German and Dutch, also in Welsh, or *x* in Greek, — somewhat like *kh.*
i	"	"	"	"	*i*	in *pin.*
í	"	"	"	"	*i*	in *pique,* or *ee* in *seen.*
j	"	"	"	"	*y*	in *yes.*
k	"	"	"	"	*k*	in *sink,* without an aspirate.
l	"	"	"	"	*l.*	

m	"	"	"	"	*m.*
n	"	"	"	"	*n.*
ň	"	"	"	"	*ñ* in Spanish (cañon) or *gn* in French (campagne); imperfectly rendered by *ny.*
o	"	"	"	"	*o* in *obey.*
ó	"	"	"	"	*ó* in *lord.*
p	"	"	"	"	*p.*
q	"	"	"	"	*q* in *question;* it occurs only in foreign words.
r	"	"	"	"	*r* in *rest;* it has a sharp, trilling sound.
ř	"	"	"	"	*rsh* (or *rzh*, as the Imperial Dictionary of the English Language has it); it is a sound proper to the Bohemian and Polish languages, which must be heard in order to be acquired correctly: the same may be said of the English sound of *th,* hard and soft.
s	"	"	"	"	*s* in *sink.*
š	"	"	"	"	*sh.*
t	"	"	"	"	*t* in *test;* it takes the sound of **ť** when followed by **ě, i** or **í.**
ť	"	"	"	"	*t* 'n the French word *tiens*, as commonly pronounced. This mellow sound of *t,* imperfectly rendered by *ty*, is also heard in the English expressions *wouldn't you, couldn't you,* when rapidly uttered, so that the terminal *t* and initial *y* are fused into one sound.
u	"	"	"	"	*u* in *push.*
ú ů }	"	"	"	"	*u* in *rude*, or *oo* in *pool.*
v	"	"	"	"	*v.*
x	"	"	"	"	*x* in *expect.*
y	"	"	"	"	*y* in *lynch.*
ý	"	"	"	"	*i* in *pique*, or *ee* in *seen.*
z	"	"	"	"	*z* in *zeal.*
ž	"	"	"	"	*z* in *azure*, or *s* in *pleasure.*

The beginner must try to master thoroughly the peculiar sound of every accented letter in the Bohemian alphabet, before proceeding with his lessons. However, it is evident that of all the accented letters only four will present a certain difficulty : **ď, ň, ť** and **ř.** The rest are simple. Among the plain consonants, the peculiar sound of **ch** must be well practiced; the combination *kh* gives it only imperfectly.

SECTION 3.
Names of the letters.

The names of the letters of the Bohemian alphabet, though of little consequence to the beginner, are given in the following table as near as can be. However, the Bohemian sounds of the letters, as explained in the foregoing section, must be well kept in mind, in order to name the letters correctly.

For instance : **b** is called *bé*, to be pronounced like *beh*, the *e* sounding like **e** in *ere*, **ai** in *air*, or **a** in *fare*, the final *h* being mute and serving only as a lengthening mark.

Two of the accents (*á, ů*), whenever they occur, signify only a prolongation of the sound; the quality of the other accents has been explained in the foregoing section.

In spelling a word, the vowels with a long accent (*á, é, í, ú, ý*) are called *long* **a,** *long* **e,** etc.; also, **a** *with a comma,* **e** *with a comma,* and so forth; **ů** is called **u** *with a ring.*

THE LETTERS NAMED.

a, á	*á (ah)*	**ch**	*khá*	**ř**	*ersh*
b	*bé*	**i, í**	*ee (in bee)*	**s**	*ess*
c	*tsé*	**j**	*yé*	**š**	*esh*
č	*ché*	**k**	*ká*	**t**	*té*
d	*dé*	**l**	*el*	**ť**	*ťé*

ď	*ďé*	**m**	*em*	**u, ú, ů**	*oo*
e, é	*é (eh)*	**n**	*en*		(in *boom*)
ě	*iyé*	**ň**	*eñ*	**v**	*vé*
f	*ef*	**o, ó**	*ó (oh)*	**x**	*ix*
g	*gé*	**p**	*pé*	**y, ý**	*ee* or *ypsilon*
	(like g in *go*)	**q**	*koo*	**z**	*zet*
h	*há*	**r**	*er*	**ž**	*žet*

SECTION 4.

Bohemian pronunciation.

After mastering the sounds of the Bohemian letters, the learner may be said to have fully conquered Bohemian pronunciation.

There is in fact only one rule : *Pronounce as it is written, sounding every letter,* — of course, giving the letters their proper Bohemian, and not their English sounds.

The English, French and German written languages abound with silent letters; the Bohemian language has practically none, that is, extremely few. Such as there are, will be pointed out in the course of the following lessons.

It is a well known rule in English, that there can be no written syllable without a vowel. In Bohemian we sometimes encounter syllables made up of consonants without any vowel.

. "How in the world can you pronounce that ?"

Not infrequently have we heard such a question from persons, having no idea of any language but their own.

But it is just as easy to pronounce such syllables in Bohemian, as it is in English to give utterance to syllables with a mute vowel. An example will elucidate it:

Trn means *thorn.* This word is evidently of the same derivation in both languages.

Now, the Bohemian word **trn** being composed of three consonants and no vowel, how is it pronounced ?

In the same way, as the second syllable of the English words *bittern, slattern,* where the vowel *e* is silent. We hear in that second syllable only the sounds of *t-r-n,* the sound of the vowel *e* disappearing entirely; and this explains exactly the pronunciation of Bohemian words of one syllable, or syllables, without a vowel. Syllables with silent vowels abound in English as well as in German,—not quite so in French; — and they are constantly pronounced with the same ease, as the syllables having no vowel sounds in Bohemian.

It is to be observed that such syllables **always** contain one of the two consonants **l** and **r** which are sometimes called "half-vowels", because in such cases they almost take the place of vowels. In a prolongation of the sound we hear in Bohemian somewhat indistinctly the vowel **e** before the proper sound of those consonants, as if we wrote and partially pronounced :

t'rn* instead of **trn** (thorn)

r'lk* ,, **vlk** (wolf)

The number of monosyllabic words without a vowel is not large; but syllables consisting of two or three consonants occur quite often.

For instance : **trčeti, strčiti,** means in English *to stick out, to push.* Each of these words is composed of three syllables : **tr-če-ti, str-či-ti;** and the first syllable of each contains only consonants : **tr, str.**

How are they pronounced ?

Just like *ter* and *ster* in the English words *bitter, blister.* Nobody finds any difficulty in passing over the silent *e* and saying *bittr, blistr.*

Among the Bohemian vowels there are some, which are called *soft.* namely : **e, ě, i, í;** and others **(a, o, u, y)** which are called hard or broad.

Of the soft vowels the last three, **ě, i** and **í,** have a softening influence upon some preceding consonants, particularly **n, d, t,** which they change into the soft sounds of **ň, ď, ť,** as noticed in section 1. For instance :

2

saně (sleigh) is pronounced as if spelt **saňe;**

pani (mistress, lady) is pronounced as if spelt **paňí;**

dělo (cannon) sounds like **ďelo;**

dilo (work)............... **ďílo;**

tělo (body) .... **ťelo;**

tisk (printing) .... **ťisk;**

This will always be plainly indicated in the pronouncing columns of the practical lessons contained in Part II.

Care must be taken to give every long vowel (á, é, í, ý, ó, ú, ů) its proper *long* sound, because a shortened sound would often make the word unintelligible or change its meaning, the same as in English in numerous cases. For instance :

pata means *heel;* **pátá** means the *fifth* (in the feminine gender). The only difference is in the length of the vowels. Likewise in English : **lid** and **lead** have the same vowel sound, the only difference being in its length or quantity. —

We have said all it is necessary to say about Bohemian pronunciation and in closing we again enjoin the only rule, which obtains in Bohemian with very few exceptions : Pronounce as it is written, — giving every letter its proper Bohemian sound.

SECTION 5.

Parts of speech.

In Bohemian the parts of speech or classes of words are the same as in English, excepting the article.

In English we have the definite article *the* and the indefinite article *a, an*. (In French, masculine, feminine, *le, la, — un, une ;* in German, masculine, feminine and neutre, *der, die, das, — ein, eine, ein.*)

In Bohemian there is no article, definite or indefinite. In this regard, Bohemian agrees with Latin.

We say in English : *the house, the houses, a house :* in Bohemian **dům, domy, dům.**

SECTION 6.

Gender.

But, having no article, the Bohemian noun suffers nevertheless from the useless infliction of grammatical gender in the same degree as the German, Latin and Greek. It has three genders, namely : masculine, feminine and neutre.

The English language has rejected all distinction of gender, attributing sex to living beings only, which is one of the greatest advantages the English language has over all other European tongues, ancient and modern.

In the absence of an article in Bohemian, if we want to designate the gender of a noun, we use the indicative pronoun *this* or *that,* namely : **ten** for the masculine, **ta** for the feminine and **to** for the neutre gender. Hence we say :

ten dům	*this* (or *that*) *house*
ta bouda	*this* (or *that*) *hut*
to okno	*this* (or *that*) *window*

In the plural it is **ti** for living masculine beings :

ti muži, *these* (or *those*) *men;*

ty for inanimate masculine things and for the feminine gender : **ta** for the neutre :

ty domy, *these* or *those houses;*

ty boudy, *these* or *those huts;*

ta okna, *these* or *those windows.*

However, in colloquial parlance, **ty** is heard in the plural regardless of gender. —

Always remember, that the article has no existence in Bohemian; and that the words **ten, ta, to, — ti, ty, ta,** when used before a noun, are simply indicative pronouns and nothing else.

SECTION 7.

Grammatical rules in general.

Bohemian is one of the highly inflected languages, like German or the classic tongues, which is doubtless a disadvantage, to be deplored especially from the standpoint of the learner. On account mainly of the useless distinction of gender, which permeates the whole structure of the Bohemian language, grammatical forms and rules are numerous, forming the principal difficulty encountered in the study of the language.

But to some extent, at least, that difficulty is offset by colloquial usage, which largely disregards the artificial distinction of gender in the employment of pronouns, adjectives and verbs, as they relate to nouns of different gender. This serves to simplify the matter somewhat for the learner of Bohemian as commonly spoken.

In the following lessons we try to imitate the natural method of learning a language. We do not teach the child grammatical rules and complications before it knows how to speak. We teach it words and their connection in phrases, expressing thoughts.

Consequently we do not intend to cram the beginner at the outset with all sorts of grammatical rules. There are not thousands but millions of people using the Bohemian language and knowing little of the rules and perplexities of its grammar. The same is true of every other living tongue.

This Course being designed solely for practical purposes, it will be our aim to impart to the learner some practical knowledge of the language in the easiest, most natural and most direct way possible. We shall therefore interpolate in the following lessons only such grammatical rules, as may appear to be indispensable to facilitate the student's progress and which may easily be mastered *en passant*, or, so to say, by a method of easy induction.

A more extended and methodical review of the Bohemian grammar will be found in the last part of this book. After acquiring to a certain degree a practical knowledge of the language, the learner will find it much easier to grapple with the details of its grammar, which in the beginning would serve only to perplex him unnecessarily and to dampen his ardor. And when a moderate knowledge of the tongue is attained, the progressive student will naturally take a Dictionary of the English and Bohemian languages to his aid, which will make further progress rapid and pleasing.

The main difficulty is in the start, as in every other language. It requires earnestness of purpose and perseverance. The beginner must not allow himself to be discouraged by such initial difficulties, as he is sure to meet with; and whenever the pronunciation of an accented letter or a word, as given in this book, seems to be a stumbling-block, we would advise him to ask some neighbor or acquaintance, who speaks Bohemian, to pronounce it for him repeatedly, so that his ear may grow accustomed to the sound and the same may become quite familiar to him. If he fails to catch it forthwith, let him try again and again, until he succeeds. Let him remember, that the thousands of Bohemians who learn English find similar difficulties in their way; and numbers of those, who at first felt discouraged, thinking they could never master the intricacies of the English tongue, to-day speak and write it tolerably well, — many of them with fluency and grace.

SECTION 8
The accent.

In the Bohemian language the accent is always placed upon the first syllable; consequently its rules, which in English have to be closely studied, do not offer any difficulty whatever. Only when a noun is preceded by a preposition of one syllable, the accent is transferred and placed upon that preposition.

SECTION 9.

Ty and vy, — *thou* and *you*.

The personal pronoun **ty** of the second person singular is used in Bohemian in family circles, and in addressing familiar or intimate friends It expresses endearment, familiarity or close friendship.

But among the Bohemians in America it is very often improperly employed instead of **vy** (*you*) in addressing others, which latter word in Bohemian has the same general usage as in English. By a curious mistake most of the original Bohemian settlers in America, like many of the Germans, translated the English *you* by **ty,** fancying the meaning to be identical and supposing that in English the second person singular is used in addressing another person, instead of the second person *plural*, as is the proper custom in Bohemian. But the rule in ordinary discourse is almost the same in English as in Bohemian, the second person plural (*you*, vy) being employed in addressing others and always combined with a plural verb, there being only a few exceptions in Bohemian as stated above. The French language follows exactly the same rule as the Bohemian ; but in German discourse the third person plural is used in speaking to another (**Sie,** *they*).

This explanation, though somewhat lengthy, has been deemed necessary at the outset.

SECTION 10.

In vulgar language, the sound of the consonant **v** is often improperly placed before the initial vowel **o,** so that for instance, in place of a pure **on, ona, ono** (he, she, it) we hear **von, vona, vono.** It is something similar to the vulgar English custom to place the sound of **h** before an initial vowel : *H'englishman, h'eye-tooth,* instead of Englishman, eye-tooth.

PART II.

PART II.

Rules of pronunciation.

The following rules must constantly be kept in mind :

1 — The Bohemian pronunciation in the following lessons is always given in *italics*.

2 — We proceed upon the supposition that section 2, part I, explaining the sounds of all the Bohemian letters, and particularly the sounds of accented vowels, has been fully digested by the beginner.

3 — Consequently we do not attempt, in the following lessons, to give English equivalents for the long vowels á and é, which are of very frequent occurrence, because it would be a useless complication. For the long vowels í and ý, whose sound is identical, the English *ee* as heard in *seen* will have to answer. But it is to be observed that in ordinary Bohemian discourse the sound of ý is frequently (in fact, nearly always) changed into **ej**, i. e. *ey* as heard in *they*, *obey*. The word **sýr** (cheese), for instance, is properly pronounced *seer*, but commonly *seyr*.

4 — The sound of the Bohemian short vowels **a, e, o,** is represented by *ă, ĕ, ŏ:* but the marked characters *ă, ĕ, ŏ* are avoided when their use appears to be superfluous. For instance the pronunciation of words like **tento** (this one), **pense** (pension), **ponor** (draught of a ship) is sufficiently indicated by *tentŏ, pensĕ, ponor*, to an English-speaking beginner; and it would by superfluous to write *tĕntŏ, pĕnsĕ, pŏnŏr*.

5 — The short sound of i is given by *i*, as heard in *pin*. When the long English sound of *i* (as heard in *dine*) is to be employed a full-face **i** or **I** will stand for it, — which however is of rare occurrence.

6 — Short y always retains its SHORT English sound as heard in the word **lynch,** and we use for it in the pronouncing column either *i* or *y*, as may be more appropriate. The combination **ej** will commonly be represented by *ey*, which must always be pronounced like *ey* in *they*, *whey*, *obey*.

7 — The short vowel **u** is represented by *ŭ*, but frequently also by *oo*, where a slight lengthening of the sound is not only admissible, but conducive to a clear enunciation. Long **ú** and **ů** are naturally always rendered by *oo*, as heard in *boot*.

8 — The vowel **ě,** when preceded by **d, n, t,** changes them into **ď, ň, ť,** and has then the sound of a simple **e.** When it retains its proper sound of ě, 'we commonly write it *ye* in the pronouncing column. The student must be careful always to sound it like *ye* in the English words *yes*, *yet*, *yell*, and **NEVER** like the word *ye*, meaning "you". For instance : **mě, právě,** (me, just), *mye, práeye* (*myĕ, práeyĕ*).

The syllable **je** is identical in pronunciation with **ě,** and is also rendered by *ye*; for example : **jen** (only), *yen*. **Je** is generally used in common discourse as an abbreviation of **jest,** *yest* (is); to guard against possible mispronunciation, we will always write it *ye*.

9 — The sound of the soft consonants **ď, ň, ť** is represented by the combination *dy, ny, ty,* when practicable, which is rarely the case. Whenever this is found impracticable, or when it would only serve to obscure instead of facilitating matters, a full-face **ď, ň, ť** is used in the pronouncing column and the student must try his best to give it the proper Bohemian sound.

Inflexible rule : When the soft vowels **ě, i, í** follow after **d, n, t,** these consonants are softened into **ď, ň, ť,** and will be so marked.

10 — To represent the sound of **ch,** the combined letters *kh* are invariably employed, for want of a better substitute. The sound of **ř** is given by *rsh*, for the same reason.*)

---

*) The letter **ř** was unknown in the old Bohemian language and is wisely rejected by the Slovaks, who use the letter **r** in its place. In many cases also, where its use is insisted upon by strict and pedantic grammarians, it is avoided by the practical common sense of the people.

11 — For the letter *č* we use *ch* or *tch* as heard in *chap, wretch;* for *š* the English equivalent *sh* is used; for the Bohemian **j,** the letter *y* as heard in *yonder* is made to answer. A final *s* in Bohemian has always the sharp hissing sound and will be marked *ss.*

12 — For the sound of *ž* the Imperial Dictionary gives *zh* as a substitute; but we retain the full-face Bohemian *ž* in the pronouncing column, as nothing would be gained by such a substitution. It is always pronounced like *z* in *azure,* or *s* in *pleasure.* But in some cases, when terminating a word or a syllable, the letter *ž* takes the sharper sound of *sh* and will be so noted.

The diphthong ou.

This is the only diphthong in the Bohemian language, and it must always be pronounced like *ou* in *dough,* or like the word *owe,* — never like *ou* in *pound* or *ghoul.* We shall commonly mark it *oů.*

Abbreviations

will be avoided as much as possible, and their meaning will in every case be self-evident. — The letters *m, f, n* beside a noun denote gender (masculine, feminine, neutre). — *Sing.* means singular number: *pl.* means plural number.

The Hyphen.

Syllables without a vowel — but always containing one of the so-called "semi-vowels" l and **r,** as before observed, — are separated from other syllables of the same word by a hyphen, to make their separate pronunciation apparent. For instance: **brzo** (soon), *br-zŏ,* — the syllable *br* being pronounced exactly like *bor* in the English words *labor, neighbor.*

However, a silent *e* will often be interpolated in such syllables, to elucidate their pronunciation; for instance: **prší,** *p*e*rshee,* it rains.

The apostrophe

will be used to prevent a collusion of two letters, into which an English-speaking beginner might easily be entrapped, and to keep them separate; as, for example: **měl jsem** (I had), pronounced *m'yell sěm,* — and not *my-ell sěm.*

LESSON I.

Já	*yá*	I		ona	*ŏná*	she
ty	*ty*	thou (*improperly* you)		ono	*ŏnŏ*	it
on	*ŏn*	he		ten, ta, to,	*ten, tă, tŏ,*	this, that

ty *ty*, that *or* those
tu, zde *tŭ*, *zdĕ* here
a, i *ă*, *i* and
ano, ne *ănŏ*, *nĕ* yes, no
za *ză* for; půl *pool* half
na *ná* on

Já mám,	*yá mám,*	I have *or*		on má,	*ŏn má,*	he has *or*	
mám	*mám*	I have got		má	*má*	he has got	
mám ?	*mám?*	have I ?		má !	*má?*	has he ?	
ty máš,	*ty másh,*	thou hast *or*		ona má,	*ŏná má,*	she has *or*	
máš	*másh*	thou hast got		má	*má*	she has got	
		(*improperly:* you have)		ono má,	*ŏnŏ má,*	it has *or*	
máš	*másh*	hast thou? (have you?)		má	*má*	it has got	

dollar, m.	*dollăr.*	dollar		účet, m.	*oo-chet*	bill, account
půl-dollar, m.	*pool-d.*	half-a-dollar		dluh, m.	*dlooh*	debt
cent, m.	*tsent*	cent		na dluh	*ná-dlooh*	on trust, on credit
peníze, pl.	*peñeczě*	money *or* cash		na účet	*ná-oochet,*	on trust, on credit
hotové	*hŏtŏvé*	cash		maso, n.	*másŏ*	meat

chleb,	m.	*khleb*		bread	**pivo,**	n.	*peevŏ*	beer
chleba		*khlebā*			**víno,**	n.	*veenŏ*	wine
sýr,	m.	*seer*	cheese		**soda,**	f.	*sodā*	soda
máslo,	n.	*māslŏ*	butter		**voda,**	f.	*vodā*	water

Note 1. Pronounce **má** like *mā'a,* the vulgar abbreviation of Mamma; and **mám** like *mā'am,* the vulgar abbreviation of Madam; it will assist in catching the true sound.

Note 2. In Bohemian, **míti** *meetǐ* (to have), is not an auxiliary verb as in English, but always an independent verb.

Note 3. **Soda** is commonly used as an abbreviation of **sodovka,** soda-water. — In vulgar speech, the expression **jo,** *yŏ,* (from the German *ja*) is often heard instead of **ano, yes.**

Note 4. The long vowel **ú,** *oo,* which occurs only at the beginning of a word or syllable, is often changed into **ou,** *oŏ,* and so pronounced. Hence we frequently hear **ouček,** *oŏchet,* instead of **úček,** *oochet,* and the like.

EXERCISES.

Já mám peníze. I have money.
Mám peníze, I have money.
Ty máš peníze, thou hast money (sometimes *improperly* used for: you have money. See Section 7. Part I).
On má hotové, he has the cash.
Ona má chleba, she has bread (*or* the bread).
Ona má dollar, she has a dollar.
Ona má cent, she has a cent.
Já mám účet, I have the bill.
Já mám dluh, I have a debt.

Ty máš dluh, thou hast (you have) a debt.
On má dluh, he has a debt.
Já mám ten účet, I have the bill.
Mám ten účet? have I that bill?
Mám, I have.
Máš ten účet? hast thou (have you) that bill?
Mám, I have.
Máš dollar? hast thou (have you) a dollar?
Já mám půl-dollar, I have half-a-dollar.

Máte peníze? have you money?
Má peníze? has he money?
Má on ty peníze? has he that money?
On má dollar, he has a dollar.
On má ten dollar, he has that dollar.
Ona má ty peníze, she has that money.
Ona má dluh, she has a debt.
Ona má zde účet, she has an account here.
Ona má ten účet, she has that bill.
Mám chleba, I have bread.
A já mám maso, and I have meat.
Máš chleba? hast thou (have you) bread?
Ano, mám; yes, I have.

Máš maso? hast thou (have you) meat?
Ne, no.
Mám chleba a maso, I have bread and meat.
A já mám pivo, and I have beer.
To pivo, that beer (*or* this beer).
To pivo a to víno, that beer and that wine.
Chleba za peníze bread for cash
a pivo na dluh, and beer on trust.
Maso za hotové meat for cash and
a víno na účet wine on account.
Má ten chleb has he that bread
a to máslo? and that butter?
Chleb i voda, bread and water.
Máslo a sýr, butter and cheese.

Note 5. *Gender of the nouns.* It will be observed that the nouns

dollar	**účet**	**chleb**
cent	**dluh**	**sýr**

are all of the masculine gender, and using the indicative pronoun we say: **ten dollar, ten cent,** etc.

Nouns terminating in consonants are mostly of the masculine gender.

The nouns **voda, soda,** are of the feminine gender: **ta voda, ta soda.**

Nouns terminating in a are always of the feminine gender.

But some feminine nouns also terminate in ě and in consonants: for instance **země,** earth (land, country); **kosť,** bone; **daň,** tax.

The nouns **maso, máslo, pivo, víno,** are neutre: **to maso, to máslo,** etc.

Nouns terminating in o are always of the neutre gender.

But some neutre nouns have the termination **e, ě** or **í;** for instance **pole,** field : **doupě,** den : **osení,** crop.

Note 6. The noun **peníze** (money) is in the plural: the singular **peníz,** *peñeez,* means either "a coin" or "an amount".

LESSON II.

My	*me*	we	**máme**	*mámě*	we have
vy	*vy*	you	**máte**	*mátě*	you have
oni	*ŏñí*	they	**mají**	*má-yee*	they have

Note 1. In the third person plural **oni** *ŏñí* (they) is used in the masculine gender for animate creatures; **ony,** *ŏny* (they) in the feminine gender, and in the masculine for inanimate things : **ona** *ŏná* (they) in the neutre gender.

But in common discourse no such grammatical distinction is made and the masculine form **oni** is employed in all cases.

papír,	m.	*pápeer*	paper	**plac,**	m.	*plăts*) place or
pero,	n.	*perŏ*	pen	**místo,**	n.	*meestŏ* ! room
inkoust,	m.	*inkoŭst*	ink	**stůl,**	m.	*stool* table

vůz,	m.	*rooz*	wagon	**seno,**	n.	*sénŏ*	hay
bič,	m.	*bitch*	whip	**obilí,**	n.	*ŏbe-lee*	grain
pytel,	m.	*pitĕll*	sack	**potah,**	m.	*potăh*	team

čas, m. *chăss* time

tam	*tăm*	there	**dost** *dŏst* enough
jen, jenom,	*yen, yenŏm*	only	**každý** *kăždee* every one

všichni, *fshikhŭi*

EXERCISES.

My máme papír,	we have paper.	**Zde máte stůl,**	here you have a table.
Máte pero?	have you a pen?	**Máme vůz,**	we have a wagon.
Ano, mám;	yes, I have.	**On má bič,**	he has a whip.
Máte inkoust?	have you ink?	**Ona má pytel,**	she has a sack.
Mám,	I have.	**Mají potah,**	they have a team.
Máte peníze?	have you money?	**Oni mají obilí a seno,**	they have grain and hay.
Zde máte plac,	here you have a place		
Tam máte místo,	there you have a place.	**Mají obilí a seno?**	have they grain and hay?
Zde má každý místo,	here every one has a place.	**Mají jen seno,**	they have only hay.
Tam mají všichni místo,	there they all have a place.	**Oni mají jenom pytel,**	they have only a sack.
		Máme čas,	we have time.

Note 2. As observed in **všichni** (all), when a word commences
with the letter **v** followed by another *consonant*, the initial **v** takes the
sharp sound of an **f,** whenever the facility of pronunciation naturally requires that modification of the sound.

LESSON III.

Kde	*gdě*	where	**ne**	*ně*	no, not
kdy	*gdy*	when	**proč**	*prŏch*	why
kdo	*gdŏ*	who	**proto že**	*protŏ žě*	because
teď	*teď*	} now,	**ani**	*ăňi*	} no, not one, not even, neither---nor
nyní	*nyňí*	} at present			
nemám	*nemám*	I have not, I have not got	**nemáme**	*nemámě*	we have not
nemáš	*nemásh*	thou hast (you have) not	**nemáte**	*nemátě*	you have not
nemá	*nemá*	he (she, it) has not	**nemají**	*nemăyee*	they have not

Note 1. In the words **kde, kdy, kdo** the hard consonant **k** is pronounced like **g** in *go*. In **nemám, nemáš,** etc., *nem* has exactly the same sound as in the word *nemesis*.

Note 2. Negation is always expressed by the prefix **ne.**

EXERCISES.

Nemám peníze. I have no money.

Nemáš peníze? hast thou no money?

Nemáte peníze? have you no money?

Ne; no.

Proč nemá peníze? why has he (she, it) no money?

Proto že nemá obilí, because he has no grain.

Nemáme účet, we have no account.

Nemáte hotové? have you no cash?

Nemáte ani dollar? have you not even a dollar?

Nemá ani cent? has he not a cent?

Nemám ani dollar, I have not a dollar.

Nemá ani cent, he has not a cent.

Nemají ani chleb, ani máslo; they have neither bread nor butter.

Nemají chleba, ani máslo, ani sýr; they have no bread, no butter and no cheese.

Nemáme papír, pero, ani inkoust; we have no paper, no pen and no ink.

Nemáte plac? have you no place?

Zde nemáme místo, we have no place here.

Tam nemáme místo, we have no place there.

Máš čas? hast thou time?

Máte čas? } have you time?
Máte kdy?

Nemám čas, } I have no time.
Nemám kdy,

Teď nemáme čas, we have no time now.

Nyní nemají čas, they have no time now.

Kdy máte čas? when have you time?

Kdy máme čas? when have we time?

Nyní; now.

Kdo má peníze? who has money?

Kdo má čas? who has time?

Kde máš peníze? where hast thou the money?

Kde máte peníze? where have you the money?

Kdo nemá peníze? who has no money?

Kdo má dluh? who has a debt?

Kde máte dluh? where have you a debt?

Proč nemáte hotové? why have you not the cash?

LESSON IV.

Co	*tsŏ*	what	**moc**	*mŏts*	}	much, many
co to	*tsŏ tŏ*	what is it (that)	**mnoho**	*mnohŏ*		
něco	*ñetsŏ*	something	**tuze**	*toozě*	very; too
nic	*ñits*	nothing	**jak**	*yăk*	how
pranic	*prăñits*	nothing at all	**tak**	*tăk*	so

EXERCISES.

Já mám něco, I have something.

Já nemám nic. Nemám nic. I have nothing.

Já mám dollar, I have a dollar.

Nemám ani dollar, I have not even a dollar.

Nemám pranic, I have nothing at all.

Nemáš nic, thou hast nothing.

Nemáte nic, you have nothing.

Oni nemají nic, they have nothing.

Co to máš? what is it thou hast got?

Máš něco? hast thou anything?

Co to máte? what have you? (what is it you have? what have you got?)

Máte něco? have you anything?

Co to mají? what have they got?

Nemáte nic? have you nothing?

Nemáte pranic? have you nothing at all?

Tak vy nemáte nic, so you have nothing.

Nic nemám, I have nothing.

Pranic nemáme, we have nothing at all.

Pranic nemají, they have nothing at all.

Ani víno, ani pivo nemají; they have neither wine, nor beer.

Mám moc, I have much.

Máme mnoho, we have much.

Ty nemáš moc, thou hast not much.

Vy nemáte moc, you have not much.

Oni nemají mnoho, they have not much.

Jak moc? Jak mnoho? how much?

Tuze moc. Tuze mnoho; very much.

Ne moc. Ne mnoho; not much.

Ne tuze moc, not very much.

Ne tuze mnoho, „ „ „

Ne tak tuze moc, not so very much.

Máš dost? hast thou enough?

Máte dost? have you enough?

Ano, mám dost; yes, I have enough.

Nemám dost, I have not enough.

To je tuze mnoho, co máte; that is very much, what you have got.

LESSON V.

---

někdo	*ňegdŏ*	somebody, some one	někde	*ňegdě*	somewhere, anywhere
nikdo	*ňigdŏ*		nikde	*ňigdě*	nowhere
žádný	*žádnee*	nobody, no one	nikdy	*ňigdi*	never

vždy	*vždi*		always, all the time, ever	stále	*stálě*
vždycky	*vždi-tski*)*			pořád*)	*porshád*
práce,	f.	*prátse*	work	co dělat	*tsŏ d'elát* to do.

EXERCISES.

Máte něco? have you something?

Máte někde něco? have you got something, anywhere?

Nemáme nikde nic, we have got nothing, nowhere.

Kdo má něco? who has something?

Žádný nic, nobody (has) anything.

Nikdo nemá nic, nobody has anything.

Nemáme žádný nic; nobody (none of us) has anything.

Nikdo nemá tuze moc, nobody has too much.

Nemám nikde nic, I have not anything anywhere.

Ty nemáš nikdy nic, thou never hast anything.

Vy nemáte nikdy nic, you never have anything.

Mám vždy (dycky) něco, I always have something.

Máte vždycky něco, you always have something.

Pořád něco máte, you always have something.

Ty pořád něco máš, thou hast always something.

Stále něco máte, you always have something.

Neustále něco mají, they always have something.

Nemám pořád nic, I never have anything.

Stále nemá nic, he never has anything.

---

*) Colloquially **dycky,** *dit-ski;* **porád,** *porád.*

Pořád nemají nic, they never have anything.

Proč nemáš nic? why hast thou nothing?

Proč nemáte nic? why have you nothing?

Proč nemáte něco? why have you not something?

Proto že nemám, because I have not.

Nemáš dollar? hast thou not a dollar?

Nemáte peníze? have you no money?

Proč nemáte peníze? why have you no money?

Já mám půl-dollar, I have half-a-dollar.

On má dollar a půl, he has a dollar and a half.

Nikdy nemám čas, I never have time.

Proč nemáte nikdy čas? why have you never time?

Proto že mám moc práce, because I have much work (much to do).

Proto že mám mnoho co dělat, because I have much to do.

Proto že mám tuze moc práce, because I have very much to do.

Jak moc? Jak mnoho? how much (many)?

Tak moc. Tak mnoho. So much (many).

Tak tuze moc, so very much.

Proč tak moc? why so much?

Stále tak tuze moc, always so very much.

Žádný nemá tak mnoho, nobody has so much.

Ne tuze moc, not too much.

Co to? what is that?

Nic, nothing.

Note 1. It will be observed that in Bohemian there is a double negation expressed in a negative sentence:

Já nemám nic; *literally,* I have not nothing, (*actually,* I have nothing).
Žádný nemá nic; nobody has not nothing, (nobody has anything).
Nemáte nikdy nic; you never have not nothing, (you never have anything).

Note 2. The order of the words in a sentence is much less rigid than in English, and may often be changed at pleasure or according to the stress we wish to lay upon a certain word, without changing the sense. For instance:

**Žádný nemá mnoho;   mnoho nemá žádný;
nemá žádný mnoho.**

This is always one and the same sentence, the words fitting together at the pleasure of the speaker. But in English we are rigidly bound to a certain order : *nobody has much.* It would be impossible to transpose the words and say : *much has nobody; has nobody much.*

Of course, not every Bohemian sentence yields to transposition to the same extent, but nearly every one yields more or less. Let us take another illustration at random from the foregoing exercises :

Proto že mám moc práce, *because I have much work* (*much to do*) may be expressed as follows, without changing the sense :

proto že moc práce mám;

proto že práce moc mám;

proto že moc mám práce;

proto že práce mám moc.

In the English sentence no transposition is possible. What an immense help this freedom of transposition is, especially in poetry, will be apparent to the student.

LESSON VI.

Já jsem, jsem	*yá sěm* *sěm*	} I am	**ty jsi** jsi	*ty si* *si*	} thou art	

on jest,	*ŏn yest;*	**on je,**	*ŏn yě;*	**jest, je**	he is
ona ,,	*ŏná ,, ;*	**ona ,,**	*ŏná ,, ;*	,, ,,	she is
ono ,,	*ŏnŏ ,, ;*	**ono ,,**	*ŏnŏ ,, ;*	,, ,,	it is

My jsme, jsme	*me smě* *smě*	} we are	**vy jste** jste	*vee stě* *stě*	} you are

oni (ony, ona) jsou, jsou	*ŏňí (ŏny, ŏná) soŭ,* *soŭ*	} they are			

Note 1. The verb **býti**, *beeťi* (to be) is the only auxiliary verb in the Bohemian language.

Jsem, jsi, jsme, jste, jsou, as shown above, are pronounced: *sem, si, smě, stě, soŭ.* In spelling the initial **j** is also frequently omitted, even by some of the best writers : **sem, si, sme, ste, sou.**

---

dobrý, á, é	*dobree*	good	**také, taky**	*tŭke*	also, too;
špatný, á, é	*shpătnee*	bad	**ale**	*ălě*	but
drahý, á, é	*drăhee*	dear	**zde, tu, tady**	*zdě, tŭ, tăde,*	here,
laciný, á, é	*lătsinee*	cheap			present;
čerstvý, á, é	*cherstvee,*	fresh	**teda**	*tĕdă*	well then;
doma	*dŏmă*	at home	**už, již**	*ŭsh, yeež*	already

není *nĕñi* (colloquially : **nejní**, *neyñi*), he (she, it) is not
pravda *prăvdă* true, truth

EXERCISES.

Jsem zde,	I am here.
Zde jsem,	here I am.
Já jsem už zde,	I am here already.
Jsi zde?	art thou here?
Už jsem tu,	I am here already.
Jste už tady?	are you already here?
Už jsme tady,	we are here already.
My jsme už také zde,	we are also here already.
Jsou už zde?	are they already here?

Ano, už jsou tu!	Yes, they are here already.
Teda jsou všichni zde;	well, then they are all here.
Proč jsme zde?	why are we here? (what are we here for?)
Proč vy jste tu!	why are you here?
A proč on tady je?	and why is he present?
Proč jsou ty zde?	why are those here?

Máme dobrý chleb,	we have good bread.
Je ten chleba dobrý?	is this bread good?

Ano, je dobrý;	yes, it is good.
Ale je drahý,	but it is dear.
My máme chleba doma,	we have bread at home.

Je čerstvý?   is it fresh?

Ano, ten chleba je čerstvý; yes, that bread is fresh.

Ale proč je tak drahý? but why is it so dear?

Není drahý,   it is not dear.

Jest tuze drahý,   it is very dear.

Vždyť (dyť) není drahý; but it is *not* dear.

Ale vždyť není drahý; why, it ain't dear at all.

Je laciný,   it is cheap.

Je dost laciný, it is cheap enough.

Je tuze laciný, it is very cheap.

Ten sýr je dobrý, that cheese is good.

Ta voda je dobrá, that water is good.

Ano, je tuze dobrá; yes, it is very good.

Je čerstvá,   it is fresh.

To pivo je taky dobré, that beer is also good.

Ano, to je pravda; yes, that is true.

Je čerstvé,   it is fresh.

Ale ta soda není dobrá, but this soda-water is not good.

To víno je špatné, that wine is bad.

Proč není to víno také tak dobré? why is that wine not just as good?

My máme dobré víno, we have good wine.

Kde mají dobré pivo? where do they have (keep) good beer?

Zde všude,   here everywhere.

Je to pravda?   is it true?

Ano, to je pravda; yes, that is true.

Zde všude mají dobré pivo, here they everywhere have good beer.

Ale víno nemají dobré, but their wine is not good (*literally:* but wine they have not good).

Proč nemáte dobré víno? why have you not good wine?

Note 2. It will be observed that the termination of the adjectives **dobrý, drahý** etc. changes according to gender.

The masculine gender terminates in   **ý**
the   feminine   ,,   ,,   ,,   **á**
the   neutre   ,,   ,,   ,,   **é**

dobrý sýr (masc.),   *dobree seer,*   good cheese;

dobrá voda (fem.),   *dobrá vŏdǎ,*   good water;

dobré pivo (neut.)   *dobré (eh) pivŏ,* good   beer.

The feminine and neutre will always be indicated by placing **á, é** after the masculine adjective, as above.

In common conversation, however, the masculine termination is also used in the neutre gender : **dobrý pivo;** so that practically we hear only the two terminations **ý** and **á** : **dobrý, dobrá.**

Note 3. In ordinary speech the final *ý* of all adjectives in the masculine gender is pronounced *ey* (as in *they*), and such is in fact the prevalent custom in relation to the long letter *ý*, no matter where it occurs, as stated in the "Rules of Pronunciation". Hence we hear *dobrey*, *dráhey* in the masculine gender, instead of *dobree*, *dráhee*. This is the general colloquial usage, by no means confined to the uneducated classes. It has sprung up quite naturally because the sound of *ey* is not only easier, but also more euphonious than the sound of *ee*, in most such cases. Listening to the common conversation of Bohemians, the beginner will almost constantly hear the long *ý* pronounced *ey*.

LESSON VII.

Rád	*rád*	glad	**nemíti rád**	*nemeeťi rád,*	(*nemeet*	
nerad	*nerád*	sorry		*rád*), to dislike		
rádi	*ráďi* } (the same		**býti rád**	*beeťi rád, (beet rád),* to		
neradi	*neraďi* } in plural)			be glad		
míti rád	*meeťi rád (meet rád)* to like		**býti nerad**	*beeťi nerád (beet nerád),* to be sorry		

vždyť	*vždiť* } but, well, yet		**veliký,**	**á, é**	*velikee* }	large,	
dyť (colloquial)	*dyť* }		**velký**		*velkee* }	great, big	
tak	*täk*	so, such	**malý,**	**á, é**	*mälee*	small, little	
také tak } *täkě täk* { just so,			**dlouhý,**	**á, é**	*dloŭhee*	long	
taky tak } { just as			**krátký,**	**á, é**	*krátkee*	short	
			pravý,	**á, é**	*prävee*	right, genuine	
všude	*fshudě*) every-		**falešný,**	**á, é**	*fäleshnee*	false	
všade	*fshădě* { where		**plný,**	**á, é**	*pl-nee*	full	
všudy	*fshudy*)		**prázný,**	**á, é**	*práznee*	empty	

i	*e*	oh, well	nebo	*něbŏ*	or
že	*žě*	that	jako	*yăkŏ*	as, like
že je	*žě yě*	that he (she, it) is	skoro	*skorŏ*	almost
zase	*zá-sě*		tomu	*tŏmŭ*	of it
zas	*záss*	again	žádné	*žádné*	none
opět	*op-yet*		dlužen	*dloožen*	indebted

EXERCISES.

Já jsem rád, I am glad.

To sem rád! I am so glad!

Tuze rád! very glad!

Jsme tomu rádi, we are glad of it.

Tuze jsme tomu rádi, we are very glad of it.

Oni jsou tomu moc rádi, they are very glad of it.

Jsi rád nebo ne? art thou glad or not?

Jste tomu rádi? are you glad of it?

Máte to rád? (speaking to *one* person) do you like it?

Máte to rádi? (speaking to *more than one* person) do you like it?

Nemám to rád, I do not like it.

Nic to nemám rád, I do not like it at all.

Nemají to rádi. Oni to nemají rádi. They do not like it.

Jsem rád že mám peníze; I am glad (that) I have money.

Ten dollar je falešný; that dollar is false.

Není, je pravý; no, it is genuine.

Já mám vždycky dobré peníze, I have always good money.

Máte vůz plný? have you a full wagon (is your wagon full)?

Vůz není plný, the wagon is not full.

On je skoro prázný, it is almost empty.

On je rád že má prázný vůz; he is glad that he has an empty wagon.

Já mám dluh, I have a debt.

Mám jen malý dluh, I have only a small debt.

Ale ty máš (vy máte) velký dluh; but thou hast (you have) a big debt.

Mám také tak velký dluh jako vy; I have just as large a debt as you.

Vždyť máte peníze! but you have money!

I nemám žádné; oh, I have none (well, I have none).

On je všude dlužen, he is indebted everywhere (he owes everybody).

Už zase máme peníze, again we have (some) money.

Ale vy zas už nemáte peníze, but you again have no money.

Já sem tuze rád, že mám peníze! I am very glad that I have money!

On je tuze nerad, že je dlužen; he is very sorry, that he is in debt.

Proč je dlužen? why is he in debt?

Proto že nemá peníze, because he has no money.

Vždyť (dyť) on nemá skoro žádný dluh; well, he has almost no debt (is almost out of debt).

To je pravda, that is true.

On není dlužen, he is not in debt.

Mám velký dluh, nebo malý? have I a large debt or a small one?

Tu jest účet, here is the bill.

To není dlouhý účet, that is not a long bill.

Je jenom krátký, it is only short.

Ano, velmi krátký; yes, very short.

Máte jen tak malý účet? have you only such a small bill?

Nemám rád velký účet, I do not like to have a large account.

Je velký dost, it is large enough

Nemám mnoho, I have not much.

To je nic, that is nothing.

To je jako nic, that is like nothing.

To že je nic? this you call nothing (*literally:* that this is nothing)?

Oni jsou rádi, že tam není žádný dluh; they are glad, that there is not any debt there.

I je tam dluh, ale malý; well, there is a debt there, but a small one.

Pravda, jenom malý: true, only a small one.

Ano, tak to je; yes, it is so.

Ne, tak to není; no, it is not so.

Účet je pravý, the bill is right.

Ten účet není pravý, that bill is not right.

Je falešný, it is false.

A proč? and why?

Proto že je! because it is!

LESSON VIII.

Nejsem	*neysem*	I am not	nejsme	*neysmě*	we are not
není	*neyñi*	he (she, it) is not	nejste	*neystě*	you are not
nejsi	*neysi*	thou art not	nejsou	*neysoñ*	they are not

Note. Always pronounce *ney*, in the pronouncing column, like the English word *neigh*.

otec	*otĕts*	father	strýc	*streets, streyts*	uncle
matka	*mătkă*	mother	teta	*tĕtă*	aunt
bratr	*bră-tr*	brother	hoch	*hŏkh*	} boy
sestra	*sest-ră*	sister	chlapec	*khlăpets*	
syn	*syn*	son	holka	*holkă*	} girl
dcera	*tsĕră*	daughter	děvče, n.	*ďefchĕ*	

	docela	*dotsĕlă*	all, quite
	pryč	*pritch*	away, gone
	i	*e*	both…and

EXERCISES.

Nejsem rád,   I am not glad.
Nejsem tomu rád,   I do not like it.
Nejsi rád?   art thou not glad?
Nejste rád? (addressing *one* person;) **nejste rádi?** (addressing *more than one* person;) are you not glad?
Jsem sám,   I am alone?
Docela sám?   all alone?
Ano, docela samoten; yes, all alone.
Není otec doma? is father not at home?
Ne, on není doma; no, he is not at home.
Není žádný doma? is nobody at home?
Matka, ani bratr, ani sestra nejsou doma; neither mother, nor brother or sister are at home.
Kde jsou?   where are they?
Pryč; gone.
Všichni jsou pryč? are they all gone?
Ano, všichni; yes, all of them.

Je strýc doma? is uncle at home?
Nebo teta? or aunt?
Jsou taky pryč; they are gone, too.
Ten hoch je tu sám; the boy (this, that boy) is here alone.
Ta holka je pryč; the girl (that girl) is gone.
To děvče je doma samotno, that girl is at home alone.
Proč tu není bratr? why is the brother (her brother) not here?
On není doma, on je pryč; he is not at home, he is gone.
Dcera není zde docela samotna, the daughter is not here all alone.
Matka je zde také; the mother (her mother) is here, too.
Je někdo doma? is somebody at home?
Není; no.
Dnes jsou všichni pryč, to-day they are all gone.

A kde jsou? and where are they?	**Proč jste tu samotna?** (fem.) why
Někde pryč, somewhere away.	are you here alone?
Práve jsem tu sama (fem.); I am	**Protože otec i matka jsou pryč,** be-
here·just alone.	cause both father and mother are
	gone.

LESSON IX.

Byl jsem *bill sĕm* ⎫ I have
(byla, f. *billă* ,, ⎬ been;
bylo, n.) *billŏ* ,, ⎭ I was

byl jsi *bill si* ⎧ thou hast
(abbr.) **byl's,** m. *billss* ⎬ been;
,, **byla's,** f. *billăss* ⎭ thou wast

byl (a, o) *bill (ă, ŏ)* ⎧ he (she, it) has been;
he (she, it) was

byli jsme *billy smĕ* ⎫ we have
(byly, f. ⎬ been;
byla, n.) ⎭ we were

byli jste *billy stĕ* ⎱ you have been;
you were

byli (y,a) *billy(y,ă)* ⎱ they have been;
they were

Nebyl jsem *nĕ-bill sĕm* ⎫ I have not
been;
I was not

Nebyli jsme *nĕ-billy smĕ* ⎫ we have not
been;
we were not

etc.

Kde jsem byl? *gdĕ sĕm bill* ⎱ where have I been?
where was I?

Kde jsme byli? *gdĕ smĕ billy?* ⎱ where have we been?
where were we?

etc.

Míti, to have: **mám,** I have;

měl jsem,	*m'yell sĕm,*	⎱ I have had; I had;
měla jsem, f.	*m'yellă sĕm,*	
měli jsme,	*m'yelli smĕ,*	we have had; we had;

and so forth, using **měl, měli** in place of **byl, byli.**

Note 1. There is in Bohemian no such formal difference between the perfect and imperfect tense as in English: *I have been; I was.*

Note 2- There is a distinction of gender in the past tense, which does not exist in English. **I have been, I was,** is used in all cases. In Bohemian however, when a man speaks, he says: **byl jsem,** *bill sěm;* when a woman speaks, she says: **byla jsem,** *billǎ sěm.* And this rule covers every verb in the language. For instance, a man says :

jedl jsem,	*yěd'l sěm,*	I ate; I have eaten;
sedl jsem,	*sěd'l sem,*	I sat down; I have sat down;
šel jsem,	*shell sem,*	I went; I have gone;
šil jsem,	*shill sem,*	I sewed; I have sewn;
viděl jsem,	*vid'el sem,*	I saw; I have seen.

A woman says :

jedla jsem,	*yědlǎ sěm;*		**šla jsem,**	*shlǎ sem;*
sedla jsem,	*sědlǎ sem;*		**šila jsem,**	*shillǎ sem;*
	viděla jsem,	*vid'elǎ sem.*		

In the third person of the past tense we say in English :

he was, he has been; she was, she has been; it was, it has been.

In Bohemian we must say : **on byl, ona byla, ono bylo,** according to gender. This rule holds good in the conjugation of every verb.

For instance :

Jedl, *yed'l,* he has eaten; he ate;	**šel,** *shell,* he has gone; he went;
jedla, *yedlǎ,* she has eaten; she ate;	**šla,** *shlǎ,* she has gone; she went;
jedlo, *yedlǒ,* it has eaten; it ate;	**šlo,** *shlǒ,* it has gone; it went.

In the *plural* number the distinction of sex is simply grammatical and perfectly useless; in the ordinary spoken language there is none whatever. In grammatical theory

byli jsme,	**byli jste,**	**byli,**	is	masculine;
byly jsme,	**byly jste,**	**byly,**	is	feminine;
byla jsme,	**byla jste,**	**byla,**	is	neutre.

But in the living tongue, or at least in ordinary conversation, we hear in all three genders :

byli jsme, *billi smě;* **byli jste,** *billi stě;* **byli,** *billi.*

There is no difference of pronunciation between **byli** and **byly;** and this orthographical distinction as well as the form **byla** in the third person neutre are only maintained by the pedantry of theoretical grammarians, opposing changes which a living tongue has actually undergone and which always tend in the direction of practical simplicity. That artificial and useless distinction of gender is found in writing, but not in conversation.

Note 3. The form of the second person plural as given above (**byli jste,** *billi stě*) is of course used when several persons are meant or spoken to; but when employing **vy,** *you,* in addressing a single person, we leave the main verb in the singular, whereas in English it is put in the plural, as if several persons were addressed : **byl jste,** *bill stě,* you have been, you were, (meaning only one person). And so in all Bohemian verbs ; for instance :

jedli jste, *yed'li stě,* you have eaten, you ate, (meaning several persons);

jedl jste, *yed'l stě,* you have eaten, you ate, (meaning one person, addressed **vy,** *you*).

Ráno	*ránŏ*	in the morning	**včera**	*fcheră*	yesterday
v poledne	*fpŏlednĕ*	at noon	**včera večer**	*fcheră vĕcher,*	last evening; last night
večer	*vĕcher*	in the evening			
venku	*venkŭ*	outside, out of doors	**zima**	*zimă*	cold
			oba	*ŏbă*	both

Exercises.

Byl jsem doma,	I was at home.
Byl jsem stále doma,	I have been at home all the time.
Byl jsi doma ? (*abbreviated :* **byl's doma?**)	hast thou been at home? wast thou at home?

Ne, nebyl jsem doma; no, I was not at home.

Ale bratr byl doma, but brother was at home.

Kde jsi byl? (*abbreviated:* **kde's byl?** *gděs bil?*) where hast thou been? where wast thou?

Kde jste byl? Kde jste byla? (fem.) (*when addressing one person*) where have you been? where were you?

Byl jsem pryč, I was away.

Byla jsem pryč (fem.) I was away.

Byli jsme právě pryč, we were just gone.

Byli jsme všichni pryč, we were all gone; we have all been away.

Kde byl otec? where was father?

Byl venku, he was out of doors.

A matka? and mother?

Matka byla také pryč, mother also was gone.

Oba byli pryč, they were both gone.

Žádný nebyl doma, nobody was at home (*literally:* nobody was not at home).

Všichni byli pryč, all were gone.

Ráno byli jsme doma a v poledne pryč; in the morning we were at home and at noon we were gone.

Byli jste večer doma? (*addressing one person:* **byl jste večer doma?**) Were you at home in the evening?

Nebyli jsme doma, we were not at home.

Nebyl jsem doma, I was not at home.

Proč jsi nebyl doma? why wast thou not at home?

Proč jste nebyl doma? why were you not at home?

Kdo byl doma? who was at home?

Bratr a sestra byli oba doma, brother and sister were both at home.

Proč nebyli venku? why were they not out of doors?

Proto že bylo zima, because it was cold.

Nebylo zima včera večer, it was not cold last evening.

Že nebylo? wasn't it?

Ba bylo! oh yes, it was!

Včera bylo zima, yesterday it was cold.

Nebylo tuze, it was not very.

LESSON X.

It will doubtless be self-evident to the student, that the past tense in the preceding lesson may at pleasure be connected with the personal pronoun, as is the rule in English.

(*Instead of:*)		(*we can say:*)	
byl jsem,	I have been	já jsem byl,	*yá sěm bill*
byl jsi,	thou hast been	ty jsi byl,	*ty si bill*
		(*abbrec.* ty's byl,	*tyss bill*)
byl, a, o,	he (she, it) has been	on (ona, ono) byl, a, o,	*ŏn bill*
byli jsme,	we have been	my jsme byli,	*me smě billy*
byli jste,	you have been	vy jste byli,	*vee stě billy*
byli, y, a,	he (she, it) has been	oni byli,	*ŏñi billy*

The sense is not changed thereby, only more emphasis is laid on the subject.

Then again, in the *first* person of the second form, both singular and plural, the auxiliary **jsem, jsme** is commonly left out.

(*Instead of:*)		(*we say :*)	
já jsem byl,	*yá sěm bill*	já byl,	I have been; I was;
my jsme byli,	*me smě billy*	my byli,	we have been; we were;
já jsem měl,	*yá sěm m'yell*	já měl,	I have had; I had;
my jsme měli,	*me smě m'yelli*	my měli,	we have had; we had;
já jsem šel,	*yá sěm shell*	já šel,	I have gone; I went;
my jsme šli,	*me smě shli*	my šli,	we have gone; we went.

u mě	*ŭm'yě*	by me,	with me,	at my house (*or* place)
u tebe	*ŭtěbě*	by thee,	with thee,	at thy house
u něho	*ŭñehŏ* ⎫	by him,	with him,	at his house
u něj	*ŭñey* ⎭			
u ní	*ŭñee*	by her,	with her,	at her house
u nás	*ŭnáss*	by us,	with us,	at our house
u vás	*ŭváss*	by you,	with you,	at your house
u nich	*ŭñikh*	by them,	with them.	at their house
rodiče	*roďichě*	parents	celý den	*tsělee den*	all day
domu	*dŏmŭ*	home	až	*ăsh*	till, until
nic než	*ñits něsh*	nothing but	pak	*păk*	then

EXERCISES.

Já byl doma, I was at home.

Byl jsem doma celý den, I was at home all day.

Byl jsem pořád doma, I have been at home all the time.

Byl otec doma? was father at home?

Ano, byl; yes, he was.

A kdy byl doma? and when was he at home?

Skoro celý den, nearly all day.

Já šel domu ráno, I went home in the morning

Kdy sestra šla domu? when did sister go home?

Ona šla domu večer, she went home in the evening.

Nešla domu až večer, she didn't go home till evening.

Byl strýc doma? was uncle at home?

Nebyl; he was not.

Byl's u něho? wast thou at his house?

Byl jste u něho? were you at his house?

Ano, byl jsem tam; yes, I was there.

Sestra byla zde, sister was here.

Byla u mě, she was at my house.

Byla také u vás? was she also at your house?

Byla tam v poledne, she was there at noon.

Teta u nás nebyla, aunt was not at our house.

Ale její hoch tam byl, but her boy was there.

My byli včera u ní, we were at her house yesterday.

Rodiče byli včera ráno doma, our parents were at home yesterday morning.

Pak šli pryč, then they went away.

A my jsme šli taky pryč, and we went away, too.

Byl někdo u nich? was anybody at their house?

Žádný u nich nebyl, nobody was at their house.

V poledne někdo tam byl, ale šel pryč; at noon somebody was there, but went away.

Já měl dnes maso a pivo, I had to-day meat and beer.

Sestra měla maso a chleba, sister had meat and bread.

Ten malý hoch neměl nic, that little boy had nothing.

Proč neměl nic? why did he have nothing?

Neměli jsme nic pro něho, we had nothing for him.

Byl zde ten chlapec? was that boy here?

4

Byl tu,	he was here.	**Docela sám,**	all alone.
Co měl?	what did he have?	**Měli jste dnes víno?**	have you had wine to-day?
Nic neměl;	he had nothing.		
Byl zde pořád?	has he been here all the time?	**Ne, my jsme měli pivo;**	no, we had beer.
Ano, byl tu stále;	yes, he has been here all the time.	**A co oni měli?**	and what did they have?
Kdy šel pryč?	when did he go away?	**Také pivo;**	beer, also.
Šel večer,	he went in the evening.	**My neměli nic,**	we had nothing.
Šel sám?	did he go alone?	**Ale pranic!**	not a thing!

LESSON XI.

Budu	*budŭ*	I shall be, ,, will ,,	**budeme**	*bŭdemĕ*	we shall be, ,, will ,,
budeš	*bŭdesh,*	thou will be	**budete**	*bŭdĕtĕ*	you will be
bude	*bŭdĕ*	he (she, it) will be	**budou**	*bŭdoŭ*	they will be

nebudu *nĕbŭdŭ*, I shall (will) not be; etc.

neb	*neb*	or	**snad**	*snăd*	perhaps
nebo	*nĕbŏ*		**sotva**	*sŏtvă*	hardly
brzo	*br-zŏ*	soon	**zítra**	*zeetră*	to-morrow
brzy	*br-ze*		**zejtra**	*zeytră*	
hned	*hned*	presently, right away	**letos**	*letŏs*	this year
až	*ăsh*	when	**dobře**	*dobrshĕ*	well, right, it is well, all right.
když	*gdiž*				

dělati	*ďelă-ťi*	to do	**prodávati**	*prodávă-ťi*	to sell; to be selling;
platiti	*plăti-ťi*	to pay			
kupovati	*kŭpovă-ťi*	to buy; to be buying;	**chtíti**	*khťee-ťi*	to want.

Note 1. English verbs in the infinitive have various endings: *to do, to pay, to sell, to speak, to converse, to understand,* etc.

Bohemian verbs invariably end in **ti.** However, in ordinary discourse the final **i** is nearly always dropped, and very often it is also omitted in spelling; the preceding **t** in such cases should indeed be written and pronounced **ť**; but it generally retains its common *hard* sound:

dělat	*d'elát*	to do	kupovat	*kúpovát*	to buy
platit	*plať'it*	to pay	prodávat	*prodávát*	to sell
	chtít	*khť'eet*	to want.		

Note 2. **Budu, budeš,** etc., connected as an auxiliary with the infinitive of another verb forms the future tense of this verb:

budu dělati	⎰ I shall (will) do	bude kupovat	he will buy
,, dělat	⎱	budeme prodávat	we shall (will) buy
budeš platit	thou wilt pay	budete chtít	you will want
	budou chtíti	they will want.	

Zde jsem, here I am.

Už jste tu? are you here already?

Je zde taky bratr? is brother also here?

Není, ale bude tu hned; he is not, but he will be here presently.

To bude dobře, that will be all right.

Kdy zde bude otec? when will father be here?

Dnes sotva, hardly to-day.

Snad zejtra, perhaps to-morrow.

Proč tu bude? why will he be here?

Kupovat obilí a seno, to buy grain and hay.

Budete mít letos víno? will you have wine this year?

Nebudeme mít žádné víno, we shall have no wine.

Co budou u vás prodávat? what will they sell at your place?

Nebudou nic prodávat, they will sell nothing.

Máte čerstvé*) máslo? have you fresh butter?

Dnes nemáme, to-day we have not.

Nemáme žádné, we have none.

Ale budeme mít zejtra, but we shall have (some) to-morrow.

---

*) See lesson VI. note 2.

Co budete dĕlat dnes veĕer? what will you do this evening?

Nebudu dĕlat nic, I shall do nothing.

A proĕ? and why?

Nemám co dĕlat, I have nothing to do.

Až bude zase práce, budu dĕlat; when there will be work again, I shall work.

LESSON XII.

Míti	*meeťi*	} to have	**chtíti**	*khťeeťi*	} to want
mít[1]	*meet*		**chtít**[1]	*khťeet*	

chci	*khtsi*	I want	**chceme**	*khtsĕmĕ*	we want
chceš	*khtsĕsh*	thou wantst	**chcete**	*khtsĕtĕ*	you want
chce	*khtsĕ*	he wants	**chtĕjí**	*khťe-yee*	they want

chtĕl jsem[2]	*khťel sĕm*	I wanted	**chtĕli jsme**	*khťeli smĕ*	we wanted

budu chtíti[3]	*budŭ khťeeťi*	}	I shall (will) want
„ **chtít**	„ *khťeet*		

budeme chtíti	*budĕmĕ khťeeťi*	}	we shall (will) want.
„ **chtít**	„ *khťeet*		

Note 1. Irregular verbs in the Bohemian language are far less numerous than in English. There is not a full dozen of them, whereas in English we find nearly two hundred. On the other hand, regular verbs have only one conjugation in English, whereas in Bohemian there are several conjugations, as we shall see in due time.

Chtíti and **míti** are irregular verbs.

---

1) See Lesson XI, Note 1.
2) See Lesson IX. **Chtĕl** simply takes the place of **byl.**
3) See Lesson XI, Note 2.

Od	*ŏd*	since, from	**nůž**	*noož*	knife
pro	*prŏ*	for	**vidlička**	*vidlichkă*	fork
více	*veetsĕ*	more	**jídlo**	*yeedlŏ*	someting to eat; victuals; meal
ještě	*yesh-ťe*	still, more, another	**jíst (jísti)**	*yeest*	to eat
trochu	*trokhŭ*	some, somewhat	**krájet (i)**	*kráyet*	to cut
spolu	*spŏlŭ*	together	**mluvit (i)**	*mlŭvit*	to speak
dlouho	*dloŭhŏ*	long	**dát (i)**	*dát*	to give
už dávno	*ŭsh dávnŏ*	already long (a long time already)	**dejte mi**	*deyťĕ me*	give me
			kůň	*kŭň*	horse
na prodej	*nă prodey*	for sale	**koně*)**	*koňe*	of the horse; for the ,,
nový, á, é	*nŏvee*	new	**ani**	*ăňi*	not one; not even; neither
starý, á, é,	*stăree*	old	**asi**	*ăssi*	about, probably
dříví	*drshee-vee*	wood	**se, s**	*sĕ*	with
stavivo	*stăvivŏ*	lumber	**opravdu**	*oprăvdŭ*	truly, really
míti hlad	*meeťi hlăd*	to be hungry	**muž**	*moož*	man

EXERCISES.

Máte peníze? have you money?

Mám asi dollar, I have about a dollar.

Nic více? nothing more?

Ani cent, not a cent.

Co s dollarem? what (can you do) with a dollar?

Aha, zde je ještě půl dollaru; ah, here is half a dollar more.

Bude to dost? will that be enough?

Sotva, hardly.

Ani to nebude dost, even that will not be enough.

Já mám hlad (literally: *I have hunger*), I am hungry.

Chci něco jíst, I want something to eat.

Máte nějaké jídlo? have you something to eat?

Tu máte maso, here you have (some) meat.

Dejte mi nůž, give me a knife.

Zde máte nůž a tu je vidlička; here you have a knife and here is a fork.

Nožem můžete dobře krájet, with the knife you can cut well.

Tu je kůň a vůz, here is a horse and a wagon.

Vy máte zde koně, you have a horse here.

---

*) The plural of the noun **kůň** is also **koně**, *koňe* (the horses).

Ano, jsem tu s koněm; yes, I am here with the horse.

To je dobrý kůň, that is a good horse.

Tuze dobrý; a také není na prodej; very good; and he is not for sale.

Máte nový vůz? have you a new wagon?

I ne; to je starý vůz; o no; that is an old wagon.

Ale jako nový; but (it looks) like a new one.

Opravdu? really?

Co máte na voze (ve voze)? what have you got in the wagon?

Dříví, wood.

Stavivo, lumber.

Trochu obilí je tam, some grain is in there.

Budete něco kupovati? will you buy something (will you make some purchases)?

Koně pro syna a vůz pro strýce, a horse for my son and a wagon for my uncle.

Chci dáti synovi dobrý potah, I want to give my son a good team.

Chtěl jsem to už dávno; I wanted (to do) it long ago.

On je zde se strýcem, he is here with uncle.

Jsou tu spolu, they are here together.

Jak dlouho jsou tu? how long are they here?

Od večera, since evening.

A jak dávno vy jste tu? and how long are you here?

Od poledne, since noon.

Tam ten muž má koně na prodej, that man there has a horse to sell.

Chcete vidět toho (*tŏhŏ*) muže? do you want to see that man?

Chci mluvit s tím (*s'tím*) mužem; I want to speak with that man.

Je na koni, he is on horseback.

Dobře že je tu s tím koněm; it is well he is here with that horse.

Je to velký kůň; it is a big horse.

Note 2. In the English language the noun remains nearly unchanged in all its relations, there being only a slight change in the genitive or possessive case: *brother, brother's* (of the brother); but this form of the possessive case is being more and more limited. The relations of one person or thing to another are expressed by separate words, called prepositions: *of a brother; to a brother; with a brother.*

In Bohemian these relations are expressed by changes in the termination of the noun, which process is called declension: **bratr,** *brother;* —**bratra,** *of a brother;* **bratru,** *to a brother;* **bratrem,** *with a brother.*

This is a heavy encumbrance which the Bohemian language shares with the German and Latin. The declension of the nouns is followed by that of the adjectives joined to the nouns, which are subject to corresponding changes in their terminations. Pronouns also have declensions, and these continue to exist even in the English tongue.

Note 3. The declension of Bohemian nouns varies according to their gender and the termination of their nominative; there is, besides, a slight variation between animate and inanimate nouns of the masculine gender.

The following table will bring before the student's eyes the different changes of the termination of Bohemian masculine nouns, in the singular, omitting the vocative case. A glance over the same now and then may assist him to become more rapidly familiar with the different endings and their signification in English; but only frequent use in common sentences during the further progress of these lessons will make them handy to him.

Inanimate nouns:

Dollar,	**vůz**	*dolăr,*	*vooz*	the dollar, the wagon;
dollaru,	**vozu**	*dolărŭ.*	*vŏzŭ*	of the dollar, the dollar's; of the wagon, the wagon's; (**v dollaru,** in the dollar: **ve voze,** in the wagon; etc.)
dollarem,	**vozem**	*dolărem.*	*vŏzem*	(or **s dollarem, s vozem**), with the dollar, with the wagon.

Animate nouns:

Syn,	**muž**	*syn,*	*moož*	the son, the man;
syna,	**muže**	*synă,*	*moožĕ*	of the son, the son's; of the man, the man's; also in the *accusative:* the son, the man);
synu,	**muži**	*synŭ,*	*mooži*	to the son, to the man; (**v synu, v synovi,** in the son; etc.)
——ovi,	**——ovi**	*synŏvi,*	*moožŏvi*	
synem,	**mužem**	*synem,*	*moožem*	(or **se synem, s mužem**), with the son, with the man.

Note 4. It will be observed that the letter ů in the nominative case of a monosyllable changes into **o** in the inflected cases :

vůz,	the wagon;	**vozu, -e**	of the wagon;
kůň,	the horse;	**koně,**	of the horse;
nůž,	the knife;	**nože,**	of the knife;

Nůž and similar nouns (masculine inanimate and ending in a soft consonant) are declined just like **muž;** only in the dative and locative case we cannot use the long form like **mužovi, v mužovi** (to the man, in the man), but must always employ only the short form: **noži, v noži, nŏži, cnŏži** (to the knife, in the knife); and the accusative agrees with the nominative: **nůž—nůž.**

Note 5. Prepositions consisting of a single consonant (**v, s, k,** simply abbreviations of **ve, se, ke,** — in, with, to) are always joined in pronunciation to the succeeding syllable; hence we write: **v synu, s koněm;** and pronounce: *vsynů* (or *fsinů*), *skoňem;* in the son, with the horse.

It may hardly be necessary to mention that the locative case does not always appear with the preposition **v** or **ve,** but employs also different other prepositions. For instance: **ve voze,** in the wagon; **na voze,** on the wagon; **o voze,** about the wagon.

LESSON XIII.

Museti	*mŭseťi*)	⎫		**jíti**	*yeeťi*	⎫
	mŭset	⎬ must, to have to			*yeet*	⎬ to go, to come.
musiti	*mŭsiťi*	⎭				⎭

musím	*mŭseem*	I must	**jdu**	*dŭ*		I go
musíš	*mŭseesh*	thou must	**jdeš**	*děsh*		thou goest
musí	*mŭsee*	he must	**jde**	*dě*		he goes
musíme	*mŭseemě*	we must	**jdeme**	*děmě*		we go
musíte	*mŭseetě*	you must	**jdete**	*dětě*		you go
musí	*mŭsee*	⎱ they must	**jdou**	*doŭ*		they go
musejí	*mŭsě-yee*	⎰				

*) The letter **s** has the same sharp sound as in *must*.

muset platiti		to have to pay	šel	*shell*	he has gone;
budu museti	*bñdñ mñžet.*	I shall			he went
		have to; I shall	půjdu	*pñydñ*	(colloquially
		be obliged.			*pñdñ*) I shall go
musel jsem	*mñžell žĕm*	I was o-	půjdeš, půjde, půjdeme, půjdete,
		bliged	půjdou;	*pñydesh, pñydĕ, pñy-*
musel	*mñžell*	he was obliged	*dĕmĕ, pñydĕtĕ, pñydoñ;* (collo-
muset jíti		to have to go, to be	quially: *pñdesh, pñdĕ, pñdĕmĕ,*
		obliged to go	*pñdĕtĕ, pñdoñ*);
šel jsem	*shell žĕm*	I have gone;	jdi	*ď'i*	go (thou)
		I went	jděte	*ď'etĕ*	go (you)

Note 1. All Bohemian verbs in the infinitive (as stated in Lesson XI, Note 1) end in **ti**, which becomes a simple **t** in ordinary discourse :

dělati, to do, to make; **platiti**, to pay; **kupovati**, to buy, to be buying; **prodávati**, to sell, to be selling; **museti**, must.

Note 2. Leaving out **ti** and putting **l** in its place (**la** for the feminine, **lo** for the neutre gendre), we get the past tense of every regular verb, using the auxiliary **jsem, jsi** in the first and second person singular, **jsme, jste** in first and second person plural, and changing **l** into **li** in the *plural* (feminine **ly**, neutre **la**, — of no account in ordinary conversation); in the third person singular and plural no auxiliary is used:

dělal	*ď'elñl*	he made;	he has made;
dělali	*ď'elñli*	they made;	they have made;
dělal jsem	*ď'elñl sem*	I made;	I have made;
dělal jsi	*ď'elñli ži*	thou madest;	thou hast made;
dělali jsme	*ď'elñli smĕ*	we made;	we have made;
dělali jste	*ď'elñli stĕ*	you made;	you have made;
platil	*plñť'il*	he paid;	he has paid;
kupoval	*kñpocñl*	he was buying;	he has been buying;
prodával	*prodñvñl*	he was selling;	he has been selling;
musel	*mñsell*	he had to;	he was obliged.

Ho	*hŏ*	him, it; of it;
ven	*ven*	out
venku	*venkŭ*	out of doors
prý	*pree*	they say;
(colloq. **prej**) *prey*		it is said
náš, m. ·	*násh*	our, ours
naší, f.	*náshee*	of our
dobře	*dobrshĕ*	well; right
tuze dobře	*toozĕ dobrshĕ*	very well
časně	*chăsśńe*	early
nějaký, á, é	*ňeyăkee*	some
(colloq. ňákej) *ňákey*		
pohromadě	*pŏ-hromăďe*	together
najednou	*năyednoŭ*	at once
dál	*dál*	in, farther
ať	*ăť*	let him be, let her be, let it be
po	*pŏ*	after
do	*dŏ*	to, before

žena	*žená*	woman
služka	*slŭshka*	servant girl
země, f.	*zemyĕ*	land, earth
snídaně, f.	*sňeedańe*	breakfast
oběd, m.	*ob·yĕd*	dinner
večeře, f.	*vĕchershĕ*	supper
kosť, f.	*kŏst*	bone
kus, m.	*kŭss*	piece
oděv, m.	*oďef*	clothing
oblek, m.	*oblĕk*	suit of clothes
kabát, m.	*kăbát*	coat
kalhoty, pl.	*kălhŏty*	pants
vesta, f.	*vestă*	vest
klobouk, m.	*kloboŭk*	hat
boty, pl.	*botty*	boots
škoda	*shkŏdă*	pity
hotov, a, o	*hŏtof*	ready
ke	*kĕ*	to

---

podívat se	*poďeevăt se*	to take a look
spáti	*spáťi, spát*	to sleep
státi	*stáťi, stát*	to stand
čekati	*chekăťi, chekăt*	to wait
viděti	*viďeťi, viďet*	to see
dívati se	*ďeevăt sĕ*	to look, to be looking

dělati	*ďelăťi, ďelăt*	to make
myslím	*mysleem*	I think
koupiti	*koŭpit*	to buy
kupovati	*kŭpŏvăt*	to be buying
prodati	*prodăt*	to sell
prodávati	*prodávăt*	to be selling

EXERCISES.

Musím jít ven.	I must go out.
Půjdu se podívat ven.	I shall go and look out.
Je někdo venku?	Is somebody out of doors?

Kdo je venku?	Who is out of doors?
Nějaká žena je tam.	Some woman is there.
Co chce ta žena?	What does that woman want?

Chce viděti dceru. She wants to see (her) daughter.

Je to matka naší služky. It is the mother of our servant girl.

Ať jde dál. Let her come in.

Proč nejde dál? Why doesn't she come in?

Chce něco jíst? Does she want anything to eat?

Dejte ženě jíst a pít. Give that woman to eat and to drink.

Maso na kosti a pivo. Meat on the bone and beer.

Až bude oběd. When dinner is (shall be) ready.

Bude zde spáti? Will she sleep here?

Já myslím. I think so.

Dobře teda. Very well, then.

Musí spáti se služkou. She must sleep with the servant girl.

Chci něco koupit. I want to buy something.

Chci si něco koupit. I want to buy me something.

Co si chcete koupit? What do you want to buy (yourself)?

Myslím že nějaký oděv. I think (that) some clothing.

Už jdu. I am going already.

Jdete taky? Are you going, too?

My taky jdeme. We are going, too.

Oni všichni jdou. They are all going.

Holka má mnoho práce. The girl has much to do.

Bude sotva do večera*) hotova. She will hardly be done before evening.

Myslím že bude s prací hotova. I think she will be done with the work.

Po večeři nemusí dělat nic. After supper she need not do anything.

Ať je večeře brzy hotova. Let supper be soon ready.

Bude zde ta ženská ke snídani? Will that woman be here to breakfast?

Myslím že bude. I think (that) she will.

Budeme míti snídani brzy ráno. We shall have breakfast soon in the morning.

Ano, časně ráno. Yes, early in the morning.

Kabát, kalhoty, vestu, klobouk. A coat, (a pair of) pants, a vest, a hat.

Snad také boty. Perhaps also (a pair of) boots.

Celý oblek. A whole suit.

Pravda, bude dobře koupit oblek. True, it will be well to buy a suit.

Myslím že sestra půjde taky. I think that sister will go, too.

Ano, půjde s tetou. Yes, she will go with auntie.

---

*) **Do večera**, instead of **do večeru**. — **Večer** has the same endings in the singular as the animate noun **syn**, excepting **-ovi** in the dative and locative.

Půjdeme všichni pohromadě.   We | Jděte se tam zase podívat. Go (you)
will all go together. | there and see again.
Jdi se podívat zdali jsou hotovi. Go | Už jdou; tu jsou. They are coming
(thou) and see if they are ready. | already; here they are.
My zde nebudeme stát a čekat. We | Půjdou všichni najednou. They will
shall not stand here and wait. | all go together.

Ten dům chci prodat.   That house | Škoda že museli sme ho prodat. It
I want to sell. | is a pity we had to sell it.
A proč to?   And why? | Náš nový dům nebude na prodej.
Je malý; musím ho prodat.   It is | Our new house will not be for sale.
small, I must sell it. | Není dobře prodávat nový dům. It
Myslím že je trochu malý. I think | is not well to sell (to be selling)
it is somewhat small. | a new house.
Ten starý dům byl dost velký. The | Budeme mít u domu kus země. We
old house was large enough. | shall have by (our) house a piece
                                   | of land.

   Note 3. The changes of endings of feminine nouns, excepting
the vocative case, are shown in the following exhibit:

1. **Žena**   *žena,*   the woman;

   ženy   *ženy,*   of the woman;

   ženu   *ženu,*   the woman, (accusative);

   ženě   *žeňe,*   to the woman, (v **ženě,** in the woman, etc.);

   ženou *ženou,*   (or se **ženou**) with the woman.

2. **Země**   *zemyě*   the earth, of the earth;

   zemi   *zemi,*   to the earth, (v **zemi,** in the earth, etc);

   zemí   *zemee,*   (or se **zemí**) with the earth.

3. **Kosť**   *kǒst,*   the bone;

   kosti *kosťi,*   of the bone, to the bone, (v **kosti** *fkosťi,* in the
                          bone, etc.);

   kostí *kosťee*   (or s **kostí** *skosťee*) with the bone.

Nouns ending in **e** (like **růže** *roože*, the rose) agree with **země**.

Nouns ending in **ka** change the hard consonant **k** into **c** *ts*, when the final **a** changes into **e :**

| matka, | služka, | *mátkă,* | *slŭshka,* | the mother, | the servant girl |
| matce, | služce, | *mátsě,* | *slŭshtsě,* | to the mother, | to the servant girl |

Nouns ending in **sť**, like **kosť**, are ALWAYS of the feminine gender.

Note 4. The verb **jíti** is irregular. Its future tense is formed by the prefix **pů**, and not by the auxiliary **budu**. The formation of the future by means of prefixes occurs quite often. as will be seen hereafter.

Note 5. The verbs **prodávati, kupovati** (to be selling, to be buying) are in fact reiterative forms of **prodati** (to sell, to make a sale) and **koupiti** (to buy, to make a purchase).

Common indefinite verbs, denoting a continuous action, may, as a rule, be changed into REITERATIVES, denoting a repeated action, by inserting **va** before the final syllable **ti** (or the final **t**) and lengthening the preceding vowel, if it be short. For instance:

dělati,	to make;	**dělávati,**	*ďelăcăťi* or *ďelăcăt,*	to use to make, to be in the habit of making;
platiti,	to pay;	**platívati,**	*plăťeevăt,*	to use to pay;
spáti,	to sleep;	**spávati,**	*spăcăt,*	to use to sleep;
jísti,	to eat;	**jídávati,**	*yeedăvăt,*	to use to eat; (irregular verb).

Note 6. In English, verbs are sometimes formed by prefixes joined to other verbs, to vary their signification; for instance:

| to deck — to bedeck | to judge — to prejudge | to sell — to undersell |
| to grow — to outgrow | to stand — to withstand | to turn — to overturn. |

The same rule finds application in Bohemian in a much higher degree. Prefixes may be joined to most of the verbs in order to modify or change their meaning; and it is astonishing how many new verbs are sometimes derived from the original verb by that process. As an example, let us take the verb **jíti**, to go :

dojíti,	*dŏ-yeeťi,*	to go (get, reach) somewhere; to make an errand;
najíti,	*nă-yeeťi,*	to find;
nadejíti,	*nădĕ-yeeťi,*	to gain, to get ahead, to head off;
obejíti,	*obĕ-yeeťi,*	to go round;
odejíti,	*odĕ-yeeťi,*	to go away, to leave;
pojíti,	*pŏ-yeeťi,*	to perish, to die;
podejíti,	*podĕ-yeeťi,*	to deceive, to cheat;
přejíti,	*prshĕ-yeeťi,*	to pass over, to pass by;
předejíti,	*prshĕdĕ-yeeťi,*	to come before, to get ahead, to anticipate;
přijíti,	*prshi-yeeťi,*	to come;
projíti,	*pro-yeeťi,*	to pass through;
rozejíti se,	*rŏzĕ-yeeťi sĕ,*	to part, to disperse;
ujíti,	*ŭ-yeeťi,*	to escape;
vejíti,	*vĕ-yeeťi,*	to go in, to come in;
vyjíti,	*vy-yeeťi,*	to go out, to come out;
zajíti,	*ză-yeeťi,*	to go down, to set, to pass behind;
zajíti si,	*ză-yeeťi si,*	to go out of one's way.

This shows the immense adaptability of the Bohemian verb, and certainly looks somewhat perplexing at first sight; but it is only necessary to fix in one's mind the meaning of a dozen of prefixes, which recur in all such cases, in order to have a key to the whole system. The same is true in English; a knowledge of the signification of the prefixes used in connection with verbs explains the modified meaning. Verbs formed by prefixes are in most cases contained separately in Bohemian dictionaries, the same as in English.

Note 7. An indefinite verb like **jíti,** *to go,* denotes a continuous action. When a new verb is formed by means of a prefix, it is definite, denoting a completed action: **dojíti,** to go (get, reach) somewhere; **najíti,** to find; etc. The present form of these verbs denotes, in fact, a *future* action : **dojdu,** I shall go or get somewhere; **najdu,** I shall find. Hence it is actually the future tense, there being no present, and the auxiliary **budu** can never be used. Such compound verbs have therefore only a past with the auxiliary **jsem,** and a simple future:

došel jsem, *dŏshell sem,* I went (got, reached) somewhere;

dojdu, *doydŭ,* I shall go (get, reach) somewhere;

našel jsem, *nŏshell sem,* I found;

najdu, *nŏydŭ.* I shall find.

LESSON XIV.

Slovo, n.	*slovŏ*	word	**teprv**	*tep^erf̌*	only, not before
horko, n.	*horkŏ*	heat; hot	**vedle**	*cědlě*	beside, next to
teplo, n.	*teplŏ*	warmth; warm	**nebe,** n.	*něbě*	heaven, sky
chladno, n.	*khlŭdnŏ*	cool	**slunce,** n.	*slŭntsě*	sun
blato, n.	*blŭtŏ*	mud	**měsíc,** m.	*myě-seets*	moon, month
město, n.	*myěs-tŏ*	city	**počasí,** n.	*pŏchŭssee*	weather
pšenice, f.	*pshě-ñitsě*	wheat	**znamení,** n.	*znŭmeñee*	sign
pole, n.	*polě*	field	**dešť,** m.	*deshť*	rain
poupě, n.	*poŭpyě*	bud	**stín,** m	*sťeen*	shade, shadow
dítě, n.	*ďeeťe*	child	**vítr,** m.	*vee-ťer*	wind
den, m.	*den*	day	**pěkný, á, é**	*pyěk-nee*	nice, fine
noc, f.	*nots*	night	**jasný, á, é**	*ydss-nee*	clear, bright
týden, m.	*teeden*	week	**hezky,**	*hessky*	nice
odpoledne	*ŏdpoledně*	afternoon	**zle**	*zlě*	bad, badly
půlnoc, f.	*poolnots*	midnight	**posud**	*pŏsŭd*	till now, still
dnes v noci	*dness vnotsi*	to-night	**okolo**	*ŏkolŏ*	about
západ slunce	*zápŭd slŭntsě*	sunset	**na**	*nŭ*	on, in
cesta, f.	*tsestŭ*	way, road	**s tím**	*sťeem*	with that
radost	*rŭdost*	pleasure	**za**	*zŭ*	behind, beyond
les	*less*	forest, timber	**zase, zas**	*zŭssě, zŭss*	again
			o	*ŏ*	at, on.
vidím	*viďeem*	I see	**svítiti**	*sweeťit*	to shine
pršeti	*p^ershěťi*	to rain	**svítí**	*sweeťee*	shines
prší	*p^ershee*	it rains	**už není**	*ŭsh neyñee*	is no more

choditi	*khŏďit*	to walk	dej mu	*dey mŭ* give (thou) him
chodím	*khŏďeem*	I walk	dejte mu	*deytě mŭ* give (you) him
chodí	*khŏďee* he (she, it) walks			

Note 1. Pršeti, pršet, *persheťi, pershet,* to rain; vítr, *veeter;* e is silent and placed there simply to elucidate the pronunciation. See Sec. 4, Part I.

EXERCISES.

Včera byl špatný den. Yesterday was a bad day.

Dnes je hezky. To-day is nice.

Opravdu, je pěkné počasí. Truly, it is fine weather.

Myslím že bude tak celý den. I think it will be so all day.

Bude teplo celý den. It will be warm all day.

Odpoledne bude horko. In the afternoon it will be hot.

Rád jsem venku za tepla. I like to be out when (it is) warm.

V horku nerad jdu do města. In the heat I do not like to go to town.

Já také ne. Neither do I.

Nebude tak zle s tím horkem. It won't be so bad with the heat.

Cesta je pěkná. The road is fine.

Není žádné blato. There is no mud.

Včera bylo ještě dost blata. Yesterday there was still enough mud.

Nerad chodím v blatě. I do not like to walk in mud.

Náš hoch rád chodí blatem. Our boy likes to walk through mud.

To snad každé dítě. Perhaps every child (likes that).

To je radost dítěte. That is a child's pleasure.

Ano, to dělá radost dítěti. Yes, it makes pleasure to a child.

Je nebe jasné? Is the sky clear?

Bylo, ale už není. It was, but is no more.

Vidím na nebi znamení deště. I see in the sky a sign of rain.

Ale slunce ještě svítí. But the sun is still shining.

Po slunce západu snad bude pršet. After sunset perhaps it will rain.

Je silný vítr. There is a strong wind.

Je skoro chladno ve stínu. It is almost cool in the shade.

No slunci je posud horko. In the sun it is still hot.

Dnes v noci svítí měsíc. To-night the moon shines.

Teprv o půlnoci. Only at (i. e. not before) midnight.

Ano, okolo půlnoci. Yes, about midnight.

Zde je náš dům. Here is our house.
Vedle domu je stodola. Beside the house there is a barn.
Za stodolou máme pole. Behind the barn we have a field.
Na tom poli je pšenice. On that field there is wheat.
Za tím polem máme kus lesa. Beyond that field we have a piece of timber.
Je to dobrý kus lesa. It is a good piece of timber.

Pak je zase kus pole s obilím. Then there is again a piece of a grainfield (*literally:* of a field with grain).
Jděte na pole. Go to (on) the field.
Jdi s tím dítětem. Go (thou) with the child.
Dej dítěti poupě z růže. Give (thou) the child a rose-bud (*literally:* a bud from the rose).
Otec je na poli. The father is in the field.

Note 2. The following little scheme shows the changes of the endings of *neutre* nouns, which in the nominative always end in **o, e, ě** or **í:**

slovo,	*slŏvŏ,*	the word;
slova,	*slŏvá,*	of the word;
slovu,	*slŏvŭ,*	to the word;

ve slovu,	*vĕ slŏvŭ*	in the word;(o slovu, about the word);
,, slově,	*vĕ slŏvyĕ*	
slovem,	*slŏvem,* (or **se slovem**) by *or* with the word.	

poupě,	*poŭpyĕ,*	the bud;
poupěte,	*poŭpyetĕ,*	of the bud;

poupěti,	*poŭpyeťi,* to the bud; (**v poupěti,** in the bud; etc.)
poupětem,	*poŭpyĕtĕm* (or **s poupětem**) with the bud.

pole,	*pŏlĕ,* the field; of the field;
poli,	*pŏli,* to the field; (**v poli,** in the field; etc.)

polem,	*polem,* (or **s polem**) with the field.

znamení,	*znămeñee,* the sign; of the sign; (**ve znamení,** in the sign; etc.);

znamením,	*znămĕ-ñeem* (or **se znamením**), with the sign.

LESSON XV.

Jeden	*yĕden*	one	**můj,** m.	*mooy*		my, mine
jedna, f.	*yĕdnă*	,,	**moji,** pl.	*moye*		my, mine, pl.
dva	*dwă*	two	**mých,** pl.	*meekh*		of my
dvě, f. & n.	*dwyĕ*	,,	**mým,** pl.	*meem*		to my
tři	*trshi*	three	**mými,** pl.	*meemi*		with my
čtyry	*shtiri*	four	**ty**	*ty*		those
pět	*pyĕt*	five	**k těm**	*kťem*		to those
šest	*shĕst*	six	**těch**	*ťekh*	} of those, from
sedm	*sedŭm*	seven	**z těch**	*sťekh*		those
osm	*osŭm*	eight	**v těch**	*fťekh*		in those
devět	*dev-yet*	nine	**od nás**	*od náss*		from us, from
deset	*desset*	ten				our place
oba, m.	*obă*	} both	**jaký, á, é**	*yăkee*		what, what kind
obě, f. & n.	*obyĕ*		**tamhle**	*támlĕ*		there, over there
pár	*pár*	} some, a few	**hned**	*hnĕd*		right away
několik	*ñekolik*		**a sice**	*ă sitsĕ*		that is, namely
mnoho	*mnohŏ*	a good deal	**možná**	*mŏžná*		perhaps, possibly
mnoho-li	*mnohŏ-li*	how much	**dokonce**	*dŏkontsĕ*		perhaps even
kolik	*kŏlik*	how many	**ještě něco?**	*yeshťe ñetso*		anything
asi tak	*ăsi tăk*	about				else?
tolik	*tŏlik*	so many, so much	**nejmíň**	*neymeeñ*		at least, least of all
k, ke, ku	*kĕ, kŭ*	to, unto	**mu, jemu,**	*mŭ, yĕmŭ,*		to him
i	*e*	oh! well	**v, ve**	*vĕ*		in
s, se	*sĕ*	with	**z, ze**	*zĕ*		from, of

Mluviti	*mlŭvit*	to speak	**utratil**	*ŭtrăťil*	spent
mluvil*)	*mlŭvil*	spoke	**prodati**	*prodăt*	to sell
utratiti	*ŭtrăťit*	to spend	**prodal**	*prodăl*	sold

*) See Lesson XIII, Note 2.

koupiti	*koŭpit*	to buy	hospoda, f.	*hŏspodă*	saloon, tavern
koupil	*koŭpil*	bought	mouka, f.	*moŭkă*	flour
koupím	*koŭpeem*	I shall buy	cena, f.	*tsĕnă*	price, value
rozuměti	*rozŭmyet*	to understand	podpora, f.	*pŏdporă*	support
rozuměl	*rozŭm'yell*	understood	drobné, pl.	*drŏbné*	change
rozumím	*rozŭmeem*	understand	výběr, m.	*veeb-yer*	choice
jezditi	*yezd'it*	to drive, to ride	tucet, m.	*tŭtset*	dozen
jezdil	*yezd'il*	drove, rode	domu	*domŭ*	home
jezdím	*yezd'eem*	I drive, I ride	na venku	*nă venkŭ*	in the country
znám	*znám*	I know, I am acquainted	spokojen	*spŏkŏyen*	satisfied
			můžete	*moožĕtĕ*	you can, you may
vím to	*veem tŏ*	I know it			
dělá	*d'elă*	makes	počitejme	*pocheeteymĕ*	let us count
člověk, m.	*chlŏ-vyĕk*	man	sto	*stŏ*	a hundred
pán	*pán*	gentleman	víc, více	*veets, veetsĕ*	more
farma, f.	*farmă*	farm	stojí	*stŏyee*	costs

EXERCISES.

Tady jsme zas. Here we are again.

Jaký pěkný den! What a nice day!

Máte ještě peníze? Have you still (some) money?

I ještě něco mám. Well, I have still something.

Mnoho-li asi máte? About how much have you?

Ne mnoho. Not much.

Mám ještě dva dollary. I have still two dollars.

Já taky mám pár dollarů. I also have a few dollars.

Kolik dollarů? How many dollars?

Asi tak čtyry dollary. About four dollars.

Žádné drobné? No change?

Mám také pár centů. I have also a few cents.

Utratil jsem mnoho. I have spent a good deal.

Jak mnoho asi? About how much?

Nejmíň pět nebo šest dollarů. At least five or six dollars.

Já také utratil několik dollarů. I also spent a few dollars.

Víc než já? More than I?

Možná asi sedm dollarů. Perhaps about seven dollars.

Nebo dokonce osm. Or perhaps even eight.

K dollarům počítejme čas. To the dollars let us count the time.

Ten má taky cenu v dollarech. It also has a price (value) in dollars.

Co stojí ten vůz? How much is that wagon? (*literally:* what costs that wagon?).

Sto dollarů. A hundred dollars.

Za sto dollarů můžete koupit dva vozy. For a hundred dollars you can buy two wagons.

Zde je můj syn. Here is my son.

Oba moji synové jsou tu. Both my sons are here.

Ano, myslím že jsou. Yes, I think (that) they are.

Jeden z mých synů právě šel ven. One of my sons has just gone out.

Dejte mým synům oběd; a sice hned. Give (to) my sons a dinner; I mean right away.

Ano, dáme pánům dobrý oběd. Yes, we shall give to the gentlemen a good dinner.

Koupil jsem mouku. I bought (some) flour.

Chcete koupit ještě něco? Do you want to buy anything else?

Půjdu a koupím dva nože. I shall go and buy two knives.

Já půjdu taky a koupím tucet nožů. I shall go, too, and buy a dozen knives.

To dělá mnoho. That makes much.

Devět nebo deset dollarů je pryč. Nine or ten dollars are gone.

Dost možná. Very likely.

Já rozumím vozům. I understand wagons.

Je velký rozdíl ve vozech. There is a great difference in wagons.

Já jezdím s vozy už dávno. I drive wagons a long time already.

V synech (mých) mám nyní podporu. In my sons I have now a support.

To je dobře. That is well.

Jsem spokojen se syny. I am satisfied with (my) sons.

Jsme všichni na farmě. We are all on the farm.

Synové jsou rádi na farmě. My sons like it on the farm.

Jsme všichni rádi na venku. We all like it in the country.

Ale k nožům také vidličky. But to the knives also forks.

Tamhle mají velký výběr v nožích. Over there they have a large choice in knives.

Ano, vím to; mají tuze dobré nože. Yes, I know it; they have very good knives.

Máte pravdu. You are right (*literally:* you have right).

Tamhle v hospodě jsou tři muži. Over there in the saloon there are three men.

Znám ty muže. I know those men.

Jeden z těch mužů je od nás. One of those men is from our place.

Prodal jsem mu koně. I sold (to) him a horse.

Jaký je to člověk? What kind of a man is that?

Je dobrý muž. He is a good man.

Jděte k těm mužům. Go to those men.

Půjdu; chci mluvit s těmi muži. I will go; I want to speak with those men.

Myslím že ti mužové půjdou brzy domu. I think that those men will soon go home.

Note 1. The formation of the *plural* of masculine inanimate and animate nouns, and the changes of their endings in different cases, are seen in the following table:

dollar, *dollär*, the dollar; **vůz,** *vooz*, the wagon; **syn,** *syn*, the son; **muž,** *moož*, the man;

dollary	*dollüry*	the dollars
vozy	*vŏzy*	the wagons
.syni	*syñi*	the sons
——ové	*synŏvé*	
muži	*mooži*	the men;
——ové	*moožoré*	

REMARK. The long termination **ové** belongs to animate nouns; only in poetic language or solemn expression does it sometimes appear connected with inanimates.—
In the accusative or objective case animate nouns have **syny, muže:** **Mám syny zde,** I have my sons here; **vidím ty muže,** I see those men.— **S dollary, s vozy, se syny, s muži;** *sdollüry, svŏzy, sě syny, smooži;* with the dollars, with the wagons, with the sons, with the men.

dollarů	*dollüroo*	of the dollars
———ův	*dollüroof*	
vozů	*vŏzoo*	of the wagons
——ův	——*f*	
synů	*synoo*	of the sons
——ův	——*f*	
mužů	*mŭžoo*	of the men
——ův	——*f*	

REMARK. Both animate and inanimate nouns use the long termination **ův,** — but never in ordinary discourse and seldom in the spoken language generally.

dollarům	*dollăroom*	to the dollars	**synům**	*synoom*	to the	sons
vozům	*vŏzoom*	to the wagons	**mužům**	*mŭžoom*	to the	men;

v dollarech	*vdollărekh*	in the dollars	REMARK. Also with other preposi-
ve vozech	*vě vŏzěch*	in the wagons	tions: **o dollarech,** about the dol-
v synech	*vsyněkh*	in the sons	lars; **po dollarech,** after the dollars
v mužích	*vmŭžeekh*	in the men.	(*or* dollar by dollar); etc.

Note 2. The prepositions **k, s, v, z,** consisting of a single consonant, are simply abbreviations of **ke, ku, se, ve, ze,** as before explained. Their use is almost arbitrary, in cases where they can easily be connected and pronounced with the succeeding syllable; hence they are nearly always used when the following word begins with a vowel or with a consonant followed by a vowel: **v obleku,** *vŏ-blě-kŭ,* in the suit of clothes; **v dollarech,** *vdol-lă-rěkh,* in the dollars; **v synech,** *vsy-někh,* in the sons; —— **s oblekem,** *sŏ-blě-kem,* with the suit of clothes; **s dollarem,** *sdol-lă-rem,* with the dollar; **s mužem,** *smoo-žem,* with the man; —— **k obleku,** *kŏ-blě-kŭ,* to the suit of clothes; **k vozu,** *kvŏ-zŭ,* to the wagon; etc.

We can never say **v vozu, s synem, k koni** (in the wagon, with the son, to the horse), because it could not be pronounced; the letter **e** has to be retained and it is ridiculous to leave it out in writing as a silent letter, as it can never be silent. We speak and write: **ve vozu** (or **ve voze**), *vě vŏzŭ* (*vŏzě*), in the wagon; **se synem,** *sě syněm,* with the son (*or* with my son); **ke koni,** *kě kŏñi,* to the horse.

On the other hand, the long form **ke, ku, ve, ze** may nearly always be employed, when the following word begins with a consonant; we can say and write **ve dollarech, ve synech;** but it is not customary. The sound of **v** connects easily with every other consonant without the help of an **e.** However, the short prepositions **k, s, z** are being limited in their use and the proper long form **ke, ku, se, ze** is employed wherever practicable.

Note 3. The letters **h, ch, k, r** are called *hard* consonants "par excellence". When they occur in a MASCULINE ANIMATE noun, or in its ultimate syllable, they are changed or softened in the nominative plural after the following manner:

h   changes   into   z | k   changes   into   c
ch   ,,   ,,   š   r   ,,   ,,   ř

The following examples will explain it:

soudruh,	*soŭdrŭh* (*soŭdrŭkh*),	a comrade;	**soudruzi,**	*soŭdrŭzi,*	comrades;
hoch,	*hŏkh,*	a boy;	**hoši,**	*hŏ-she,*	boys;
kluk,	*klŭk,*	a boy, an urchin;	**kluci,**	*klŭtsi,*	boys, urchins;
bratr,	*brat^er,*	a brother;	**bratři,**	*brăt-rshi,*	brothers;

But whenever the long form of the nominative plural **(ové)** is employed, the hard consonant remains unchanged: **soudruhové,** the comrades; **bratrové,** the brothers. In the other cases (excepting the vocative, which is like the nominative: **o soudruzi!** o comrades!) the hard consonant also retains its place: **soudruhů, hochů, kluků, bratrů,** of the comrades (boys, brothers); **soudruhům,** and so forth.

LESSON XVI.

Líbí se mi	*leebee sĕ me*	I like it (him, her, etc)
nésti	*nesťi*	to bring, to yield
nesou	*nessoŭ*	they bring, they yield (*or* pay)
přines	*prshi-ness*	bring (thou)
přinesu	*prshi-nessŭ*	I shall bring
vede se	*vĕdĕ sĕ*	thrives
čítám	*cheetám*	I read (i. e. I use to read)
rád čítám	*rád cheetám*	I like to read
sednu	*sednŭ*	I sit down
bavím se	*băveem sĕ*	I amuse myself
dejte	*deytĕ*	give, put
posázím	*posázeem*	I shall set out
povídá	*poveedá*	says
letos	*letoss*	this year
v loni	*vloňi*	last year
hodně	*hodňe*	much, many, a good deal
(the same as **mnoho)**		
třeba	*trshĕ-bă*	it needs, needed, necessary
i třeba	*e trshĕ-bă*	I don't care
všeho druhu	*vshĕhŏ drŭhŭ*	of all kinds
krajina, f.	*krăyină*	country

soused, m.	*soŭsed*	neighbor	půda, f.	*poodă*	land, soil
užitek, m.	*ŭžitek*	profit	prairie, f.	*prairiě*	prairie
kukuřice, f.	*kŭkŭrshitsě*	corn	bahno, n.	*băhnŏ*	swamp
korna, f.	*kornă*	corn	řezník, m.	*rshěz-ñeek*	butcher
brambory, pl.	*brămbory*	potatoes	kniha. f.	*kñihă*	book
oves, m.	*ovess*	oats	knihovna, f.	*kñihŏvnă*	library
ječmen, m.	*yěchmen*	barley	milovník, m.	*milŏv-ñeek*	lover
sklizeň, f.	*sklizeň*	crop	záliba, f.	*zálibă*	pleasure
slad, m.	*slăd*	malt	růže, f.	*roože*	rose
trh, m.	*terh*	market	pivonka, f.	*pivonkă*	piony
u cesty	*ŭ tsěsty*	by the road / near the road	okno, n.	*oknŏ*	window
			poklad, m.	*poklăd*	treasure

samý, á, é	*sămee*	nothing but	kdykoli	*gdi-koli*	whenever
úrodný, á, é	*oo-rodnee*	fertile	ještě jeden	*yeshťe yěden*	one more, another
obzvláště	*ob-zlăshťe*	especially,			
obzvlášť	*ob-zlăshť*	particularly	před	*prshěd*	before
zvláštní	*zlăsht-ñe*	special, particular	bez	*běz* or *bess*	without
zpátky	*spátke*	back	za	*ză*	beyond, behind

EXERCISES.

Zde se mi líbí.	I like it here.
Zde je pěkná krajina.	This is (here is) a nice country.
Každý to povídá.	Everybody says so.
My máme zde farmu.	We have a farm here.
Strýc je náš soused.	Uncle is our neighbor.
On má zde dvě farmy.	He has two farms here.

Má velký užitek z těch farem? Has he a large profit from those farms?

Myslím že má. I think (that) he has.

Myslím že nesou mu hodně. I think (that) they yield (i. e. pay) him a good deal.

V loni měl mnoho sklizně (*skliz-ně*, of the c.) všeho druhu. Last year he had a large crop of all kinds.

Je to tuze úrodná farma. It is a very fertile farm.

Měl mnoho sena, pšenice, kukuřice i brambor. He had a great deal of hay, wheat, corn and potatoes.

Letos bude míti také oves, ječmen a žito. This year he will also have oats, barley and rye.

Ječmen na slad má vždycky (dycky, *dit-ski*) dobrý trh. Barley for malt has always a good market.

Na farmách zde ječmen vede se dobře. On the farms here barley thrives well.

Za farmami u cesty je kus špatné půdy. Beyond the farms by the road there is a piece of bad land.

Já myslel, že je to úrodná prairie. I thought (that) it was a fertile prairie.

Není; je to skoro samé bahno. It is not: it is almost nothing but swamp.

Knihy jsou poklad. Books are a treasure.

Rád čítám knihy. I like to read books.

Obzvláště když jsem doma. Especially when I am at home.

Jste teda milovník knih. You are then a lover of books.

To je pravda. That is true.

Máte mnoho knih? Have you many books?

Má knihovna je veliká. My library is large.

Jaké knihy máte? What books have you?

Mám knihy všeho druhu. I have books of all kinds.

Sednu ke knihám kdykoli mám čas. I sit down to the books whenever I have time.

Teda máte zálibu ve knihách. Then you have (you find) pleasure in books.

Ano, tuze rád bavím se s knihami. Yes, I like very much to amuse myself with books.

Máte růže před oknem. You have roses before the window.

Máme tam hodně růží. We have many roses there.

K růžím dejte pivonky. To the roses put pionies.

V růžích mám zvláštní zálibu. In roses I have (I take) particular pleasure.

Posázím ještě jeden záhon růžemi. I shall plant another bed with roses.

Byl jsem u řezníka. I was at the butcher's.

Koupil jsem maso od řezníka. I bought (some) meat from the butcher.

Tu je to maso. Here is that meat.

To je samá kost. That is nothing but bone.

Jsou tu nějaké kosti. There are some bones here.

Ano, kostí je dost. Yes, there are bones enough.

K těm kostím třeba více masa. To the bones (besides the b.) we need more meat.

Na těch kostech není ho mnoho. On these bones there is not much of it.

Co s kostmi? What (can we do) with the bones?

Nechceme tolik kostí. We do not want so many bones.

Přines maso bez kostí. Bring meat without bones.

Půjdu zpátky a přinesu ho. I shall go back and bring it.

Note 1. The formation of the plural of feminine nouns, and the changes of their endings in different cases, are shown in the following table:

cena, *tsĕnă*, the price;   **růže,** *roožĕ*, the rose;   **kosť,** *kŏst*, the bone;

ceny	*tsĕny*	the prices
růže	*roožĕ*	the roses
kosti	*kosťi*	the bones;

cen	*tsĕn*	of the prices
růží	*roožee*	of the roses
kostí	*kosťee*	of the bones;

REMARK. When two consonants terminate the noun in the genitive, an e is interpolated: **farmy,** the farms; **farem** (instead of **farm**), of the farms;—**matky,** the mothers; **matek** instead of **matk**), of the mothers.

cenám	*tsĕnám*	to the prices
růžím	*roožeem*	to the roses
kostem	*kostem*	to the bones;

v cenách	*ftsĕ-nákh*	in the prices
v růžích	*vroo-žeekh*	in the roses
v kostech	*fkos-tĕkh*	in the bones;

REMARK. Also with other prepositions: **o cenách,** about prices; **při cenách,** at the prices; etc.

cenami	*tsĕnámi*	with the prices
růžemi	*roožemi*	with the roses
kostmi	*kostmi*	with the bones.

REMARK. Usually with the proposition s (with): **s cenami**, *stsĕ-námi;* **s růžemi**, *sroo-žemi;* **s kostmi**, *skost-mi.*

LESSON XVII.

Vám	*vám*	to you	bohactví, n.	*bŏháts-tvee*	richess
jim	*yim*	to them	štěstí, n.	*shťess-ťi*	happiness,
mi, mě	*me, myĕ*	to me			luck, good fortune
moje, mé	*moyĕ, mé*	mine, my	moudrost, f.	*moŭdrost*	wisdom
naše	*nášhĕ*	our, ours	váha, f.	*váhá*	weight
vaše	*váshĕ*	your, yours	poupě, n.	*poŭpyĕ*	bud
s těmi	*sťemi*	with those	poupata	*poŭpátá*	buds
tohle	*tŏhlĕ*	this here	plot, m.	*plŏt*	fence
tam ty	*tăm ty*	those over there	obtíž, f.	*ob-ťeež*	trouble
tuze	*toozĕ*	very much	mýlka, f.	*meelkă*	mistake
blíže	*bleežĕ*	nearer	máte pravdu	*máte prăvdŭ*	you are
nikoli	*ñikoli*	no, not at all			right (*literally:* you
kolem	*kŏlem*	round			have right;)
pojď me	*poďmĕ*	let us go	není třeba	*neñi trshĕ-bă*	it is not
jde	*dĕ*	comes			necessary
hleďte	*hleďtĕ*	see, look	obalený, á, é	*obálĕnee*	covered
vidím	*viďeem*	I see	drátěný, á, é	*drá-ťenee*	of wire
vidíte	*viďeetĕ*	you see	hluboký, á, é	*hlŭbŏkee*	deep, pro-
znám	*znám*	I know			found.
znáte	*znátĕ*	you know	zdravý, á, é	*zdrăvee*	healthy, well,
přidám	*prshi-dám*	I shall add			sound
řeknu	*rshek-nŭ*	I shall tell	děvče	*ďef-chĕ*	girl
slyšet	*slishet*	to hear	děvčata	*ďef-chătă*	girls
postačí	*postă-chee*	is sufficient	dobře	*dobrshĕ*	well, all right
roste	*rostĕ*	grows	slovem	*slŏvem*	in a word

EXERCISES.

Já vám něco řeknu. I will tell'you something.

Bohactví není štěstí. Riches are not happiness.

To jsou slova moudrosti. These are words of wisdom.

Znáte váhu těch slov? Do you know the weight of those words?

K těm slovům nic více není třeba. To those words nothing more is needed.

V těch slovech je hluboká pravda. In those words there is a profound truth.

Chcete slyšeti více? Do you want to hear more?

Nikoli; ta slova postačí. Not at all; those words suffice.

Jsem spokojen s těmi slovy. I am satisfied with those words.

Slovem: máte pravdu! In a word: you are right!

Tam ty růže už mají poupata. The roses over there already have buds.

Ano, mají mnoho poupat. Yes, they have many buds.

Letos jsou obaleny poupaty. This year they are covered with buds.

V loni byly skoro bez poupat. Last year they were almost without buds.

Pojďme blíže k těm poupatům. Let us go nearer to those buds.

Vidím něco na těch poupatech. I see something on the buds.

To není nic. That is nothing.

Máte pravdu; poupata jsou zdravá. You are right; the buds are sound.

Ano, jsou; yes, they are.

Aha, zde je moje děvče! Ah, here is my girl!

Jsou vaše děvčata zdravá? Are your girls well?

Obě naše děvčata jsou zdravá. Both our girls are well.

Přines děvčeti poupě. Bring (thou) to the girl a bud.

Jsou zde dvě děvčata. There are two girls here.

Přineste jim několik poupat. Bring (you to) them some buds.

Tady jde s těmi poupaty. Here he comes with the buds.

Tu je pár poupat. Here are some buds.

Dobře. All right.

Hleďte! See !

Ty pole co vidíte jsou moje. The fields you see are mine.

Kolem těch polí je nový plot. Around those fields there is a new fence.

Je to drátěný plot. It is a wire fence.
K těm polím je dobrá cesta. To those fields there is a good road.
Co bude na těch polích? What will there be on those fields?
Na těch polích bude obilí a kukuřice. On those fields there will be grain and corn.

Co je tohle? What is this here?
Nějaká znamení. Some signs.
To jsou moje znamení. These are my signs.
Já něco přidám k těm znamením. I shall add something to those signs.

Jste spokojen s těmi poli? Are you satisfied with those fields?
Jsem tuze spokojen. I am very much satisfied.
Všechno dobře roste na těch polích. Everything grows well on those fields.

Není mýlka v těch znameních? Is there no mistake in those signs?
S těmi znameními je někdy obtíž. With those signs there is sometimes trouble.
Pravda, je někdy obtíž. True, there is sometimes trouble.

Note. The formation of the plural of neutre nouns, and the changes of their endings in different cases, will appear from the following table:

slovo	*slŏvŏ*	the word	**pole**	*polĕ*	the field
poupě	*pŏŭpyĕ*	the bud	**znamení**	*znămĕñee*	the sign;
slova	*slŏvă*	the words	**pole**	*pŏlĕ*	the fields
poupata	*pŏŭpătă*	the buds	**znamení**	*znămĕñee*	the signs;
slov	*slof*	of the words	**polí**	*pŏlee*	of the fields
poupat	*pŏŭpăt*	of the buds	**znamení**	*znămĕñee*	of the signs;
slovům	*slŏvoom*	to the words	**polím**	*pŏleem*	to the fields
poupatům	*pŏŭpătoom*	to the buds	**znamením**	*znămĕñeem*	to the signs;

ve slovech *vĕ slŏvĕkh* in the words
v poupatech *fpŏŭpătĕkh* in the buds
v polích *fpoleekh* in the fields
ve znameních *vĕ znămĕñeekh* in the signs;

REMARK. Also with other prepositions: **o polích,** about the fields; **na polích,** on the fields.

slovy	*slŏvy*	with the words
poupaty	*poŭpăty*	with the buds
poli (-emi)	*poli (-ĕmi)*	with the fields
znamenimí	*znăměñeemi*	with the signs.

REMARK. Also with the preposition se, s: se slovy, *se slŏvy;* s poupaty, *spoŭpăty;* s polemi, *spolĕmi;* se znamenimí, *sĕ znăměñeemi.*—Instead of polemi, the short forms polmi and poli (*polmi, polli*) are also used.

LESSON XVIII.

Mrak, m.	*mrăk*	cloud
mráček, m.	*mrá-chek*	little cloud
žena	*ženă*	wife
míle*), f.	*meelĕ*	mile
hodina*), f.	*hŏd'ină*	hour, o'clock
jízda, f.	*yeezdă*	drive, ride
k večeru	*kwĕchĕrŭ*	toward evening
za světla	*ză swyĕt-lă*	by daylight
tma	*tmă*	dark, darkness
pozdě	*pŏzd'e*	late
dobrá !	*dobrá*	very well!
krásný, á,	*é krássnee*	beautiful
s námi	*snámi*	with us
brzy	*bᵉr-zy*	soon
po svém	*pŏ swém*	after one's business
ještě	*yeshťe*	still, yet.

já pravil	*yá prăvil*	I said
jářku	*yá-rshkŭ*	I said, I say (like the colloq. "says I'.)
jeti	*yeťi, yet*	to drive, to ride
pojedem	*pŏyĕdem*	we shall drive, we shall ride
pojeďme	*poyĕd'mĕ*	let us drive, let us ride
vyjeti	*ve-yeťi, ve-yet*	to drive out, to ride out, to start
vyjeli jsme	*ve-yelli smĕ*	we started
vrátíme se	*vráťeemĕ sĕ*	we shall return, we shall come back
vrátil mi	*vráťil me*	he returned to me (something);
půjčené peníze	*pŭychĕné peñeezĕ*	the money loaned;

*) Jedna, dvě, tři, čtyry míle, *yednă, dvŏĕ, trshi, shtiri meelĕ,* one, two, three, four miles; pět mil, *pyĕt mill,* five miles; šest mil, *shĕst mill,* six miles; and so forth.

Jedna hodina, *yednă hoďină,* one hour, one o'clock; dvě, tři, čtyry hodiny, *dvŏĕ, trshi, shtiri hoďiny,* two, three, four hours; two, three, four o'clock; pět hodin, *pyĕt hoďin,* five hours; five o'clock; šest hodin, *shĕst hoďin,* six hours, six o'clock; — and so forth.

EXERCISES.

Včera byl krásný den; — nebe bylo jasné, — ani mráčku nikde.

Yesterday was a beautiful day; — the sky was clear, — not a cloud anywhere.

Jářku, ženo! dnes pojedem do města.

I said: wife, to-day we will drive to town.

Ano, pojeďme! pravila žena; — je den tak krásný!

Yes, let us drive! said (my) wife; — the day is so beautiful!

Máme deset mil do města.

It is ten miles to town (*literally:* we have ten miles to town).

Brzy po snídani vyjeli jsme; — bylo právě osm hodin.

Soon after breakfast we drove out (we started); — it was just eight o'clock.

Soused pan Rohan byl s námi.

(Our) neighbor Mr. Rohan was with us.

Já pravil: sousede, jak brzy budeme ve městě?

I said: neighbor, how soon shall we be in the city?

V deset hodin jsme tam! pravil pan Rohan.

At ten o'clock we are there! said Mr. Rohan.

A byli jsme.

And we were.

Je to as dvě hodiny jízdy, když cesta je dobrá.

It is about a two hours' ride, when the road is good.

Ve městě soused šel kupovat něco a my také šli po svém.

In the city, the neighbor went to buy something, and we also went after our business.

Půjčil jsem mu pět dollarů.

I loaned to him five dollars.

Jářku, sousede! kdy se vrátíme?

I said: neighbor, when shall we return?

Myslím pozdě odpoledne, nebo k večeru; — to bude dost času.

I think late in the afternoon or towards evening; — that will be time enough.

Dobrá; vrátíme se asi v sedm hodin večer, — ještě za světla.

Very well; we shall return about seven o'clock in the evening, — still by daylight.

Ale bylo už tma, když jsme se vrátili.

But it was already dark, when we returned.

Soused šel domu a vrátil mi půjče- **né peníze.**	The neighbor went home and re- turned to me the money I loaned him.

Note 1. The noun **mráček** is a diminutive of **mrak.** In English only a few nouns have their proper diminutives; for instance: man, *manikin;* eagle, *eaglet;* river, *rivulet;* goose, *gosling.*

In Bohemian, diminutives are exceedingly numerous; and very often a noun has two, sometimes three diminutives, differing in degree. For example:

dům, m.	*dŭm,* a house; **domek,** *dŏmĕk,* a small house; **domeček,** *dŏ-mĕchek,* a very small house.
hoch,	*hŏkh,* a boy; **hošík,** *hŏsheek,* a small boy; **hošíček,** *hŏshee-chek,* a very small boy.
ruka, f.	*rŭkă,* a hand; **ručka,** *rŭchkă,* a small hand; **ručička,** *rŭ-chich-kă,* a very small hand.
oko, n.	*ŏkŏ,* an eye; **očko,** *ŏch-kŏ,* a small eye; **očičko,** *ŏchich-kŏ,* a very small eye.

Diminutives, however, are often used simply as expressions of fondness and endearment, apart from any relation of size or degree.

Note 2. The genitive or possessive case of **mráček** is **mráčku,** not **mráčeku.** All nouns ending in **ek** drop the letter **e** in their declension. They are all of the masculine gender (as observed in Lesson I, Note 5), and the animate have **ka,** the inanimate **ku** in the genitive:

ptáček,	*ptáchek* (colloq. *ftáchek*), a small bird; **ptáčka,** *ptáchkă* (*ftáchkă*), a small bird's;
svátek,	*swátek,* a holiday; **svátku,** *swát-kŭ,* a holiday's.

Note 3. Reflexive verbs in English are followed by reflexive pronouns; for instance: to forswear *one's self;* I forswore *myself;* he forswore *himself;* they forswore *themselves;* etc.

In Bohemian, the reflexive pronoun is always **se,** without any variation. But many verbs, which are reflexive in Bohemian, are not so in English; and vice versa.

Vrátiti se, *vráťit sě* (to return, to come back), is a reflexive verb; we say: **vrátím se,** *vráťeem sě,* I shall return; **vrátíme se,** *vráťeemě sě,* we shall return; **vrátíte se,** *vráťeetě sě,* you will return; **vrátí se,** *vráťee sě,* they will return.

Note 4. In the foregoing exercises, **sousede, ženo,** are the vocative cases of **soused** (neighbor), **žena** (wife). The noun is put in the vocative case, when the person or thing is addressed: o Lord! o heavens!

In Bohemian, the vocative case in the singular is very often, in the plural *always* like the nominative, as will be seen from the following comparison:

Nominative.			Vocative.		
soused,	*soŭsed,*	the neighbor	**sousede!**	*soŭsedě,*	o neighbor!
muž,	*moož,*	the man	**muži!**	*mooži,*	o man!
žena,	*ženă,*	the woman	**ženo!**	*ženŏ,*	o woman!
kost, f.	*kŏst,*	the bone	**kosti!**	*kŏsťi,*	o bone!
růže, f.	*roožě,*	the rose	**růže!**	*roožě,*	o rose!
slovo, n.	*slŏvŏ,*	the word	**slovo!**	*slŏvŏ,*	o word!
pole, n.	*pŏlě,*	the field	**pole!**	*pŏlě,*	o field!
znamení,	*znămeñee,*	the sign	**znamení!**	*znămeñee,*	o sign!

In the plural number, the nominative and vocative always agree:

sousedi*),	*soŭsedi,*	the neighbors;	o neighbors!
muži (-ové),	*mooži,*	the men;	o men!
ženy,	*žěny,*	the women;	o women!
kosti,	*kŏsťi,*	the bones;	o bones!
růže,	*roožě,*	the roses;	o roses!
slova,	*slŏvă,*	the words;	o words!
pole,	*pŏlě,*	the fields;	o fields!
znamení,	*znămĕñee,*	the signs;	o signs!

---

*) **Sousedé,** *soŭsedé,* is the proper grammatical form, this noun forming an exception; but **sousedi** is the common usage.

6

Note 5. The Latin noun has six cases; the Bohemian noun has six cases corresponding perfectly with the Latin, and an additional case called "instrumental", because it denotes by whom, with whom or through whom (by means of what or through what) something happens or is done: **mužem, s mužem,** by the man, with the man; **dollarem, s dollarem,** with the dollar.

The nature of the six cases of the Bohemian noun apart from the vocative will appear more distinctly by stating the questions to which they respond.

The *nominative* case, of course, responds to the question **kdo? co?** *gdŏ, tsŏ;* who? what?
> **dollar, muž, žena, slovo;** the dollar, the man, the woman, the word;—**dollary, muži, ženy, slova;** the dollars, the men, the women, the words.

The *genitive* or *possessive* case responds to the question **čí? čcho?** *chee, chěhŏ;* whose? of what?
> **dollaru, muže, ženy, slova;** of the dollar, the man's, the woman's, of the word; — **dollarů (-ŭv), mužů (-ŭv), žen, slov;** of the dollars, the men's, the women's, of the words.

The *dative* case responds to the question **komu? čemu?** *kŏmŭ, chěmŭ;* to whom? to what?
> **dollaru, muži, ženě, slovu;** to the dollar, to the man, to the woman, to the word; — **dollarům, mužům, ženám, slovům;** to the dollars, to the men, to the women, to the words.

The *accusative* or *objective* case responds to the question **koho? co?** *kŏhŏ, tsŏ;* whom? what?
> **dollar, muže, ženu, slovo;** the dollar, the man, the woman, the word; — **dollary, muže, ženy, slova;** the dollars, the men, the women, the words.

The *locative* case responds to the question **v kom? v čem? (na kom? na čem? — o kom? o čem?),** *fkŏm, fchěm;* in whom? in what? (on whom — what? about whom — what?)
> **v dollaru, v muži, v ženě, ve slovu (-ě);** in the dollar, in the man,

in the woman, in the word; — v dollarech, v mužích, v ženách, ve slovech; in the dollars, in the men, in the women, in the words.

The *instrumental* case responds to the question kým? čím? — s kým? s čím? *keem, cheem, skeem, scheem;* by whom? by what? with whom? with what?

dollarem, mužem, ženou, slovem; with the dollar, with the man, with the woman, with the word; — dollary, muži, ženami, slovy; with the dollars, with the men, with the women, with the words.

LESSON XIX.

Pan	*pán*	Mr. (mister)	blízký, á, é	*bleeskee*		near
pán	*pán*	gentleman	hodný, á, é	*hodnee*		nice, good
paní	*pāñee*	Mrs.(missis); lady	jiný, á,, é	*ye-nee*		another
člověk	*chlŏvyĕk*	man; one;	letný, á, é	*letnee*		aged
Karel	*kárell*	Charles	bohatý, á, é	*bŏhátee*		rich
Anna	*ánă*	Anna	chudý, á, é	*khŭdee*		poor
Marie	*mariĕ*	Mary	poctivý, á, é	*pots-ťivee*		honest
dceruška	*tserŭshkă*	little daughter	mladý, á, é	*mlădee*		young
hošik	*hŏsheek*	little boy	četný, á, é	*chetnee*		numerous
sousedka	*soŭsedkă*	female neighbor	pilný, á, é	*pillnee*		industrious
vdova	*vdŏvă*	widow	poslušný, á, é	*poslŭshnee*	obedient
vdovec	*vdŏ-vĕts*	widower	ještě tři	*yeshťe trzhi* {	three other
domov, m.	*dŏmof*	home			}	three more
rok, m.	*rŏk*	year	usazen	*ŭssăzen*		settled
leta	*letă* }	years*)	jmenuje se	*menŭyĕ sĕ*		is called
let	*let* }		v skutku	*fskŭt-kŭ* {	indeed, in
náklonnost, f.	*náklŏnnost*	inclination	opravdu	*oprăvdă* }	fact, really
několik	*ñekolik*	several, some, a few	má být	*má beet*		ought to be
			máte rád	*mátĕ rád*		you like

---

*) **Dvě leta,** *dwyĕ letă,* two years; **tři leta,** *trzhi letă,* three years; **čtyry leta,** *shtiri letă,* four years; **pět let,** *pyĕt let,* five years; **šest let,** *shĕst let,* six years; **sedm let,** *sĕdŭm let,* seven years; and so forth.

Máte to rád?	*mátě tŏ rád?*	do you like it?
mám vždycky rád,	*mám dit-ski rád,*	I always like;
dávno,	*dávnŏ,*	a long time;
jak dávno,	*yăk dávnŏ*	how long;
nesklame se,	*nessklămě sě,*	will not be disappointed;
jednám,	*yed-nám,*	I deal;
jedná,	*yed-ná,*	deals;
váš,	*vásh,*	your, yours;
její,	*yěyee,*	her, hers.

EXERCISES.

Tak zde je váš domov!	So here is your home!
Kdo je váš soused?	Who is your neighbor?
Pan Hodan je můj soused.	Mr. Hodan is my neighbor.
On je náš blízký soused.	He is our near neighbor.
Je pan Hodan hodný muž?	Is Mr. Hodan a nice man?
Ano, je hodný muž; a paní Hodanová je hodná žena.	Yes, he is a nice man; and Mrs. Hodan is a nice woman.
Mají děti?	Have they children?
Mají jednu dcerušku.	They have one little daughter.
Jak se jmenuje?	What is her name?
Myslím že jmenuje se Marie; je to hodné dítě.	I think she is called Mary; she is a nice child.
Jiný soused náš je pan Braun.	Another neighbor of ours is Mr. Brown.
Jak dávno je zde usazen?	How long is he (has he been) settled here?
Je zde usazen asi rok nebo dvě leta.	He has been settled here about a year or two (years).
Je pan Braun bohatý?	Is Mr. Brown rich?
Není; on je chudý člověk.	He is not; he is a poor man.
Je chudý a tuze poctivý.	He is poor and very honest.
Je letný muž?	Is he an aged man?
Ne, pan Braun je mladý muž a paní Braunová je mladá žena.	No; Mr. Brown is a young man, and Mrs. Brown is a young woman.
Ale rodina je už četná.	But the family is already numerous.
Mají několik dětí.	They have several children.

Karel je asi deset let a pak mají ještě tři děti.	Charles is about ten years, and then they have three more children.
Karel je poslušný a pilný hoch.	Charles is an obedient and industrious boy.
Anna je také poslušná a pilná.	Anna is also obedient and industrious.
Je jí asi osm let.	She is (*literally:* it is to her) about eight years.
Dítě má být poslušné a pilné.	A child should be obedient and industrious.
Ano, má být; ale někdy není.	Yes, it ought to be; but sometimes it is not.
Vdova Borošová je také naše blízká sousedka.	The widow Borosh is also our near neighbor.
Její bratr, pan Bloch, je také vdovec.	Her brother, Mr. Bloch, is also a widower.

Teda máte rád pana Hodana? (*pána hodana,*—accusative).	So you like Mr. Hodan?
Mám vždycky rád hodného muže, a hodnou ženu také.	I always like a nice man, and a nice woman too.
K hodnému muži a k hodné ženě máme vždy náklonnost.	Toward a nice man and a nice woman we always have an inclination.
A je také pravda, že v hodném muži a v hodné ženě se člověk nikdy nesklame.	And it is also true, that in a good man and in a good woman one is never disappointed.
S hodným mužem a hodnou ženou každý rád jedná.	With a nice man and a nice woman everybody likes to deal.
Též rád jednám s hodným dítětem.	I also like to deal with a nice child.
Pana Brauna hošík je v skutku hodné dítě.	Mr. Brown's little boy is really a good child.

Note 1. In Lesson VI, Note 2, it was explained that the termination of adjectives changes according to the gender of the nouns which they qualify:

hodný muž,	*hodnee moož,*	a nice man;
hodná žena,	*hodná ženǎ,*	a nice woman;
hodné dítě,	*hodné ďeeťe,*	a nice child (in ordinary discourse **hodný dítě,** like the masculine).

Adjectives, also, are declined and agree in number and case with the nouns. The changes of termination in the singular number appear in the following table:

hodný muž,	*hodnee moož,*	a nice man;
hodné dítě,	*hodné ďeeťe,*	a nice child;
hodného muže,	*hodnéhǒ moožě,*	of a nice man,
,, dítěte,	,, *ďeeťetě,*	of a nice child;

REMARK. The accusative or objective agrees with the possessive in the masculine, and with the nominative in the neutre gender:
vidím hodného muže, *viďeem hodnéhǒ moožě,* I see a nice man;
vidím hodné dítě, *viďeem hodné ďeeťe,* I see a nice child.

hodnému muži,	*hodnémǔ mooži,*	to a nice man,
,, dítěti,	,, *ďeeťeťi,*	to a nice child;
v hodném muži,	*vhodném mooži,*	in a nice man,
,, ,, dítěti,	,, *ďeeťeťi,*	in a nice child;
s hodným mužem,	*shodneem moožem,*	with a nice man,
,, ,, dítětem,	,, *ďeeťetem,*	with a nice child.

hodná žena,	*hodná ženǎ,*	a nice woman;
hodné ženy,	*hodné ženy,*	of a nice woman;
,, ženě,	,, *žeñe,*	to a nice woman;
v ,, ženě,	*v ,, ,, ,*	in a nice woman;
hodnou ženu,	*hodnoǔ ženǔ,*	a nice woman (*accusative*);
s hodnou ženou,	*shodnoǔ ženoǔ,*	with a nice woman.

Note 2. In common discourse no distinction whatever is made between the masculine and neutre gender, and the terminal ý does not change. We hear:

hodný muž,	hodný dítě;	a nice man,	a nice child;
hodnýho muže,	hodnýho dítěte;	of a nice man,	of a nice child;
hodnýmu muži,	hodnýmu dítěti;	to a nice man,	to a nice child;
hodnýho muže,	hodný dítě; *(accusative);*	a nice man,	a nice child;
v hodným muži,	v hodným dítěti;	in a nice man,	in a nice child;
s hodným mužem,	s hodným dítětem;	with a nice man,	with a nice child.

In the feminine gender, we hear: **hodná žena, hodnou ženu** (accus.), **s hodnou ženou;** but in the other cases:

hodný	ženy,	of a good woman;
hodný	ženě,	to a good woman;
v hodný	ženě,	in a good woman.

The ordinary usage of the people evidently rejects all artificial, and unnecessary grammatical distinctions, always tending to simplicity; and it will be noticed that there is much more consistency in this common rule as applied to the declension of adjectives. when we come to treat of their plural number.

Note 3. In Bohemian, the adjective may be placed either before or after the noun, according to the speaker's pleasure:

pan Hodan je hodný muž;
pan Hodan je muž hodný; } Mr. Hodan is a nice man;

je to letný muž;
je to muž letný; } he is (*literally*, it is) an aged man.

It is usually placed after the noun when the speaker wishes to lay particular stress upon the adjective (*hodný, letný*) qualifying the noun.

LESSON XX.

Sousedstvo, n.	*soŭsedstvŏ*	neighborhood
celý, á, é	*tsellee*	whole, all
milý, á, é	*millee*	pleasant, pleasing, dear
příjemno, f.	*prshee-yĕmnŏ*	agreeable, pleasant
nehodný	*nĕhodnee*	naughty
bydleti	*bidlet*	to live, to reside
vše	*fshĕ*	} everything, all
všechno	*fshekh-nŏ*	
však	*fshăk*	but
však je	*fshăk yĕ*	but there is (there are)
nad	*năd*	over
není nad	*nĕñi năd*	there is nothing better than ....; nothing like ....;
velmi	*velmi*	very
jich	*yikh*	of them
nám	*nám*	to us
vám	*vám*	to you
vejde	*veydĕ*	enters, calls
rád vejde,	*rád veydĕ,*	likes to call
rád promluví,	*rád promlŭvee,*	likes to talk (to have a chat)
má rád	*má rád*	he likes
má ráda	*má rádă*	she likes
doufám	*doŭfám*	I hope
ba právě	*bă právyĕ*	that is so; to be sure;
ba věru	*bă vyĕrŭ*	certainly; no doubt of it;
v pořádku	*fpo-rshád-kŭ*	right; all right;
dobrá vůle	*dobrá voolĕ*	good will
na štěstí	*nă shťesťi*	happily, fortunately;
je na to čas,	*yĕ nă tŏ chăss,*	there is time for it.
že ne?	*žĕ nĕ?*	} isn't it so? is it not? are they not?
to víš	*tŏ veesh*	thou knowest
to víte	*tŏ veetĕ*	you know

REMARK. When standing alone and used as a rejoinder, **to víš** and **to víte** signify: *of course; to be sure.*

EXERCISES.

Myslím že všichni vaši sousedi jsou hodní.	I think that all your neighbors are nice.
Pravda; celé sousedstvo je hodné.	True; the whole neighborhood is nice.
Pak je příjemno bydleti zde.	Then it is agreeable to live here.
Opravdu, velmi příjemno.	Truly, very agreeable.
A jaké je sousedstvo vaše?	And what kind is *your* neighborhood?
My také máme pár hodných sousedů.	We also have some nice neighbors (i. e. some *of* the nice neighbors).
Myslím že je vám to také milé.	I think (that) it is also agreeable to you.
Je nám to tuze milé.	It is very agreeable to us.
Člověk rád vejde k hodným sousedům.	One likes to call on nice neighbors; (*literally:* one likes to enter to nice neighbors).
Každý má rád hodné sousedy.	Everybody likes good neighbors.
Ba právě; a v hodných sousedech vždycky (*dit-ski*) má podporu.	To be sure; and in good neighbors one always has (finds) a support.
Když je na to čas, člověk rád promluví s hodnými sousedy.	When there is time for it, one likes to have a chat with good neighbors·
Není nad hodné sousedy!	There is nothing like good neighbors!

Má žena je zde velmi spokojena.	My wife is very much satisfied here.
Vaše sousedky jsou všechny hodné, že ne?	Your female neighbors are all nice, are they not?
Naše sousedky jsou hodné.	Our female neighbors are nice.
To víte, že mezi hodnými sousedkami je dobrá vůle.	You know that among nice female neighbors there is good will.
Není nad dobrou vůli v sousedstvu.	There is nothing like good will in a neighborhood.
To víte.	Of course (i. e. you know).
Když sousedi také mají hodné děti, všechno je v pořádku.	When the neighbors also have nice children, everything is all right.

Máme opravdu mnoho hodných dětí v sousedstvu.	We have indeed many nice children in the neighborhood (i. e. many *of the* nice children)*).
Však je také několik nehodných.	But there are also a few naughty (ones).
Doufám že není jich mnoho.	I hope (that) there are not many of them.
Na štěstí není jich mnoho.	Fortunately there are not many of them.
Je jich jen pár; ale je to dost.	There are only a few; but it is enough.
Ba věru.	No doubt of it.

Note 1. In the plural, the masculine gender of an adjective changes the terminal **ý** into an **í** :

hodný muž, *hodnee moož,* a nice man; **hodní muži,** *hodňee mooži,* nice men.

The feminine gender changes the terminal **á** into an **é** :

hodná žena, *hodná žená,* a nice woman; **hodné ženy,** *hodné ženy,* nice women.

The neutre gender changes the terminal **é** into an **á** :

hodné děcko, *hodné ďet-sko,* a nice child; **hodná děcka,** *hodná ďet-ská,* nice children.

Dítě, ďeeťe, (child,) follows the feminine in the plural: **hodné děti,** *hodné ďeťi,* nice children.

Note 2. Adjectives containing in their last syllable the hard consonants **h, ch, k, r,** change these consonants in the plural of the masculine animate gender into **z, š, c, ř,** in the same manner as stated in Lesson XV, Note 3. For example:

---

*) **Mnoho, málo, pár, kolik, několik,** (many, few, a few, how many, some), as well as all numbers after "four" (see foot-notes in Lessons XVIII and XXIX) govern the *genitive or possessive* case; hence the noun, or pronoun, adjective, which follows them, must always appear in that case.

dlouhý had, *dloŭhee hăd,* a long snake; **dlouzí hadi,** *dloŭzee hăďi,* long snakes;

hluchý muž, *hlŭkhee moož,* a deaf man; **hluší muži,** *hlŭshee mooži,* deaf men;.

velký hoch, *velkee hŏkh,* a big boy; **velcí hoši,** *veltsee hŏ-she,* big boys;

dobrý soused, *dobree soŭsed,* a good neighbor; **dobří sousedi,** *dob-rshee soŭseďi,* good neighbors.

Note 3. The following table presents a complete view of the plural number of adjectives ending in **ý (á, é).**

The *nominative* and *accusative* cases :

> **hodní muži** (*accus.* **hodné muže**), *hodňee mooži, (hodné moožĕ),* nice men;
> **hodné ženy,** *hodné žĕny,* nice women;
> **hodná děcka,** *hodná ďetská,* nice children.

The *genitive* or possessive case :

> **hodných mužů, žen, děcek,** *hodneekh moožoo, žen,* **ďetsek,** of the nice men, women, children.

The *locative* case :

> **o hodných mužích, ženách, děckách,** *ŏ hodneekh moožeekh, ženákh,* **ďetskákh,** about the nice men, women, children..

The *instrumental* case:

> **s hodnými muži, ženami, děcky,** *shodneemi mooži, ženămi,* **ďetski,.** with the nice men, women, children.

Note 4. In common discourse, however, the grammatical distinction of gender in the nominative plural of this class of adjectives is treated as perfectly useless, which in fact it is. The Bohemian language, as it lives in the daily intercourse of millions, employs the masculine singular fcrm of the adjective in all three genders of the plural, recognizing only one form of declension :

hodný muži, hodný ženy, hodný děti (or děcka); the nice men, women, children;

hodných mužů, žen, dětí; of the nice men, women, children;

and so forth.

LESSON XXI.

Sousedův, m. *soŭsedoof*
sousedova, f. *soŭsedŏvă*
sousedovo, n. *soŭsedŏvŏ*
sousedovi, pl. *soŭsedŏvi*
} the neigh-bor's.

bratrův, m. *brătroof*, the brother's

plný, á, é *pl-nee* full

nový, á, é *nŏvee* new

falešný, á, é *făleshnee* false

co nového? *tsŏ nŏvéhŏ*, what is the news?

noviny, pl. *nŏviny* news, news-paper

tiskárna, f. *ťiskárnă* printing office

list *list* paper, sheet, leaf

hlas, m. *hlăss* voice

sloupec, m. *sloŭpets* column

sloupce *sloŭp-tsĕ* columns

čísti *cheesťi, cheest*, to read

čteme *chtĕmĕ* we read

v tom, m. & n. *ftŏm*
v té, f. *fté*
} in that

proto *prŏtŏ* hence, therefore

proto ale přece, *prŏtŏ ălĕ prshĕ-tsĕ*, in spite of that, notwith-standing that

denní *dĕñee* daily

týdenní *teedĕñee* weekly

denník, m. *dĕñeek*, daily paper

týdenník, m. *teedĕñeek* weekly „

dnešní *dnesh-ñee* to-day's

včerejší *fchĕreyshee* yesterday's

poslední *pŏsledñee* last

volba, f. *volbă* election

zpráva, f. *správă* advice

den co den, *den tsŏ den*, day by day

co, něco *tsŏ, ñetsŏ* something

brzo hotovi, *bᵉrzo hotŏvi*, soon done

přinesl *prshi-nessl* he brought

dopadnouti, *dŏpădnoŭt*, to come out, to result

podívej se, *pŏďeevey sĕ*, look (thou)

podívejte se, *pŏďeevĕytĕ sĕ*, look (you)

pokaždé, *pŏkăždé*, every time

též *též* also

věřiti, *vyĕ-rshiťi, vyĕ-rshit*, to be-lieve

nesmíte *nĕsmeetĕ* you must not

pracovati *prătsŏvăt* to work

pracuje *prătsŭyĕ* works

EXERCISES.

Kdo to byl?	Who was it?
To byl sousedův syn.	That was (our) neighbor's son.
Přinesl něco?	Has he brought something?
Přinesl nám noviny.	He brought (to) us a newspaper.
Sousedovy noviny?	Our neighbor's newspaper?
Ano, sousedovy noviny.	Yes, our neighbor's paper.
Jsou to denní nebo týdenní noviny?	Is it a daily or a weekly newspaper?
Je to denník.	It is a daily.
Jaký je to denník?	What daily is it?
Je to Denní Hlas.	It is the Daily Voice.
Bratrův hoch pracuje v té tiskárně, myslím.	My brother's boy works in that printing-office, I think.
Ano, a sousedova dcera též.	Yes, and (our) neighbor's daughter also.
Bratrova dcera chce tam pracovat též.	My brother's daughter wants to work there also.
A Hodanova Marie také.	And Mary Hodan too.

Je to dnešní list?	Is it to-day's paper?
Je dnešní; ale sousedův Jan také přinesl včerejší list.	It is to-day's; but (neighbor's) John also brought yesterday's paper.
Co je nového? Podívej se do dnešního listu.	What is the news? Look (thou) into to-day's paper.
Ve dnešním listu není mnoho nového; — jen něco o poslední volbě.	In to-day's paper there is not much news; only something about the last election.
Jak dopadla poslední volba?	How did the last election come out?
Hned to budu čísti.	I shall read it right away.
Budeme brzy hotovi s dnešním listem.	We shall soon be done with to-day's paper.

Denní listy vždycky (*dít-ski*) mají něco nového.	Daily papers always have something new.
Pravda, v denních listech je pokaždé co čísti.	To be sure, in daily papers there is every time something to read.

Ale nesmíte vždy věřiti denním listům.	But you must not always believe the daily papers.
S denními listy je to tak : sloupce musí býti plné den co den.	With the daily papers it is so: the columns must be full day by day.
Proto jsou někdy falešné zprávy v denních listech.	Hence there are sometimes false advices in daily papers.
Proto ale přece rádi čteme denní listy.	In spite of that we like to read the daily papers.
Cteme několik denních listů (*genit. case,* — "of the daily papers").	We read several daily papers.

Note 1. Adjectives ending in **í**, like **denní, dnešní, poslední, včerejší,** have the same termination in all genders and both numbers; and in the singular of the feminine gender they remain unchanged in all cases; in the masculine and neutre gender the genitive case is characterized by the termination **ího,** the dative by **ímu,** the locative and instrumental by **ím,** — corresponding with **ého, ému, ém & ým** of the main order of adjectives.

In the plural, their declension is the same in all three genders, showing the termination **ích** in the genitive and locative, **ím** in the dative, and **ími** in the instrumental case.

Note 2. There is also a class of adjectives derived *from nouns* denoting persons or animals, by means of the suffixes **ův, ova, ovo,** according to gender. They are called "possessive adjectives", and their sense is rendered in English by the "possessive case" of the noun :

sousedův syn,	*soŭsedoof syn,*	the neighbor's son;
sousedova dcera,	*soŭsedŏvă tsĕră,*	the neighbor's daughter;
sousedovo dítě,	*soŭsedŏvŏ ďeeťe.*	the neighbor's child;
sousedovi synové,	*soŭsedŏvi synŏvé,*	the neighbor's sons;
sousedovy dcery (děti),	*soŭsedŏvi tsĕry (ďeťi),*	the neighbor's daughters (children).

From feminine nouns they are derived by the suffixes **in, ina, ino** (**iny** in the plural, in colloquial usage):

ženin klobouk, *žeňin kloboůk,* the woman's (or wife's) bonnet;
ženiny šaty, pl. *žeňiny sháty,* the woman's (or wife's) clothes *or* dress.

Grammatically, these adjectives have their own mode of declension; but colloquially, they are declined just like adjectives of the main order: **hodný, á, é.**

Note 3. A few more examples of such possessive adjectives as are commonly in use, in connection with nouns of different gender, will make the student sufficiently familiar with them:

Otec, *ŏtěts,* the father :

otcův klobouk, m.	*ŏtsoof kloboůk,*	the father's hat;
otcova čepice, f.	*ŏtsová chěpitsě,*	the father's cap;
otcovo místo, n.	*ŏtsovŏ meestŏ,*	the father's place;

Matka, *mátká,* the mother;

matčin pokoj, m.	*mátchin pŏkoy,*	the mother's room;
matčina stolice, f.	*mátchiná stolitsě,*	the mother's chair;
matčino slovo, n.	*mátchinŏ slovŏ,*	the mother's word.

Sestra, *sestrá,* the sister :

sestřin šál, m.	*sest-rshin shawl,*	the sister's shawl;
sestřina taška, f.	*sest-rshiná táshká,*	the sister's satchel;
sestřino piano, n.	*sest-rshinŏ piáno,*	the sister's piano.

Hoch, *hŏkh,* the boy :

hochův míč, m.	*hŏkhoof meech,*	the boy's ball;
hochova mapa, f.	*hŏkhová mápá,*	the boy's map;
hochovo pero, n.	*hŏkhovŏ perŏ,*	the boy's pen;

Holka, *holká,* the girl :

holčin kufr, m.	*holchin kůffer,*	the girl's trunk;
holčina postel, f.	*holchiná postell,*	the girl's bed;
holčino prádlo, n.	*holchinŏ prádlŏ,*	the girl's linen.

Remark. It will be noticed that in the derivatives from feminine nouns ending in **ka, ra,** the hard consonants **k, r,** change into the soft consonants **č, ř: matka, matčin; sestra, sestřin.**

LESSON XXII.

Mladý, á, é	*mlădee*	young		**přítel,** m.	*prshee-tel*	friend
mladší	*mlăd-shee*	younger		**obchod,** m.	*ob-khŏd*	business
nejmladší	*ney-mlăd-shee*	youngest		**obchodník,** m.	*ob-khŏd-ñeek,*	mer-
starý, á, é	*stăree*	old				chant, business man;
starší	*stăr-shee*	older		**krám,** m.	*krám*	store
nejstarší	*ney-stăr-shee*	oldest		**sklad,** m.	*sklăd*	warehouse
bohatší	*bohăt-shee*	richer		**zboží,** n.	*zbožee*	goods, stock
nejbohatší	*ney-bohăt-shee*	richest				of goods;
chudší	*khŭd-shee*	poorer		**železný, á, é**	*žeľĕznee,*	of iron;
nejchudší	*ney-khŭd-shee*	poorest		**železné zboží,**	*žeľĕzné zbožee,*	hard-
nejposlednější	*ney-posled-ñeysheĕ*					ware;
	last of all, the very last			**konkurent,** m.	*concŭrent,*	compet-
jak se jmenuje?	*yăk sĕ menŭyĕ,*					itor;
	what is his name?			**lidi, lidé,**	*liďi, lidé,*	people
buď jak buď,	*bŭď yăk bŭď,*	be it		**jeden z (ze),**	*yĕden z (zĕ),*	one of
	as it may; no matter how it is;			**jeho**	*yĕhŏ*	his
není-li pravda?	*neyñi-li prăvdă,*			**zatím**	*zăťeem*	on the contrary
	isn't it so?			**naopak**	*nă-opăk*	
je-li možná!	*yelli mŏžná,*	is it pos-		**mezi**	*mĕzi*	among
	sible!			**přes**	*prshĕs*	over, across
já myslel,	*yá mis-lel,*	I thought		**skoupý, á, é**	*skoŭpee*	miserly
oni myslí,	*oñi mislee,*	they think		**štědrý, á, é**	*shťedree*	liberal
bydlíte	*bidleetĕ*	you live (reside)		**patří**	*pătrshee*	belongs.

známý, á, é, *známee,* known; (used as a noun) acquaintance;
půl leta, *pool letă,* half a year; ze všech, *zĕ fshĕkh,* of all.

EXERCISES.

Jsem rád že jste tu.

Vy bydlíte teda v B.?

Ano; už přes rok.

Já mám přítele*) v B.

Je bohatý obchodník; — má veliký sklad — a krám plný zboží na Washington ulici.

Jaký má obchod?

Železné zboží. (Obchod v železném zboží).

Jak se jmenuje?

Jmenuje se Josef Baldwin; — znáte ho?

Znám ho; — je bohatý, — ale jeho konkurent p. Adams je bohatší, — a pan Fleming je nejbohatší.

Buď jak buď, pan Baldwin patří mezi nejbohatší obchodníky ve městě B.

Ano, jest jeden z nejbohatších obchodníků, — to je pravda.

Ale není pravda, že je skoupý; — naopak, — on je tuze štědrý.

Jeho soused přes ulici, pan Wild, je také můj známý; — myslím že je posud chudý muž.

Ano, je prý chudší než lidi myslí; — však není ten nejchudší obchodník ve městě.

I am glad that you are here.

You live, then, in B.?

Yes; already over a year.

I have a friend in B.

He is a rich merchant; — he has a large warehouse — and a store full of goods on Washington street.

What business has he?

Hardware. (A hardware business).

What is his name?

His name is Joseph Baldwin; — do you know him?

I know him; — he is rich, — but his competitor Mr. Adams is richer, — and Mr. Fleming is the richest.

Be it as it may, Mr. Baldwin belongs among the richest business men in the city of B.

Yes, he is one of the richest merchants, — that is true.

But it is not true, that he is miserly; — on the contrary, — he is very liberal.

His neighbor across the street, Mr. Wild, is also my acquaintance; — I think that he is still a poor man.

Yes, he is said to be poorer than people think ; — but he is not the poorest business man in town.

---

*) The noun **přítel** is somewhat irregular in its declension: **přítele**, *prshee-telě*, in the genitive and accusative case (of a friend; a friend); **příteli**, the dative, also the vocative (to a friend; friend!). The plural is **přátelé**, *prshá-telé*, the friends; **přátel**, *prshá-tel*, of the friends.

Váš Robert je klerkem*), není-li pravda?	Your Robert is a clerk, is he not?
Ano, je**) klerkem už půl leta.	Yes, he has been a clerk for half-a-year.
Myslím že Robert bude dobrý obchodník (or dobrým obchodníkem).	I think that Robert will be a good business man.
Robert je pilný hoch, — ale Frank je pilnější, — a Edward je nejpilnější ze všech.	Robert is an industrious boy, — but Frank is more industrious, — and Edward is the most industrious of all.
Není Frank starší než Robert?	Is not Frank older than Robert?
Ne; Robert je starší a Edward je nejstarší.	No, Robert is older, and Edward is the oldest.
Je-li možná! — Já myslel, že Robert je mladší než Frank, — a Frank zatím je nejmladší.	Is it possible!—I thought that Robert was younger than Frank, — and Frank, on the contrary, is the youngest.

---

*) The noun **klerk** is here used in the instrumental case, answering the question **čím je?** *cheem yě,* what is he?

This is a common construction. — We may ask: **Co je váš syn?** *what is your son?* — The answer would be: **On je klerk,** *he is a clerk.*

We may also ask: **Čím je váš syn?** (which, in English, is identical with the first question;) the answer would be: **On je klerkem,** *he is a clerk.*

In a similar manner we say in Bohemian, using the instrumental case:

Jsem farmerem,	I am a farmer;
on je farmerem,	he is a farmer;
on je obchodníkem,	he is a merchant;
je generalem,	he is a general; etc.

) **Je, on je, on jest, *he is,* the simple present tense of **býti,** *to be,* is also used in Bohemian for the perfect tense *he has been.* (See Lesson IX, Note 1.) Similarly we say:

jsem tu rok,	I have been here a year;
já jsem tu rok,	" " " " " "
jsem farmerem deset let,	I have been a farmer for ten years;
jsme doma týden,	we have been at home a week;
jsme sami přes rok,	we have been alone over a year; etc.

Máte také dcery?	Have you also daughters?
Mám dceru; je ještě mladší než hoch Frank.	I have a daughter; she is still younger than the boy Frank.
To je nejposlednější dítě.	That is the very last child.
To je má celá rodina.	That is my whole family.

Note 1. In the English language, the comparative degree of adjectives is formed either by adding **er,** or by placing **more** before them: young, *younger;* industrious, *more industrious.*

The superlative degree is formed either by adding **est (st),** or by placing **most** before the adjective: *youngest; most industrious.*

In Bohemian, the comparative degree is formed by adding **ší** or **ější** (sometimes **ejší**) in place of the final **ý (á, é):**

mladý, á, é *mlădee,* young; **mlad-ší,** *mlădshee,* younger;

pilný, á, é *pillnee,* industrious; **piln-ější,** *pillñeyshee,* more industrious.

The superlative degree is always formed by prefixing **nej,** *ney,* to the comparative degree:

nej-mladší,	*neymlădshee.*	youngest;
nej-pilnější,	*neypillñeyshee,*	most industrious.

Note 2. Some adjectives, in Bohemian as well as in English, have an irregular comparison. The most common of them are the following:

dobrý,	*dobree,*	good;	**lepší,**	*lepshee.*	better;
zlý,	*zlee,*	bad;	**horší,**	*horshee,*	worse;
malý,	*mălee,*	small;	**menší,**	*menshee,*	smaller;
velký,	*velkee,*	large;	**větší,**	*vyětshee,*	larger;
dlouhý,	*dloŭhee,*	long;	**delší,**	*delshee.*	longer;
vysoký,	*· risŏkee,*	high;	**ryšší,**	*vishee,*	higher;
hluboký,	*hlŭbokee,*	deep;	**hlubší,**	*hlŭbshee,*	deeper;
široký,	*shirokee,*	wide;	**širší,**	*shirshee,*	wider;
daleký,	*dălekee,*	far;	**další,**	*dălshee,*	farther;

blízký,	*bleeskee,*	near;	bližší,	*blishee,*	nearer;
hezký,	*hesskee,* pretty,(nice);		hezčí,	*hess-chee,*	prettier;
lehký,	*lĕhkee,*	light;	lehčí,	*lĕh-chee,*	lighter;
měkký,	*myĕkee,*	soft;	měkčí,	*myĕk-chee,*	softer.

The superlative is formed without exception by prefixing **nej** to the comparative.

LESSON XXIII.

Já jel,	*yá yell,*	I rode, I went;
čekal,	*chekăl,*	(he) waited;
pravil,	*prăvil,*	(he) said;
vešel,	*vĕshell*	went in;
psala,	*psălă,*	(she) wrote;
neviděl jsem,	*nĕviďel sem,*	I did not see;
milujem se,	*milŭyem se,*	we love each other;
postavím si,	*postăveem si,*	I shall build for myself;
ať to stojí,	*ať tŏ stoyee,*	let it cost;
řka,	*rshkă,*	saying;
řekl jsem,	*rshĕkl sem,*	I said, I told; I have said (told);
mluvil jsem,	*mlŭvil sem,*	I have spoken; I spoke;
slyšel jsem,	*slishell sem:*	I have heard; I heard;
sednouti si,	*sednoŭt si,*	to sit down;
tázati se,	*tázăt sĕ,*	to ask, to inquire;

domov, m.	*dŏmof,*	a home;
obydlí, ʃn.	*ŏbidlee,*	dwelling;
světnice, f.	*swyĕtňitsĕ*	} room;
sednice, f.	*sedňitsĕ*	
ložnice, f.	*lož-ňitsĕ,*	bedroom;
dráha, f.	*dráhă,*	road, railroad;
po dráze,	*pŏ drázĕ,*	by railroad;
nádraží, n.	*nádră-žee.*	depot;
pohodlí, n.	*pŏhodlee,*	comfort;
pohodlný, á, é,	*pŏhodᵉlnee,*	comfortable;
švagrová,	*shwăgrová,*	sister-in-law;
dítko, n.	*ďeetkŏ,*	child, baby;
nemoc, f.	*nĕmots,*	sickness;
všelico,	*fshellitsŏ,*	different things;
dlouho,	*dloŭhŏ,*	long, a long time;
onehdy,	*ŏnĕh-de,*	the other day;
zdráv, a, o,	*zdráv,*	well, healthy;
unaven, a, o,	*ŭnăven,*	tired;
takový, á, é,	*tăkovee,*	such;
vedle,	*vĕ-dlĕ,*	next to; side by side;
věru,	*vyĕrŭ,*	indeed;

zůstati, *zoostát,* to stay, to remain; | **pro,**   *prŏ,*   for.
svlékni se, *svlékñi sě,* undress; | **napřed,**   *náprshed,* first, ahead;
lehl jsem si, *lě-hl sem si,* I lied down; |

se, sebe, *sě, sěbě,* oneself; myself, thyself, himself, herself, itself;
               ourselves, yourselves, themselves;

si, sobě, *si, sŏbyě,* to oneself; to myself, etc. etc.

sebou, *sěbou,* by *or* with oneself; etc. etc.

EXERCISES.

Já jel*) onehdy do Chicago; — | I went the other day to Chicago;
mám tam bratra; — chtěl jsem ho | —I have a brother there;—I wanted
vidět, — též jeho obydlí; — on če- | to see him,—also his dwelling;—he
kal na mě v nádraží. — Já přijel | waited for me at the depot.—I came
po dráze C. & NW. | by the C. & NW. railroad.

Pravil mi : "Rád tě vidím, bra- | He said to me: "I am glad to see
tře! — Čekal jsem tebe; — ukážu | thee, brother!—I have been expect-
ti můj domov. — Dáme tobě naši | ing thee; — I will show to thee my
největší ložnici. | home.— We shall give (to) thee our
| largest bedroom.

Musíš zůstati u mě aspoň týden; | Thou must stay with me (i. e. at
— tak teda pojď se mnou." | my house) at least a week; — so,
| then, come with me."

Řekl jsem mu, že já také rád | I told him that I also was glad to
ho vidím. — Jsi zdráv? tázal jsem | see him? — Are you well? I asked
se ho. | him.

"Ano, jsem tuze zdráv", pra- | "Yes, I am very well", said he;
vil on; "má žena je také zdráva | "my wife is also well and the baby

---

*) **Jeti,** *yeťi* (commonly *yet*), to ride, to go by railroad or otherwise. **Já jsem jel,** *yá sem yell,* I rode, I went, — I have gone; **já
jel,** *yá yell,* is the past tense with the auxilliary **jsem** left out, as
explained in Lesson X. The same applies to **já přijel,** *yá prshi-yell,*
I came (by train or other means of conveyance). From the verb **jeti,**
yeťi (or *yet*), to ride, or to go by some conveyance, about as many new
verbs can be derived by prefixes as from **jíti,** *yeeťi* (or *yeet*) to go. See
Lesson XIII, Note 6.

a dítko je také zdrávo. — Jsme spokojeni a milujem se."

A věru, na něm neviděl jsem žádnou nemoc. — Švagrová psala pravdu o něm, že je zdráv.

Šel jsem s nim. — Za půl hodiny byli jsme u něho. — Já šel napřed, on za mnou. — Jeho žena též ráda mě viděla; — ona také mě čekala.

Přinesl jsem jí všelico; — něco pro ni, něco pro její dítko. — Mluvil jsem s ní dlouho o všeličem, — a slyšel jsem od ní mnoho nového.—Ono bylo skoro všecko nové pro mě.

Myslil jsem si: Mají pěkný dům, — pohodlný domov. — Tolik světnic! — Já si postavím takový dům; — malou ložnici pro sebe a dvě veliké ložnice pro rodinu. — Postavím sobě též vedle písárnu.

Ať to stojí něco; — postavím to pro sebe. — Anebo koupím si pěkný dům.

Sedl jsem si na sofa, řka: Jsem unaven!

"Udělej si pohodlí, — svlékni se," — pravil bratr.

Já se svlékl a lehl jsem si.

is well, too.—We are contented and we love each other."

And indeed, on him I didn't see any sickness.—Sister-in-law wrote the truth about him that he was well.

I went with him.—In half an hour we were at his house.—I went in first, he (followed) after me. — His wife also was glad to see me; — she also expected me.

I brought to her different things; —something for her, something for her baby.—I spoke with her long about different things, — and I heard from her many news.—It was nearly all news to me.

I thought to myself: They have a nice house,—a comfortable home. —So many rooms!—I shall build me such a house;—a small bedroom for myself, and two large bedrooms for the family. — I shall build myself also next to it an office.

Let it cost something; — I shall build it for myself.—Or, I shall buy me a nice house.

I sat down on the sofa, saying: I am tired!

"Make thyself comfortable,— undress (thyself)," — said my brother.

I undressed and lay (myself) down.

Note 1. The personal pronouns **já**, **ty**, **on (ona, ono)**, show the following variation :

Já,	*yá,*	I;	**ty,**	*te,*	thou;
mě,	*myě,*	me;	**tě, tebe,**	*tě, těbě,*	thee;
mi, mně,	*me, mňe,*	to me;	**ti, tobě,**	*t'i, těbyě,*	to thee;
se mnou,	*sě mnoǔ,*	with me;	**s tebou,**	*stěboǔ,*	with thee;
on, ono,	*ǒn, ǒnǒ,*	he, it;	**ona,**	*ǒnǎ,*	she;
ho,	*hǒ,*	him, it;	**ji, jí,**	*ye, yee,*	her, to her;
jeho,	*yěhǒ,*	his, its;	**její,**	*yěyee,*	her, hers;
mu, jemu, němu,	*mǔ, yěmǔ, ňěmǔ,*	to him, to it;			
v něm,	*vñěm,*	in him, in it;	**v ní,**	*vñee,*	in her;
s nim,	*sñim,*	with him, with it;	**s ní,**	*sñee,*	with her.

Note 2. Adjectives sometimes take an indefinite form:

on je zdráv, *ǒn yě zdráv,* he is well (or healthy);

ona je zdráva, *ǒnǎ yě zdrávǎ,* she is well;

ono je zdrávo, *ǒnǒ yě zdrávǒ,* it is well;

but when placed before a noun, the adjective must always have its definite form: **zdravý muž,** *zdrǎvee moož,* a healthy man; **zdravá žena,** *zdrǎvá žená,* a healthy woman; **zdravé dítě,** *zdrǎvé ďeeťe,* a healthy child.

The following indefinite adjectives are of common occurrence:

nemocen,	*němotsen,*	instead of	**nemocný,**	*němotsnee,*	sick;
mrtev,	*m^ertev,*	" "	**mrtvý,**	*m^ertvee,*	dead;
stár,	*stár,*	" "	**starý,**	*stǎree,*	old;
mocen,	*mǒtsen,*	" "	**mocný,**	*motsnee,*	capable;
znám,	*znám,*	" "	**známý,**	*známee,*	known;
vesel,	*vě-sell,*	" "	**veselý,**	*vesselee,*	cheerful;
práv,	*práv,*	" "	**pravý,**	*prǎvee,*	just;
bos,	*bǒs,*	" "	**bosý,**	*bosee,*	barefoot.

Adjectives ending in **vý** and **ný** frequently take the indefinite form in the nominative case, changing their termination into **v** and **en** (**va, na** in the feminine, **vo, no** in the neutre gender).

Note 3. As observed in Note 2, Lesson XIII, the past tense of regular Bohemian verbs is formed from the infinitive by an **l** in place of the usual termination **ti** :

jeti,	*yeťi or yet,*	to ride;	jel,	*yell,*	rode;
čekati,	*chekät,*	to wait;	čekal,	*chekäl,*	waited;
mluviti,	*mlŭvit,*	to speak;	mluvil,	*mlŭvil,*	spoke;

But some verbs ending in **outi** show a slight deviation from this rule, changing **outi** into **ul,** and having besides a short form of the past tense, in which the letter **l** is substituted for the whole termination **nouti,** being attached immediately to the stem of the verb :

lehnouti, *leh-noŭťi* (or *leh-noŭt*), to lie down; **lehnul, lehl,** *leh-nŭl, lě-hl,* lay down;

sednouti, *sednoŭt,* to sit down; **sednul, sedl,** *sednŭl, sedl,* sat down;

svléknouti, *svlék-noŭt,* to undress; **svléknul, svlékl,** *svléknŭl, svlékl,* undressed.

The verb **svléknouti** has also an irregular form of the infinitive: **svléci,** *svlé-tsi.* In common conversation we hear **sliknout, slikl, slečený,** *sleeknoŭt,* (to undress), *sleekl, slěchěnee* (undressed, — as past participle and adjective).

LESSON XXIV.

Ať jde,	*ať dě,*	let him (her, it) come, *or* go;	to je škoda,	*tŏ yě shkodǎ,*	that is a pity;
zůstanem,	*zoostänem,*	we shall stay;	pohostění, n.	*pohŏsťeñee,*	hospitality;
zůstaň,	*zoostäñ.*	stay (thou);			
ukaž,	*ŭkǎsh,*	show (thou), let see;	návštěva, f.	*náfshťevǎ,*	visit;
přijeti,	*prshi-yet,*	to come (by railway, etc);	často,	*chǎstŏ,*	often;
			buď...nebo,	*bŭď...nebŏ,*	either...or;
přijedem,	*prshi-yědem,*	we shall come (by some conveyance);	nemám co,	*nemám tsŏ,*	I have nothing (to....);

líbí se mi,   *leebee sě me,*   I like it (him, her); it pleases me;

bude se jim líbit, *bŭdě sě yim leebit,* they will like it; it will please them;

bude jim milé, *bŭdě yim milé,* it will please them:

doufám,   *doŭfám,*   I hope;

v Chicago*), *fchicago,* in Chicago.

přijedou, *prshi-yědoŭ,* they will come;

povídal jsem, *poveedăl sem,* I said;

slíbiti,   *sleebit,*   to promise;

tajiti,   *tăyit,*   to hide;

ukrývati, *ŭkreevăt,* to cover up, to hide, to conceal;

nemůžem, *nemoožem,* we can not;

EXERCISES.

My zůs anem v Chicago, — pravil bratr; — pro nás je to dobré místo; — ukaž nám lepší! — Ať rodina jde sem, — a zůstaň zde s námi.

Já pravil : Vy máte zde pěkný domov; — líbí se mi u vás; — myslím že často přijedem k vám, —

We shall stay in Chicago, — said (my) brother; — for us it is a good place; — show (to) us a better one! — Let (your) family come here, — and stay here with us.

I said: You have here a nice home; —I like it here (i. e. at your house, with you,—u vás);—I think that we

---

*) If we insist upon declining **Chicago** like a Bohemian noun of the neutre gender (ending in **o**), we should say in the locative case: v Chicagu, *fchicagŭ.* However, this is rather an exception among the Bohemians in America, names of places of foreign origin being usually left unchanged, the same as in English. This may not exactly satisfy unyielding grammarians, but it is a rule dictated by common sense, the inflection of such proper names being not only useless, but in many cases perfectly absurd, and often impossible. Hence we say: **do Milwaukee, v Milwaukee, za Milwaukee** (to Milwaukee, in M., beyond M.); **do Kewaunee, do Spring Valley, do Dubuque, do Des Moines,** etc. To attempt an inflection of such names, according to the rules of some declension of Bohemian nouns, would be an intolerable absurdity. The name of **Chicago,** indeed, yields easily to the Bohemian declension, and hence it is now and then declined; the same is true of some other names. There are also a few names of places well known throughout the world, which are always declined in Bohemian, presenting no difficulty to such a process; such are for instance: **New York, — v New Yorku, do New Yorku, za New Yorkem** (in New York, to N. Y., beyond N. Y.); **Boston, — v Bostonu, do Bostonu, za Bostonem; Washington, do Washingtonu;** and some others. — These names are masculine, by force of their termination.

buď já, nebo jeden z nás. — Ale zůstati s vámi nemůžem. — Náš domov je na venku.

Oni oba pravili: To je škoda!

Tázal jsem se jich, kdy přijedou k nám na návštěvu; — povídal jsem, že dáme jim také hezkou světnici; — že se jim bude líbit u nás, — jako se mně líbí u nich.

Slíbili přijeti na návštěvu. — Doufám že pohostění od nás bude milé jim, jako je milé mně od nich.

Ten den mluvil jsem s nimi dlouho; — nemám co tajiti před nimi; — nemám co ukrývati. — Tak mluvili jsme, až nebylo už co mluviti.

shall often come to you, — either I, or one of us.—But to stay with you we can not. — Our home is in the country.

They both said: That is a pity!

I asked them, when they would come to us on a visit; — I said, that we should give (to) them also a nice room; — that they will like it at our place (u **nás**), — as I like it at their house (u **nich**).

They promised to come on a visit. — I hope that hospitality from us will be pleasing *to them*, as it is pleasing *to* me *from them*.

That day I spoke with them a long time; — I have nothing to hide from them;—I have nothing to conceal.— So we spoke, until there was nothing further to speak about.

Note. The personal pronouns **my, vy, oni (ony** f., **ona,** n.) show the following variation, which has already become somewhat familiar to the student from the preceding lessons :

my,	*me,*	we;	vy,	*ve,*	you;
nás,	*nás,*	us;	vás,	*vás,*	you;
nám,	*nám,*	to us;	vám,	*vám,*	to you;
s námi,	*snámi,*	with us;	s vámi,	*svámi,*	with you;

oni, (ony, ona),	*ŏñi, (ŏne, ŏnŭ),*	they;
jich,	*yikh,*	of them, them;
jim,	*yim,*	to them;
je,	*yĕ,*	them;
v nich,	*vñikh,*	in them, (o nich, about them; od nich, from them; etc.)
s nimi,	*sñime,*	with them; (za nimi, behind or after them, etc.)

LESSON XXV.

Státi,	*stáťi (stát)*,	to stand; to cost;
stojí,	*stoyee*,	stands; costs;
stál,	*stál*,	stood; cost;
mluví,	*mlŭvee*,	speaks;
půjčil,	*pŭychil* (colloquially : *pŭchil*),	lent, loaned;
snáší se,	*snáshee sĕ*,	agrees;
smál se,	*smál sĕ*,	he laughed;
podívej se,	*poďeevey sĕ*,	look (thou);
podívejte se,	*poďeeveytĕ sĕ*,	look (you);
sejde se,	*seydĕ sĕ*,	(he, she, it) will meet;

tisíc, m.	*ťiseets*,	thousand;
stát, m.	*stát*,	state;
úcta, f.	*ootstă*,	respect;
rozprávka, f.	*ros-práfkă*	talk, conversation,
hovor, m.	*hŏvor*,	discourse;
zoubek, m.	*zoŭbek*,	little tooth;
něco,	*ñetsŏ*,	some;
než,	*nesh*,	than;
rozen, a, o	*rŏzen*	born
narozen, a, o	*nărŏzen*	
právě jako,	*právyĕ yăkŏ*,	same as;
nebyla u nás,	*nebillă ŭnáss*,	she was not at our house; she has not been to see us.

EXERCISES.

Můj bratr je posud mladý; — je mladší než já. — Já jsem o dvě leta starší než on.

My brother is still young; — he is younger than I. — I am (by) two years older than he.

Dům mého bratra stojí teprv rok; — stál pět tisíc*) dollarů; — soused půjčil něco peněz mému bratru.

The house of my brother stands only a year; — it cost five thousand dollars; — the neighbor loaned some money to my brother.

On má rád mého bratra; — on mluví o mém bratru s úctou. — S mým bratrem každý se snáší dobře.

He likes my brother; — he speaks of my brother with respect. — With my brother everybody agrees well.

---

*) **Jeden tisíc,** *yĕdęn ťiseets,* one thousand; **dva, tři, čtyry tisíce,** *dwă, trshi, shtiri ťiseetsĕ,* two, three, four thousand; **pět tisíc,** *pyĕt ťiseets,* five thousand; **šest tisíc,** *shĕst ťiseets,* six thousand; and so forth.

Moje švagrová je ze státu Indiana*), — rozena v Terre Haute; — má žena je z Ohio.

My sister-in-law is from the state of Indiana, — born in Terre Haute; my wife is from Ohio.

Mojí švagrové**) líbí se v Chicago tuze; — mé ženě líbí se více na venku.

My sister-in-law likes it in Chicago very much; — my wife likes it more in the country.

Rozprávka neb hovor s mojí švagrovou jest milý, — velmi milý, — právě jako s mojí ženou. — Nevím kdy sejde se s mou ženou zas; — nebyla u nás dávno.

A conversation or discourse with my sister-in-law is pleasant, — very pleasant, — the same as with my wife. —I don't know when she will meet (with) my wife again; — she has not been to see us a long time.

Podívejte se na moje dítko, — má už zoubek! — pravila švagrová a smála se. — Hošík také smál se na mě. — To je mé dobré dítko! pravila matka.

Look at my baby, — he has already a tooth! — said my sister-in-law and laughed. — The little boy also smiled at me. — That is my good baby! said (his) mother.

N o t e 1. The so-called possessive pronoun **můj,** *můy* (my, mine), takes in the feminine gender the form **moje, má,** and in the neutre geuder **moje, mé.** Hence we say: **můj bratr,** my brother; **moje sestra** or **má sestra,** my sister; **moje dítě** or **mé dítě,** my child. — The variation of this pronoun is shown in the following table :

můj, m.	*můy;*	moje,	má, f.	*moyě,*	*má;*	my, mine;
mého,	*méhŏ;*	mojí,	mé,	*moyee,*	*mé;*	of my;
mému,	*mémŭ;*	mojí,	mé,	"	" ;	to my;
v mém,	*vmém;*	v mojí,	v mé,	*v "*	*v " ;*	in my;
s mým,	*smeem;*	s mojí,	s mou,	*smoyee,*	*smoŭ,*	with my.

*) Or **Indiany.** See foot note in Lesson XXIV.

) ⁻ **Mojí švagrové, mé ženě, is the dative case, responding to the question **komu?** (to whom?) **Komu se líbí?** to whom is it pleasing? (whom does it please?) — **Líbí se mé švagrové;** — líbí se mé ženě; — it pleases (to) my sister-in-law; it pleases (to) my wife.

The neutre gender **moje, mé,** shows in the other cases the same variation as the masculine **můj,** excepting the accusative (or objective) and the vocative case, which are like the nominative: **to je mé dítě,** this is my child; **vidím mé dítě,** I see my child; **ó mé dítě!** oh my child!

Note 2. The possessive pronoun **tvůj,** m., *tvŭy* (**tvoje** or **tvá,** f., *tvŏyĕ, tvá;* **tvoje** or **tvé,** n., *tvé*), thy, thine, — agrees in its declension perfectly with **můj (moje, má, mé).**

The same is true of the possessive pronoun **svůj (svoje, svá,** f.; **svoje, své,** n.), *svŭy (svoyĕ, svá, své*), which means "one's own", but frequently stands for **můj, tvůj, jeho, její** (my, thy, his, her), **náš, váš, jich** (our, your, their).

Moji lidé,	*moye lidé,*	my folks;	**radši jsem,** *rádchi sem,* I like better to be;
půda, f.	*poodá,*	ground, soil;	**nejradši jsem,** *neyrádchi sem,* I like best to be;
krov, m.	*krof,*	roof;	**nerad jsem,** *nerád sem,* I do not like to be;
příbuzný, á,	*prshoo-búznee,*	relative, kinsman, relation;	**sejdu se,** *seydŭ sĕ,* I meet;
vlastní,	*vlást-ñee,*	own;	**kolem sebe,** *kolem sĕbĕ,* around me (him, her, us, etc.)
šťasten,	*shťásten,*	happy;	
nazpět,	*náspyĕt,*	back;	
spěchám,	*spyĕ-khám,*	I hasten, I hurry;	

EXERCISES.

Mí přátelé*) v Chicagu všichni rádi mě viděli; — škoda že moji lidé nebyli se mnou.

Nerad jsem pryč od mých lidí; — pokaždé spěchám nazpět k mým lidem.

Rád vidím své přátele; — rád se sejdu se svými příbuznými; — ale

My friends in Chicago all liked (were glad) to see me; — it is a pity that my folks were not with me.

I do not like to be away from my folks; — every time I hasten back to my folks.

I like to see my friends;—I like to meet (with) my relatives;—but I like

---

*) See foot-note in Lesson XXII.

radši jsem doma. — Opravdu, nej- radši jsem doma s mými lidmi.	better to be at home. — Truly, I like best to be at home with my folks.
Nejradši vidím kolem sebe své lidi. — Jsem šťasten se svými lid- mi ve svém vlastním domově, — na své vlastní půdě, — pod svým vlast- ním krovem.	I like best to see around me my folks. — I am happy with my folks in my own home, — on my own ground, — under my own roof.

Note 2. The plural of **můj** m., **moje** or **má** f., and **moje** or mé n., is as follows : **moji, mí,** *moye, mee*, m.

moje, mé, *moyĕ, mé,* f.

moje, má, *moyĕ, má,* n.

In common discourse **moje, mé** is used in the neutre as well as in the feminine gender. In English, we invariably employ *my* and *mine*.

In the plural number the following variation takes place :

moji, mí; moje mé; *moyi, mee; moyĕ, mé;* — my, mine;

mých, *meekh,* of my (**od mých,** from my; **v mých,** in my; etc.), of mine;

mým, *meem,* to my, to mine;

s mými, *smeeme,* with my, with mine; (**za mými,** after or behind mine, etc.)

The plural of **tvůj** m., **tvoje, tvá** f., **tvoje, tvé** n. (thy, thine) is perfectly analogous: **tvoji, tví** m., *tvoyi, twee;* **tvoje, tvé** f. & n. *twoyĕ, twé* (thy, thine); **tvých,** *tweekh,* of thine; **tvým,** *tweem,* to thine; **s tvými,** *stweemi,* with thine.

LESSON XXVI.

Základ, ·m. *záklăd,*	foundation;	zahrada, f. *zăhrădă,*	garden
kolik světnic, *kŏlik swyĕt-ñits,* how	many rooms;	zahrádka, f. *zăhrádka,* small	garden
kuchyně, f. *kŭkhiñe,*	kitchen	strom, m. *strom,*	tree
sklep, m. *sklep,*	cellar	stromy, pl. *stromy,*	trees
		stromoví, n. *stromŏvee,*	

patro, n.	*pătrŏ,*	story	ovoce, n.	*ŏvotsĕ,*	fruit
studně, f.	*stŭdňe,*	well	ovocné,	*ŏvotsné,*	fruit-bearing
cisterna, f.	*tsisternă,*	cistern	nesou,	*nesoŭ,*	they bear
altán, m.	*ăltán,*	bower	mrva, f.	*m^ervă,*	manure
plot, m.	*plot,*	fence	v letě,	*vleťe,*	in summer
docela,	*dotselă,*	quite	v zimě,	*vzimyĕ,*	in winter
úplně,	*vop^elňe,*	perfectly	z jara,	*zyă-ră,*	in the spring
dříve,	*drshee-vĕ* (or *drsheef*)) be-		půda, f.	*poodă,*	land
prve,	*p^ervĕ,*	fore	akr, m.	*ăk^er,*	acre
je-li pravda?	*yelli prăvdă*) isn't it		zbytek, m.	*zby-tek,*	remainder
že ne?	*žĕ nĕ ?*) so?		je, jest,	*yĕ, yest,*	there is, there are;
			pouze,	*poŭzĕ,*	only.

EXERCISES.

Váš dům je nový, je-li pravda?

Your house is new, isn't it?

Ano, náš dům je docela nový.

Yes, our house is quite new.

Základ našeho domu je dobrý.

The foundation of our house is good.

Ten velký lot patří k vašemu domu, že ne?

That large lot belongs to your house, does it not?

Ten lot patří k našemu domu; — je to zbytek akru půdy co jsme měli dříve.

That lot belongs to our house; — it is a remainder of the acre of land (what) we had before.

Co je ve vašem domě? kolik světnic máte?

What is in your house? how many rooms have you?

V našem domě je kuchyně, pět světnic a dobrý sklep, — studený v letě, teplý v zimě.

In our house there is a kitchen, five rooms and a good cellar,— cold in summer, warm in winter.

Doufám že jste spokojeni s vaším domem (or se svým domem).

I hope that you are satisfied with your house.

Ano, jsme úplně spokojeni s naším domem.

Yes, we are perfectly satisfied with our house.

Váš dům má dvě patra, že ne?

Your house has two stories, hasn't it?

Ne; pouze jedno patro.

No; only one story.

Myslím že máte u vašeho domu malou zahradu a za vaším domem studni, též cisternu.	I think that you have by your house a small garden and back of your house a well, also a cistern.
Ano, naše místo je pěkné; — na naší zahradě máme altán; — kolem naší zahrady je vysoký plot. — Je to příjemná zahrádka.	Yes, our place is nice; — in our garden we have a bower; — around our garden there is a high fence. — It is a pleasant little garden.

Naši lidé mají rádi stromoví*). —Naše stromy jsou ovocué.— Z ja-ra dáváme**) mrvu k našim ovoc-ným stromům.—Rád sedám**)s na-šimi lidmi ve stínu našich stromů.	Our folks like trees. — Our trees are fruit-bearing. — In the spring we put manure to our fruit-trees. — I like to sit with our folks in the shadow of our trees.

Note 1. The possessive pronoun **náš,** (**naše,** f. and n.) shows the following variation:

(Masculine and neutre gender.)

náš, m. **naše,** n.	*násh, náshě,*	our, (ours);
našeho,	*náshěhő,*	of our; our (in the accus. or objective case);
našemu,	*náshěmŭ,*	to our;
v **našem,**	*vnáshěm,*	in our, (**o našem,** about our; etc);

(Feminine gender.)

naše,	*náshě,*	our, ours;
naši,	*náshi,*	our (in the accus. or objective case);
naší,	*náshee,*	of our, to our; (**v naší,** in our; **s naší,** with our; etc.)

---

*) **Stromoví,** *stromővee,* is a collective noun and means trees (**stromy**) in general.

) **Dáti, *dáťi,* to give; **dávati,** *dávắťi,* to give repeatedly, to use to give; **dáváme,** *dávámě,* we use to give; we are giving. See Lesson XIII, Note 5. — **Seděti,** *seďeťi,* to sit; **sedati,** *sedắťi,* to sit repeatedly, to use to sit; **sedám,** I use to sit.

(*Plural of all genders.*)

naši, m. **naše,** f. & n.   *nåshi, nåshĕ,*   our, ours;

našich,   *nåshikh,*   of our;   (**v našich,** in our;   etc.)

našim,   *nåshim,*   to our;

s našimi,   *snåshimi,*   with our;   (**za našimi,** beyond or back of our; etc.)

Note 2. The pronoun **váš** (**vaše,** f. and n.) is perfectly analogous with **náš** in its declension.   (Instrumental case m. & n. gender singular, omitted above: **s našim, s vašim,** *snåsheem, svåsheem,* with ours, with yours.)

The English words *their* and *theirs* are both expressed by **jich,** — in common discourse nearly always **jejich;** *yikh, yĕyikh.* This is in fact the genitive of the personal pronoun **oni (ony, ona),** *they,* and naturally remains unchanged.   For instance:

Jich dům, jich domy, or **jejich dům, jejich domy;** *yikh dům, dŏmi; yĕyikh dům, dŏmi;* their house, their houses.

Ten dům jest jejich, *ten dům yest yĕyikh,* that house is theirs. — **Ty domy jsou jejich,** *ty dŏmi soů yĕyikh,* those houses are theirs.

LESSON XXVII.

The student is already somewhat acquainted with the indicative pronouns **ten, ta, to,** this *or* that; plural: **ti, ty, ta, ťi,** *ty, tå,* these *or* those (in common discourse **ty** for all genders).   Hence, in a short practical review of their variations he will only meet old acquaintances.

Lidé,	*lidé*	people	**kuželua,**	*kůželnå,*	bowling-alley;
lidi,	*liďi*		**zábava,**	*zábåvå,*	amusement;
stavěti,	*ståvyĕt,*	to build	**bydlí,**	*bidlee,*	lives; they live;
staveni,	*ståvĕñee,*	building	**co bydlí,**	*tsŏ bidlee,*	who lives
zděný dům,	*zďenee dům*	brick			(*lit.* what lives);
cihelný dům,	*tsihelnee dům*	house	**nic nechybí,**	*ñuts nĕkhibee,*	nothing
střecha,	*strshĕ-khå,*	roof			is wanting;

šindel,	*shindell,*	shingle		může,	*moožě,*	can, may;
učitel,	*ŭchitell,*	teacher		býti za dobré,	*beeťi zá dobré,*	to be
pokojný, á, é,	*pokoynee,*	quiet				on good terms;
prázný, á, é,	*práznee,*	vacant		na pravo,	*ná prăvŏ,*	to the right;
jistě,	*yisťe,*	surely, certainly;		na levo,	*ná lĕvŏ,*	to the left.

Exercises.

Ten dům je věru pěkný; — je to zděný dům.

That house is indeed nice; — it is a brick house.

Střecha toho domu je ze šindele, není?

The roof of that house is of shingle (i. e. covered with shingles), is it not?

Myslím že je. — Nic nechybí tomu domu; — jest příjemno bydleti v tom domě; — s tím domem každý může býti spokojen.

I think it is.—Nothing is wanting to that house; — it is agreeable to live in that house;—with that house everybody can be satisfied.

Ta zahrada má velkou cenu. — V té zahradě je mnoho ovocného stromoví.

That garden has a large value. — In that garden there are many fruit-trees.

Tu zahradu mám radši než park. — Máme také kuželnu v té zahradě, pro naši (or pro svou) zábavu.

That garden I like better than a park.—We have also a bowling-alley in that garden, for our amusement.

To místo s tím stavením a s tou zahradou má vysokou cenu.

That place with the building and garden has a high value.

Ti lidé co bydlí vedle nás, jsou pokojní sousedé; — žádný z těch lidí není zlý; — se všemi těmi lidmi jsme za dobré.

The people who live next to us, are quiet neighbors; — nobody (not one) of those people is bad;—with all those people we are on good terms.

Viděl jsem doktora jíti k těm lidem na pravo od nás; — jistě někdo je nemocen.

I saw the doctor go to those people to the right of us;—surely somebody is sick.

Kdo jsou ti lidé na levo? — Na levo od nás bydlí učitel, pan Stanton, se svou (i. e. s jeho) rodinou.

Ty loty za námi jsou prázné; — ale budou prý stavět na těch lo-tech.

Kolik těch lotů je? — Myslím že je šest těch lotů.

Who are those people to the left? — To the left of us lives a teacher, Mr. Stanton, with his family.

Those lots back of us are vacant; — but, it is said, they will build on those lots.

How many of those lots are there? —I think that there are six of those lots.

Note 1. The variation of the indicative pronouns employed in the foregoing is shown to be as follows:

ten, m. **to,** n.	*těn, tŏ,*	this, that;	**ta,** f.	*tă,*		this, that;
tolio,	*tŏhŏ,*	of this, of that;	**tu,**	*tŭ,*		this, that (accus.
tomu,	*tŏmŭ,*	to this, to that;				or objec. case);
v tom,	*ftŏm,*	in this, in that;	**té,**	*té,*	to this, to that; **v té,** in	
		(o tom, about that; etc)			that; o té, about that; etc.	
s tím,	*st'eem,*	with this, with that; (za tím, beyond that; etc.	**s tou,**	*stoŭ,*	with this, with that; za tou, behind that; etc.	

Plural:

ti, ty, ta, these, those;

těch, *t'ekh,* of those; **v těch,** *ft'ekh,* in those; etc.

těm, *t'em,* to those;

s těmi, *st'emi,* with those;

za těmi, behind those; etc.

These indicative pronouns often occur in a compound form: **tento, tato, toto,** always meaning "this one"; in the plural: **tito, tyto, tato,** "these ones". Their inflection remains the same, with the suffix **to** attached to the original pronoun in every case: **tohoto,** to this one; **tomu-to,** of this one; and so forth.

Note 2. The numeral **jeden** (f. and n. **jedna, jedno**), *yĕden, yĕdnă, yĕdnŏ,* one, — agrees perfectly with **ten, (ta, to)** in its inflection:

jeden člověk tam byl, one man was there;

viděl jsem jen jednoho (accus. or objective case), I saw only one;

dal jsem to jednomu z nich (*zñikh*), I gave it to one of them;

v jednom z nich se mejlím*), in one of them I am mistaken;

šel jsem s jedním z nich, I went with one of them.

Jedna žena je zde, one woman is here; — **vidím jednu ženu,** I see one woman; — **mám to od jedné z nich,** I have it from one of them (f.); — **mluvil jsem s jednou,** I spoke with one (f.).

LESSON XXVIII.

Sem,	*sĕm,*	hither, here;
sám,	*sám,*	alone;
čekáte,	*chĕkátĕ,*	you expect, you await (*or* you wait);
nečekám,	*nĕchekám,*	I do not expect;
že přijde,	*žĕ prshiy-dĕ,*	that he will (*or* would) come;
na ulici,	*nă ŭlitsi,*	on the street;
že jste?	*žĕ stĕ?*	you say you are?
že s nikým?	*žĕ sñikeem,*	(*literally:* that with nobody?) you say with nobody?

lék, m.	*lék,*	medicine;
lahev, f.	*lăhev,*	bottle;
v lahvi,	*vlăh-vi,*	in the bottle;
dávka, f.	*dáfkă,*	dose;
po dávkách,	*pŏ dáfkăkh,*	in doses;
nastuzen,	*năstŭzen,*	having a cold;
jste nastuzen,	*stĕ năstŭzen,*	you have a cold;
nastuzení, n.	*năstŭzeñee,*	a cold;
kašel, m.	*kăshell,*	cough;
dáti vinu,	*dáťi vinŭ,*	to charge to; to blame (for);
mysliti,	*mysliťi,*	to think;

---

*) **Mejliti se, mýliti se,** *meylit sĕ, meelit sĕ,* to be mistaken; **mejlím se,** *meyleem sĕ,* I am mistaken. — **Zmejliti se, zmýliti se,** *zmeylit sĕ, zmeelit sĕ,* to make a mistake; **zmejlil jsem se,** *zmeylil sem sĕ,* I made a mistake.

neotevru,	*něo-tev-rŭ,*	I shall not open;
jindy,	*yindy,*	before; at other times;
tohle,	*tŏhlě,*	this here;

mazati se,	*măzăt'i sě,*	to rub oneself;
užívat,	*ŭžeevăt,*	to take medicine, (otherwise: to use);
mazat se,	*măzăt sě,*	to rub one's self.

EXERCISES.

Myslím že někdo jde sem; — kdo je to?

I think that somebody is coming here; — who is it?

Nevím; — koho čekáte?

I do not know; — whom do you expect?

Nečekám nikoho; — dnes chci býti sám; — nechci viděti nikoho.

I do not expect anybody; — to-day I want to be alone; — I do not want to see anybody.

Komu poslal jste to pozvání? — Nikomu.

To whom did you send that invitation? — To nobody.

O kom myslil jste včera, že přijde? — O nikom.

Of whom did you think yesterday, that he would come? — Of nobody.

S kým mluvil jste dnes ráno na ulici? — S nikým.

With whom did you speak this morning on the street? — With nobody.

Že s nikým? — Vy se mejlíte. — Viděl jsem vás státi s někým na ulici.

You say, with nobody? — You are mistaken. — I saw you standing with somebody on the street.

Pravda; ale dnes nečekám nikoho. — Je někdo zde, opravdu?

That is true; but to-day I do not expect anybody. — Is somebody here, really?

I ne; žádný tu není. — Nevidím žádného a neotevru žádnému. — Já vím, že dnes nechcete mluvit se žádným.

O no; nobody is here. — I do not see anybody, and I shall not open to anybody. — I know that to-day you do not want to speak with anybody.

Zde něco máte; — co to je?	Here you have something;—what is it?
To je lék.	That is medicine.
Jste nemocen?	Are you sick? .
Mám nastuzení a zlý kašel.	I have a cold and a bad cough.
Že jste nastuzen? — od čeho to je?	You say you have a cold?—what is it from?
Nevím čemu dáti vinu.	I do not know, to what I should charge it.
K čemu je ten lék?	What is that medicine for?
Budu ho užívat po dávkách.	I shall take it in doses.
A co je v tom? — V čem? — V té malé lahvi. — To je liniment.	And what is in that?—In what?—In that small bottle. — That is a liniment.
Co s tím budete dělat? — S čím? S tím linimentem.	What will you do with that? — With what?—With that liniment.
Tím se budu mazat.	With that I shall rub myself.
Čím jste se jindy mazal? — Ničím.	With what did you rub yourself before? — With nothing.

Note. The student is, by this time, quite familiar with the interrogative pronouns **kdo, co,** *gdŏ, tsŏ,* (who, what). This lesson is designed simply to serve as a review of their variation, already shown in Note 5, Lesson XVIII.

Kdo, co,	*gdŏ, tsŏ,*	who, what;
koho, čeho,	*kŏhŏ, chĕhŏ,*	whose, whom; of what; **od koho, (čeho),** from whom (what);
komu, čemu,	*kŏmŭ, chĕmŭ,*	to whom, to what; **k čemu,** *kchĕmŭ* what for;
v kom, v čem,	*fkom, fchem,*	in whom, in what; **o kom, o čem,** about whom (what); etc.
kým, čím,	*keem, cheem,*	by whom, by what; **s kým, s čím,** with whom, with what.

LESSON XXIX.

Číslo, n.   *oheesslŏ,*   number;
pověra, f.   *povyěrā,*   superstition;
u stolu,   *ŭstolŭ,*   at (*or* by) the table;
roku,   *rŏkŭ,*   in the year;
po roce,   *pŏ rotsě,*   after a year, in a year;
všecko,   *fshětsko,*   everything, all;
nynější,   *nyñeyshee,*   present;
sousední,   *soŭsedñee,*   neighboring;
společně,   *spolechñe,*   jointly, together;
přes,   *prshěs,*   over;
před,   *prshěd,*   before, ago;
teda,   *tědā,*   therefore;
o to více,   *ŏ tŏ veetsě,* so much more;
pouhý, á, é,   *poŭhee,*   pure, mere;
nešťastný, á, é *něshťāstnee,* unlucky, unfortunate;

zdálo se,   *zdálŏ sě,*   it seemed;
stěhovat se,   *sťehovāt sě,*   to move;
vystěhovat se, *vy-sťehovāt sě,* to emigrate;
přestěhovat se, *prshě-sťehovāt sě,* to remove;
usadit se,   *ŭsāďit sě,*   to settle;
odtud,   *ŏtŭd* } from here,
odsud,   *ŏtsŭd* } from there;
odtamtud,   *ŏtāmtŭd,*   from there;
kolik je,   *kŏlik yě,*   how many are; how much is;
vám je,   *vám yě,*   you are;
že je,   *žě yě,*   (that) there is, (that) there were;
to prý je,   *tŏ pree yě,* that is said to be.

Jedenáct,	*yědenátst,*	eleven	čtyrycet,	*shtiritset,*	forty
dvanáct,	*dwănátst,*	twelve	padesát,	*păděsát,*	fifty
třináct,	*trshinátst,*	thirteen	šedesát,	*shěděsát,*	sixty
čtrnáct,	*shtˈernátst*	fourteen	sedmdesát,	*sedŭmděsát,*	seventy
patnáct,	*pătnátst,*	fifteen	osmdesát,	*osŭmděsát,*	eighty
šestnáct,	*shěstnátst,*	sixteen	devadesát,	*děvăděsát,*	ninety
sedmnáct,	*sedŭmnátst,*	seventeen	sto jeden,	*stŏ yěden,*	one hundred and one
osmnáct,	*osŭmnátst,*	eighteen			

devatenáct, *dĕvătĕnátst*, nineteen

dvacet, *dwătset*, twenty

dvacet jeden, *dwătset yĕden*, twenty one

dvacet dva, *dwătset dwă*, twenty two

třicet, *trshitset*, thirty

třicet jeden, *trshitset yĕden*, thirty one

třicet dva, *trshitset dwă*, thirty two

sto dva, *stŏ dwă*, one hundred and two

sto dvacet, *stŏ dwătset*, one hundred and twenty

dvě stě, *dwyĕ st'e*, two hundred

tři sta, *trshi stă*, three hundred

čtyry sta, *shtiri stă*, four hundred

pět set, *pyĕt set*, five hundred;

šest set, *shest set*, six hundred; etc.

---

tisíc, *t'iseets*, a thousand

tisíc jedno sto, *t'iseets yednŏ stŏ*, one thousand one hundred;

tisíc pět set, *t'iseets pyĕt set*, one thousand five hundred;

dva tisíce, *dwă t'iseetsĕ*, two thousand;

tři tisíce, *trshi t'iseetsĕ*, three thousand;

čtyry tisíce, *shtiri t'iseetsĕ*, four thousand;

pět tisíc, *pyĕt t'iseets*, five thousand; etc.

tisíc osm set devadesát, *t'iseets osŭm set dĕvădĕsát*, one thousand eight hundred and ninety;

milion, *milliŏn*, a million;

dva miliony, *dwă milliŏny*, two millions;

tři miliony, *trshi milliŏny*, three millions;

čtyry miliony, *shtiri milliŏny*, four millions;

pět milionů, *pyĕt milliŏnoo*, five millions;

šest milionů, *shest milliŏnoo*, six millions; etc.

Jednotka, *yĕdnotkă*, a unit;

dvojka, *dwoykă*, a two; the figure two;

trojka, *troykă*, a three;

čtyrka, čtverka, *shtirkă, shtwerka*, a four;

pětka, *pyĕtkă*, a five;

desítka, *dĕseet-kă*, a ten;

dvacítka, *dwătseetkă*, a twenty;

třicítka, *trshitseetkă*, a thirty;

čtyrycítka, *shtiritseetkă*, a forty;

padesátka, *pădĕsátkă*, a fifty; etc.

stovka, *stofkă*, a hundred;

tisícovka, *t'iseetsofkă*, a thousand.

EXERCISES.

Kolik je nás u stolu? — Je nás dvanáct. — To je dobře; já myslel že je nás třináct a to prý je nešťastné číslo.	How many are we at the table?— There are twelve of us. — That is right; I thought there were thirteen of us, and that is said to be an unlucky number.
I, to je pouhá pověra!	O, that is a mere superstition.

Kolik akrů má vaše farma? — Sto šedesát akrů. — A farma vašeho otce? — Otec má tři čtyrycítky; já mám o čtyrycet akrů více.	How many acres has your farm?— One hundred and sixty acres.—And the farm of your father? — Father has three forties; I have forty acres more.
Moje farma stála o tisíc dollarů více, nežli farma otcova.	My farm cost one thousand dollars more than my father's farm.
Oba máte dobré farmy; — obě farmy jsou dobré. — To jsou dvě pěkné farmy.	Both of you have good farms; — both farms are good. — Those are two nice farms.
Jaká je asi nynější cena těch dvou farem? — Asi devět tisíc dollarů.	What is about the present price of those two farms?—About nine thousand dollars.
Nám dvoum*) také patří osmdesátka lesa v sousedním townshipu.	To us two also belongs an eighty of forest in the neighboring township.
Vám oboum*)? — Ano, nám dvoum*) společně.	To both of you?—Yes, to us two jointly.
Kdy jste se tu usadili?	When did you settle here?
Otec usadil se tu před čtyrmi lety; — já též; strýc před dvouma*) nebo třemi lety.	Father settled here four years ago;— I also; uncle two or three years ago.

---

*) In ordinary discourse always: **dvoum, oboum,** *dwoŭm, oboŭm,* to the two, to both; **před dvouma, před obouma,** *prshĕd dwoŭmă, prshĕd oboŭmă,* before two, before both. — The precise grammatical form is: **dvěma, oběma,** *dwyĕmă, obyĕmă;* **před dvěma, před oběma.**

Nám třem zdálo se, že musíme bydleti pohromadě.

To us three it seemed that we must live together.

My vystěhovali se z Evropy[2]) do Ameriky[2]), — usadili se v Ohio, — po roce přestěhovali jsme se do státu Illinois, odtud po dvou nebo třech letech do Nebrasky[2]), a odtud po pěti letech do Kansasu.

We emigrated from Europe to America, — settled in Ohio, — after a year we removed to the state of Illinois, from there after two or three years to Nebraska, and from there after five years to Kansas.

Kdy jste narozen? — Roku tisíc osm set padesát dva. — Teda je vám třicet osm let.

When were you ("are you") born? — In the year one thousand eight hundred fifty two. — Then you are thirty eight years.

Jak starý je váš otec? — Můj otec je přes šedesát; — můj strýc je skoro sedmdesát let stár; — je o pět let starší než můj otec.

How old is your father? — My father is over sixty; — my uncle is nearly seventy years old;—he is five years older than my father.

Já jsem jen o rok starší než má sestra a o tři leta starší než můj bratr.

I am only one year older than my sister and three years older than my brother.

Note 1. We have seen that the numeral jeden is declined (Note 2, Lesson XXVII). The same is true of the numerals dva, tři, čtyry and oba. The feminine and neutre gender of dva and oba is dvě, obě; but the inflected cases are the same in all three genders. Čtyry is used in the feminine and neutre gender, and in connection with *inanimate* nouns of the masculine gender: čtyry ženy, čtyry děti, čtyry domy (four women, four children, four houses); whereas the masculine animate use čtyři; for instance: čtyři muži, čtyři hoši (four men, four boys). Colloquially, however, čtyry is used without any discrimination.

---

[2]) Evropa, Amerika, *évropá, ámeriká;* z Evropy do Ameriky, *zěvropy dǒ ámeriky,* from Europe to America. Nebraska, do Nebrasky, to Nebraska. Kansas, do Kansasu, to Kansas. — Evropa, Amerika, Nebraska, are feminine, Kansas is masculine, by reason of their termination. See also foot-note in Lesson XXIV.

The variation of these numerals is set forth in the following exposé:

dva, oba m.,   **dvě, obě,** (f. & n.)   *dwă, obă, dwyě, obyě,*   two, both;

dvou, obou,   *dwoŭ, oboŭ,*   of two, of both;

dvěma, oběma, (colloq. **dvoum, oboum**), *dwyěmă, obyěmă (dwoŭm, oboŭm),* to two, to both; **se dvěma, s oběma, (se dvouma, s obouma)** with two, with both; etc.

---

tři, čtyři (čtyry),   *trshi, shtirshi (shtiri),* three, four;

tří, třech; čtyr, čtyrech; *trshee, trshekh; shtir, shtirekh;* of three, of four; **ve třech, ve čtyrech,** in three, in four; etc.

třem, čtyrem, *trshem, shtirem,* to three, to four;

se třemi, se čtyrmi, *sě trshěmi, sě shtirmi* (colloq. **se třema, se čtyrma**), with three, with four.

Note 2. The adverbial numerals *once, twice, three times, four times.* etc., are formed in Bohemian by adding the suffix **krát** to the cardinal number: **jedenkrát, dvakrát, třikrát, čtyrykrát,** etc.

In place of **jedenkrát,** *yědenkrát* (once), the shorter form **jednou,** *yědnoŭ,* is generally employed:

Kolikrát jste tam byl? how many times have you been there? — **Jen jednou;** only once.

Kolikrát se to stalo? how many times has it happened? — **Myslím že dvakrát;** I think (that) twice.

Note 3. The ordinal numbers are as follows:

první,	*pᵉrvňee,*	first	**šestý,**	*shěstee,*	sixth
druhý,	*drŭhee,*	second	**sedmý,**	*sedmee,*	seventh
třetí,	*trshěťee,*	third	**osmý,**	*osmee,*	eighth
čtvrtý,	*shtvᵉrtee,*	fourth	**devátý,**	*děvátee,*	ninth
pátý,	*pátee,*	fifth	**desátý.**	*dessátee,*	tenth

From eleven to nineteen they are formed by appending **ý** to the cardinal number (corresponding with the English *th*): **jedenáctý,** *yĕdenátstee,* eleventh; etc.

Dvacet, třicet, čtyrycet have **dvacátý, třicátý, čtyrycátý,** *dwătsátee, trshitsátee, shtiritsátee* (twentieth, thirtieth, fourtieth). The rest of the tens are regular: **padesátý,** *pădĕsátee* fiftieth), etc. — **Stý,** *stee,* one hundredth; **tisící,** *ťiseetsee,* one thousandth.

Dvacátý první, twenty first; **dvacátý druhý,** twenty second; etc. Both tens and units take the ordinal form.

There is also a distinction of gender, the feminine terminating in **á** and the neutre in **é** (in place of the masculine **ý**), corresponding exactly with the adjectives: **dobrý, á, é** (see Note 2, Lesson VI).

Hence we say: **druhý muž, druhá žena, druhé dítě,** the second man, the second woman, the second child.

The plural form **druzí, druhé,** *drůzee, drůhé,* means "the others".

První, třetí, have the same termination in every gender, like adjectives ending in **í.** (See Note 1, Lesson XXI.)

Ordinal numbers are declined like adjectives of a corresponding termination: **prvního muže,** of the first man; **druhého dne,** of the second day (or: on the next day); **druhé ženy,** of the second woman (or wife); **druhého dítěte,** of the second child; **druhému,** to the second; **v druhém,** in the second; **s druhým,** with the second.

Note 4. The adverbs formed from cardinal numbers by means of the suffix **fold,** denoting multiplication, are in Bohemian called special numerals and formed as follows:

dvojí,	*dwoyee,*	twofold	**paterý,**	*pătĕree,*	fivefold
trojí,	*troyee,*	threefold	**šesterý,**	*shĕstĕree,*	sixfold
čtverý,	*shtwĕree,*	fourfold	**sedmerý,**	*sedmĕree,*	sevenfold:

and so forth, always appending **erý** to the cardinal number (in the feminine gender **erá,** in the neutre **eré**).

From these there is derived a distinct class of multiplicative numerals by changing **erý** into **ero** and appending **násobný** (which in English also means *fold*), only the first three forming an exception:

dvojnásobný,	*dwoy-násobnee,*	twofold	(double);
trojnásobný,	*troy-násobnee,*	threefold	(treble);
čtvernásobný,	*shwer-násobnee,*	fourfold	(quadruple);
pateronásobný,	*păterŏ-násobnee,*	fivefold	(quintuple); etc.

LESSON XXX.

Všecek,	*fshĕtsek,* m.	} all, (whole)	**silný,**	*silnee,*	strong
všecka,	*fshĕtskă,* f.		**silně,**	*silñe,*	strongly
všecko, vše, *fshĕtsko, fshĕ,* n.			**silněji,**	*silñeyi,*	more strongly
prodej, m.	*prodĕy,*	sale	**nejsilněji,**	*neysilñeyi,*	most strongly
výprodej, m.	*veeprodĕy,*	selling out;	**pěkně,**	*pyĕkñe,*	nicely
zásoba, f.	*zásobă,*	stock	**hluboký,**	*hlŭbokee,*	deep
látka, f.	*látkă,*	stuff	**hluboko,**	*hlŭbŏkŏ* } deeply	
látka na šaty, *látkă nă shăte,*		dress-goods;	**hluboce,**	*hlŭbotsĕ* }	
			velice,	*vĕlitsĕ,*	greatly
známka, f.	*známkă,*	label	**hezký,**	*hesskee,* nice, pretty, fine;	
kupec, m.	*kŭpets,* buyer, purchaser;		**hezky,**	*hesske,* nicely, prettily, finely	
(**kupci,** pl.	*kŭptsi*)		**český,**	*chesskee,*	Bohemian
odkupník, m.	*odkŭpñeek,*	customer	**česky** (adv.),	*chesske,*	"
věc, f.	*vyĕts,*	thing, article;	**po česku,**	*pŏ chesskŭ,*	in Bohemian
výdělek, m.	*veeďelek,*	profit	**anglicky** (adv.),	*ănglitske,*	English
vůle, f.	*voolĕ,*	will	**francousky,**	*frăntsoŭske,*	French
základ, m.	*zăklăd,*	foundation	**španělsky,**	*shpăñelske,*	Spanish
základní,	*zăklădñee,* fundamental		**německy,**	*ñemetske,*	German
kámen, m.	*kámen,*	stone	**pozdě,**	*pozďe,*	late
zármutek, m.	*zármŭtek,*	sorrow	**později,**	*pozďeyi,*	later

psáti,	*psáťi, psát,*	to write
učiti se,	*účtt sě,*	to learn
vyprodán, a, o,	*veprodán, ă, ŏ,*	sold out
kladli jsme,	*klădli smě,*	we were laying;
položili jsme,	*pŏložili smě,*	we laid

dal jsem,	*dăl sěm,*	I gave, I put;
ručím (za),	*ručesm,*	I warrant;
dojat,	*doyăt,*	moved
trápilo*),	*trápilŏ,*	it grieved
zbylo*),	*zbylŏ,*	remained, was left
zemřel,	*zemrshel,*	died
vál,	*vál,*	blew

EXERCISES.

Měl jsem výprodej. — Můj krám je všecek vyprodán; — všecka zásoba je vyprodána; — prodal jsem všecko zboží lacino. — Vyprodal jsem všecko za hotové.

I had a selling out. — My store is all sold out; — the whole stock is sold out; — I sold all goods cheaply. — I sold out every thing for cash.

Ze všeho zboží zbylo jen něco látky na šaty.

Of all the goods there only remained some dress-goods.

Ke všemu zboží dal jsem ceny; — známky byly na všem. — Jsem teď hotov se vším.

To all the goods I put (i. e. attached) prices;—labels were on every thing.—I have now done with everything.

Všichni kupci, doufám, budou spokojeni; — všecky věci byly dobré; — na všech věcech měl jsem jen malý výdělek.

All the buyers, I hope, will be satisfied; — all articles were good; — on all articles I had only a small profit.

Všem svým odkupníkům ručím za zboží; — chci míti se všemi dobrou vůli.

To all my customers I warrant my goods; — I want to have with all a good will.

---

*) **Trápiti,** *trápiťi, (trápit),* to grieve, to trouble, to torment; **trápil, a, o,** (he, she, it) grieved, troubled, etc.

      Zbýti, *zbeeťi (zbeet),* to remain, to be left; zbyl, a, o, (he, she, it) remained, was left; zbylo, there remained. — See Note 2, Lesson IX.

Dnes je hezký den. — Ano, dnes je hezky; — slunce svítí hezky.

Doufám že zítra bude také pěkný den a že slunce bude pěkně svítit.

Včera byl silný vítr. — Ráno vítr vál silně, odpoledne ještě silněji a nejsilněji k večeru.

Váš dům má hluboký základ. — Ano, položili jsme základy hluboko.

Když jsme kladli základní kámen, náš hošík zemřel a byl jsem hluboce dojat.

Byl to veliký zármutek; — trápilo nás to velice.

Kolik let mu bylo?*) — Bylo mu dvanáct let.

Mluvil anglicky i česky, — také psal po anglicku i po česku.

Později chtěl učiti se též francousky, španělsky i německy, — aspoň čísti a psáti trochu.

To-day is a fine day.—Yes, to-day it is nice;—the sun is shining nicely.

I hope that to-morrow will be also a nice day, and that the sun will shine nicely.

Yesterday there was a strong wind. — In the morning the wind blew strongly, in the afternoon more strongly yet, and most strongly toward evening.

Your house has a deep foundation. —Yes, we laid the foundations deep.

When we were laying the foundation stone, our little boy died, and I was deeply moved.

It was a great sorrow;—it grieved us greatly.

How old was he?—He was twelve years.

He spoke English and Bohemian, — he also wrote in English and in Bohemian.

Later he wanted to learn also French, Spanish and German, — at least to read and write a little.

Note 1. Grammarians call **všecek** (all) an indefinite numeral; it also takes the form of **všechen** or **všecken** (feminine, **všechna, všeckna;** neutre, **všechno, všeckno**). The plural is **všickni, všecky, všecka,** *všitskňí, vshětski, vshětská.* In common discourse **všecky** or **všeci** is used in the plural in all three genders.

*) **Kolik let mu bylo?** (*literally:* how many years was it to him?), the same as: **jak byl stár?** how old was he? **Bylo mu,** the same as **byl,** he was.

This numeral is also declined and presents the following variation of form:

Singular:

všeho, m. & n. *fshěhŏ* (vší, f. *fshee*) of all (of the whole, of everything); všemu, *fshěmŭ*, to all; ve všem, *vě fshěm*, in all; se vším, *sě fsheem*, with all.

Plural:

všech, *fshěkh*, of all; ve všech, *vě fshěkh*, in all; všem, *fshěm*, to all; se všemi, *sě fshěmi* with all.

Note 2. Adverbs (qualifying verbs) are often derived from adjectives, qualifying nouns. This rule obtains in Bohemian as well as in English.

Such adverbs are formed in English by adding **ly** to the adjective: *strong, strongly; nice, nicely.* In Bohemian, the terminal **ý** of the adjective is changed into an **ě**:

silný, silně; pěkný, pěkně.

In some cases, however, the final **ý** changes into an **o**, or the final syllable **ký** into **ce**: hluboký, hluboko, hluboce, *deep, deeply;* veliký, velice, *great, greatly.* In a few cases the formation of adverbs is wholly irregular: dobrý, *good*; dobře, *well.*

Sometimes the long **ý** simply changes into a short **y**: hezký, hezky, *nice, nicely.* This is generally the case, whem the adjective is derived from the name of a nation: anglický národ, *the English nation;* mluvím anglicky, *I speak English;* — český jazyk, *the Bohemian tongue;* mluvím česky, *I speak Bohemian.* In these cases we can also use the form: po anglicku, po česku.

In common discourse, the distinction between such adjectives and adverbs as hezký — hezky, český — česky, etc., is obliterated, their pronunciation being the same.

Note 3. Many adverbs of quality have a comparison, like adjectives, in order to express various degrees of quality. In regular comparison, the second degree is formed by adding **ji** to the adverb, and the third degree by prefixing **nej** to the second degree : **silně,** *strongly;* **silněji,** *more strongly;* **nejsilněji,** *most strongly.* Some adverbs have an irregular comparison, which must be learned and remembered. The following are mostly in use :

dobře, *dobrshě,* well; **lépe,** *lépě,* better; **nejlépe,** *neylépě,* best; **líp,** *leep,* " ; **nejlíp,** *neyleep,* " ;

zle, *zlě,* badly; **hůře,** *hoorshě,* worse; **nejhůře,** *neyhoorshě,* worst; **hůř,** *hoorsh,* " ; **nejhůř,** *neyhoorsh,* " ;

brzo, *berzŏ,* soon; **dříve,** *drsheevě,* sooner; **nejdříve,** *neydrsheevě,* soonest; **dřív,** *drsheef,* " ; **nejdřív,** *neydrsheef,* " ;

dlouho, *dloŭhŏ,* long; **déle,** *délě,* longer; **nejdéle,** *neydélě,* longest; **dýl,** *deel,* " ; **nejdýl,** *neydeel,* " ;

blízko, *bleeskŏ,* near; **blíže,** *bleežě,* nearer; **nejblíže,** *neybleežě,* nearest; **blíž,** *bleež,* " ; **nejblíž,** *neybleež,* " ;

daleko, *dălěkŏ,* far; **dál,** *dál,* farther; **nejdál,** *neydál,* farthest;

vysoko, *vysŏkŏ,* high; **výše,** *veeshě,* higher; **nejvýše,** *neyveeshě,* highest;

hluboko, *hlŭbŏkŏ,* deep, deeply; **hloub,** *hloŭb,* deeper; **nejhloub,** *neyhloŭb,* deepest;

snadno, *snădnŏ,* easily; **snáz,** *snáz,* more easily; **nejsnáz,** *neysnáz,* most easily;

mnoho, *mnŏhŏ,* much; **víc, více,** *veets, veetsě,* more; **nejvíc, nejvíce,** *neyveets, neyveetsě,* most;

málo, *málŏ,* little; **méně, míň,** *méne, meeñ,* less; **nejméně, nejmíň,** *neyméne, neymeeñ,* least;

draho, draze, *drăhŏ, drăzě,* dear, dearly; **dráže,** *drážě,* dearer; **nejdráže,** *neydrážě,* dearest.

LESSON XXXI.*)

Nesti (or nésti), *to carry, to bear*, is a verb denoting a CONTINUOUS action.

By means of prefixes numerous other verbs are derived from it (see Note 6, Lesson XIII), denoting a FINITE or finished action, or a solitary act of that nature:

přinesti,	*prshinesťi,* or *prshinest,*	to bring, to fetch;
přenesti,	*prshě-nest,*	to carry over; to transplace;
nanesti,	*nănest,*	to bring a heap; to pile on;
odnesti,	*ŏdnest,*	to carry away; to take away;
donesti,	*dŏnest,*	to carry to a place; to carry to somebody;
podnesti,	*pŏdnest,*	to carry under;
přednesti,	*prshed-nest,*	to carry before; (hence: to lay before, to submit, to deliver;)
pronesti,	*prŏnest,*	to carry through; **pronesti se,** to grow heavy, to tire out (said of a burden which is carried);
roznesti,	*rŏznest,*	to carry round; to scatter or spread; to deliver;
unesti,	*ŭnest,*	to carry off, to kidnap; (also: to be able to carry);
vynesti,	*vinest,*	to carry out;
zanesti,	*zănest,*	to carry behind, away, i. e. out of sight; (also: to enter in a book or list).

*) We bespeak the student's particular attention for this Lesson, designed as a systematic but easy and popular introduction to a complete mastery of the Bohemian verb, which is the most important and the most complicated part of the language. To a great extent, this introduction will only appear as a review of what has already been learned about the verb in the preceding lessons, and hence will be the more readily mastered by the student. There being only a few hundred verbs used in the ordinary intercourse in any language, their acquisition for practical every-day purposes is, after all, only a matter of a few weeks' application.

As before observed, the meaning of these derivatives becomes in most cases self-evident, when we bear in mind the signification of the prefixes, which constantly recur in this process of formation of new verbs:

do, *dŏ,* to;	**pře,** *přshĕ,* over;	**pod,** *pŏd,* under;
od, *ŏd,* from, off;	**při,** *přshi,* to, by, at;	**nad,** *năd,* over, up, above;
na, *nă,* on;	**před,** *přshed,* before;	**pro,** *prŏ,* through;
ve, *vĕ,* in;	**ob,** *ŏb*) round,	**roz,** *rŏz,* apart, asunder;
vy, *ve,* out;	**o,** *o*) about;	**za,** *ză,* behind, away, into.

The prefix **za** very often denotes a solitary action or sudden manifestation; for example:

pěti, zpívati, *pyĕťi, speevaťi,* to sing; **zapěti, zazpívati,** *zăpyĕt, zăspeevăt,* to sing a song;

zvoniti, *zwŏñit,* to ring; **zazvoniti,** *zăzwŏñit,* to give a ring; to pull the bell once.

The prefix **u** denotes: 1. an action separating a part from the whole: **seknouti,** *seknoŭťi,* to make a cut; **useknouti,** *ŭseknoŭťi,* to cut off; — 2, a diminutive, momentary, or solitary action: **Šklebiti se,** *shklĕbiťi sĕ,* to frown;— **ušklebiti se,** to make a frown; 3. a progressive destruction or disappearance: **páliti,** *páliťi,* to burn; **upáliti,** to burn up, to burn at the stake; — 4. a completion or carrying out of something: **dělati,** *ďelăťi,* to do, to make, to work; **udělati,** to make or finish something; to do a certain act.

These are the main modifications due to the prefix **u,** connected with verbs; there are, besides, two or three minor or incidental ones, which it is not necessary to mention.

The principal parts of a Bohemian verb, from which the entire conjugation may easily be formed by means of the proper endings, are the following:

The infinitive: **nesti,** to carry;	the perfect indicative: **nesl,** carried;
the present indicative: **nesu,** I carry;	the imperative: **nes,** carry (thou).

Nesu,	*nessŭ,*	I carry,	**nesl*)jsem,**	*nessl sem,*	I carried,
neseš,	*nessesh,*	thou carriest,	**nesl jsi,**	*nessl si,*	thou carriest,
nese,	*nessĕ,*	(he, she, it) carries,	**nesl,**	*nessl,*	he carried,
neseme,	*nessĕmĕ,*	we carry,	**nesli**)jsme,**	*nessli smĕ,*	we carried,
nesete,	*nessĕtĕ,*	you carry,	**nesli jste,**	*nessli stĕ,*	you carried,
nesou,	*nessoŭ,*	they carry;	**nesli,**	*nessli*	they carried;

nes,	*ness,*	carry (thou),
ať nese,	*ăť nessĕ,*	let him (her, it) carry,
nesme,	*nessmĕ,*	let us carry,
neste,	*nesstĕ,*	carry (you),
ať nesou,	*ăť nessoŭ,*	let them carry.

Note 1. The future tense of nesti is usually not formed by means of the auxiliary **býti** (to be) in connection with the infinitive: **budu nesti, budeš nesti,** etc.; but by means of the prefix **po,** connected with the present tense: **ponesu,** *pŏnessŭ,* I shall carry; **poneseš,** *pŏnessesh,* thou wilt carry; and so forth.

The derivatives mentioned above, formed by means of prefixes, have in fact no present, but only a past and a simple future tense; for example:

přinesti, to bring; **přinesl jsem,** I brought; **přinesu,** I shall bring; — **odnesti,** to carry away; **odnesl jsem,** I carried away; **odnesu,** I shall carry away. (See Notes 4 and 7, Lesson XIII.)

---

*) Feminine **nesla,** *nesslă;* neutre **neslo;** — see Note 2, Lesson IX. — **Já jsem nesl, já nesl,** I carried; **ty jsi nesl, ty's nesl,** thou carriedst; **vy jste nesli,** you carried. See Lesson X.

As already mentioned in Note 1, Lesson IX, the distinction between the perfect tense, so difficult and puzzling for the student of the English language, does not exist in Bohemian. **Nesl jsem** means both *I carried* and *I have carried;* it also means *I did carry,* and *I was carrying,* — when the latter relates to a separate action.

Likewise the present, **nesu,** means not only *I carry,* but also: *I am carrying, I do carry;* or, if used interrogatively: **nesu?** *do I carry?*

The same observations apply to all other verbs, there being *only one form* of the present tense, and of the past tense, in Bohemian.

) Feminine **nesly; neutre **nesla;** see Note 2, Lesson IX.

The verbs **lezu,** I crawl; **vezu,** I carry; **jedu,** I ride; **kvetu,** I blossom; **rostu,** I grow, — and some others, usually form their future in the same way as **nesu,** I carry. Hence we do not say **budu lezti,** etc; but we say :

polezu, *polĕzŭ*, I shall crawl; **povezu,** *povĕzŭ*, I shall carry; **pojedu,** *poyĕdŭ*, I shall ride; **pokvetu,** *pokwetŭ*, I shall blossom; **porostu,** *porostŭ*, I shall grow.

In the sequel we shall give the principal parts of every verb, from which the student can form the whole conjugation without any difficulty. There being a slight irregularity in the formation of the present tense from the infinitive in some cases, this course will obviate any confusion which might arise therefrom, for a beginner.

Vezti,	*vĕzťi, vezť*),	to carry (in a vehicle);	**plesti se,**	*p. sĕ,*	to be mistaken, confused; etc.**)
vezti se,	*vĕzťi sĕ,*	to ride;	**másti,**	*másťi,*	to confuse;
vesti,	*vessťi,*	to lead;	**másti se,**	*másti sĕ,*	to be mistaken;
lezti,	*lĕzťi,*	to crawl, to climb;	**mésti,**	*mésťi,*	to sweep;
kvesti,	*kwesťi,*	to blossom;	**klásti,**	*klásťi,*	to lay;
čísti,	*cheesťi,*	to read;	**krásti,**	*krásťi,*	to steal;
rŭsti,	*rousťi* }	to grow;	**pásti,**	*pásťi,*	to herd, to tend, to pasture.
rosti,	*rosťi* }				
plesti,	*plessťi,*	to twist, to knit; to confuse, to mix up;	**pásti se,**	*p. sĕ,*	to graze, to browse;

vezu, *vĕzŭ*, I carry; **vezl jsem,** *vĕzl sem,* I carried, *or* I have carried; **vez,** *vĕz,* carry (thou)***);

---

*) See Note 1, Lesson XI.

**) This and many other verbs have a variety of significations, which cannot here be explained. We refer the student to the Dictionary of the Bohemian and English languages, by Charles Jonas, *second edition.*

***) The reflexive form of a verb is conjugated in the same way as the ordinary form, with **se** added: **vezu se,** I ride; **vezl jsem se,** I rode; **povezu se,** I shall ride; **vez se,** ride (thou)!

The student is already well aware that negation is always expressed by the prefix **ne,** which stands for the English *do not, does not, did not:* **nevezu,** I do not carry; **nevezl jsem,** I did not carry; **nepovezu,** I shall not carry; **nevez!** do not carry!

vedu, *vĕdŭ*, I lead; **vedl jsem,** *vĕdl sĕm*, I led; **veď,** *veď*, lead;

lezu, *lĕzŭ*, I crawl; **lezl jsem,** *lĕzl sem*, I crawled; **lez,** *lĕz*, crawl;

kvete, *kwĕtĕ*, it blooms; **kvetl,** *kwĕtl*, it bloomed; **kveť,** *kwĕť*, bloom;

čtu, *chtŭ*, I read; **četl jsem,** *chĕtl sem*, I read; **čti,** *chťi*, read;

rostu, *rostŭ*, I grow; **rostl jsem,** *rostl sem*, I grew; **rosť,** *rosť*, grow;

pletu, *pletŭ*, I knit; (**pletu se,** I get mixed up, etc.); **pletl jsem,** I knit- ted; **pleť,** *pleť*, knit;

matu, *mătŭ*, I confuse; **matl jsem,** *mătl sem*, I confused; **mať,** *măť*, con- fuse;

metu, *metŭ*, I sweep; **metl jsem,** *metl sem*, I swept; **meť,** *meť*, sweep;

kladu, *klădŭ*, I lay: **kladl jsem,** *klădl scm*, I laid; **klaď,** *klăď*, lay;

kradu, *krădŭ*, I steal; **kradl jsem,** *krădl sem*, I stole; **kraď,** *krăď*, steal;

pasu, *păsŭ*, I herd; **pasl jsem,** *păsl sem*, I herded; **pas,** *păs*, herd.

Pasák, m.	*păssák*,	the cowboy, the herdsman;	**datum,** n.	*dătŭm*,	the date
dobytek, m.	*dŏbytek*,	the cattle	**škola,** f.	*shkolă*,	the school
chodník, m.	*khodñeek*,	the sidewalk	**novela,** f.	*novellă*)	the novel
zloděj, m.	*zloďey*,	the thief	**román,** m.	*rŏmán*)	
červ, m.	*cherf*,	the worm	**zem,** f.	*zem*)	the floor
jabloň, m.	*yăbloň*,	the appletree	**podlaha,** f.	*podlăhă*)	
ptáci, pl.	*ptátsi*,	the birds	**pastva,** f.	*păstwă*,	the pasture
dějepis, m.	*ďeyĕpis*,	the history	**ruka,** f.	*rŭkă*,	the hand
cestopis, m.	*tsestŏpis*,	the book of travels;	**noha,** f.	*nŏhă*,	the foot
stádo, n.	*stádŏ*,	the herd	**mléko,** n.	*mlékŏ*,	the milk
ovce, n. s. & pl.	*oftsĕ*,	the sheep	**zeleniny,** f. pl.	*zĕlĕñiny*,	the vege- tables;
sotva,	*sotwă*,	hardly, scarcely;	**zamésti,**	*zămésťi*,	to sweep up;
snadno,	*snădnŏ*,	easily	**dočísti,**	*dŏcheesťi*,	to finish reading;
nikam,	*ñikăm*,	nowhere	**může,**	*moožĕ*,	he (she, it) can
			zábavný, á, é	*zábăvnee*,	entertaining.

EXERCISES.

Co neseš? (co to neseš?)

What doest thou carry? (what is it thou carriest?)

Nesu oběd pro otce*).

I carry dinner for my father.

Co vezete na trh? — Vezu trochu obilí.

What do you carry to market? — I carry some grain.

Co veze váš soused? — On veze brambory.

What does your neighbor carry? — He carries potatoes.

Kam vedete toho chlapce*)? — Vedu ho do školy. — Ze školy povedu ho zas domu.

Where do you lead (or "take") that boy? — I lead him to school. — From school I shall lead him home again.

Nelez na strom! — Já nelezu. — Nelezl jsem nikam. — Viděl jsem tě lezti.

Do not climb (on) the tree!—I do not (climb). — I did not climb anywhere. — I have seen thee climb.

Co to zde leze? — Červi zde lezou.

What is that crawling here? — Worms are crawling here.

Všecko kvete. — Stromy už kvetou. — Loni náš jabloň kvetl krásně; — nevím jak pokvete letos.

Everything blossoms. — The trees are blooming already.—Last year our appletree blossomed beautifully; — I don't know how it will bloom this year.

Co to čteš? — Já čtu zábavnou knihu; — a co vy čtete? — Dějepis Spojených Států**).

What is it thou readest?— I read an entertaining book; — and what do you read? — A history of the United States.

---

*) The rule stated in Note 2, Lesson XVIII, applies also to nouns ending in ec (declined like **muž**), the vowel e being dropped in the inflected cases: **otec**, *ŏtets*, the father (or "my father"); **otce**, *ŏtsě*, of the father; **pro otce**, *for the father*; **otcové**, *ŏtsŏvé*, the fathers; — **chlapec**, *khlăpets*, the boy; **chlapce**, *khlăptse*, of the boy (or "the boy", in the objective case).

) **Spojené Státy, *spoyěné státy*, the United States; **Spojených Států**, *spoyěneekh státoo*, of the United States; **ve Spojených Státech**, *vě spoyěneekh státekh*, in the United States.

Včera četl jsem román; — večer jsem ho dočetl; — zítra budu čísti nějaký cestopis.	Yesterday I read a novel; — in the evening I finished reading it; — to-morrow I shall read some book of travels.
Když je teplo, všecko roste rychle. — Ty zeleniny rostou rychle; — po dešti porostou ještě rychleji.	When it is warm, everything grows fast.—Those vegetables grow fast; —after a rain they will grow still faster.
Já často se pletu v datum. — Člověk snadno se plete; — já také často se matu.	I am often mistaken in the date. — One is easily mistaken; — I also am frequently mistaken.
Zameť krám. — Zametl jsem ho už; — chodník zametu hned.	Sweep the store. — I have swept it already; — the sidewalk I shall sweep presently.
Ptáci nyní kladou vejce.	The birds now lay eggs.
Zloděj krade kde může. — Zloději kradou vše.	The thief steals where he can. — Thieves steal everything.
Pasák pase stádo. — Dobytek se pase. — Ovce se pasou.	The cowboy tends the herd. — The cattle are grazing.—The sheep are browsing.
Rád pasu krávy, kde je dobrá pastva.	I like to pasture cows where there is a good pasture.

Bíti,	*beeťi,*	to beat, to strike;	krýti,	*kreeťi,*	to cover;
píti,	*peeťi,*	to drink;	tříti,	*trsheeťi,*	to rub;
líti,	*leeťi,*	to pour;	příti se,	*prsheeťi sě,*	to dispute;
síti,	*seeťi*	} to sow, to seed;	šíti,	*sheeťi,*	to sew;
seti,	*seťi*		žíti,	*žeeťi,*	to live*).
mýti,	*meeťi,*	to wash;			

*) Notes 1 and 2, Lesson XIII, explain that in common discourse the final ì of the infinitive is nearly always dropped. Consequently we hear: beet, instead of beeťi; peet, instead of peeťi; and so forth. Mýti is often pronounced *meyt*, krýti — *kreyt*. (See Note 3, Lesson VI.)—There is no difference of pronunciation between bíti (to beat), and býti (to be), except when the latter is vulgarly pronounced *beyt*.

biju (or **biji**), *biyŭ*, I beat; **bil jsem,** *bill sem,* I beat (have beaten);
bij, *biy* or *be,* beat (thou);

piju (or **piji**), *piyŭ,* I drink; **pil jsem,** *pill sem,* I drank; **pij,** *piy* (or *pee*), drink;

liju or **leju,** *liyŭ* or *leyŭ,* I pour; **lil jsem,** *lil sem,* I poured; **lij** or **lej,** *liy, ley,* pour;

siju or **seju,** *siyŭ, seyŭ,* I sow; **sil jsem,** *sil sem,* I sowed; **sej,** *sey,* sow;

myju*), *miyŭ,* I wash; **myl jsem,** *mill sem,* I washed; **myj,** *miy,* wash;

kryju*), *kriyŭ,* I cover; **kryl jsem,** *krill sem,* I covered; **kryj,** *kriy,* cover;

tru*), *trŭ,* I rub; **třel jsem,** *trshell sem,* I rubbed; **tři,** *trshi,* rub;

pru se*), *prŭ sě,* I dispute; **přel jsem se,** *prshell sem sě,* I disputed; **při se,** *prshi sě,* dispute;

šiju, *she-yŭ,* I sew; **šil jsem,** *shil sem,* I sewed; **šij,** *shiy* (or *she*), sew;

žiju, *žiyŭ,* I live; **žil jsem,** *žil sem,* I lived; **žij,** *žiy* (or *ži*), live;

Note 2. The paradigm of the present indicative of **bíti** would be: **biju, biješ, bije, bijeme, bijete, bijou** (I beat, thou beatest, he beats, we beat, you beat, they beat). In the written language, the forms **biji** and **bijí** (*biyi, biyee*) are frequently employed in the first person singular and third person plural, in place of **biju, bijou** (*biyŭ, biyoŭ*), which are always used in conversation. The same is true of the other verbs of this class.

Exercises.

Proč biješ to dítě? — Nebij ho! — Já ho nebiju.	Why do you beat that child? — Do not beat him! — I do not beat him.
Hodiny**) bijou deset. — Už bilo deset.	The clock strikes ten. — It has already struck ten.

---

*) Colloquially also **meju, kreju, třu, přu se,** *meyŭ, kreyŭ, trshŭ, prshŭ sě;* **mej, krej,** *mey, krey,* (do) wash, (do) cover.

) **Hodiny (the clock) is a plural noun; the following verb must therefore be put in the plural: **bijou** or **bijí** (they strike).

Co piješ? — Piju pivo; — co vy pijete? — Pijeme víno; — děti pijou vodu. — Ráno všichni pili jsme mléko.	What doest thou drink? — I drink beer; — what do you drink?—We drink wine; — the children drink water. — In the morning we all drank milk.
Lijeme mléko do kávy.	We pour milk in coffee.
Služka myje zem. — Kryjeme podlahu kobercem.	The servant-girl washes the floor.— We cover the floor with a carpet.
Lil jsem liniment na ruku a třel jsem nohu.	I poured the liniment on (my) hand and rubbed (my) foot.
Seju pšenici; — soused sil ječmen. — Sejeme časně. — Co jste vy seli? — Nic ještě; — budeme síti oves.	I sow wheat;—(my) neighbor sowed barley. — We sow early. — What have you sowed? — Nothing as yet;—we shall sow oats.

Note 3. All verbs consisting of a simple *root* or *stem*, to which the termination **ti** is directly attached, belong to the first conjugation.

They may be divided in two leading classes, slightly diverging in their inflection, but following the same general principle, as shown in the preceding two groups of examples; namely, 1. those terminating generally in **sti,** and 2. those terminating generally in **íti :**

1. **nesti,** to carry (nes in the root or stem); — **nesu, neseš, nese,** I carry, thou carriest, he carries; **neseme, nesete, nesou,** we carry, you carry, they carry; — **nesl jsem,** I carried; — **nes,** carry;

2. **píti,** to drink (pí is the root or stem); — **piju, piješ, pije,** I drink, thou drinkest, he drinks; **pijeme, pijete, pijou,** we drink, you drink, they drink; — **pil jsem,** I drank; — **pij,** drink.

Note 4. A few exceptional verbs of this conjugation, with the grammatical termination of **ci** (but popularly **cti**) in their infinitive, show a slight deviation from the above paradigms. For instance:

peci, *petsi,* to bake; — **peku, pečeš, peče, pečeme, pečete, pekou,** *pěkŭ, pěchesh, pěchě, pěchěmě, pěchětě, pěkoŭ* (I bake, thou bakest, he bakes, we bake, you bake, they bake); **pekl jsem,** *pěkl sem,* I baked; **peč,** *pěch,* bake;

teci, *tetsi,* to flow; **teče, tekou, tekl, teč,** *těchě, tekoŭ, tekl, těch* (it flows, they flow, it flowed, flow).

But colloquially, the forms **peču, pečou, tečou** (I bake, they bake, they flow) are used in place of **peku, pekou, tekou.**

LESSON XXXII.

Minouti, *minoŭťi,* to pass by; — **minu,** *minŭ,* I pass by; (**mineš, mine,** *minesh, mině,* thou passest by, he passes by; **mineme, minete, minou,** *minŏmě, minŏtě, minoŭ,* we, you, they pass by); — **minul*) jsem,** *minŭl sem,* I passed by *or* I have passed by; **miñ,** *miň,* pass (thou) by.

hynouti, *hynoŭťi,* to perish (or rather: to be perishing); — **hynu,** *hynŭ,* I am perishing; **hynul jsem,** I was perishing; **hyñ,** *hyň,* perish.

zdvihnouti, *zdwihnoŭťi,* to pick up, to raise; — **zdvihnu,** *zdwihnŭ**),* I shall pick up; I shall raise; **zdvihnul jsem** (also **zdvihl jsem,** like the first conjugation), *zdwihnŭl sem* (*zdwihl sem*), I picked up, I raised; **zdvihni,** *zdwihňi,* pick up, raise.

kopnouti, *kopnoŭťi,* to kick; — **kopnu**),** I shall kick; **kopnul jsem** (also **kopl jsem**), *kopnŭl sem,* I kicked; **kopni,** *kopňi,* kick.

Dálka, f.	*dálkă,*	the distance	**osení,** n. *osseñee,* growing crops;
planina, f.	*plăñină,*	the plain	**takto,** *tăktŏ.* in this way;

---

*) Feminine **minula,** *minŭlă;* neutre **minulo,** *minŭlŏ;*—see Note 2, Lesson IX.

) The present tense having a *future* meaning, **zdvihnu, kopnu, is in fact the simple future tense of these verbs. See Note 7, Lesson XIII.

hruška, f. *hrŭshkă,*   the pear
jablko, n. *yăblkŏ* (colloq. *yăbkŏ*),
                 the apple
sucho, n.   *sŭkhŏ,*   drought (as an
              adverb: dry);

než,   *nesh,*   before;
hleděti,   *hleďet,*   to look;
pes, m.   *pess,* the dog; psa, *psă,*
            of the dog, the dog
                 (obj. case).

EXERCISES.

Než hodina mine, budu zde, — pravil.

Before an hour passes by, I shall be here, — he said.

Hodina minula, — dvě hodiny minuly, — pět hodin minulo (i. e. *it* passed), — den minul, — a nebyl zde.

An hour passed,—two hours passed, — five hours passed, — the day passed by, — and he was not here.

Až mineme ten les, budeme viděti více.

When we pass that forest, we shall see more.

Jak brzy minuli jste les?

How soon did you pass the forest?

Minuli jsme ho za hodinu; — pak viděli jsme celou planinu.

We passed it in an hour; — then we saw the whole plain.

Ti lidé nás brzy minou*). — Mineš mnoho lidí (*liďee,* gen. case).

Those people will soon pass us. — Thou wilt pass many people.

Je sucho; — všecko hyne; — osení hyne; — zeleniny hynou.

It is dry; — everything is perishing; — the crops are perishing; — the vegetables are perishing.

Bylo sucho a všecko hynulo.

There was a drought, and everything was perishing.

Takto všecko bude hynouti.

In this way everything will be perishing.

Zdvihni to jablko. — Už jsem ho zdvihnul (or zdvihl).—Zdvihnula (or zdvihla) jsem dvě jablka a hrušku.

Pick up that apple. —I have picked it up already. — I picked up (*fem.*) two apples and a pear.

---

*) It is self-evident that this present tense of the verb **minouti** also has a *future* meaning, denoting an action which is expected to take place.

Zdvihli jsme se a hleděli do dálky. — Zdvihni se! — Zdvihněte se! — Zdvihněte ruku (plural ruce, *rŭtsĕ*).	We raised ourselves and looked into the distance. — Raise thyself! — Raise yourself!—Raise your hand (your hands).
Kopni toho psa! — Kopnul jsem ho trochu.	Kick that dog! — I kicked him a little.

Note 1. The root or stem of the verb **minouti** is **min,** to which the termination **outi** is attached. All verbs ending in **outi** belong to the second conjugation.

Some of the verbs of this class are derived from adjectives, and their imperative is always formed like that of **zdvihnouti : zdvihni.** For · example :

bled-ý, *bledee,* pale; **bled-nouti,** *blednoŭťi,* to grow pale; (**blednu,** I grow pale; **blednul jsem,** I grew pale; **bledni,** do grow pale);

bohat-ý,	*bohătee,*	rich;	**bohat-nouti,**	*bohătnoŭťi,*	to grow rich;
chud-ý,	*khŭdee,*	poor;	**chud-nouti,**	*khŭdnoŭťi,*	to grow poor;
mlad-ý,	*mlădee,*	young;	**mlád-nouti,**	*mládnoŭťi,*	to grow young;
star-ý,	*stăree,*	old;	**stár-nouti,**	*stárnoŭťi,*	to grow old;
slab-ý,	*slăbee,*	weak;	**sláb-nouti,**	*slábnoŭťi,*	to grow weak;
měk-ký,	*myĕkee,*	soft;	**měk-nouti,**	*myĕknoŭťi,*	to grow soft;
tvrd-ý,	*twerdee,*	hard;	**tvrd-nouti,**	*twerdnouťi,*	to grow hard.

Viděti,	*viďeťi,*	to see;	**slyšeti,**	*slishĕťi,*	to hear;
seděti,	*seďeťi,*	to sit;	**slušeti,**	*slŭshĕťi,*	to fit, to become;
běžeti,	*byĕžeťi,*	to run, to go hurriedly;	**styděti se,**	*stiďeťi sĕ,*	to be ashamed;
			uměti,	*ŭmyĕťi,*	to know; can;
držeti,	*deržeťi,*	to hold;	**rozuměti,**	*rozŭmyĕťi,*	to understand;
mlčeti,	*melcheťi,*	to be silent;	**házeti,**	*házeťi,*	to throw (con-
hořeti,	*horshĕťi,*	to burn;			tinually);
pršeti,	*pershĕťi,*	to rain;	**poroučeti,**	*poroŭcheťi,*	to command.

Vidím, *veďeem,* I see; — **vidíš, vidí,** *viďeesh, viďee,* thou seest, he sees; **vidíme, vidíte, vidí,** (colloq. also **vidějí**) *viďeemě, viďeelě, viďee,* colloq. *viďeyee,* we (you, they) see; — **viděl jsem,** *viďel sem,* I saw, *or* I have seen; **viz,** see (being an irregular imper.).

sedím, *seďeem,* I sit; **seděl jsem,** *seďel sem,* I sat; **seď,** sit.

běžím, *byěžeem,* I run; **běžel jsem,** *byěžel sem,* I ran; **běž,** *byěž,* run;

držím, *děržeem,* I hold; **držel jsem,** *děržel sem,* I held; **drž,** *děrž,* hold;

mlčím, *mělcheem,* I am silent, **mlčel jsem,** *mělchel sem,* I was silent; **mlč,** *mělch,* be silent;

hoří, *horshee,* it burns; **hořel,** *horshel,* burned; **hoř,** *horsh,* burn;

prší, *pershee,* it rains; **pršelo,** *pershělǒ,* it rained; **prš,** *persh,* rain;

slyším, *slisheem,* I hear; **slyšel jsem,** *slishel sem;* I heard; **slyš,** *slish,* hear;

sluší, *slǔshee,* it fits; **slušelo,** *slǔshěllǒ,* it fitted.

stydím se, *stiďeem se,* I am ashamed; **styděl jsem se,** *stiďel sem sě,* I was ashamed; **styď se,** shame on thee!

umím, *ǔmeem,* I know, I can; **uměl jsem,** *ǔmyěll sem,* I knew; **uměj,** *ǔmyěy,* know;

rozumím, *rozǔmeem,* I understand; **rozuměl jsem,** *rozǔmyěll sem,* I understood; **rozuměj,** *rozǔmyěy,* understand;

házím, *házeem,* I throw (I am throwing); **házel jsem,** *házel sem,* I was throwing; **házej,** *házey,* throw;

poroučím, *poroǔcheem,* I command; **poroučel jsem,** *poroǔchel sem,* I commanded; **poroučej,** *poroǔchey,* command.

Vlak, m.	*vlăk,*	the train;	**pevně,**	*pevňe,*	tightly, fast;
opratě, f. pl.	*oprăťe,*	the lines;	**silně,**	*silňe,*	strongly, hard;
povyk, m.	*pǒvik,*	the cry;	**výborně,**	*veeborňe,*	very well, excellently;
jazyk, m.	*yăzik,*	the tongue;			
prádlo, n.	*prádlǒ,*	the linen;	**špinavý, á, é**	*shpinǎvee,*	dirty;
šaty, pl.	*shăty,*	suit of clothes;	**jiný, á, é**	*yinee,*	other, different;
kamení, n.	*kămeňee,*	stones (collectively);	**zapomněl jsem,**	*zăpom-ňel sem,*	I forgot;

před tím,	*prshed ťeem,* before that;	**hráti,**	*hráťi,*	to play;
za něj,	*zá ñey,* for him, of him, (for it, of it);	**už ne,**	*ŭsh ně,* not any more.

Vidíš něco? — Co vidíš? — Nevidím nic*).

Doest thou see something? — What doest thou see?—I do not see anything.

Vidíte dobře? —Ano, vidím všecko. — Oni to vidí dobře.

Do you (*or* can you) see well?—Yes, I can see all.—They see it well.

Viděli jsme vlak; — viděli jste ho také?

We have seen a train; — have you seen it too?

Neviděli jsme ho; — děti ho viděly.

We have not seen it; — the children saw it.

Zde budeme viděti všecko. — Naši přátelé budou viděti nás hned.

Here we shall see all. — Our friends will see us immediately.

Kdo tu sedí?— To jsem já. — Proč tu sedíš? — Běž ven; — běžte oba ven.

Who sits here?—It is I.—Why doest thou sit here?—Run out;—go out both (of you).

Seděli jste pořád; — večer budete seděti zas.

You have been sitting all the time; —in the evening you will sit again.

Drž koně a mlč. — Držte opratě a mlčte. — Držíte pevně? — Držíme pevně.

Hold (thou) the horse and keep still. — Hold (you) the lines and keep still. — Do you hold fast? — We hold fast.

Oni nás slyší. — Žádný nás neslyší. — Ta holka nás slyšela. — Slyšeli nás.

They hear us.—Nobody hears us.— That girl has heard us. —They have heard us.

Prší; slyším to. — Slyšíte dešť?

It rains; I hear it.— Do you hear the rain ?

Neprší ještě; ale bude pršeti. — Včera pršelo silně; — před tím nepršelo už dávno.

It does not rain yet; but it will rain. — Yesterday it rained hard; — before that it had not rained for a long time.

---

*) There is a double negation in Bohemian, similar to the vulgar English way of speaking: *I don't see nothing.* See Note 1, Lesson V.

Ty šaty sluší vám výborně.	That suit of clothes fits you very well.
Ten klobouk mi nesluší; stydím se za něj.	That hat does not fit me; I am a-shamed of it.
Nestyď se; sluší ti dobře dost.	Do not be ashamed; it fits thee well enough.
Tvé prádlo je špinavé; nestydíš se? Styď se !	Thy linen is dirty; art thou not a-shamed?—Shame on you !
Umíš česky? — Ano já umím česky.	Doest thou know Bohemian?—Yes, I know Bohemian.
Umíte anglicky ? — Trochu.	Do you know English? — A little.
Umíte německy ? — Uměl jsem dobře; ale zapomněl jsem trochu.	Do you know German?—I knew it well; but I have forgotten it some-what.
Umíš hráti na piano? — Neumím. — Umíte zpívati ? — Neumím.	Doest thou know how to play on the piano? — I do not. — Can you sing? — I can not.
Naše děti umějí česky a anglicky, — a žádný jiný jazyk.	Our children know Bohemian and English, — and no other tongue.
Rozumějí německy ? — Nerozumě-jí.	Do they understand German?—they do not (understand).
Házej kamení za plot. — Neházej kamení na cestu.	Throw (thou) the stones behind the fence. — Do not throw the stones on the road.
Házejte ty pytle dolu. — Neházejte tak rychle.	Throw (you) the sacks down. — Don't throw so fast.
Házeli jsme dříví na hromadu, — a budeme házeti zas. — Otec to poroučí.	We have been throwing the wood on a heap, — and we shall throw again. — Father commands it.
Házejí ti hoši kamení ? — Neháze-jí. — Už neházejí.	Are those boys throwing stones? — They are not. — They are not throwing any more.
Už dávno neházejí.	They have not been throwing for a long time (i. e. they stopped throw-ing long since).

Note 2. The root or stem of the verb **viděti** is **vid,** to which the termination **ěti** is attached. All verbs ending in **ěti** or **eti** belong to the third conjugation.

The root of the verb is the usual form of the imperative: **běž,** run (thou); **seď,** sit; **drž,** hold; etc. — The third person singular and plural of the present tense are alike: **vidí,** he (she, it) sees; **vidí,** they see. But in colloquial usage it commonly takes the longer form: **vidějí,** se-dějí (they see, they sit).

In some cases the imperative is formed by cutting off the terminal **ti** and adding **j: uměti, — uměj,** know; **házeti, — házej,** throw; etc. These verbs always use the long form in the third person plural : **umí,** he (she, it) knows; **umějí,** *ŭmyěyee,* they know; —**házejí,** *házěyee,* they throw.

LESSON XXXIII.

Činiti,	*chiñiťi,*	to do;	**souditi,**	*souďiťi,*	to judge;
choditi,	*khoďiťi,*	to walk; to go (frequently);	**platiti,**	*plaťiťi,*	to pay; to rule, prevail, be in force;
mluviti,	*mlŭviťi,*	to speak, to tell;	**svítiti,**	*sweeťiťi,*	to shine;
věřiti,	*vyĕrshiťi,*	to believe;	**buditi,**	*bŭďiťi,*	to wake;
učiti,	*ŭchiťi,*	to teach;	**blázniti,**	*blázňiťi,*	to fool; to be crazy;
učiti se,	*ŭchiťi sĕ,*	to learn (i. e. to teach one's self);	**modliti se,**	*modliťi sĕ,*	to pray.

Činím, *chiñeem,* I do; — **činíš,** *chiñeesh,* thou doest; **činí,** *chiñee,* he (she, it) does; **činíme, činíte, činí** (colloquially also **činějí**), *chiñeemĕ, chiñeetĕ, chiñee* or *chiñeyee,* we, you, they do; — **či-nil jsem,** *chiñil sem,* I did, *or* I have done; **čiň,** do (thou); **čiňte,** *chiñtĕ,* do (you);

chodím, *khoďeem,* I walk; **chodil jsem,** *khoďil sem,* I walked; **choď,** walk;

10

mluvím, *mlŭveem,* I speak; **mluvil jsem,** *mlŭvil sem,* I spoke; **mluv,** *mlŭf,* speak;

věřím, *vyĕrsheem,* I believe; **věřil jsem,** *vyĕrshil sem,* I believed; **věř,** believe;

učím, *ŭcheem,* I teach; **učil jsem,** *ŭchil sem,* I taught; **uč,** teach;

učím se, *ŭcheem sĕ,* I learn; **učil jsem se,** *ŭchil sem sĕ,* I learned; **uč se,** learn;

soudím, *soŭďeem,* I judge; **soudil jsem,** *soŭďil sem,* I judged; **suď, sŭď,** judge;

platím, *plăťeem,* I pay; **platil jsem,** *plăťil sem,* I paid; **plať,** pay;

svítím, *sweeťeem,* I shine (I light); **svítil jsem,** *sweeťil sem,* I shined (lighted); **sviť,** shine (light);

budím, *bŭďeem,* I wake; **budil jsem,** *bŭďil sem,* I waked; **buď,** wake;

blázním, *blázñeem,* I am crazy; **bláznil jsem,** *blázñil sem,* I was crazy; **blázni,** *blázñi,* be crazy;

modlím se, *modleem sĕ,* I pray; **modlil jsem se,** I prayed; **modli se,** pray.

Učitel*), m.	*ŭchitel,*	the teacher;	**kresliti,**	*kressliťi,*	to draw;
učitelka, f.	*ŭchitelkă,*	a female teacher;	**živý, á, é**	*živee,*	living;
			nahlas,	*năhlăs,*	aloud;
žák, m.	*žák,*	the scholar;	**pilně,**	*pilñĕ,*	diligently;
soudce, m.	*soŭtsĕ,*	the judge;	**právě,**	*právyĕ,*	rightly;
zákon, m.	*zákon,*	the law;	**křivě,**	*krshivyĕ,*	wrongly;
kostel, m.	*kŏstel,*	the church;	**podle,**	*pŏdlĕ.*	according to;
lampa, f.	*lămpă,*	the lamp;	**dříve,**	*drsheevĕ,*	formerly.

---

*) **Učitel,** the teacher; **učitele,** *ŭchitellĕ,* of the teacher; **učiteli,** *ŭchitelli,* to the teacher; (plural) **učitelé,** *ŭchitellé,* the teachers; — like **přítel, přátelé** (see foot-note on page 97).

EXERCISES.

Čiň dobré a budeš šťasten.	Do good and thou shalt be happy.
Co jsi učinil? Neučinil jsem nic. — On to učinil.	What hast thou done? — I have not done anything. — He has done it.
Chlapec chodí do školy; — obě děti chodí do školy.	The boy goes to school; — both children go to school.
Chodíte často do města? — Dříve chodil jsem tam často; — nyní tam nechodím.	Do you often go to town? — Formerly I went there often; — now I do not go there.
Proč nechodíte? — Nemám čas.	Why do you not go? — I have no time.
Mluv nahlas; já tě neslyším.	Speak loud; I do not hear thee.
Mluvil jsi s učitelem? — Nemluvil; ale mluvil jsem s učitelkou.	Hast thou spoken with the teacher? — I have not (spoken); but I spoke with the lady teacher.
Věří ti učitel? — On vždy mi věří, protože mluvím pravdu. — To rád slyším.	Does the teacher believe you? — He always believes me, because I speak the truth. — I like to hear that.
Učitel učí nás mluviti pravdu. — Učil nás tomu vždycky.	The teacher teaches us to speak the truth. — He has taught us that always.
Uč se pilně. — Učte se dobře. — Učme se společně.	Learn(thou) diligently.—Learn(you) well. — Let us learn together.
Co se učíš*)? — Zeměpis. — Co vy se učíte? — Kresliti. — Kreslíte dobře. — Žák kreslil pěkně.	What doest thou learn? — Geography.— What is it you learn?—To draw. — You draw well. — The scholar drew nicely.
Soudil jsem křivě. — Vy jste soudili právě. — Soudce soudil podle zákona.	I judged wrong. — You judged right. — The judge judged according to law.

---

*) This is the colloquial expression. In the written language, **učiti** and **učiti se** govern the dative case, responding to the question **čemu?** (See page 82.) Hence we should write: **čemu se učíš?** what doest thou learn? **čemu učíte?** what do you teach? And the answer would be: **zeměpisu.**

Zákon platí, vždy platil a musí vždy platit.	The law rules, always ruled, and must always rule.
Budil jsem každé ráno celou rodinu časně.	I waked up every morning the whole family early.
Myslím že blázníš. — Ten člověk blázní. — Neblázni! — Bláznil jsi? — Ba bláznil jsem!	I think that thou art crazy. — That man is crazy. — Don't be crazy! Wast thou crazy? — Surely, I was crazy!
Měsíc ještě svítí; svítil celou noc. — Ta lampa svítí špatně; včera svítila dobře.	The moon still shines; it has been shining all night. — That lamp shines badly; yesterday it shined well.
Modli se! — Modleme se! — Lidé modlí se v kostele. — Kněz modlil se za živé*) i za mrtvé. .	Pray! — Let us pray! — People pray in church. — The priest prayed for the living and for the dead.

Note 1. The root or stem of the verb **činiti** is **čin**, to which the termination **iti** is attached. All verbs ending in **iti** belong to the fourth conjugation.

The root of the verb is the common form of the imperative: **čiň**, do; **choď**, walk; **mluv**, speak; etc. In some cases, however, only the final ti is thrown off to form the imperative: **blázni**, be crazy; **modli se**, pray.

Note 2. The verbs **bydliti, mysliti, musiti** (to reside, to think, must) are also written **bydleti, mysleti, museti,** and in popular language this form is always employed. This does not materially modify their inflection, as the third and fourth conjugation are essentially almost identical. For instance :

---

*) **Živý,** living; plural: **živí,** in the objective case **živé.** These distinctions, however, disappear in common discourse. This adjective also has an indefinite or short form (see Note 2, Lesson XXIII): **živ, a, o.** For instance: **je posud živ,** he is still living; **matka je živa,** the mother is living; **dítě je živo,** the child is living. The expression **živ a zdráv,** pronounced *živ a zdráv,* is frequently heard.

(Third conjugation)

sedĕti,	sẽd'ẽt'i,	to sit
sedím,	sẽd'eem,	I sit
sedĕl jsem,	sẽd'el sem,	I sat
sed',	sed',	sit (thou)
budu sedĕti,	bŭdŭ sẽd'et'i	I shall sit

(Fourth conjugation)

činiti,	chiñit'i,	to do
činím,	chiñeem,	I do
činil jsem,	chiñil sem,	I did
čiň,	chiñ,	do (thou)
budu činiti,	bŭdŭ chiñit'i,	I shall do.

The above three verbs, in colloquial discourse, always take in the third person plural the form: **bydlejí, myslejí, musejí,** *bidlẽyee, mislẽyee, mŭsẽyee* (they reside, they think, they must); whereas the proper grammatical form is like the third person singular: **bydlí, myslí, musí.**

LESSON XXXIV.

Volati,	colãt'i,	to call;
bĕhati,	byẽhãt'i,	to run (about);
čekati,	chekãt'i,	to wait;
dĕlati,	d'elãt'i,	to do, to make, to work;
hledati,	hlẽdãt'i,	to seek, to look for;
doufati,	doŭfãt'i,	to hope;

prodati,	prodãt'i,	to sell;
prodávati*),	prodãvãt'i,	to be selling;
povídati,	povedãt'i,	to say, to tell;
trestati,	trestãt'i,	to punish;
znáti,	znãt'i,	to know;
ptáti se,	ptãt'i sẽ,	to ask, to inquire;
plovati,	plovãt'i,	to swim.

Volám, *volãm,* I call; **voláš,** *volãsh,* thou callest; **volá,** he (she, it) calls; **voláme, voláte, volají,** *volãmẽ, volãtẽ, volãyee,* we, you, they call; — **volal jsem,** *volãl sem,* I called; **volej,** *voley,* call (thou); **volejte,** *voleytẽ,* call (you);

bĕhám, *byẽhãm,* I run; **bĕhal jsem,** *byẽhãl sem,* I was running; **bĕž,** *byẽž,* run;

čekám, *chekãm,* I wait; **čekal jsem,** *chekãl sem,* I waited; **čekej,** *chekey,* wait;

dĕlám, *d'elãm,* I do, I make; **dĕlal jsem,** *d'elãl sem,* I did, I made; **dĕlej,** *d'eley,* do, make;

---

*) Reiterative form of **prodati;** see Note 5, Lesson XIII.

hledám, *hlĕdám*, I seek; hledal jsem, *hlĕdăl sem*, I sought; hledej, *hlĕ-dey*, seek;

doufám, *doŭfám*, I hope; doufal jsem, *doŭfăl sem*, I hoped; doufej, *doŭfey*, hope;

prodám, I shall sell (having a future meaning; see Note 7, Lesson XIV; prodal jsem, *prodăl sem*, I sold; prodej, *prodey*, sell;

prodávám, I am selling: prodával jsem, *prodávăl sem*, I was selling: pro-dávej, *prodávey*, sell;

povídám, *poveedám*, I say; povídal jsem, *poveedăl sem*, I said; povídej, *poveedey*, tell;

trestám (also tresci, *trestsi*), I punish; trestal jsem, *trestăl sem*, I pun-ished; trestej, *trestey*, punish;

znám, I know; znal jsem, *znăl sem*, I knew; znej, *zney*, know;

ptám se, I ask; ptal jsem se, *ptăl sem sĕ*, I asked; ptej se, *ptey sĕ*, ask.

Květina, f. *kwyĕťină*	} flower	
kvítko, n. *kweetko*		
kytka, f. *kitkă*,	bouquet;	
majetek, m. *măyĕtek*,	property;	
na přesrok, *nă prshĕsrok*,	next year	
před lety, *prshed lety*,	years ago;	
druzí, *drŭzee*,	the others;	
naši, *năshi*,	our folks;	

spatřiti, *spătrshiťi*, to see (or to meet);

věděti, *vyĕďeťi*, to know;

poslušný, á, é *poslŭshnee*, obedient;

neposlušný, disobedient;

tento (f. tato, n. toto), *tentŏ*, this one, this here.

EXERCISES.

Voláš mě? — Koho voláš? — Koho jsi volal?

Doest thou call me? — Whom doest thou call?— Whom didst thou call?

Volám hocha; kde je? — Běhá ven-ku; všechny děti běhají venku.

I call the boy; where is he? — He is running outside (i. e. out of doors); — all the children are running out-side.

Volal jsem tě; kde's (abbrev. of kde jsi) byl?

I called thee; where hast thou been?

Běhal jsem na zahradě; — čekal jsem až mě budete volati.

I was running in the garden;— I was waiting until you would call me.

Co jsi dělal na zahradě? — Nedělal jsem nic; — hledal jsem květiny.

What wast thou doing in the garden? — I was not doing anything; — I was looking for flowers.

Je tam mnoho květin? — Ano.

Are there many flowers there?—Yes.

Co druzí dělali na zahradě? — Hledali květiny se mnou.

What have the others been doing in the garden? — They were looking for flowers with me.

Hledej pěkné květiny a dělej kytky. — Jděte*) oba, ty a Karel, a hledejte kvítka.

Look for nice flowers, and make bouquets. — Go both of you, — thou and Charles, and look for flowers.

Doufám že na přesrok budeme živi a zdrávi. — Doufejme!

I hope that next year we shall be alive and well. — Let us hope!

Doufal jsem spatřiti vás zde. — Všichni doufali sme sejíti se s vámi.

I hoped to see (or meet) you here. — We all hoped to meet you.

Prodám svůj majetek. — Prodejte ho brzy. — Můj bratr prodal svůj majetek lacino.

I shall sell my property. — Sell it soon.—My brother sold his property cheap.

Naši prodali farmu a povídají že půjdou do města.

Our folks have sold the farm, and they say that they will go to the city.

Povídal jsem mu, že mám dům na prodej. — Prodávám všecko co mám.

I told him that I had a house for sale. — I am selling everything I have.

Tento majetek není na prodej. — Kdo to povídal? — Kdo vám to povídal?

This property is not for sale. — Who said so? — Who told you so?

Každý to povídá. — Všichni to povídají.

Everybody says so. — They all say so.

Znáš mě? — Znám tě dobře; — znal jsem tě už před lety.

Doest thou know me?—I know thee well; — I knew you already years ago.

---

*) The infinitive is **jíti**, *yeeťi*, to go; see Lesson XIII.

Každý mě zná; — všichni mě znají.	Everybody knows me; — they all know me.
Znáte mého otce? — Neznám ho. — Znal jste mou matku? — Neznal jsem ji.	Do you know my father? — I do not know him. — Did you know my mother? — I did not know her.
Proč se ptáš? — Ptám se, protože chci věděti.*)	Why doest thou ask? — I ask because I want to know.
Ptáte se po mě? — Ptal jsem se kde bydlíte; — povídali mi, že prodal jste svůj dům. — Neprodal jsem ho ještě.	Do you ask for me? — I asked where you lived; — they told me that you had sold your house. — I have not sold it yet.
Neptám se co učitel povídal; já to vím.	I do not ask what the teacher said; I know it.
Věděl jsem, že chlapec je neposlušný; — víte že musel jsem trestati ho.	I knew that the boy was disobedient; — you know that I was obliged to punish him.
To víme. — Všichni víme, že trestal jste ho často.	We know that. — We all know that you punished him often.

Note 1. The root or stem of the verb **volati** is **vol**, to which the termination **ati** is attached. Verbs ending in **ati** belong to the fifth conjugation.

Note 2. Some verbs ending in **áti** form their present like the verbs of the first conjugation ending in **íti**, (**bíti**, to beat; **biju, biješ, bije**, etc.); for example:

hráti, *hráťi*, to play: **hraju*), hraješ, hraje,** *hrăyŭ, hrăyesh, hrăyĕ,* I play, thou playest, he plays; **hrajeme, hrajete, hrajou**)** *hrăyemĕ, hrăyetĕ, hrăyoŭ,* we, you, they play; — **hrál jsem,** *hrál sem,* I played; **hraj,** *hrăy,* play.

---

*) **Věděti** (to know) is one of the thoroughly irregular verbs: **vím, víš, ví,** *veem, veesh, vee,* I know, thou knowest, he (she, it) knows; **víme, víte, vědí,** *veemĕ, veetĕ, vyĕďee,* we, you, they know; — **věděl jsem,** *vyĕďĕl sem,* I knew; **věz,** *vyĕz,* know thou; **vězte,** *vyĕzte,* know you.

) **Hraji, hrají, I play, they play) are considered the pure grammatical forms of the first person singular and third person plural; but **hraju, hrajou,** are exclusively used in the popular language.

However, this verb also follows the rule of the fifth conjugation in the present tense: **hrám, hráš, hrá; hráme, hráte, hrají** (I play, thou playest, he plays; we, you, they play).

A few verbs modify the letter á in the present tense:

hřáti, *hrsháťi,* to warm; — **hřeju** (or **hřeji) hřeješ, hřeje; hřejeme, hře-jete, hřejou** (or **hřejí); I** warm, thou warmest, he warms; etc. — **hřál jsem,** *hrshál sem,* I warmed; **hřej,** *hrshey,* warm;

přáti, *prsháťi,* to wish; — **přeju** (or **přeji), I** wish; **přál jsem,** I wished; **přej,** wish;

smáti se, *smáťi sě,* to laugh; — **směju se** (or **směji se),** *smyěyŭ sě,* I laugh; **smál jsem se,** *smál sem sě,* I laughed; **směj se,** *smyěy sě,* laugh.

Note 3. There are some verbs essentially belonging to this con-jugation, which show a considerable deviation in the present tense and imperative. The following are most frequently met with:

bráti, to take; — **beru, bereš, bere, bereme, berete, berou,** *berŭ, beresh, berě, berěmě, berětě, berou* (I take, thou takest, etc); **bral jsem,** *brál sem,* I took; **ber,** take;

práti, to wash; — **peru,** *perŭ,* I wash; **pral jsem,** *prál sem,* I washed; **per,** wash;

psáti, to write; — **píšu,** *peeshŭ,* I write; **psal jsem,** *psál sem,* I wrote; **piš,** *pish,* write;

kázati, to preach (or to command); — **kážu,** *kážŭ,* I preach; **kázal jsem,** I preached; **kaž,** preach;

tázati se, to ask; — **tážu se,** *tážŭ sě,* I ask; **tázal jsem se,** *tázál sem sě,* I asked; **taž se,** ask;

plakati, to weep; — **pláču,** *plăchŭ* (but also **plakám)** I weep; **plakal jsem,** *plăkál sem,* I wept; **plač,** *plăch,* weep;

skákati, to jump; — **skáču,** *skáchŭ* (but also **skákám),** I jump; **skákal jsem,** *skákál sem,* I was jumping; **skákej,** *skákey,* jump;

stonati, to be sick; — **stůňu,** *stooňŭ* (but also **stonám,** *stŏnám),* I am sick; **stůněš,** *stooňesh,* thou art sick; **stůně,** *stooňě,* he is sick, etc.; **stonej,** *stŏney,* be sick.

LESSON XXXV.

Milovati, *milŏvắťi,*	to love;	**pracovati,** *prắtsŏvắťi,* to work;
děkovati, *ďekŏvắťi,*	to thank;	**radovati se,** *rắdŏvắťi sě,* to rejoice;
litovati, *litŏvắťi,* to be sorry, to		**opakovati,** *ŏpắkŏvắťi,* to repeat;
	regret;	**pamatovati,** *pắmắtŏvắťi,* to remem-
jmenovati, *menŏvắťi,* to name, to		ber;
	call;	**podporovati,** *pŏdporŏvắťi,* to sup-
jmenovati se, *m. sě,* to be called;		port, to assist;
kupovati, *kŭpŏvắťi,* to be buying;		**ztravovati,** *strắvŏvắťi,* to board.

Miluju (or **miluji***) *milŭyŭ,* I love: **miluješ,** *milŭyesh,* thou lovest; **milu-je,** *milŭyě,* he (she, it) loves; **milujeme, milujete, milujou** (or **miluji***) *milŭyěmě, milŭyětě, milŭyoŭ,* we, you, they love; — **miloval jsem,** *milŏvắl sem,* I loved; **miluj,** *milŭy,* love; **milujte,** *milŭytě,* love (you);

děkuju (or **děkuji),** *ďekŭyŭ,* I thank; **děkoval jsem,** *ďekŏvắl sem,* I thank-ed; **děkuj,** *ďekŭy,* thank;

lituju (or **lituji),** *litŭyŭ,* I regret; **litoval jsem,** *litŏvắl sem.* I regretted; **lituj,** *litŭy,* regret;

jmenuju (or **jmenuji),** *menŭyŭ,* I name; **jmenoval jsem,** *menŏvắl sem,* I named; **jmenuj,** *menŭy,* name;

jmenuju se, *menŭyŭ sě,* I am called; **jmenoval jsem se,** *menŏvắl sem sě.* I was called; **jmenuj se,** *menŭy sě,* call yourself;

kupuju (or **kupuji),** *kŭpŭyŭ,* I am buying; **kupoval jsem,** *kŭpŏvắl sem,* I was buying; **kupuj,** *kŭpŭy,* buy (or rather: keep buying);

---

*) **Miluju, milujou** (I love, they love) is always used in ordinary conversation; **miluji, milují,** *milŭyi, milŭyee* (I love, they love) prevails in the written language, being considered the proper grammatical form. This applies to all verbs of this conjugation: **děkuju, děkujou,** or **děkuji, děkují** (I thank, they thank); **lituju, litujou,** or **lituji, litují** (I regret, they regret); etc.

pracuju (or **pracuji**), *prătsŭyŭ*, I work; **pracoval jsem,** *prătsŏvăl sem*, I worked; **pracuj, prătsŭy,** work;

raduju se (or **raduji se**), *rădŭyŭ sĕ*, I rejoice; **radoval jsem se,** *rădŏvăl sem sĕ*, I rejoiced; **raduj se,** *rădŭy sĕ*, rejoice;

opakuju (or **opakuji**), *ŏpăkŭyŭ*, I repeat; **opakoval jsem,** *ŏpăkŏvăl sem›* I repeated; **opakuj, ŏpăkŭy,** repeat;

pamatuju (or **pamatuji**), *pămătŭyŭ*, I remember; **pamatoval jsem,** *pămătŏvăl sem*, I remembered; **pamatuj, pămătŭy,** remember;

podporuju (or **podporuji**), *pŏdporŭyŭ*, I support; **podporoval jsem,** *pŏdporŏvăl sem*, I suported; **podporuj, pŏdporŭy,** support;

žaluju (or **žaluji**), *žălŭyŭ*, I complain; **žaloval jsem,** *žălŏvăl sem*, I complained; **žaluj, žălŭy,** complain.

Bůh*) m.	*booh,*	God;	**osud,** m.	*osŭd,*	fate;
bližní**) m.	*bleežñee,* the fellow man, (neighbor);		**vychování,** n. *vykhŏváñee,* education;		
král,	*král,*	the king;	**díl,** m.	*ďeel,*	a part;
královna,	*králŏvnă,*	the queen;	**výdělek,** m. *veeďelek,* earnings, wages, profit;		
žebrák, m.	*žĕbrák,*	the beggar:	**který, á, é** *kteree* or *keree,* which, what, who;		
kamarád, m. *kămărád,* the comrade;					
objevitel, m. *obyĕ-vitel,* the discoverer;			**vespolek,** *vespŏlek,* { all together; one another;		
svět, m.	*swyĕt,*	the world;	**nazpamět,** *năspămyĕt,* by heart;		
země, f.	*zemyĕ,* the country; the earth:		**z paměti,** *spămyĕťi,* from memory;		
vlast, f.	*vlăst,*	one's country;	**svobodný, á, é** *swŏbodnee,* free; single;		
dávati,	*dăvăťi,* to give, to offer;		**Řimané,** *rshimăné,* the Romans:		
život, m.	*živŏt,*	life;	**Václav,** *vátslăv,* Venceslaus,		
válka, f.	*válkă,*	war;			Wencel.

---

*) **Bůh, Boha, Bohu, s Bohem** (*booh, bŏhă, bŏhŭ, sbŏhem*), God, of God (God's), to God, with God.

) Nouns having the termination of adjectives are declined like adjectives of the corresponding termination. Hence we decline: **bližní, — bližního, of (our) fellow man *or* neighbor; **bližnímu,** to (our) neighbor; **s bližním,** with (our) neighbor. See Note 1, Lesson XXI.

Exercises.

Miluj blížního svého*). — Milujte se vespolek.

Love thy neighbor. — Love (you) one another.

Miluješ rodiče své? — Miluju je velmi.

Doest thou love thy parents? — I love them greatly.

Matka miluje své dítě. — Děti milují matku svou.

The mother loves her child. — The children love their mother.

Washington miloval svou vlas'. — Řimané milovali válku.

Washington loved his country. — The Romans loved war.

Co kupuješ? — Kupuji obilí. — Co kupoval jsi onehdy? — Kupoval jsem pár koní.

What art thou buying? — I am buying grain. — What wert thou buying the other day?—I was buying a pair of horses.

Kdo kupoval tento dům? — Naši kupovali ten dům; — dávali za něj dva tisíce.

Who has been buying this house?— Our folks were buying that house; —they offered for it two thousand.

Chceš něco jísti? — Nechci nic, děkuju.

Doest thou want something to eat?— I do not want anything, thank you.

Dal jsem žebráku pět centů a on děkoval mi.

I gave (to) the beggar five cents and he thanked me.

Děkujme Bohu, že jsme zdrávi. — Děkuj svému osudu, že jsi rozen ve svobodné zemi.

Let us thank God that we are healthy. — Thank thy fate that thou wast born in a free country.

Děkujte rodičům za dobré vychování.

Thank (your) parents for a good education.

Lituju že musím pryč. — Litoval jsem, že musil jsem odejíti. — Zůstaň zde, povídali všichni, nebo budeš litovati.

I am sorry that I must (go) away. — I was sorry that I had to leave. — Stay here, they all said, or thou wilt be sorry.

---

*) This is the objective case, responding to **koho?** *whom?* It agrees with the possessive case; see Remark on page 86.

Jak se jmenuješ? — Jmenuju se Václav Zeman. — A jak vy se jmenujete? — Já se jmenuju Staněk. — Jmenuj mi pět dílů světa.

What is thy name? — My name is WencelZeman.—And what is your name? — My name is Staněk. — Name (to me) the five parts of the world.

Jak se jmenoval objevitel Ameriky? — Krištof Kolumbus.

What was the name of the discoverer of America? — Christopher Columbus.

Jak se jmenoval král, který ho podporoval? — Ferdinand. — A královna? — Isabella.

What was the name of the king who assisted him?— Ferdinand.—And of the queen? — Isabella.

Pracuj pilně a budeš radovati se nad výdělkem.

Work diligently, and thou wilt rejoice over (thy) earnings.

Rád pracuješ? — Ano, ale můj kamarád nerad pracuje; — on pořád žaluje, že musí pracovati.

Doest thou like to work?— Yes; but my comrade does not like to work; — he always complains that he must work.

Pracovali jsme celý den.

We worked (or have been working) all day.

Učitel žaloval mi, že jsi neposlušný; — opakuju, že musíš býti poslušný; — pamatuj si to!

The teacher complained to me that thou art disobedient; — I repeat that thou must be obedient; — remember that!

Pamatuj co se učíš; — pamatuješ si to? — Pamatuju to dobře; — učím se to nazpamět.

Remember what thou learnest; — doest thou remember it? — I remember it well;-I learn it by heart.

Pamatujme na chudé; — podporujme je. — Pamatujte že život jest krátký.

Let us remember the poor; — let us support them. — Remember (you) that life is short.

Note. The root or stem of the verb **milovati** is **mil,** to which the termination **ovati** is attached. Verbs ending in **ovati** (when this termination is attached to the *root*) belong to the sixth conjugation.

LESSON XXXVI.

(Já) bych	*bikh*	I should	Abych (já)	*ăbikh*	that I should
(ty) bys	*bis*	thou wouldst	abys (ty)	*ăbis*	that thou shouldst
(on) by	*bi*	he would	aby (on)	*ăbi*	that he should; etc.

(my) bychom	*bikhŏm*	} we should	Kdybych	*gdibikh*	if I should
,, bysme	*bismĕ*		kdybys	*gdibis*	if thou wouldst
(vy) byste	*bistĕ*	you would	kdyby	*gdibi*	if he would (or
(oni) by	*bi*	they would			simply "if").

Byl*) bych	*bill bikh*	I should be	Abych byl	*ăbikh bill*	that I should be
byl bys	*bill bis*	thou wouldst be	abys byl	*ăbis bill*	that thou
byl by	*bill bi*	he would be;			shouldst be
		etc.	aby byl	*ăbi bill*	that he should be; etc.

Byl bych byl,	} I should have	Kdybych byl,	if I were,
byl bych býval	} been:	kdybys byl,	if thou wert,
byl bys býval,	thou wouldst have	kdyby byl,	if he were; etc.
	been; etc.		

Nesl bych,	*nessl bikh,*	I should (or "would") carry;	nesli bychom (or bysme), *nessli bikhŏm,* we should (or "would")carry
minul bych,	*minăl bikh,*	I should pass	minuli bychom, *minăli bikhom,* we should pass
viděl bych,	*vid'el bikh,*	I should see	viděli bychom, *vid'eli bikhŏm,* we should see
činil bych,	*chiñil bikh,*	I should do	činili bychom, *chiñili bikhŏm,* we should do
volal bych,	*vŏlăl bikh,*	I should call	volali bychom, *vŏlăli bikhŏm,* we should call
miloval bych,	*milŏvăl bikh,*	I should love	milovali bychom, *milŏvăli bikhŏm,* we should love.

---

*) In the feminine gender **byla bych, byla bys, byla by;** third person neutre: **bylo by,** it would be. See Lesson IX.

Byl bych nesl, I should have carried;   **byl bych činil,** I should have done;
byl bych minul, I should have passed;   **byl bych volal,** I should have called;
byl bych viděl, I should have seen;   **byl bych miloval,**   I should have loved.

Kdyby,	*gdibi,*	if	**kufr,** m.	*kŭf'er,*	the trunk
kterýkoli, *kťereekŏli,*		whichever, any	**košík,** m.	*kosheek,*	the basket
kdož (same as **kdo**),	*gdŏž,*	who	**list,** m.	*list,*	the letter
či, čili,	*chi, chilli,*	or	**vodopád,** m.	*vŏdŏpád,*	a waterfall
říci,	*rsheetxi,*	to say, to tell	**krajina,** f.	*krǎyinǎ,*	a section of country
řekni,	*rshěkñi,*	say, tell (thou)			
řekněte,	*rshěkñetě,*	say, tell (you)	**počasí,** n.	*pŏchǎxsee,*	the weather
těžký, á, é	*ťeshkee,*	heavy, hard	**štěkati,**	*shťekǎťi,*	to bark.

Exercises.

Nesl bych ten kufr, kdyby nebyl tak těžký. — I would carry that trunk, if it were not so heavy.

Byl bych nesl ten kufr, kdybyste byli chtěli. — I should have carried that trunk, if you had wanted it.

My bysme nesli košík a vy byste nesli pytel. — We should carry the basket, and you would carry the sack.

Četl bys tu knihu? — Četl bych ji rád, kdybych ji měl. — Wouldst thou read that book? — I would like to read it, if I had it.

My bychom (or my bysme) rádi četli dnešní noviny. — We should like to read to-day's newspaper.

Které noviny byste rádi četli? — Kterékoliv. — What newspaper would you like to read? — Any newspaper.

Byli bychom (or byli bysme) četli ten list, ale byl tuze dlouhý. — We should have read that letter, but it was too long.

Pil bych pivo, kdybych ho měl. — Pil byste*) čaj? — Nepil bych nic. — I should drink beer, if I had it. — Would you drink tea? — I would not drink anything.

---

*) Speaking to one person and using the second person plural: **vy,** *you;* speaking to several persons, we should say: **pili byste** (would you drink).

Kdyby bylo pěkně, sil bych pšenici.	If it were nice*), I should sow wheat
Kdyby pes štěkal, kopnul bych ho.	If the dog barked, I should kick him.
Viděl bych rád vodopád Niagaru.	I should like to see the Niagara Falls.
Na cestě do Iowy viděli bysme řeku Mississippi.	On (our) way to Iowa we should see the river Mississippi.
Kdybyste přijeli k nám, viděli byste hezkou krajinu.	If you would come to us, you would see a nice country.
Kdybych věděl, jaké počasí bude, řekl bych vám.	If I knew what kind of weather it will be, I should tell you.
Chodil bych k tobě, kdybys chtěl.	I should come to thee (i. e. "come to to see thee often"), if thou wouldst wish it.
On by chodil k vám často. — Proč by nechodil? — Jen ať chodí!	He would come to you often.— Why should he not come?— Do let him come!
Věřil bys tomu? — Věřil byste že nemám čas? — Nevěřil bych to**). —	Wouldst thou believe it? — Would you believe that I have no time? — I should not believe it.
Věřili by nám? — Myslím že věřili by vám to.	Would they believe us?—I think that they would believe you (it).
Prodal bych rád můj obchod. — Těžko byste prodal nyní.	I would like to sell my business. — You would find it hard to sell now.
Litoval bych, kdybyste prodal ten obchod. — Já bych nelitoval nic.	I should be sorry, if you would sell that business. — I should not be sorry at all.
Je čas, abych šel. — Řekni mu aby šel.	It is time that I should go.—Tell him to go, *or* to come (i. e. tell him that he should go).
Chci abys přišel brzy. — Chci abyste odešli.	I want thee to come soon. — I want you to leave.
Chcete abych to koupil?	Do you want me to buy that?

---

*) That is, "if the weather were nice".

) **Věřiti to (accus. case), **věřiti tomu** (dative case); both are used with equal propriety.

| Kdybys byl zde býval, byl bys viděl všelico. | If thou hadst been here, thou wouldst have seen different things. |
| Kdybych tam byl, bylo by dobře.— Kdybych tam byl býval, byl bych rád. | If I were there, it would be well.—If I had been there, I should be glad. |

Note 1. The English conjunctions *if*, *whether*, used to introduce a conditional sentence, are expressed in Bohemian by the suffix **li**, or by **jestli, zdali, pakli,** *yestli, zdáli, pákli* :

Jsem-li,	*sem-li*	if I am,	jsme-li,	*smě-li*	if we are,
jestli jsem,	*yestli sem*	whether I	jestli jsme,	*yestli smě*	whether
zdali jsem,	*zdáli sem*	am;	zdali jsme,	*zdáli smě*	we are;

byl-li jsem,	*bill-li sem*	if I	byli-li jsme,	*billi-li smě*	if we
jestli jsem byl,	*yestli sem bill*	was, if I	jestli jsme byli,	*yestli smě billi*	were, if we
zdali jsem byl,	*zdáli sem bill*	have	zdali jsme byli,	*zdáli smě billi*	have
pakli jsem byl,	*pákli sem bill*	been.	pakli jsme byli,	*pákli smě billi*	been;

| budu-li, | *búdů li* | if I shall | budeme-li, | *búděmě-li* | if we shall |
| jestli budu, | *yestli búdů* | be; etc. | jestli budeme, | *yestli búděmě* | be; etc. |

| nesu-li, | *nessů-li* | if I carry; | nesl-li jsem, | *nessl-li sem* | if I carried |
| jest-li nesu, | *yestli nessů* | | jestli jsem nesl, | *yestli sem nessl* | |

Arci (že),	*artsi*	of course,	směti,	*smyěťi,*	to be allowed,
ovšem (že),	*ofshěm*	to be sure;			to dare;
nikam,	*ñikám,*	nowhere;	smím-li,	*smeemli,*	if I may;
nikdo jiný,	*ñigdő yinee,*	no one else;	víte-li,	*veetěli,*	if you know;
ani my,	*áñi me,*	not even we,	slíbiti,	*sleebiťi,*	to promise;
		neither we;	pověděti,	*povyěďeťi,*	to tell;
zač je,	*zách yě,*	what is it worth;	pověz,	*povyěz,*	tell (thou);
zač jsou,	*zách soů,*	what are they worth;	utratiti,	*útráťiťi,*	to spend;
			vzíti si,	*vzeeťi si,*	to take (to
mouka, f.	*moůká,*	the flour;			one's self);
tuna, f.	*tůná,*	a ton;	vezmu si,	*vězmů si,*	I shall take
přijeti,	*prshiyěťi,*	to arrive (by			(to myself).
		some conveyance);			

Note 2. The pronoun **si** has the same meaning as **sobě,** *sobyě* "to one's self", "for one's self". It often accompanies verbs, denoting the closest relation between the subject and its predicate, somewhat after the manner of reflexive verbs (connected with **se,** the same as **sebe,** one's self). For instance :

Vzíti means simply "to take"; **vzíti si** means "to take to one's self", — to take for one's own use or exclusive possession. — **Vzíti kytku,** to take a flower; **vzíti si kytku,** to take (and keep for one's self) a flower. — **Vzíti si ženu,** to take to one's self a wife; **vzal si ženu,** he took unto himself a wife.

Vezmi si peníze, take (to thyself) money, *or* the money; **vezměte si piva,** take (yourself) some beer; **vezměme si vína,** let us take (ourselves) some wine.

Koupím klobouk, I shall buy a hat; **koupím si klobouk,** I shall buy (myself) a hat,—I shall buy me a hat; **kup si klobouk,** buy (thyself) a hat.

Dej udělat obraz (*děy uďelňt obráz*), let (thou) a picture be made; order a picture to be made; **dej si udělat obraz,** let a picture be made for thyself. — **Dejte udělat šaty,** have a suit of clothes made; **dejte si udělat šaty,** have a suit of clothes made for yourself.

Note 3. The *finite* verb **vzíti** (to take) has only a past and future tense, — the *continuous* verb **bráti** (to take) supplying the present: **beru,** I take. See Note 3 on page 153.

Vzal jsem, vzal jsi, vzal, I took, thou tookest, hee took; **vezmu, vezmeš, vezme,** I shall take, thou wilt take, he will take; **vezmi, vezměte,** take (thou, you).

In common discourse we often hear **vemu, vemeš, veme,** *věmů, věmesh, věmě,* in place of **vezmu, vezmeš, vezme;** and **vem, vemte,** *věm, věmtě,* in place of **vezmi, vezměte.**

EXERCISES.

Ptáte se, jsem-li rád? — Ovšem že jsem rád.	You ask if I am glad? — Of course I am glad.
Ptal jsem se, jsou-li naši zde.— Arci že jsou, — pravil pan Hronek.	I asked if our folks were here. — Of course they are, — said Mr. Hronek.

Rád bych věděl, jestli sestra při-
jela.

Ráda bych věděla (f.), zdali bratr
přijel.

Rád bych slyšel, je-li můj syn živ
nebo mrtev.

Co myslíte, bude pršet? — Kdož ví,
bude-li pršet čili nebude.

Myslíte-li že bude pršet, nepůjdu
nikam.

Chci vědět má-li peníze; — nemá-
li, ať odejde.

Dám-li mu peníze, utratí je. — Dá-
me-li mu dollar, bude spokojen.
— Dáte-li mi něco, budu rád.

Podívám se, zdali je otec doma. —
Pověz mi pak, je-li doma nebo
není.

Povězte mi, musím-li jíti domu
nebo ne. — Ať poví ti, musíš-li
jíti do školy.

Povězte mi, smím-li vzíti si růži.
— Smíš; ale nikdo jiný nesmí.

Vezmi si tu kytku. — Já nesmím.

Proč nesmíš? — Nesmíš-li ty, nesmím já.

Nesmí-li nikdo, nesmíme ani my.

Nevím smíme-li, nebo nesmíme.

To nesmíš dělat! — Jestli nesmím,
teda nebudu.

Otec slíbil mi dollar, budu-li hodný.

I should like to knew, if sister has
arrived.

I should like to know if brother has
arrived.

I should like to hear whether my
son is alive or dead.

What do you think, will it rain? —
Who knows if it will rain or not.

If you think that it will rain, I shall
not go anywhere.

I want to know if he has money; —
if he has not, let him go away.

If I give him money, he spends it.—
If we give him a dollar, he will be
satisfied. — If you give me something, I shall be glad.

I shall see if father is at home.— Tell
me then if he is at home or not.

Tell me whether I must go home or
not. — Let him tell thee, whether
thou must go to school.

Tell me if I may take a rose. — Thou
mayest; but nobody else may.

Take that flower. — I dare not (I
must not).

Why must thou not?— If thou must
not, I must not.

If nobody is allowed, then we too
are not allowed.

I don't know whether we may or
not.

Thou must not do that!— If I must
not, than I shall not.

Father promised me a dollar if I am
(i. e. shall be) good.

Jestli ti ho slíbil, dá ti ho.	If he has promised it (to thee), he will give it to thee.
Povězte mi, víte-li zač je tuna sena. — Víte-li pak, zač jsou prasata?	Tell me if you know what is a ton of hay worth. — Do you know what hogs are worth?
Znáte-li pak mě? — Víte-li*) pak, že jsem zde dávno?	Do you know me? — Do you know that I have been here a long time?

Note 4. The present participle *being* varies in Bohemian according to gender and number:

jsa, *sa*, m. — **jsouc,** *soûts*, f. and n. — **jsouce,** *soûtsě*, pl. of all three genders.

The past, *having been*, is rendered thus:

byv, *bif*, m. — **byvši,** *bifshi*, f. and n. — **byvše,** *bifshě*, pl. of all three genders.

The following models will amply suffice for the verbs of all conjugations:

nesa	*nessa*, m.	carrying	**sedě**	*seďe*, m.		sitting
nesouc	*nessoûts*, f. & n.	"	**sedíc,**	*seďeets*, f. & n.		"
nesouce	*nessoûtsě*, pl.	"	**sedíce**	*seďeetsě*, pl.		"
pije	*piyě*, m.	drinking	**volaje**	*volâyě*, m.		calling
pijíc	*piyeets*, f. & n.	"	**volajíc**	*volâyeets*, f. & n.		"
pijíce	*piyeetsě*, pl.	"	**volajíce**	*volâyeetsě*, pl.		"
miluje	*millâyě*, m.	loving	**Piv**	*pif*, m.	having drank	
milujíc	*millâyeets*, f. & n.	"	**pivši**	*pifshi*, f. & n.		"
milujíce	*millâyeetsě*, pl.	"	**pivše**	*pifshě*, pl.		"

seděv, *seďef*, having sat; **volav,** *volâf*, having called; etc.

---

*) We may ask, for instance: **víte zač je mouka?** "do you know what flour is worth?" But if we ask: **víte-li pak zač je mouka?** or **zdali pak víte, zač je mouka?** there is a peculiar emphasis in the question, as if we say in English: "I wonder if you know what flour is worth?" — **Znáte mě?** "do you know me?" **Znáte-li pak mě?** or **zdali pak mě znáte?** "I wonder if you know me!"

Viděti, "to see", is irregular, forming its partic. like **nesti : vida** m., **vidouc** f. & n., **vidouce,** pl. (*vidá, vidouts, vidoutsĕ*), seeing.

These participles occur in the written language and sometimes in solemn discourse, but are never used in ordinary conversation. Expressions may be greatly shortened and made incisive by their use; for instance :

"As he was going away from here, he fell down", — may be translated into Bohemian: **Jda odsud, upadl.** In common discourse, however, people would say : **Když šel odsud, upadl** (or **upadnul.*)**

A verbal adjective is formed in Bohemian by adding an **i** to the present participle (f. and n.): **jsouci,** *soutsee,* being; **nesouci,** *nessoutsee,* carrying; **pijíci,** *piyeetsee,* drinking; **volajíci,** *volayeetsee,* calling; **milujíci,** *milliyeetsee,* loving. — They are rarely employed in common conversation, but frequently in writing:

Muž nesouci kufr minul mě; a man carrying a trunk passed me. — **Rodiče milujíci své děti jsou starostlivi o ně;** parents loving their children are anxious about them.

--- - ---

LESSON XXXVII.

THE PASSIVE VERB. In English the "past participle" is also the *passive participle,* employed to form the "passive voice" or passive verb-phrases : *I am carried; I was carried; I shall be carried.*

In Bohemian there is a special "passive participle", ending in **n** (**na** in the feminine, **no** is the neutre gender, — **ni, ny, na** in the plural), by which the passive voice of transitive verbs is formed :

Jsem nesen, *sem nessĕn* (**nesena,** *nessĕná* f.. **neseno,** *nessĕnŏ* n.), I am carried; **jsme neseni, y, a,** *smĕ nesseñi,* we are carried;

byl jsem nesen, *bill sem nessĕn,* I was carried;

budu nesen, *budŭ nessĕn,* I shall be carried.

*) **Padnouti,** *pádnouťi,* to fall; **upadnouti,** *upádnouťi,* to fall down. As repeatedly stated in preceding lessons, the colloquial usage drops the final **i** of the infinitive, and the letter **t** has its ordinary hard sound: *pádnout, upádnout.*

Jsem viděn, *sem viďen,* I am seen; | **jsem volán,** *sem volín,* I am called;
jsem učen, *sem účhen,* I am taught; | **jsem milován,** *sem millován,* I am loved.

The passive participle of verbs of the first conjugation ending in **íti,** and of verbs of the second conjugation (ending in **outi**) terminates in **it** and **ut;** for instance, — **bíti, minouti** (to beat, to pass):

Jsem bit, *sem bit,* I am beat (whipped or punished); **byl jsem bit,** I was beat; **budu bit,** I shall be beat ;

jsem minut, *sem minůt,* I am passed; **byl jsem minut,** I was passed; **budu minut,** I shall be passed.

The imperative of the passive voice is expressed in Bohemian by **ať,** which is already familiar to the student as an equivalent of the English "let":

Ať jsem nesen, a, o,	*ať sem nessěn,*	let me be carried;
ať jsem bit, a, o,	*ať sem bit,*	let me be whipped;
ať jsem volán, a, o,	*ať sem volín,*	let me be called;
ať jsem milován, a, o,	*ať sem milován,*	let me be loved.

In English the past or passive participle is often used as an adjective; for example : "An *invited* guest."

In Bohemian every passive participle may be changed into an adjective by adding **ý** (and changing **a** into **á** in the feminine, **o** into **é** in the neutre gender). For instance :

nesen, a, o : nesený, á, é, carried | **viděn, a, o : viděný, á, é,** seen
bit, a, o : bitý, á, é, beaten | **volán, a, o : volaný, á, é,** called
minut, a, o : minutý, á, é, passed | **milován, a, o : milovaný, á, é,** loved, beloved.

In the termination **án, ána, áno** the long vowel **á** is shortened when the participle changes into an adjective :

volán m., **volána** f. **voláno,** n. } called (as past participle and adjective).
volaný m. **volaná** f. **volané,** n.

POTENTIAL FORMS.

The potential mood employing the auxiliary *may* is formed in Bohemian by means of the verb **moci,** *motsi* (commonly **mocti,** vulgarly **moct,** *mŏtst*), which has an irregular inflection :

Mohu,	*mŏhŭ,*	I may	**můžeme,**	*moožĕmĕ,*	we may
můžeš,	*moožexh,*	thou mayest	**můžete,**	*moožĕtĕ,*	you may
může,	*moožĕ,*	he (she, it) may	**mohou,**	*mŏhoŭ,*	they may;

mohl, (a, o) bych,	*mŏhl, (ŭ, ŏ) bikh,*	I might	**mohli, (y, a) bychom**	(or **bysme**), *mŏhli bixmĕ,*	we might
mohl bys,	*mŏhl bis,*	thou mightest	**mohli byste,**	*m. bistĕ,*	you might
mohl by,	*mŏhl bi,*	he might	**mohli by,**	*m. bi,*	they might.

Mohu býti nesen, I may be carried **mohl bych býti nesen,** I might be carried

mohu býti bit, I may be whipped **mohl bych býti bit,** I might be whipped

mohu býti viděn, I may be seen **mohl bych býti viděn,** I might be seen

mohu býti milován, I may be loved **mohl bych býti milován,** I might be loved.

Mohl jsem býti nesen, *mŏhl xem beeťi nesxĕn,* I might have been carried;

mohl jsem býti bit, *mŏhl xem beeťi bit,* I might have been whipped.

Otherwise **moci** has the meaning of "can" or "to be able":

Mohu to udělati; — nemohu to udělati;	I can do it; — I cannot do it;
mohl jsem to udělati; — nemohl jsem to udělati;	I could do it (or: I could have done it); — I could not do it;
budu moci to udělati; — nebudu moci to udělati.	I shall be able to do it; — I shall not be able to do it;
Můžete přijíti? — Nemůžeme přijíti.	Can you come? — We cannot come.
Mohou choditi? — Nemohou choditi.	Can they walk? —They cannot walk.

In common discourse **mohu** (I can), and **mohou** (they can) are displaced by **můžu** and **můžou**, *moožŭ, moožoŭ*, making the present tense consistent, if not regular.

REITERATIVE FORM.

The English reiterative form of "used to" is rendered in Bohemian:

1. — By reiterative verbs derived from simple verbs as explained in Note

5, Lesson XIII; for instance : **hráti** means "to play"; **hrávati** means "to play often", to use to play ;

hrál jsem tam; hrával jsem tam; — hráli tam; hrávali tam.	I played there; I used to play there; — they played there; they used to play there.

2. — By verbs having in themselves a reiterative meaning; for instance : **přicházeti,** *prshikházěťi,* means "to come often" (also 'to be coming"); **docházeti,** *dŏkházěťi,* means "to go often somewhere", to make frequent calls, (also "to be on the decline");

on přichází k nám; on přicházel k nám; — my docházeli k němu; budeme docházeti k němu.	he often comes to us; he used to come to us; — we used to go to him; we shall often go to him.

LESSON XXXVIII.

English participles may be used substantively, or changed into nouns; for instance :

speaking, — *the speaking;* sitting, — *the sitting;* calling, — *the calling.*

In Bohemian, nouns are derived from verbs in two different ways, illustrated by the following examples :

1.

bíti,	*beeťi,*	to beat; —	**bití,**	*biťee,*	the beating;
píti,	*peeťi,*	to drink; —	**pití,**	*piťee,*	the drinking;
šíti,	*sheeťi,*	to sew; —	**šití,**	*shiťee,*	the sewing;
žíti,	*žeeťi,*	to live; —	**žití,**	*žiťee,*	the living;
bod-nouti,	*bodnoŭťi,*	to stab; —	**bod-nutí,**	*bodnŭťee,*	the stabbing, a stab;
hyn-outi,	*hinoŭťi,*	to be perishing; —	**hyn-utí,**	*hinŭťee,*	the perishing;
kop-nouti,	*kopnoŭťi,*	to kick; —	**kop-nutí,**	*kopnŭťee,*	the kicking, a kick;

2.

nes-ti,	*nesstʼi,*	to carry; —	nes-ení,	*nesseñee,*	the carrying;
pás-ti,	*pástʼi,*	to herd; —	pas-ení,	*pǎsseñee,*	the herding;
vid-ěti,	*vidʼetʼi,*	to see; —	vid-ění,	*vidʼeñee,*	the seeing; the vision;
slyš-eti,	*slishětʼi,*	to hear; —	slyš-ení,	*slishěñee,*	the hearing;
mluv-iti,	*mlǔvitʼi,*	to speak; —	mluv-ení,	*mlǔvěñee,*	the speaking;
vol-ati,	*volátʼi,*	to call; —	vol-ání,	*volǎñee,*	the calling or call,
milov-ati,	*milovátʼi,*	to love; —	milov-ání,	*milǒváñee,*	the loving.

The simple rules of derivation are apparent from the above list.

1. Verbs terminating in **íti** (forming a subdivision of the first conjugation; Note 3, p. 138;) are changed into nouns by a simple transfer of the long **í** : **píti,** to drink, — **pití.** the drinking.

2. Verbs ending in **outi** (which belong to the second conjugation) become nouns by a change of this termination into **uti** : **bodnouti,** to stab, (**bodnu,** I shall stab), — **bodnutí,** the stabbing, or "a stab".

3. Verbs ending in **ěti, eti, iti** (which form the third and fourth conjugations) become nouns by changing their termination into **ění** or **ení** : **viděti,** to see, — **vidění,** the seeing, or "the vision"; **mluviti,** to speak, — **mluvení,** the speaking.

4. Verbs ending in **ati** (which form the fifth and sixth conjugations) become nouns by changing that termination into **ání** : **volati,** to call, — **volání,** the calling, or "the call".

When the long vowel **á** occurs in the root of a simple verb, it is shortened in the process of deriving a noun :

pás-ti, *pástʼi,* to herd (or "to pasture"); **pas-ení,** *pǎsseñee,* the herding; **psá-ti,** *psátʼi,* to write; **psa-ní,** *psáñee,* the writing.

In some cases the derivation of nouns from verbs of the first conjugation is somewhat irregular, the same as the formation of the tenses; for instance :

čísti, *cheesťi*, to read; (čtu, čteš, čte, *chtŭ, chtĕsh, chtŏ,* I read, thou readest, he reads); — čte-ní, *chtĕñee,* the reading;

plesti, *plesťi,* to twist; (pletu, pleteš, plete, I twist, thou twistest, he twists); — plete-ní, *plĕtĕñee,* the twisting;

klásti, *klásťi,* to lay; (kladu, kladeš, klade, I lay, thou layest, he lays); — klade-ní, *klŭdĕñee,* the laying;

másti, *másťi,* to confuse (to mix up); mate, he confuses; — matení, *mŭtĕñee,* the confusion or mixing up;

mesti, *mesťi,* to sweep; mete, he sweeps;—metení, *mĕtĕñee,* the sweeping;

vesti, *vessťi,* to lead; vede, he leads; — vedení, *vĕdĕñes,* the leading.

LESSON XXXIX.

VERBS CLASSIFIED.

1. — As before observed (in Lesson XXXI) nesti, "to carry" or "to be carrying", is a verb denoting a CONTINUOUS action.

2. — By means of prefixes other verbs are derived therefrom, which denote a limited or FINISHED action and are called FINITE verbs; for example :

donesti, *dŏnessťi,* to carry somewhere or to somebody ;
přinesti, *prshinessťi,* to bring, to fetch.

3. — Many continuous verbs have a corresponding form denoting a REPEATED or reiterated action; for instance :

nesti,	*nessťi,*	to carry;	nositi,	*nossiťi,*	to carry repeatedly;
vezti,	*vezťi,* to carry (in a vehicle);		voziti,	*voziťi,*	" "
vesti,	*vessťi,*	to lead;	voditi,	*voďiťi,*	to lead repeatedly;
čísti,	*cheessťi,*	to read;	čítati,	*cheetŭťi,*	to read repeatedly;
pásti,	*pássťi,*	to herd;	pásati,	*pássŭťi,*	to herd repeatedly;
letěti,	*letĕťi,*	to fly;	lítati,	*leetŭťi,*	to fly repeatedly;
jeti,	*yeťi,*	to ride;	jezditi,	*yezďiťi,*	to ride repeatedly.

There are, besides, reiterative verbs derived in the manner explained in Note 5, page 61, and denoting so to say a CUSTOMARY action; for instance:

nositi,	to carry repeatedly,	nosí-va-ti, *nosseevat'i,* to use to carry,
voziti,	to carry repeatedly (in a vehicle),	vozí-va-ti, *vozeevat'i,* to use to carry,
voditi,	to lead repeatedly,	vodí-va-ti, *vod'eevat'i,* to use to lead,
čítati,	to read repeatedly,	čítá-va-ti, *cheetávat'i,* to use to read,
pásati,	to herd repeatedly,	pásá-va-ti, *pássávat'i,* to use to herd,
lítati,	to fly repeatedly,	lítá-va-ti, *leetávat'i,* to use to fly,
jezditi,	to ride repeatedly;	jezdí-va-ti, *yezd'eevat'i,* to use to ride.

4. — Certain verbs denote an action which is simply MOMENTARY. As a rule they terminate in **iti**, belonging to the fourth conjugation. For instance: **skočiti,** *skŏchit'i,* to jump, to leap, — that is, to make a jump or leap.

From these are derived FINITE verbs in the same manner as from continuous verbs (1.), namely by prefixes. For instance :

kročiti,	to make a step,	zakročiti,	*zakrŏchit'i,*	to step between, to interfere;
skočiti,	to jump,	vyskočiti,	*viskŏchit'i,*	to jump out *or* up;
střeliti,	to shoot (once),	zastřeliti,	*zastrshellit'i,*	to shoot dead;
strčiti,	to push,	vystrčiti,	*vistˀrchit'i,*	to push out;
pustiti,	to let go,	vypustiti,	*vipŭst'iti,*	to let out;
chytiti,	to catch,	zachytiti,	*zakhit'it'i,*	to catch up, to snatch;
chybiti,	to err,	pochybiti,	*pŏkhibit'i,*	to commit an error.

Note 1. Such is the general classification of Bohemian verbs in regard to the duration of the action or process they denote. But for practical purposes it is sufficient to distinguish two great classes of verbs, namely:

1. CONTINUOUS VERBS, denoting a continued or repeated action. This class comprises the simple verbs of all conjugations except some ending in **outi** and **iti**. For instance: **nesti,** to carry; **plouti,** to float; **viděti,** to see; **činiti,** to do; **volati,** to call; **milovati,** to love.

2. FINITE VERBS, denoting a finished or momentary action or process. This class comprises many verbs of the second and fourth conjuga-

tions, ending in **ou⁴i** and **iti;** for instance: **minouti,** to pass; **bodnouti,** to stab; **skočiti,** to leap; **střeliti,** to shoot (to discharge a shot).

Most of the verbs derived from others by prefixes also belong to this class; for example: **vyskočiti,** to jump up; **donesti,** to carry somewhere; **pominouti,** to pass over; **uviděti,** to catch a sight; **učiniti,** to do a certain act; **zavolati,** to call out or up; **pomilovati,** to fondle a little.

The finite verbs have in fact only a past and a future tense, and no present, because their present *form* denotes a *future action:*

donesu, I shall carry somewhere;	**uvidím,** I shall see:
minu, I shall pass ;	**učiním,** I shall do;
udělám, I shall make;	**skočím,** I shall jump;
zavolám, I shall call;	**vyskočím,** I shall jump up;
pomiluju (or **pomiluji**) I shall fondle;	**střelím,** I shall shoot.

LESSON XL.

Every language has peculiar ways or modes of expression, which cannot be taken literally, or translated closely into another language. They are called idiomatic expressions or IDIOMS. Many of them are of frequent occurrence in ordinary intercourse.

The student will naturally desire to know the Bohemian equivalents of such English expressions as are in constant use in common conversation. He will find most of them in the following list, the English expression always preceding the Bohemian, in order to facilitate their study. The beginner should often peruse these phrases until he has a perfect command of them, or — to use an English idiom — until "he has them at his fingers' ends."

All along,	**venkoncem, veskrze,**	*venkŏntsĕm, veskᵉrzĕ;*
all over,	**všude,**	*vshŭdĕ;*
all is over,	**je po všem,**	*yĕ pofshĕm;*
all in all,	**vůbec,**	*voobets;*
all one,	**vše jedno,**	*fshĕ yednŏ;*
all the same,	" "	" "

all the time,	stále, pořád,	*stáľ, pŏrsháď;*
all the better,	tím líp,	*ťecm leep;*
all hollow,	na dobro,	*nă dŏbrŏ;*
all of a sudden,	najednou, z nenadání,	*nădyednoŭ, znĕnădáñi;*
along-side,	vedle,	*vĕdlĕ;*
as far as I can,	pokud mohu,	*pŏkăd mŏhŭ;*
as far as possible,	pokud možná,	*pŏkăd možná;*
as far as I am concerned	co se mě týče,	*tsŏ sĕ myĕ tcechĕ;*
as far as that is concerned,	co se toho týče,	*tsŏ sĕ tŏhŏ teechĕ;*
at any rate, at all events,	} buď jak buď,	*băď yăk băď;*
at last, at length,	} konečně,	*kŏnechñĕ;*
at once, all at once,	} hned, najednou,	*hnĕd, nădyednoŭ;*
at large,	vůbec, celkem,	*voobets, tselkem.*

Be it as it may,	buď jak buď; ať je jakkoli;	*băď yăk băď; ăť yĕ yăkkoli;*
be perfectly easy,	buďte bez starosti,	*băďtĕ bestărŏsťi;*
by and by,	hnedle, znenáhla,	*hnedlĕ, znĕnáhlă;*
by the bye,	} mimo to,	*mimŏ tŏ,*
by the way,	} apropos,	*ăpropo;*
by day,	za dne,	*ză dnĕ;*
by night,	v noci,	*vnotsi;*
by the day,	na den,	*nă den;*
by the week,	na týden,	*nă teeden;*
by the piece,	od kusu,	*ŏd kăsŭ;*
by all means,	na všechen spůsob,	*nă fshĕkhen spoosob.*

Call for me,	stavte se pro mě,	*stăftĕ sĕ pro myĕ;*
can it be possible?	je-li možná?	*yelli možná?*
can't do it!	nejde to!	*nĕydĕ tŏ!*

| come on, come along, | } pojď ! pojďte ! | *poyď, poyďtě*);* |
| come and see us, | přijďte nás navštívit, | *prshiďtě nás náfshťee-vit.* |

Don't you hear?	což neslyšíte?	*tsŏsh něslisheetě ?*
don't you see ?	což nevidíte?	*tsŏsh něviďeetě ?*
don't you know it?	což to nevíte?	*tsŏsh tŏ něveetě ?*
don't mention it !	to nestojí za řeč,	*tŏ nestoyee zá rshěch;*
dear me !	o jemine !	*o yěmině !*
day and night,	ve dne v noci,	*vě dně vnotsi;*
day by day,	den co den,	*den tsŏ den;*
do as you please,	dělejte jak myslíte,	*ďěleytě yák misleetě;*
drop me a line,	pište mi pár řádek,	*pishtě me pár rsháděk.*

Excuse me !	odpusťte !	*odpůstě!*
every now and then,	každou chvíli,	*káždoŭ khweeli;*
Farewell !	} s bohem!—na zdar !	*sbŏhem ! — ná zdár !*
Good-bye !		
get up !	zhůru !—vstaňte !	*zhoorů !—fstáňtě!*
get out !	ven !—pojďte ven !	*ven !—pŏďtě ven !*
get ready !	připravte se !	*prshipráftě sě !*
give me a rest !	dejte mi pokoj !	*deytě me pŏkoy !*
go ahead !	} jen dál !	*yen dál !*
go on !		

Help yourself !	poslužte si ! vemte si ! račte !	*poslůshtě si ! vemtě si ! ráchtě!*
here and there,	sem tam,	*sem tăm,*
hurry up !	honem !	*hŏnem !*
he is good at it !	on to umí ! on to zná !	*ŏn tŏ ŭmee ! ŏn tŏ zná!*

*) Colloquially *pŏď, pŏďtě,* (thou, you) come on. — **I pojďte už !** *i pŏďtě ŭsh!* come on, now! do come along!

he is good for nothing;	není k ničemu;	neyňi kňichěmú;
he is on the lookout;	on číhá;	ǒn cheehá;
he is well off;	on se má dobře;	ǒn sě má dǒbrshě;
he means no harm;	on to zle nemyslí;	ǒn tǒ zlě němislee;
he took a hint;	dovtípil se;	dǒfťeepil sě;
he keeps out of sight;	on se straní;	ǒn sě strāňee;
he has a head of his own;	on má vlastní hlavu;	ǒn má vlástňee hlǎvǔ;
how do you do ?	} jak se máte ?	yǎk sě mátě?
how are you ?		

I am glad of it!	to mě těší!	tǒ myě ťěshee!
I bet, — I guess,	vsadím se, — myslím,	fsǎďeem sě, — misleem,
I don't care;	nedbám; to je mi jedno;	nědbám; tǒ yě mi yednǒ
I have a mind,	hodlám,	hodlám,
I made up my mind,	odhodlal jsem se,	ǒdhodlǎl sem sě,
I can't afford it;	nejsem s to;	neysem stǒ;
I can't stand it (meaning: I hate it);	nemohu to vystát (vystáti);	němǒhǔ tǒ vistát;
I can do without it;	mohu být bez toho;	mǒhǔ beet bes tǒhǒ;
I have taken a fancy to it;	zalíbilo se mi to;	zǎleebilǒ sě mi tǒ;
I have no hand in it;	nemám s tím co dělat;	němám sťeem tsǒ ďělǎt;
I had some words with him;	měl jsem s ním hádku;	myěl sem sňim hádkǔ;
I had rather	} raději bych	rǎďěy bikh
I would sooner		
I am no match for him;	já s něho nejsem;	yá sňěho neysem;
I am very anxious;	mám starost;*) — tuze rád bych**)	mám stǎrost; — toozě rád bikh;
I am sorry for it;	lituju toho;	litǔyǔ tǒhǒ;
I will make him do it;	já ho donutím;	yá hǒ dǒnǔťeem;

*) When it means an anxiety, care or suspense about something.
**) When it means an impatience to do or to know something.

I will see you paid;	postarám se o váš plat;	*postārám sě o vāsh plāt;*
I am in no hurry;	nemám na spěch;	*němám nā spyěkh;*
I must be off;	musím pryč;	*mūseem prich;*
I think much of him;	já si ho moc vážím;	*yā si hŏ mots vāžeem;*
if you please;	prosím; — račte;	*proscem; — rāchtě;*
indeed;	opravdu; — skutečně;	*oprāvdū; — skŭtechñě;*
it is all over;	je po všem;	*yě pofshem;*
it is of no use;	není to nic platné (*meaning:* it will do no good); — není to k ničemu (*meaning:* it is of no service);	*neyñi tŏ ñits plātné; — neyñi tŏ kñichěmŭ;*
it is none of your busi-nes;	vám po tom nic není;	*vám pŏ tŏm ñits neyñi;*
it is your turn;	teď je na vás;	*teď yě nā vāss;*
it is a bargain;	zůstane při tom;	*zoostāně prshitŏm;*
it is a pity;	to je škoda;	*tŏ yě shkŏdā;*
it grew into a habit;	stalo se zvykem;	*stālo sě zwikem;*
it wears well (of a dress or stuff);	dobře se nese;	*dobrshě sě nessě;*

Keep still! keep in line!	Ticho!—Buďte zticha! do řady!	*ťikhŏ! — bŭďtě sťikhā! dŏ rshādy!*
Let it go; — let go!	nechte to být; — pusťte!	*nekhtě tŏ beet; — pŭstě!*
let me alone;	nechte mě;	*nekhtě myě;*
let me in;	pusťte mě tam;	*pŭstě myě tām;*
let me know;	dejte mi vědět;	*deytě me vyěďět;*
look here;	hleďte;	*hleďtě;*
look out!	pozor!	*pŏzor!*
Mind you;	pamatujte;	*pāmātŭytě;*
No doubt;— no matter;	zajisté; — nic nedělá;	*zāyisté; — ñits něďělá;*
no matter how it is;	ať je to jakkoli;	*ať yě tŏ yāckŏli;*
no matter who it is;	ať je to kdokoli;	*ať yě tŏ gdŏkŏli;*
never mind;	nic nedělá; — co na tom;	*ñits něďělá; — tsŏ nā tŏm;*

not yet; — not at all;	ještě ne, — dokonce ne;	*yeshťě ně; — dŏkontsě ně;*
now and then;	časem, — chvílemi;	*chăssem; — khweelemi,*
now we are even;	teď jsme kvit;	*teď smě kwit;*
Of course;	ovšem; — to se rozumí;	*ofshěm; — tŏ sě rozŭmee;*
on a sudden;	náhle; — z nenadání;	*náhlě; — zněnădáñi;*
on purpose;	schválně; — naschvál.	*skhwálñě; — náskhwál;*
on the contrary;	naopak;	*năopăk;*
on the wing;	v letu;	*vletŭ;*
once for all;	jednou na vždy;	*yednoŭ nă vždy;*
one by one;	po jednom; — jeden za druhým;	*pŏ yědnom; — yěden ză drŭheem;*
Piece by piece;	po·kusu;	*pŏ kŭsŭ;*
plenty time!	dost času!	*dost chăssŭ!*
Send me word:	zkažte mi;	*skăshtě me;*
served him right!	dobře tak!	*dobrshě tăk!*
Take care!	pozor! — dejte pozor!	*pŏzor! — deytě pŏzor!*
the more the better;	čím víc tím líp;	*cheem veets ťeem leep;*
the other day;	onehdy;	*ŏněhdy;*
the time is up;	čas prošel;	*chăss proshell;*
that's it! — that will do;	to je to! — to je dost; to dostačí;	*tŏ yě tŏ; — tŏ yě dost; tŏ dŏstăchee;*
that's right!	to je dobře!	*tŏ yě dobrshě!*
that is out of my way;	to je mi z ruky;	*tŏ yě me z rŭky;*
they like to show off;	rádi se ukazují;	*ráďi sě ŭkăzŭyee;*
to be short about it;	krátce řečeno;	*krátsě rhěchěnŏ;*
to be sure!	zajisté!	*ză̆yisté!*
to call and see, (to pay a visit);	navštívit;	*năfshťeevit;*
to find fault;	vytýkat;	*vyteekăt;*
to get rid (of something);	zbavit se (čeho);	*zbăvit sě;*
to give a blowing;	vymluvit,	*vymlŭvit;*
to come about;	státi se,	*státi sě;*
to no purpose;	zbytečně.	*zbytěchñě;*

Well?— Very well.	nuže? — dobře;	*nŭžĕ? — dŏbrshĕ;*
well to do, well off;	zámožný,	*zámožnee;*
what of that? — what does it matter?	co na tom? co z toho?	*tsŏ nă tom? tsŏ stŏhŏ?*
what is the matter?	co se děje? (i. e. what is happening?)	*tsŏ sĕ ďĕyĕ?*
what is the question?	oč se jedná? oč běží?	*ŏch sĕ yednă?—ŏch byĕžee?*
what is the matter with you?	co je vám?	*tsŏ yĕ vám?*
what next?	co dále?	*tsŏ dálĕ?*
what will become of us?	co z nás bude? co se s námi stane?	*tsŏ znáss bŭdĕ? tsŏ sĕ snámi stănĕ?*
we had better go;	abysme raději šli;	*ăbysmĕ răďĕy shli;*
we had better go and see;	abysme se raději podívali (i. e. šli podívati);	*ăbysmĕ sĕ răďĕy poďeevăli;*

You are right;	máte pravdu;	*mátĕ prăvdŭ;*
you are wrong, you are mistaken;	} mejlíte se;	*meyleetĕ sĕ;*
you are late;	jdete pozdě;	*dĕtĕ pozďĕ;*
you are safe;	jste v tom dobře;	*stĕ ftom dŏbrshĕ;*
you are gone up!	s vámi je konec!	*svámi yĕ kŏnets!*
you are welcome to it;	vemte si to; — přeju vám to;	*vemtĕ si tŏ; — prshĕyŭ vám tŏ;*
year by year;	rok co rok;	*rŏk tsŏ rŏk;*
you must not find fault;	nesmíte dělat výčitky;	*nesmeetĕ ďĕlăt veechitky;*
you ought to be glad; — you ought to be gone;	měl byste být (or býti) rád;—měl byste být pryč;	*m'yell bystĕ beet rád; — m'yell bystĕ beet prich.*

PART III.

~~~~~~~~

Bohemian Conversation.

———

Note 1. In the following conversations we shall invariably observe the common rule of politeness, which requires the use of the personal pronoun **vy** (you) in addressing another person. Hence all verbs employed in the same will appear in the second person plural (for instance: **jste, máte,** (you are, you have), and not in the second person singular **jsi*),** **máš,** (thou art, thou hast), which is properly confined to familiar or very intimate intercourse, as fully set forth in Section 9, Part I; otherwise the use of the second person singular (**ty,** thou) is out of place and in fact vulgar, although freely indulged in by some ill-informed or ill-bred persons among the Bohemians in America.

Throughout these conversations we give the Bohemian pronunciation in full**). It is true that the student, having advanced so far, may be supposed to be able to pronounce every word and to read Bohemian without difficulty; but the pronouncing column will nevertheless continue to be an aid, especially welcome in such cases as may appear to be somewhat obscure or doubtful.

———

*) In common discourse we frequently hear **ty jseš,** *ty sěsh,* in place of **ty jsi.** — **Ty jseš velký,** *ty sěsh velkee,* thou art tall. — **Jseš rád** (instead of **jsi rád)?** *sěsh rád?* art thou glad? — **Jseš zdráv?** *sesh zdráf?* (f. **jseš zdráva?** *sěsh zdráva?*) art thou well? — **Jseš hotov?** *sěsh hŏtof?* (f. **jseš hotova?** *sěsh hŏtŏva?*) art thou ready?

**) The rules given in Sections 2 and 4, Part I, are supposed to have been thoroughly digested and practiced by the student, as well as the forty introductory lessons contained in Part II. Unless that is done, it will be useless and disappointing to proceed with this eminently practical part of our Bohemian Course.

In regard to the pronunciation of Bohemian infinitives (for instance: **míti,** to have; **činiti,** to do; **dělati,** to make) we again remind the student of the explanation given in Note 1, Lesson XI. In the pronouncing column of these conversations we shall as a rule follow the colloquial custom of dropping the final **i,** to simplify matters and to present the sentences as they are generally heard in actual intercourse.

The student will always bear in mind that Bohemian orthography and pronunciation are on the whole governed by the rule which appears to be the ideal of many would-be reformers of English orthography, namely:

A sound for every letter and a letter for every sound, and no silent letters. —

In regard to capital letters the rules in Bohemian are the same as in English, excepting that adjectives derived from names of nations or countries are not written with a capital letter; for example: English, Bohemian, European, **anglický, český, evropský** (*ănglitskee, chesskee, ĕvropskee*).

Bohemian and English.
ČEŠTINA a ANGLIČINA.

The Bohemian language;—the Bohemian tongue.	**Česká řeč; — český jazyk.**	*chesská rshĕch;—chesskee yăzyk.*
Do you know Bohemian? — do you speak Bohemian?	**Umíte česky? — mluvíte česky?**	*ŭmeetĕ chesske? — mlŭveetĕ chesske?*
Yes, I speak Bohemian well.	**Ano, mluvím česky dobře.**	*ănŏ, mlŭveem chesske dŏbrshĕ.*
Do you speak English?	**Mluvíte anglicky?**	*mlŭveetĕ ănglitske?*
Perfectly ;— a little; — not much.	**Dokonale; — trochu; — ne mnoho.**	*dŏkŏnălĕ; — trokhŭ; — nĕ mnŏhŏ.*
Do you understand English? — I do.	**Rozumíte anglicky? — Rozumím.**	*rozŭmeetĕ ănglitske? — rozŭmeem.*

In America everybody has to know English.	V Americe každý má u- měti*) anglicky.	*vámeritsě každee má ů- myet ánglitske.*
I am learning English.	Učím se anglicky.	*ůcheem sě ánglitske.*
Do you learn Bohemian?	Učíte se česky?	*ůcheetě sě chesske?*
I want to learn Bohemian.	Chci se učiti česky.	*khtsi sě ůchit chesske.*
I want to know (i.e. to acquire) Bohemian.	Chci uměti česky.	*khtsi ůmyet chesske.*
I would like to learn Bohemian.	Rád bych učil se čes- ky.	*rád bikh ůchil sě chess- ke.*
I would like to know Bohemian.	Rád bych uměl česky.	*rád bikh ůmyell chess- ke.*
I must learn (i. e. ac- quire) Bohemian.	Musím se naučiti čes- ky.	*můseem sě náůchit chesske.*
Yes, do learn Bohemian I am learning Bohemi- an.	Ano, naučte se česky. Učím se česky.	*áno, náůchtě sě chesske ůcheem sě chesske.*
How long have you been learning**) Bo- hemian?	Jak dlouho učíte se česky?	*yák dloůhö ůcheetě sě chesske?*
I have been learning Bohemian since last year.	Učím se česky od lou- ska.	*ůcheem sě chesske öd lonská.*
How long did you learn English?	Jak dlouho učil jste se anglicky?	*yák dlöůhö ůchil stě sě ánglitske?*
I learned (or: I was learning) English one year.	Učil jsem se anglicky rok.	*ůchil sem sě ánglitske rök.*

---

*) **Míti** (to have) often in connection with another verb signifies obligation or necessity, the same as in English: **Mám uměti,** I have to know, I am obliged or expected to know; **mám jíti,** I have to go; — **má uměti,** he has to know; **každý má uměti,** everybody has to know.

) The present tense in Bohemian is also used for the English per- fect tense: **(jak dlouho) učíte se, — (how long) have you been learning. See second foot-note on page 98.

I learned (i. e. acquired) English in one year.	Naučil jsem se anglicky za rok.	*năŭchil sem sě ănglitske ză rŏk.*
To learn English is not difficult.	Naučiti se anglicky není těžké.	*năŭchit sě ănglitske neyñi ťěshké.*
Neither is Bohemian.	Česky také ne.	*chesske tăké ně.*
How soon shall I learn Bohemian?	Jak brzo naučím se česky?	*yăk bᵉrzo năŭcheem sě chesske?*
If you will be (*or* if you are) diligent, you will learn it soon.	Budete-li pilný, naučíte se brzo.	*bŭdětě-li pilnee, năŭcheetě sě bᵉrzŏ.*
About how soon?	Jak brzo asi?	*yăk bᵉrzŏ ăsi?*
In a few months.	Za pár měsíců.	*ză pár myěseetsoo.*
I have been learning Bohemian only two months, and already I know a good deal.	Učím se česky teprv dva měsíce, a už umím hezky.	*ŭcheem sě chesske tepᵉrf dwă myěseetsě, ă ŭsh ŭmeem hesske.*
I am getting along well.	Jde to dobře.*)	*dě tŏ dobrshě.*
Already I understand nearly all.	Už rozumím skoro všecko.	*ŭsh rozŭmeem skŏrŏ fshětskŏ.*
It is not difficult; — it is easy.	Není to těžké; — je to lehké.	*neyñi tŏ ťěshké; — yě tŏ lehké.*
Only plenty of exercise! then you make good progress.	Jen hodně cviku! pak to jde*)!	*yen hodñě tswikŭ! păk tŏ dě!*
Do you understand Bohemian?	Rozumíte česky?	*rozŭmeetě chesske?*
I understand a little.	Rozumím trochu.	*rozŭmeem trokhŭ.*
I understand already a good deal.	Rozumím už hodně.	*rozŭmeem ŭsh hodñě.*
I understand already nearly all.	Rozumím už hnedle všecko.	*rozŭmeem ŭsh hnedlě fshětsko.*
Do you understand German?	Rozumíte německy?	*rozŭmeetě ñěmetske?*

---

*) **Jde to dobře**; *literally:* it goes well. **Pak to jde:** then it goes.

I do not.—I understand a little bit.	Nerozumím. — Rozumím něco málo.	něrozŭmeem. — rozŭmeem ñětsŏ málŏ.
Do you know (how) to write Bohemian?	Umíte psáti po česku?	ŭmeete psát pŏ chesskŭ?
Not yet; but I shall learn (it).	Ještě ne; ale budu se učiti.	yeshťě ně; ǎlě bŭdŭ sě ŭchit.
I shall know (it) soon.	Budu uměti brzo.	bŭdŭ ŭmyet berzŏ.
I must know both to read and to write Bohemian.	Musím uměti čísti i psáti po česku.	mŭseem ŭmyet cheest i psát pŏ chesskŭ.
You will learn that easily.	To se naučíte snadno.	tŏ sě nǎŭcheetě snǎdnŏ.
I expect to learn it in half a year.	Hodlám se to naučiti za půl leta.	hodlám sě tŏ nǎŭchit zǎ pool letǎ.
Why does not John learn English?	Proč se Jan neučí anglicky?	prŏch sě yǎn něŭchee ǎnglitske?
He is going to learn;—he must learn it well.	On se bude učiti;—musí se naučiti dobře.	ŏn se bŭdě ŭchit;— musee sě nǎŭchit dobrshě.
When will he commence to learn?	Kdy se začne učiti?	gdy sě zǎchně ŭchit?
Shortly.	Co nevidět.	tsŏ něviďět.
My neighbor's boy speaks English perfectly and understands also Latin.	Sousedův hoch mluví anglicky dokonale a rozumí také latinsky.	soŭsedoof hŏkh mlŭvee ǎnglitske dŏkonǎlě ǎ rozŭmee tǎké lǎťinske.
Annie is learning to read and write Bohemian.	Anna učí se česky čísti a psáti.	ǎnǎ ŭchee sě chesske cheest a psát.
Have you a Bohemian newspaper? — lend me it.	Máte české noviny?— půjčte mi je.	mátě chesské nŏviny? — pŭchtě me yě.
Lend me a Bohemian book.	Půjčte mi českou knihu.	pŭchtě me chesskoŭ kñihŭ.
What book? — Any book.	Jakou? — Jakoukoli.	yǎkoŭ? — yǎkoŭkoli.

This is Bohemian, is it not?	Tohle je česky, není?	tŏhlĕ yĕ chesske, neyňi?
What is it in English? — Tell me it in English.	Co je to po anglicku? — Povězte mi to po anglicku.	tsŏ yĕ tŏ pŏ ănglitskŭ? — Pŏvyĕztĕ me tŏ pŏ ănglitskŭ.
How is it in English?	Jak je to po anglicku?	yăk yĕ tŏ pŏ ănglitskŭ?
I don't know how to pronounce it.	Nevím jak to vysloviti.	nĕveem yăk tŏ vislŏvit.
How is it in Bohemian?	Jak je to po česku?	yăk yĕ tŏ pŏ chesskŭ?
How do you call it in Bohemian?— how in English?	Jak se to jmenuje česky? — jak anglicky?	yăk sĕ tŏ menŭyĕ chesske? — yăk ănglitske?
Speak Bohemian; — speak Bohemian with me;— speak only Bohemian.	Mluvte česky;— mluvte se mnou česky; — mluvte jenom česky.	mlŭftĕ chesske;— mlŭftĕ sĕ mnoŭ chesske;— mlŭftĕ yĕnom chesske.
Speak as you wish.	Mluvte jak chcete.	mlŭftĕ yăk khtsĕtĕ.
Do you like to speak Bohemian? — Why do you not speak English?	Mluvíte rád česky? — Proč nemluvíte anglicky?	mlŭveetĕ rád chesske? — prŏch nĕmlŭveetĕ ănglitske?
Because I cannot;— because I know it only a little. — Do speak; you will get along.	Protože neumím; — protože umím jen málo.-- Jen mluvte, půjde to.	protŏžĕ nĕŭmeem; — protŏžĕ ŭmeem yen málŏ. — yen mlŭftĕ, pŭdĕ tŏ.
Speak English or Bohemian,as you please; — I understand both;	Mluvte anglicky nebo česky, jak chcete; — rozumím obojí.	mlŭftĕ ănglitske nĕbŏ chesske, yăk khtsĕtĕ; — rozŭmĕem ŏbŏyee.
You speak Bohemian very well.	Vy mluvíte česky tuze dobře.	ve mlŭveetĕ chesske toozĕ dobrshĕ.
Speak slowly, that I may understand you.*)	Mluvte pomalu, abych vám rozuměl.	mlŭftĕ pomălŭ, ăbikh vám rozŭmyell.

*) **Abych, abys, aby,** that I should, that thou shouldst, that he should (see Lesson XXXVI), also signifies: "that I may, that thou mayest, that he (she, it) may". Hence we translate: **abych rozuměl,** that I may understand;—**abych rozuměl vám,** or **abych vám rozuměl,** "that I may understand you".

Concerning the freedom of transposition of words in Bohemian sentences see Note 2, Lesson VI.

Did you understand me? — I did not; repeat it slowly.

Do not speak so fast; I should not understand you.

Do you know what I said?—could you understand?

I could understand a little;—now I understood well.

When you don't understand, tell me; — I want to teach you.

I am glad of that; — if you will teach me, I shall soon know.

In a quarter of a year I shall understand all.

Do I pronounce it right? — did I pronounce it right?

You have a good pronunciation: — you pronounce everything right.

That was not right; see here; — I will pronounce it slowly.

Is that right?

Once again!

That's it; — now it was right; first-rate.

Very well!—you make quick progress.

Rozuměl jste mi!—Nerozuměl; opakujte to pomalu.

Nemluvte tak rychle; já bych vám nerozuměl.

Víte co jsem povídal! — porozuměl jste?

Porozuměl jsem trošku;—teď jsem rozuměl dobře.

Když nerozumíte, řekněte mi; — já chci vás učiti.

To jsem rád; —budete-li mě učiti, budu brzo uměti.

Za čtvrt leta budu všemu rozuměti.

Vyslovuju to dobře! — vyslovil jsem to dobře?

Máte dobrou výslovnost; — vyslovujete všecko dobře.

To nebylo dobře; dejte pozor; — já to vyslovím pomalu.

Je to dobře?

Ještě jednou!

Tak; — teď to bylo dobře; tuze dobře.

Výborně! — děláte rychlý pokrok.

rozŭmyell stě me? —něrozŭmyell;—ŏpŭkŭytě tŏ pomŭlŭ.

němlŭftě tŭk rikhlě; yŭ bikh vŭm něrozŭmyell.

veetě tsŏ sem poveedŭl? —pŏrozŭmyell stě?

pŏrozŭmyell sem troshku; — těd' sem rozŭmyell dŏbrshě.

* gdiž něrozŭmeetě, rshěkňetě me; — yŭ khtsi vŭs ŭchit.*

tŏ sem rŭd; — bŭdětě li myě ŭchit, bŭdŭ bᵉrzŏ ŭmyět.

zŭ shtwᵉrt letŭ bŭdŭ fshěmŭ rozŭmyet.

vislovŭyŭ tŏ dobrshě?—vislovil sem tŏ dŏbrshě?

mŭtě dŏbroŭ vceslŏvnost; — vislovŭyetě fshětskŏ dŏbrshě.

tŏ něbillŏ dŏbrshě; deytě pŏzor; — yŭ tŏ visloveem pomŭlŭ.

yě tŏ dobrshě?

yeshtě yednoŭ!

tŭk; — těd' tŏ billŏ dŏbrshě; toozě dŏbrshě.

veeborně! — dělŭtě rikhlee pŏkrok.

| I wish I had more opportunity to speak Bohemian. | Rád bych měl více příležitosti mluviti česky. | *rád bikh m'yell veetsě prsheelěžitosťi mlŭvit chesske.* |

VOCABULARY.

Slovo, n. *slovŏ,* the word
slovník, m. *slovñeek,* the dictionary
slovníček, m.*) *slovñeechek,* the vocabulary
vysloviti, *vislovit,* to pronounce
vyslovím, *vislovcem,* I shall pronounce
vyslovovati, *vislovŏvăt,* to be pronouncing;
vyslovuju (or **vyslovuji**), *vislovăyŭ,* I am pronouncing;
výslovnost, f. *veeslovnost,* the pronunciation;
čeština, f. *cheshťină,* the Bohemian language;
angličina, f. *ănglichină,* the English language;
pokrok, m. *pŏkrok,* progress;
příležitost, f. *prsheelěžitost,* opportunity;
rád bych měl, *rád bikh m'yell,* I wish I had (or: I would like to have);
hezky, *hesske,* ⎫
hodně, *hodñě,* ⎬ a good deal;
něco málo, *ñětso mălŏ,* a little bit;

učiti se, *ŭchit sě,* to learn, to be learning;
neučiti se, *něŭchit sě,* not to learn;
naučiti se, *năŭchit sě,* to learn or acquire (something);
rozuměti, *rozŭmyet,* to understand;
rozumím, *rozŭmeem,* I understand
porozuměti, *pŏrozŭmyet,* to understand; or "to catch the meaning";
začnouti, *zăchnoŭt,* ⎫ to begin, to
začíti, *zăcheet,* ⎬ commence;
začne, *zăchně,* will commence;
půjčiti, *pŭychiťi,* (colloquially: *pŭchit*), to lend;
půjčte mi, *pŭchlě me,* lend me;
povězte mi, *po-vyěztě me,* tell me.
jak se jmenuje, *yăk sě menŭyě,* how is — he, she, it — called.
těžký, á, é, *ťěshkee,* difficult, hard;
rychlý, á, é, *rikhlee* ⎫
rychle, adv. *rikhlě* ⎬ fast;
pomalu, *pomălŭ,* slowly;
hnedle, *hnedlě,* nearly, (also "soon", "quick");
co nevidět, *tsŏ něviďet,* in no time, shortly;

---

*) **Slovníček** is simply a diminutive of **slovník,** meaning "a little or short dictionary". See Note 1, Lesson XVIII.

trošku, (same as **trochu**), *trŏshkŭ,* a little;	**dokonalý, á, é,** *dŏkonálee,* perfect.	
snaduý, á, é, *snădnee,* easy.	**dokonale,*)** *dŏkonălĕ,* perfectly;	
snaduo, *snădnŏ,* easily;	**výborný, á, é** *veebornee* **výborně,** adv. *veeborňĕ* } first-rate.	

Greetings and compliments.
POZDRAVY A POKLONY.

Good morning, Sir! (gentlemen, — Madam,— Miss,— ladies).	**Dobré jitro**), pane!** (**pánové, — pauičko, —slečuo,—dámy).**	*dŏbré ye-trŏ, pănĕ! (pánŏvé, — pănichkŏ, — slĕchnŏ, — dámy, — slĕchny).*
Good afternoon, Mr. Brown!	**Dobré odpoledue, pane Braune!***)**	*dŏbré odpolĕdnĕ, pănĕ Brownĕ!*
Good evening, Mrs. Brown!	**Dobrý večer, paní Braunová!**	*dŏbree vĕcher, păňi Brownŏvá!*
My compliments!	**Má úcta!**	*mú ootstă!*
Good night, doctor!	**Dobrou noc, pane doktore⁴)!**	*dŏbroŭ nots, pănĕ doktoře!*
Good bye! — Farewell!	**S bohem!—Na zdar!**	*sbŏhem!—nă zdăr!*
Farewell!	**Mějte se dobře!**	*myĕy-tĕ sĕ dŏbrshĕ!*

*) See Note 2. Lesson XXX, about the derivation of adverbs from adjectives. In this case, as well as in some others, the final ý changes into a simple **e: dokoualý, — dokonale.**

Mostly it changes into an **ě: výborný, — výborně**; and sometimes into an **o: snaduý, — snaduo.** This, however, is rather optional, as we may equally say: **snaduě,** *snădňĕ,* (easily).

) In common conversation very often abbreviated: **dobrytro! *dŏbritro!*

***) It is proper to use the vocative case in addressing a person; but in ordinary discourse the proper name is generally left in the nominative: **dobré jitro, pane Braun!**

4) We cannot say in English "Mr. doctor", two titles in this case being incompatible; but it is customary in Bohemian to say: **pane doktore, pane professore,** or (in common parlance) **pane doktor, pane professor,** — leaving the title in the nominative case. *"Mr. editor",* — **pane redaktore,** *pănĕ redăktoře,* — is an analogous expression in English.

Good luck to you!	Na zdar vám !	nă zdăr vám!
I wish you good luck!	} Přeju vám štěstí !	prshĕyŭ vám shťěsťi!
I wish you Godspeed!		
A happy journey!	Šťastnou cestu !	shťăstnoŭ tsěstŭ!
A happy return!	Šťastný návrat !	shťăstnee návrăt !
To drink one's health.	Píti na zdraví.	peeťi nă zdrăvee.
Your health !	Na vaše zdraví !	nă văshě zdrăvee!

How do you do? How are you?	Jak se máte?	yăk sě mátě?
How are you getting along?	Jak se vám vede?	yăk sě vám vědě ?
Very well, thank you.	Tuze dobře, děkuju.	toozě dŏbrshě, ďěkŭyŭ.
How is everything with you?	Jak se vede?	yăk sě vědě ?
Tolerably well.	Projde to.—Ujde to.	proydě tŏ.—ŭydě tŏ.
How is your health?	Jak vám zdraví slouží?	yăk vám zdrăvee sloŭžee?
Are you well? Are you in good health?	Jste zdráv?	stě zdráf?
I am pretty well, thank you.	Je mi dost dobře, děkuju.	yě me dost dŏbrshě, ďěkŭyŭ.
I am all right.	Mám se hezky.	mám sě hesske.
I feel very well.	Je mi tuze dobře.	yě me toozě dŏbrshě.
I am perfectly well.	Jsem docela zdráv.	sem dotsělă zdráf.
And how are you?	A jak vy se máte?	ă yăk ve sě mátě?
I am also well, thank you.	Taky dobře, děkuju.	tăke dŏbrshě, ďěkŭyŭ.
You are looking well.	Vypadáte dobře.	vipădátě dobrshě.
I am very well; I cannot complain.	Mám se výborně; nemohu stěžovat.	mám sě veeborňe; nemŏhŭ sťěžŏvăt.
How is your wife (your lady)?	Jak se má vaše žena (vaše paní)?	yăk sě má văshě ženă (păňi)?
She is well, thank you.	Dobře, děkuju.	dŏbrshě, ďěkŭyŭ.
How is your family?	Jak se má vaše rodina?	yăk sě má văshě roďină?
They are all well.	Jsou všichni zdrávi.	soŭ fshikhňi zdrávi.

I am glad of it.	**To mě těší.**	*tŏ myě ťěshee.*
I am glad to hear it.	**To rád slyším.**	*tŏ rád slisheem.*
That is right.	**To je dobře.**	*tŏ yě dŏbrshě.*
I am very glad to see you (or: to meet you).	**Jsem tuze rád že vás vidím.**	*sem toozě rád žě váss viďeem.*
I have not seen you for a long time.	**Neviděl jsem vás už dávno.**	*neviďel sem váss ŭsh dávnŏ.*
I would like to see you often.	**Rád bych viděl vás často.**	*rád bikh viďel váss chásstŏ.*

My regards!	**Že pozdravuju!**	*žě pozdrăvŭyŭ!*
Greet him (her, them)! — Give him my regards.	**Pozdravujte ho (ji, je)!**	*pozdrăvŭyte hŏ (ye, yě)!*
Give (him, etc.) my best regards!	**Vyřiďte mé pozdraveni.**	*virshiďtě mé pozdrăvě-ñi*)*
My best regards!	**Pěkné pozdravení!**	*pyěkné pozdrăveñi!*
Give my regards to all!	**Pozdravujte ode mne všecky!**	*pozdrăvŭytě ŏdě myě fshětske!*
Remember me to your wife. — My best respects to your wife.	**Mou úctu vaší choti!**	*moŭ ootstŭ văshee khŏ-ťi!*
My best regards to your wife!	**Pěkné pozdravení manželce!**	*pyěkné pozdrăveñi mănželtsě!*
My compliments to your sister!	**Mou poklonu vaší se-stře!**	*moŭ poklŏnŭ văshee sě-strshě!*
Good bye!	**Poroučím se!**	*poroŭcheem sě!*
My best respects!	**Pěkné poručení!**	*pyěkné porŭcheñi!*

---

*) Nouns ending in **ní** are neutre (see **znamení**, Note 2, Lesson XIV). The final **í** has the long sound of *ee*. But in common discourse the length of the sound is immaterial and it is usually shortened; hence we represent it in these conversations by a simple **ñi**, instead of **ñee.**

VOCABULARY.

Pánbůh (i. e. **Pán Bůh**) *pánbooh,* the Lord God;

jitro, n. (same as **ráno**), *yitrŏ,* the morning;

pozdrav, m. *pozdrăf* ⎰ greet-
pozdravení, n. *pŏzdrăveñí,* ⎱ ing;
pozdraviti, *pozdrăvit,* to greet (once);
pozdravovati, *pozdrăvŏvăt,* to greet; to send greetings;

poklona, f. *pŏklonă,* compliment, bow;

úcta, f. *ootsta,* respect;

návrat, m. *năvrăt,* return;

zdraví, n. *zdrăvee,* health;

choť, m. & f. *khŏť,* the spouse, husband or wife;

stěžovati, *sťežovăt,* to complain;

vypadati, *vipădăt,* to look.

A call.
NÁVŠTĚVA.

Give me a call. — Call and see me.	Navštivte mě.—Přijď-te ke mě.	*năfshťiftě myě. — Prshiď-tě*) kě myě.*
Call at my house.	Přijďte ke mě domu.	*prshiďtě kě myě dŏmŭ.*
Call at my store.	Přijďte ke mě do krá-mu.	*prshiďtě kě myě dŏ krá mŭ.*
Call at my office.	Přijďte do mé písárny.	*prshiďtě dŏ mé peesár-ny.*
Did you call at my place?	Byl jste u mě?	*bill stě ŭ myě?*
I called at your house, but nobody was at home.	Byl jsem u vás, ale žádný nebyl doma.	*bill sem ŭ váss, ălě žád-nee něbill dŏmă.*
Call again.	Přijďte zas.	*prshiďtě zăss.*
And when?—Any time.	A kdy?—Kdykoli.	*ă gdy?—gdykoli.*
When will you be at home.	Kdy budete doma?	*gdy bŭdětě dŏmă?*
To-morrow surely.	Zejtra**) jistě.	*zeytră yistě.*
When will you call and see me?	Kdy mě navštívíte?	*gdy myě nafshťiveetě?*

*) Colloquially this is still more condensed and sounds like *prshi-tě.*

) **Zejtra or **zítra** (to-morrow), derived from **zjitra, zajitra,** next morning.

I shall give you a call to-morrow or day after to-morrow.	Navštívím vás zejtra nebo pozejtří.	náfshťiveem váss zeytrá něbǒ pozeytrshee.
Yes, do call; I shall be expecting you.	Ano, navštivte; budu vás očekávat.	ănǒ, náfshťiftě; búdú váss ǒchěkávăt.
Somebody is knocking. — Some one rings.	Někdo klepá. — Někdo zvoní.	ñegdǒ klěpá. — ñegdǒ zwǒñee.
Go and see who that is.	Jděte se podívat kdo to je.	ďetě sě poďeevăt gdǒ tǒ yě.
Go and open the door.	Jděte otevříti.	ďetě ǒtěvrsheet.
It is some gentleman, — some stranger.	Je to nějaký pán, — nějaký cizinec.	yě tǒ ñeyăkee pán, — ñeyăkee tsizinets.
It is Mr. Arbes.	Je to pan Arbes.	yě tǒ păn Arbes.
Let him come in.	Ať vejde!	ăť veydě!
Come in!—Walk in!	Dále !	dálě!
Come in, if you please.	Vejděte, prosím!	veyďetě, proseem!
Sit down.	Sedněte si.	sedňetě si.
Take a seat, if you please.	Posaďte se, prosím.	posăďtě sě, proseem.
Please take a seat.	Račte se posaditi.	răchtě sě posăďit.
Here is a seat.	Tady je židle.	tădy yě židlě.
Stay with us to dinner.	Zůstaňte u nás na oběd.	zoostăňtě u nás nă obyěd
Excuse me, I cannot; I have no time.	Odpusťte, nemohu; nemám čas.	odpŭstě, nemǒhŭ; nemám chăss.
Are you in a hurry?	Máte na spěch?	mătě na spyěkh?
Yes, I am in a hurry.	Ano, mám na spěch.	ănǒ, mám nă spyěkh.
Where do you hurry?	Kam spěcháte?	kăm spyěkhátě?
I have an appointment with Mr. Coleman.	Mám schůzi s panem Kolmanem.	mám skhoozi spănem Kolmănem.
Don't be in such a hurry; wait a little.	Nespěchejte tak; počkejte trošku.	nespyěkheytě tăk; pochkeytě troshkŭ.
Indeed I cannot; I shall soon call again.	Opravdu nemohu; přijdu brzo zas.	oprăvdŭ němǒhŭ; prshiydŭ berzǒ zăss.
Do so, if you please!	Prosím, přijďte!	proseem, prshiďtě!
Please, come again.	Račte přijíti zas.	răchtě prshiyeet zăss.

Drop in, when you have time.	Zaskočte sem, když máte čas.	*zăskŏchtĕ sem, gdyž mă-tĕ chăss.*
I will come here as soon as I have time.	Přijdu sem, jakmile budu mít čas.	*prshiydŭ sem, yăkmilĕ bŭdŭ meet chăss.*
Good day!	Poroučím se!	*porŏŭcheem sĕ!*

VOCABULARY.

Návštěva, f. *năfshťevă*, a call, a visit;
navštíviti, *năfshťeevit*, to visit;
očekávati, *ochĕkăvăt*, to await;
zaskočiti, *zăskochit*, to drop in;
poroučeti, *porŏŭchet*, to command;
poroučeti se, *porŏŭchet sĕ*, to take leave;
poroučím se, *porŏŭcheem sĕ*, good day !
sednouti si, *sednŏŭt si* ⟩ to sit down,
posaditi se, *posăďit sĕ* ⟩ to take a place;

cizinec, m. *tsizinets*, a stranger;
spěch, m. *spyĕkh*, the hurry;
schůze, f. *skhoozĕ*, meeting, appointment;
židle, f. *židlĕ*, the chair;
klepati, *klepăt*, to knock;
zvoniti, *zwoňit*, to ring;
otevříti, *otĕvrsheet*, to open;
odpustiti, *odpŭsťit*, to excuse, to forgive.

Time.
ČAS.

Day and night.	Den a noc.	*den ă nots.*
I worked all day.	Pracoval jsem celý den.	*prătsovăl sem tsĕlee den.*
I did not sleep all night.	Nespal jsem celou noc.	*nespăl sem tsĕloŭ nots.*
I work day and night.	Dělám ve dne v noci.	*ďelăm vĕ dnĕ vnotsi.*
We sat up late at night.	Seděli jsme dlouho do noci.	*sĕďeli smĕ dlŏŭhŏ dŏ notsi.*
He came late at night and wanted a night's lodging.	Přišel pozdě na noc a chtěl nocleh.	*prshishell pozďe nă nots a khťel notslĕh.*
The day was clear; the night was dark.	Den byl jasný; noc byla tmavá.	*den bill yăsnee; nots bil-lŭ tmăvá.*
To-day, — yesterday.	Dnes, — včera.	*dness, — fcheră.*
This morning, — this noon,— this evening, — this midnight.	Dnes ráno, — dnes v poledne, — dnes večer,—dnes o půlnoci.	*dness răno,—dness fpo-lednĕ,— dness vĕcher, — dness o poolnotsi.*

English	Czech	Pronunciation
This forenoon it rained — this afternoon it was fine.	Dnes dopoledne pršelo; —dnes odpoledne bylo hezky.	*dness dŏpolednĕ pershellŏ; — dness ŏdpolednĕ billŏ hessky.*
Until evening; — until morning.	Až do večera; — až do rána.	*ásh do vĕcherá; — ásh dŏ ránú.*
In broad daylight.	Za bílého dne.	*zá beeléhŏ dnĕ.*
To-night he will come home. — To-night he came home.	Dnes v noci přijde domu. — Dnes v noci přišel domu.	*dness vnotsi prshidĕ dŏmú. — dness vnotsi prshi-shell dŏmú.*
He came last night, — last evening, — early in the morning,—late in the evening, — about midnight.	Přišel minulou noc, — včera večer, — časně ráno, — pozdě večer, — kolem půlnoci.	*prshi-shell minúlŏú nots — fcherá vĕcher, — chassñe ránŏ,—pozďe vĕcher, — kolem poolnotsi.*
Evening before last; — night before last.	Předminulý večer; — předminulou noc.	*prshĕd-minúlee vĕcher;- prshĕd-minúlŏú nots.*
When was it? — Last night.	Kdy to bylo? — Dnes v noci.	*gdy tŏ billŏ? — dness vnotsi.*
When did it happen?— Night before last.	Kdy se to stalo?—Včera v noci.	*gdy sĕ tŏ stálŏ? — fcherá vnotsi.*
When shall I take that medicine?	Kdy mám užívati?	*gdy mám úžeevát?*
In the morning, at noon and at bed-time.	Ráno, v poledne a na noc.	*ránŏ, fpolednĕ á nú nots.*
Yesterday was a holiday. — Day before yesterday there was a fire.	Včera byl svátek. — Předevčírem hořelo.	*fcherá bill svátek. — prshĕdĕ-fcheerem horshĕlŏ.*
To-morrow I shall leave;— day after tomorrow I shall be in St. Louis.	Zejtra odjedu; — pozejtří budu v St. Louis.	*zeytrá odyĕdú; — pozeytrshee búdú v St. Louis.*

VOCABULARY.

Nocleh, *notslĕh,* a night's lodging;
svátek, *swátek,* a holiday;
státi se, *stát sĕ,* to happen, to occur;

stalo se, *stálŏ sĕ,* it happened;
stane se, *stánĕ sĕ,* it will happen;
stane-li se, *stánĕ-li sĕ,* if it happens;

13

jasný, á é, *yǎssnee*, bright, clear;
tmavý, á, é, *tmǎvee*, dark;
minulý, á, é, *minǔlee*, past, last;
předminulý, *prshěd-minǔlee*, before last;

odjeti, *ǒdyet*, to leave (by some conveyance);
užívati, *ǔžeevǎt*, to take medicine; (also "to enjoy").

This week I am in good health; — last week I was sick.	Tento týden jsem zdráv;-minulý týden byl jsem nemocen.	*tento teeděn sem zdráf; — minǔlee teeděn bill sem němotsěn.*
The last two weeks I was on the road (i. e. traveling).	Poslední dvě neděle byl jsem na cestách.	*posledňee dwyě něd'elě bill sem nǎ tsestákh.*
Next week I shall again leave.	S neděle zase odjedu.	*sněd'elě zǎssě odyědǔ.*
Next week I expect my brother.	Budoucí týden čekám bratra.	*bǔdoǔtsee teeděn chekǎm brǎtrǎ.*
In two weeks I shall get money; — in five weeks I shall be in Europe.	Za dvě neděle dostanu peníze; — za pět neděl budu v Evropě.	*zǎ dwyě ned'elě dǒstǎnǔ peñeezě; — zǎ pyět ned'el bǔdǔ věvropyě.*
In how many weeks will you return? — I shall return in about a month.	Za kolik neděl se vrátíte? — Vrátím se asi za měsíc.	*zǎ kolik ned'el sě vrá-t'eetě? — vrát'eem sě ǎsi zǎ myěseets.*
In how many months shall I see you?— In two months;—in five months.	Za kolik měsíců vás uvidím? — za dva měsíce;—za pět měsíců.	*zǎ kolik myěseetsoo vǎss ǔvid'eem? — zǎ dwǎ myěseetsě; — zǎ pyět myěseetsoo.*
When shall we meet again?— In a quarter	Kdy se sejdeme zas? —Za čtvrt leta,*) za	*gdy sě seydemě zǎss? — za shtwᵉrt letǎ, — zǎ*

---

*) Ordinarily leto, n. means "summer"; but the noun rok, m. (the year) has in the plural leta, let: dvě leta, two years or "two summers"; pět let, five years or "five summers"; etc. See Lesson XIX, and foot-note on page 88.

The same is true of fractions: čtvrt leta, *shtwᵉrt letǎ*, a quarter of a year; půl leta, *pool letǎ*, half a year; tři čtvrti leta, *trshí shtwᵉrťi letǎ*, three quarters of a year.

However, we may also say: dva roky, two years; pět roků, five years etc. Likewise: čtvrt roku, půl roku, tři čtvrti roku.

of a year,— in half a year, — in a year.	půl leta, — za rok.	*pool letů, — zů rok.*
I shall be here within a year.	Budu zde do dne do roka.	*bŭdŭ zdě dŏ dně dŏ rokŭ.*
My son has been gone five years;—he writes to me once a year (once in a year, — once yearly).	Syn je pryč pět let; — píše mi jednou do roka (or: jednou za rok, —jednou ročně).	*syn yě prich pyět let;— peeshě me yednoŭ dŏ rokŭ (or: yednoŭ zŭ rok, — yednoŭ rochñe).*
In how many years do you expect him?	Za kolik let ho čekáte?	*zŭ kolik let hŏ chekátě?*
In three years,— in six years.	Za tři leta, — za šest let.	*zŭ trshi letŭ, — zŭ shěst let.*
I think he will arrive shortly, — speedily, — before long.	Myslím že přijede za krátko, — v krátkosti, — za nedlouho.	*misleem že prshiyědě zŭ krátkŏ, —fkrátkosťi, — zŭ nedloŭhŏ.*
In a short time we shall see him.-- In a short while we shall be together.	Za krátký čas ho uvidíme. — Za krátkou dobu budeme pohromadě.	*zŭ krátkee chŭss hŏ ŭviďeemě. — zŭ krátkoŭ dŏbŭ bŭdemě pŏhromŭďe.*
It is a week since I was in New York.	Je tomu týden co jsem byl v New Yorku.	*yě tŏmŭ teeděn tsŏ sem bill v New Yorkŭ.*
It is scarcely two weeks since father was here.	Je tomu sotva dvě neděle, co zde byl otec.	*yě tŏmŭ sotvŭ dwyě něďelě tsŏ zdě bill otets.*
It will soon be a year since I was in the old country.	Bude tomu brzo rok, co jsem byl ve staré vlasti.	*bŭdě tŏmŭ b°rzŏ rŏk, tsŏ sem bill vě stŭré vlŭsťi.*
It is very near two years since I sold the farm.	Budou tomu hnedle dvě leta, co jsem prodal farmu.	*bŭdoŭ tŏmŭ hnedlě dwyě letŭ, tsŏ sem prodŭl fŭrmŭ.*
This day a year (or: a year ago to-day) Otto was here;—four years ago to-day we were together at San Francisco.	Dnes rok byl zde Otto; — dnes čtyry leta byli jsme spolu v San Franciscu.	*dness rok bill zdě Otto; — dness shtiry lětŭ billi smě spolŭ fŭanfrancisŭ.*

To-morrow it will be a year since Mary left; — two years ago yesterday mother died.

Zejtra bude rok co Mary odjela; — včera dvě leta matka zemřela.

zeytrŭ bŭdě rok tsŏ Mary od-yellŭ; — fchěrŭ dwyě letŭ mŭtkŭ zemrshellŭ.

The other week our folks were here.

Onen týden byli tu naši.

onen teedĕn billi tŭ nŭshi.

It is scarcely a week since they left;—it is just a month since they arrived.

Je tomu sotva týden co odjeli;—je tomu zrovna měsíc, co přijeli.

yě tŏmŭ sotwŭ teedĕn tsŏ od-yelli;—yě tŏmŭ zrovnŭ myěseets tsŏ prshi-yelli.

It will shortly be a month since it happened.

Hnedle bude měsíc co se to stalo.

hnedlě bŭdě myěseets tsŏ sě tŏ stŭlŏ.

It is not long since; — it was a short time since; — it was the other day.

Je to nedávno; — bylo to nedávno; — bylo to onehdy.

yě tŏ nedávnŏ;—billŏ tŏ nedávnŏ; — billŏ tŏ ŏnehdy.

How long is it since you have been here?

Jak dávno tomu co jste tu ?

yŭk dávnŏ tŏmŭ tsŏ stě tŭ ?

Day before yesterday it was a year. — It was half a year (last) Sunday. — It will be four months on Monday.—It will be eight months on Tuesday.

Přede věirem minul rok. — Minulo půl leta v neděli. — Budou čtyry měsíce v pondělí.— Bude osm měsíců v úterý.

prshĕdě fcheerem minŭl rok.—minŭlŏ pool lětŭ vněďeli. — bŭdoŭ shtiry myěseetsě fponďelee. — bŭdě osŭm myěseetsoo vooteree.

When was it?—Wednesday a week; — two weeks ago on Thursday; — a week ago last Friday; — three weeks ago last Saturday.

Kdy to bylo?—Ve středu týden; — ve čtvrtek dvě neděle; — v pátek minul týden; — v sobotu minuly tři neděle.

gdy tŏ billŏ?—vě strshĕdŭ teedĕn;—vě shtwertek dwyě neďelě; — fpátek minŭl teedĕn; — fsobŏtŭ minŭly trshi neďelě.

Before a year passes we shall be one another's (i. e. man and wife).

Než mine rok budeme svoji.

nesh mině rok, bŭdemě swoyi.

Before two years pass away, all will be over.

Než minou dvě leta, bude po všem.

nesh minoŭ dwyě letă, bŭdě pŏ fshěm.

Will it be long? — It won't be long.

Bude to dlouho? — Nebude to dlouho.

bŭdě tŏ dloŭhŏ?—nebŭdě tŏ dloŭhŏ.

Will it last long? — It won't last long.

Bude to dlouho trvati? —Nebude to dlouho trvati.

bŭdě tŏ dloŭhŏ tᵉrvăt? — nebŭdě tŏ dloŭhŏ tᵉrvăt.

It takes long.— It took long.—It didn't take long.—O yes, it did !

To trvá dlouho. — Trvalo to dlouho.—Netrvalo to dlouho. — Ba trvalo ?

tŏ tᵉrvă dloŭhŏ.—tᵉrvălŏ tŏ dloŭhŏ.— nětervălŏ tŏ dloŭhŏ. — bă tervălŏ!

How soon will it be?— It will be right away. — It is done already.

Jak brzo to bude? — Bude to hned. — Už je to.

yăk bᵉrzŏ tŏ bŭdě?—bŭdě tŏ hned.—ŭsh yě tŏ.

VOCABULARY.

Neděle, *něďelě*, Sunday
pondělí, *ponďelee*, Monday
úterý, *ootěree*, Tuesday
středa, *strshědă*, Wednesday
čtvrtek, *shwᵉrtek*, Thursday
pátek, *pátek*, Friday
sobota, *sŏbotă*, Saturday
nedávno, *nědávnŏ*, not long since
jak dávno, *yăk dávnŏ*, how long since
co, *tsŏ*, since
sotva, *sotvă*, scarcely, hardly
budoucí, *bŭdoŭtsee* ⎫
příští, *prsheesh·ťee* ⎭ future, next
dostati, *dostăt*, to get, to receive;

za krátko, *ză krátkŏ* ⎫
v krátkosti, *fkrátkŏsťi* ⎪
za nedlouho, *ză nědloŭhŏ* ⎬ shortly,
za krátký čas, *ză krátkee chăss* ⎪ in a short
za krátkou dobu, *ză krátkoŭ dŏbŭ* ⎭ time;

denně, *děňe*, daily
týdně, *teedňe*, weekly
měsíčně, *myěseechňé*, monthly
ročně, *rochňe*, yearly.
na cestách, *nă tsestăkh*, (literally : "on the roads"), traveling;
stará vlast, *stărá vlăst*, the old country.

The hour.
HODINA.

English	Czech	Pronunciation
Have you a watch? — — I have.	Máte hodinky? — Mám.	*mátě hoď'inky?— mám.*
Does it go right?— It is too slow (i. e. it goes late);—it loses;— it is (it goes) too fast.	Jdou*) dobře? — Jdou pozdě;— pozdí se; — jdou napřed.	*doŭ dobrshě? — doŭ pozď'e; — pozď'ee sě; — doŭ năprshed.*
It is a few minutes too late. — It is five min- utes too fast.	Jsou o pár minut po- zadu. — Jsou o pět minut napřed.	*Soŭ o pár minŭt pozd- dŭ. — Soŭ o pyět minŭt năprshed.*
It stopped (literally: it stands).	Stojí. — Zůstaly stá- ti.	*stoyee. — zoostăly stát.*
It is not wound up. — It was not wound up.	Nejsou nataženy. — Nebyly nataženy.	*neysoŭ nătăženy. — ně- billy nătăženy.*
Wind up the watch,— the clock.	Natáhněte hodinky, — hodiny.	*nătăhňetě hoď'inky, — hoď'iny.*
Is that clock right (lit. "does it go right")?-- I think it is.	Jdou ty hodiny dobře? Myslím že jdou.	*doŭ ty hoď'iny dŏbrshě? — mysleem žě doŭ.*
What o'clock is it (or: what time is it)? — How late is it?	Kolik je hodin? — Jak je pozdě?	*kolik yě hoď'in? — yăk yě pozď'e?*
Don't you know what o'clock it is?—I don't know.	Nevíte kolik je hodin? Nevím.	*něveetě kolik yě hoď'in? — něveem.*
See what o'clock it is.— I will see (*or* look).	Podívejte se kolik je hodin.—Podívám se.	*poď'eeveytě sě kolik yě hoď'in.—poď'eevám sě*
It is one o'clock. — It is a quarter past one.	Je jedna hodina. — Je čtvrt na dvě (or na druhou).	*yě yednă hoď'ină. — yě shtwᵉrt nă dwyě (nă drŭhoŭ).*

*) **Hodinky** (the watch) and **hodiny** (the clock) are plural nouns; consequently the succeeding verb must appear in the plural form: **jdou, jsou** (they go, they are). This has already been pointed out in a foot-note on page 137. — **Hodina, hodinka,** in the singular, means: "the hour", "the small hour".

It is half past one.— It is a quarter to two.

It is two o'clock. — Is it so late already? — Yes, it is two (o'clock) already.

It is past two o'clock — It is five minutes to three. — It is very near three o'clock.

It is past three. — It wants ten minutes to four.

At what o'clock shall we go?—We shall go at a quarter past four.

That is too soon; we shall wait till half past four. Very well, then.

We shall go at five o'clock. — All right.

We started at five o'clock in the afternoon.

Did you come in time? — Didn't you come late?

It was time enough; there was no hurry.

We came there a few minutes after six.

We arrived there before seven, — after seven, — early in the

Je půl druhé. — Jsou tři čtvrtě na dvě (or na druhou).

Jsou dvě hodiny. — Už je tak pozdě? — Ano, už jsou dvě.

Jsou dvě hodiny pryč. — Je pět minut do třech. — Jsou hnedle tři hodiny.

Jsou tři pryč.—Chybí deset minut do čtyrech.

V kolik hodin půjdeme? — Půjdeme ve čtvrt na pět.

To je tuze brzo; počkáme do půl páté.— Tak teda.

Půjdeme v pět hodin. — Třeba.

Vyšli jsme o páté hodině odpoledne.

Přišli jste v čas? —Nepřišli jste pozdě?

Bylo dost času; nebyl žádný spěch.

Přišli jsme tam pár minut po šesté.

Došli jsme tam před sedmou,—po sedmé, —s večera, — pozdě

---

yĕ pool druhé.- soŭ trshi shtw ᶜrťe na dwyĕ (na druhoŭ).

soŭ dwyĕ hoďiny.— ŭsh yĕ tŭk pozďe? — ănŏ, ŭsh soŭ dwyĕ.

soŭ dwyĕ hoďiny prich· — yĕ pyĕt minŭt dŏ trshĕkh. — soŭ hnĕdlĕ trshi hoďiny.

soŭ trshi prich.—khibee dĕxet minŭt dŏ shtyrekh.

fkolik hoďin půydemĕ? —půydemĕ vĕ shtwᵉrt nŭ pyĕt.

tŏ yĕ toozĕ bᵉrzŏ; pochkámĕ dŏ pool páté. — tŭk tĕdŭ.

půydemĕ fpyĕt hoďin. — trshĕbŭ.

vishli smĕ ŏ páté hoďi ňe ŏdpolednĕ.

prshishli stĕ fchŭss? — nĕprshishli stĕ pozďe?

billŏ dost chŭssŭ; nebill žádnee spyĕkh.

prshi-shli smĕ tŭm pár minŭt pŏ shĕsté.

dŏshli smĕ tŭm prshĕd sedmoŭ, — pŏ sedmé, — svĕcherŭ, — pozďe

English	Czech	Pronunciation
evening,—late in the evening, — at midnight.	**večer, — o půlnoci.**	*věcher,—ŏ poolnotsi.*
We got there in an hour, — in an hour and a half, — in two hours,—in five hours.	**Došli jsme tam za hodinu, — za půldruhé hodiny, — za dvě hodiny,—za pět hodin.**	*dŏshli smě tăm ză hoď'inŭ,—ză pooldrŭhé hoď'iny,—ză dwyě hoď'iny, — ză pyět hoď'in.*
We were here just at twelve o'clock.	**Byli jsme tu zrovna ve dvanáct hodin.**	*billi smě tŭ zrŏvnă vě dwănátst hoď'in.*
We were here exactly at noon.	**Byli jsme tu navlas v poledne.**	*billi smě tŭ năvlăss fpoledně.*
I must be there between one and two; — between two and three; — between four and five.	**Musím tam býti mezi jednou a druhou; — mezi druhou a třetí; —mezi čtvrtou a pátou.**	*mŭseem tăm beet mĕzi yednoŭ ă drŭhoŭ; — mĕzi drŭhoŭ ă trshěťee, — mĕzi shtwⁿrtoŭ ă pátoŭ.*
We must be there before evening, —early in the evening, — towards evening.	**Musíme tam býti před večerem, — brzo s večera, — na večer.**	*mŭseemě tăm beet prshěd věcherem, — bᵉrzo swěcheră, — nă věcher.*

The clock strikes.	**Hodiny bijou*)**	*hoď'iny biyoŭ.*
Hear how many (what o'clock) it strikes.	**Slyšte kolik bijou!**	*slishtě kolik biyoŭ!*
It strikes twelve.	**Bijou dvanáct.**	*biyoŭ dwănátst.*
Did you hear the clock strike?	**Slyšel jste hodiny bíti?**	*slishell stě hoď'iny beet?*
How many (i. e. what o'clock) did it strike?	**Kolik bilo?**	*kolik billŏ?*
It struck one;–it struck two;—it struck three; — it struck five;— it struck six.	**Bila jedna;— bily dvě; — bily tři; — bilo pět; — bilo šest.**	*billă yednă; — billy dwyě; — billy trshi; — billŏ pyět; — billŏ shěst.*

---

*) **Bijou** or **bijí** (they strike). See Note 2, and also foot-note on page 137.

It has just struck half past six.	Právě bilo půl sedmé.	*prácyě billŏ pool sedmé.*
It has already struck seven.	Už odbilo sedm.	*ůsh odbillŏ sedům.*
It is soon going to strike eight.	Hnedle bude bíti osm.	*hnedlě bůdě beet osům.*
I shall wait till half past eight.	Budu čekati do půl deváté.	*bůdů chekāt dŏ pool děváté.*
I shall wait till nine.	Počkám do devíti.	*pochkám dŏ děceeťi.*
Let us wait till ten.	Počkejme do desíti.	*porhkeymě dŏ dessecťi.*
Wait till midnight, or until morning.	Počkejte do půlnoci, nebo do rána.	*pochkeytě dŏ poolnotsi, nebŏ dŏ ránă.*
I shall wait gladly.	Rád počkám.	*rád pochkám.*
I do not like to wait.	Nerad čekám.	*nerăd chekám.*
Waiting is not agreable.	Čekání není milé.	*chekáñi neyñi milé.*
I do not like long waiting.	Nemám rád dlouhé čekání.	*nemám rád dloŭhé chekáñi.*

VOCABULARY.

Hodina, f. *hoďină,* the hour;
hodinka, f. *hoďinkă,* the small hour;
hodiny, pl. *hoďiny,* the clock;
hodinky, pl. *hoďinky,* the watch;
lék, m. *lék,* the medicine;
spěch, m. *spyěkh,* the hurry;
čekání, n. *chekáñi,* the waiting;
napřed, *năprshěd,* ahead, before;

natahnouti, *nătăhnoŭt,* to wind up;
nataženy, *nătăženy,* wound up;
čekati, *chekăt,* to wait, to be waiting;
čekám, *chekám,* I am waiting;
počkati, *pochkăt,* to wait;
počkám, *pochkám,* I shall wait;
pozadu, *pozádŭ,* behind.

Age and date.
VĚK a DATUM.

| How old are you? | Jak jste stár? Kolik je vám let? | *yăk ste stár? kolik yě vám let?* |
| I am twenty years. — I am over twenty. | Je mi dvacet let. — Je mi přes dvacet. | *yě me dwătset let. — yě me prshěs dwătset.* |

I shall soon be twenty five years.	Bude mi brzo dvacet pět let.	*bůdě me berzŏ dwătset pyět let.*
I am nearly thirty years.	Je mi málem třicet let.	*yě mi málem trshitset let.*
I am already thirty five years.	Už je mi třicet pět let.	*ŭsh yě me trshitset pyět let.*
I was forty years in January.	Bylo mi čtyrycet let v lednu.	*billŏ me shtiritset let vlednŭ.*
You are still young.	Jste ještě mladý.	*stě yeshťe mlădee.*
I shall be fifty years in February. — I am getting old.	Bude mi padesát let v únoru. — Stárnu.	*bůdě me păděsát let voonorŭ. — stárnŭ.*
That is not a great age.	To není velké stáří.	*tŏ neyñi velké stárshce.*
You look young.	Vypadáte mladý.	*vypădátě mlădee.*
You don't look so old.	Nevypadáte tak starý.	*něvypădátě tăk stăree.*
You look well for your age.	Vypadáte dobře na svůj věk.	*vypădátě dŏbrshě nă svŭy vyěk.*
When were you born?	Kdy jste*) narozen?— Kdy jste se narodil?	*gdy stě nărŏzěn? gdy stě sě nărod'il?*
What year?— In what year?	Který rok ?— V kterém roce ?	*ktěree rŏk? — fktěrém rotsě ?*
I was born in the year 1840.—I was born in May in the year 1850.	Jsem narozen roku 1840. — Jsem rozen v máji leta 1850.	*sem nărŏzěn rŏkŭ ťiseets osŭm set shtiritset.—sem rozěn v máyi letă ťiseets osŭm set păděsát.*
I was born in the month of June 1862.	Narodil jsem se v měsíci červnu 1862.	*nărod'il sem sě vmyěseetsi chervnŭ ťiseets osŭm set shěděsát dwă.*
The first of August is my birth-day.	Prvního srpna je můj den narození.	*pervñeehŏ serpnă yě mŭy den nărozěñi.*

---

*) In Bohemian the passive participle **rozen** or **narozen** is used in connection with the present tense : kdy jste rozen ? kdy jste narozen ? "when *are* you born"?

English	Czech	Pronunciation
How old is that child?	Jak staré je to dítě?	*yăk stăré yĕ to ďeeťe ?*
It is ten days. — It is two weeks (old).	Je mu deset dní. — Jsou mu dvě neděle.	*yĕ mŭ dĕset dñee.— soŭ mŭ dwyĕ nĕďelĕ.*
It is a month (old).—It is two months.—It is five months.	Je mu měsíc. — Jsou mu dva měsíce. — Je mu pět měsíců.	*yĕ mŭ myĕseets. — soŭ mŭ dwŭ myĕseetsĕ. — yĕ mŭ pyĕt myĕseetsoo.*
It is one year (old). — It is two years (old). —It is five years (old).	Je mu rok. — Jsou mu dvě leta.—Je mu pět let.	*yĕ mŭ rŏk. — soŭ mŭ dwyĕ letă. — yĕ mŭ pyĕt let.*
It will be a year in September.—It will soon be three years.	Bude mu rok v září.— Budou mu brzo tři leta.	*bŭdĕ mŭ rŏk vzárshee. — bŭdoŭ mŭ berzŏ trshi letă.*
It is going on two years (it is in its second year). — It is going on five years.	Jde mu na druhý rok. Jde mu na pátý rok.	*dĕ mŭ nă drŭhee rŏk.— dĕ mŭ nă pátee rŏk.*
How old is that girl?	Jak stará je ta holka?	*yăk stără yĕ tă holkă?*
She will be four years at Christmas. — She will be five years at Easter. — She will soon be six years.	Budou jí čtyry leta o vánocích. — Bude jí pět let o velkonocích.—Bude jí hnedle šest let.	*bŭdoŭ yee shtiry letă ŏ vánotseekh.—bŭdĕ yee pyĕt let ŏ velkŏnotseekh.— bŭdĕ yee hnĕdlĕ shĕst let.*
What day of the month is it?—what date is it?	Kolikátého je!— jaké je datum?	*kolikátéhŏ yĕ? — yăké yĕ dătum?*
To-day is the first,—the second,— the fifth.	Dnes je prvního, druhého, — pátého.	*dness yĕ pervñeehŏ, — drŭhého,—pátéhŏ.*
What day of the month is (i. e. will be) to-morrow?	Kolikátého bude zejtra?	*kolikátéhŏ bŭdĕ zeytră?*
To-morrow is ("will be") the third, — the tenth, — the twentieth.	Zejtra bude třetího,— desátého,—dvacátého.	*zeytră bŭdĕ trshĕťcehŏ, — dessátéhŏ, — dwătsátéhŏ.*
What date was yesterday?	Kolikátého bylo včera?	*kolikátéhŏ billŏ fcheră?*

Yesterday was the twenty-first.	Včera bylo dvacátého prvního.	fcherá billŏ dwătsátéhŏ pᵉrvñeehŏ.
What day of the month will be next Sunday? –The twenty-second.	Kolikátého bude v neděli? — Dvacátého druhého.	kolikátéhŏ bŭdě vněď'elï? — dwătsátéhŏ drŭhéhŏ.
On what day of the month was Frank here? — He was here on the fifteenth and he will come again on the twenty-fifth.	Kolikátého byl zde Frank?– Byl zde patnáctého a přijde zas na dvacátého pátého.	kolikátéhŏ bill zdě Frank?—bill zdě pătnáctéhŏ ă přshidě zăss nă dwătsátéhŏ pátéhŏ.
This month?— Yes; he will stay here until the last.	Tento měsíc? — Ano; zůstane tu do posledního.	tentŏ myěseets? — ăno; zoostănĕ tŭ dŏ posledñeehŏ.
On the first I shall receive new goods.	Na prvního dostanu nové zboží.	nă pᵉrvñeehŏ dŏstănŭ nové zbožee.
When will Mr. Danesh pay (his) bill? — Before the last.--On the first of next month.	Kdy pan Daneš zaplatí účet?— Do posledního. — Na prvního budoucí měsíc.	gdy păn Dănesh zăplăťee oochet? — dŏ pŏsledñeehŏ. — nă pᵉrvñeehŏ bŭdoŭtsee myě seets.
When will the agent arrive? — About the ninth.	Kdy přijede agent? — Asi devátého.	gdy přshiyědě ăkent?— ăsi děvátéhŏ.
When will the time run out? When will it be due?— About the fifteenth.	Kdy vyjde čas? Kdy vypadne lhůta? — Kolem patnáctého.	gdy veedě chăss? gdy vypădně lhootă?—kŏlem pătnátstéhŏ.
That is, about the middle of the month. — I shall pay towards the end of the month.	Teda v polou měsíce.— Zaplatím ke konci měsíce.	tědă fpoloŭ myěseetsě. - zăplăťeem kě kontsi myěseetsě.
Next month I expect to be gone. — Before two months pass away, I shall be back.	Na druhý měsíc hodlám býti pryč. — Než uplynou dva měsíce, budu nazpět.	nă drŭhee myěseets hodlám beet prich.—nesh ŭplinoŭ dwă myěseetsě, bŭdŭ năspyět.

We shall expect you some time in October; — or in the beginning of November;—at latest before the first of December.

Budeme vás čekati někdy v říjnu; — nebo počátkem listopadu; — nejdýl do prvního prosince.

bŭdĕmĕ váss chekát ñegdy frsheeynŭ; — nĕbŏ pocháŧkem listopádŭ:—neydeel dŏ pervñeeho prosintsĕ.

The fourth of July is a national holiday, — the day of independence.

Čtvrtý červenec jest národní svátek, — den neodvislosti.

shtw^ertee chervĕnets yest národñee swátek, — den nĕodvislosŧi.

Thanksgiving day is usually in November.

Den díkůvzdání bývá v listopadu.

den ďeekŭvzdáñee beevá vlistopádŭ.

On new-year's day; — before New-year's;— after New-year's.

Na nový rok; — do nového roku; — po novém roce.

nŭ novee rŏk;—dŏ nového rŏkŭ; — pŏ novém rotsĕ.

VOCABULARY.

Věk, m. *vyĕk* stáří, n. *stárshee* } the age

stárnouti, *stárnoŭt,* to grow old;

naroditi se, *nároďit sĕ,* to be born;

narození, n. *nározĕñi,* the birth:

počátek, m. *pocháŧek,* the beginning;

lhůta, f. *lhootŭ,* the given time, the term;

vánoce, pl. *vánotsĕ,* Christmas;

velkonoce, pl. *velkŏnotsĕ,* Easter;

svatodušní svátky, pl., *swŭtŏdŭshñee swátky,* Whitsuntide;

vypadati, *cypŭdŭt* vyhlížeti, *vyhleežet* } to look, to appear;

vyjíti, *viyeet,* to go out, to run out:

uplynouti, *ŭplynoŭt,* to pass away;

zaplatiti, *zŭplŭŧit,* to pay up:

někdy, *ñegdy,* sometimes;

v polou, *fpoloŭ,* in the middle:

nazpět, *nŭspyĕt* zpátky, *spátky* } back

neodvislost, f. *nĕodcislŏst,* the independence.

Leden, *ledĕn,* January
únor, *oonor,* February
březen, *brshĕzĕn,* March
duben, *dŭbĕn* april, *ŭpril* } April

květen, *kwyĕtĕn* máj, *máy* } May
červen, *chervĕn,* June
červenec, *chervĕnets,* July
srpen, *serpĕn,* August

září, *zárshee*, September
říjen, *rsheeyĕn*, October

listopad, *listopăd*, November
prosinec, *prosinets*, December.

The weather.
POČASÍ.

English	Czech	Pronunciation
How is the weather?	Jaké je počasí?	*yăké yĕ pŏchăsee?*
It is fine; — it is beautiful weather.	Je pěkně; — je krásné počasí.	*yĕ pyĕkñe; — yĕ krăssné pŏchăsee.*
It is clearing up; — it is a fine morning; — it will be a nice day.	Vybírá se; — je krásné ráno; — bude pěkný den.	*vybeerá sĕ; — yĕ krăssné ráno; — bŭdĕ pyĕknee den.*
The heaven is clear. — The sun shines, — warms (i. e. makes it warm), — burns.	Nebe je jasné. — Slunce svítí — hřeje — pálí.	*nĕbĕ yĕ yăsné. — slŭntsĕ sweeťee, — hrshĕyĕ, — pálee.*
In the sun it is hot.	Na slunci je horko.	*nă slŭntsi yĕ horkŏ.*
It is warm; — it will be hot; — there will be a great heat to-day.	Je teplo; — bude horko; — bude dnes velké parno.	*yĕ teplŏ; — bŭdĕ horkŏ; — bŭdĕ dness velké parnŏ.*
Yesterday there was a great heat.	Včera bylo silné vedro.	*fcheră bilŏ silné vĕdrŏ.*
How does the thermometer stand? — Eighty five in the shade.	Jak stojí teploměr? — Osmdesát pět ve stínu.	*yăk stoyee teplŏmyĕr? — osŭmdessát pyĕt vĕ sťeenŭ.*
The thermometer is rising, — is falling.	Teploměr stoupá, — klesá.	*teplŏmyĕr stoŭpá, — klĕsá.*
What a heat! — I am perspiring; let us go into the shade; — I feel hot.	To je horko! — Já se potím; pojďme do chládku. — Je mi horko.	*tŏ yĕ horkŏ! — yá sĕ poťeem; poďmĕ dŏ khládkŭ; — yĕ me horkŏ.*
What wind is it? — East wind, — West wind, South wind, — North wind.	Jaký je vítr? — Východní, — západní, jižní, — severní.	*yăkee yĕ veeter? — veekhodñee, — zápădñee, — yižñee, — sĕverñee.*
I think there will be a	Myslím že bude změna	*misleem že bŭdĕ zmyĕ-*

change in the weather;—the wind changes. — Now it blows from the East.

Very likely there will be a change.

It is dry; we need rain; —I wish it would rain! —There is a great deal of dust.

Is it going to rain?— It looks like it; it is getting cloudy.

It is cloudy;— the sky is clouded;— the sky is overcast; — it is damp.

Do you see those dense, black clouds?—They bring rain,— a heavy rain.

I think a rainstorm is coming, — a heavy rainstorm.

The weather is bad; — the weather is nasty; — it is wet and muddy.

It is very nasty out of doors; — it is rainy; — too much rain!

It sprinkles;—it rains a little; — it rains; — it pours;— how muddy it will be!

počasí;— vítr se mění. — Teď vane od východu.

Dost možná, že bude změna.

Je sucho; potřebujeme déšť. — Kéž by jen pršelo! — Je moc prachu.

Bude pršet? — Vypadá to tak; mračí se.

Je zamračeno;— je pod mrakem;— obloha je zatažena; — je vlhko.

Vidíte ty husté, černé mraky? — Z toho bude déšť, — hodný déšť.

Myslím že bude liják, — silný liják.

Je špatné počasí; — je škaredá povětrnost; — je mokro a blativo.

Je tam ošklivě;— je deštivo; — mnoho deště!

Krápe; — poprchává; — prší; lije se; — to bude blata!

ná pochásee; — veet^er sě myěñee.— těď váně od veekhodů.

dost možná že budě zmyěná.

yě sukhö; potrshěbůyě-mě desht'.— kéž be yen p^ershellö! — yě mots prákhů.

budě p^ershět?—vypádá tö ták; mráchee sě.

yě zámráchenö;—yě pod mrákem; — oblöhá yě zátážená;—yě v^elhko.

veďeete ty hússté, cherné mráky? — stohö budě desht', — hodnee desht'.

misleem že budě liyák, — silnee liyák.

yě shpátné pochásee; — yě shkáredá povyět^er-nost;—yě mokrö.

yě tám oshklivyě; — yě desht'ivö; — mnohö desht'e!

krápě; — pop^erkhává;— p^ershee;— liyě sě;—tö budě blátá!

It rains in torrents.—It has ceased to rain already.	Prší jen se lije. — Už přestalo pršeti.	$p^e rshee$ yen $s\breve{e}$ $liy\breve{e}$. — $\breve{u}sh$ $prsh\breve{e}st\breve{a}l\breve{o}$ $p^er\text{-}$ $sh\breve{e}t$.
That was a heavy rainstorm,—a cloudburst; —it rained in torrents. — It caused a flood.	To byl příval, — průtrž mračen; - pršelo jen se lilo. — Byla z toho povodeň.	$t\breve{o}$ $bill$ $prsheeval$,—$proo\text{-}t^ersh$ $mr\breve{a}ch\breve{e}n$;—$p^er\text{-}shell\breve{o}$ yen $s\breve{e}$ $lill\breve{o}$. — $b\breve{u}d\breve{e}$ $st\breve{o}h\breve{o}$ $p\breve{o}voden$.
It is calm,— no wind,— not a leaf is stirring. — It is sultry; the air is heavy.	Je ticho, — bez větru, —ani se list nehýbe. — Je dusno; vzduch je těžký.	$y\breve{e}$ $t'ikh\breve{o}$,— $b\breve{e}z$ $vy\breve{e}tr\breve{u}$,—$\breve{a}ni$ $s\breve{e}$ $list$ $n\breve{e}heeb\breve{e}$. — $y\breve{e}$ $d\breve{u}ssn\breve{o}$; $vzd\breve{u}kh$ $y\breve{e}$ $t'ethkee$.
The wind rises; — it is windy; — it blows hard; — there is a strong wind.	Dělá se vítr; — je větrno; — fouká hodně; — je silný vítr.	$d'el\acute{a}$ $s\breve{e}$ $veet^er$;— $y\breve{e}$ $vy\breve{e}\text{-}t^ern\breve{o}$;—$fo\breve{u}k\acute{a}$ $hod\tilde{n}e$; —$y\breve{e}$ $silnee$ $veet^er$.
A storm is brewing; — there will be a hurricane; — a cyclone is coming.	Bude z toho bouře; — bude vichřice; — cyklon se blíží.	$b\breve{u}d\breve{e}$ $st\breve{o}h\breve{o}$ $bo\breve{u}rsh\breve{e}$; — $b\breve{u}d\breve{e}$ $vikh\text{-}rshits\breve{e}$; — $tsiklon$ $s\breve{e}$ $bleezee$.
A thunderstorm is coming. — It lightens. — Now there was a flash of lightning. — What flashes of lightning!	Tahne bouřka. — Blýská se. — Teď se zablesklo. — To je blýskání!	$t\breve{a}hn\breve{e}$ $bo\breve{u}rsh\text{-}k\breve{a}$.— $bleesk\acute{a}$ $s\breve{e}$.—$te\check{d}$ $s\breve{e}$ $z\breve{a}bles\text{-}kl\breve{o}$.—$t\breve{o}$ $y\breve{e}$ $bleesk\acute{a}\tilde{n}i$!
Do you hear the thunder? — Yes, it thunders; the thunder rolls from afar; — a thunderstorm is coming.	Slyšíte hřímati?—Ano, hřímá — hrom hučí z daleka; — bouřka se blíží.	$slisheet\breve{e}$ $hrsheem\breve{a}t$? — $\breve{a}n\breve{o}$, $hrsheem\acute{a}$;—$hrom$ $h\breve{u}chee$ $zd\breve{a}lek\breve{a}$;—$bo\breve{u}\text{-}rshk\breve{a}$ $s\breve{e}$ $bleezee$.
The thunder roars; — the lightning has struck;— it has struck somewhere! — the lightning set fire.	Hrom burácí; — hrom uhodil; — někde uhodilo! — blesk zapálil.	$hrom$ $b\breve{u}r\acute{a}tsee$; — $hrom$ $\breve{u}hod'il$; — $\tilde{n}egd\breve{e}$ $\breve{u}ho\text{-}d'il\breve{o}$!—$blesk$ $z\breve{a}p\acute{a}lil$.
This is a terrible storm,	To je hrozná bouře, —	$t\breve{o}$ $y\breve{e}$ $hr\breve{o}zn\acute{a}$ $bo\breve{u}rsh\breve{e}$,—

— an awful thunder-storm.—The crashing of thunder is incessant. — Flash after flash, one thunder-clap after the other. That was a thunder-clap —a thunderbolt from a clear sky.	strašné hromobití.— Hrom bije neustále. — Blesk za bleskem, rána za ranou.	străshné hromobiťee. —hrom biyĕ nĕŭstálĕ. — blesk ză bleskem, rănă ză rănoŭ.
It hails. — This is a big hailstorm. It will destroy the crops —the hail will destroy everything. — The hail-storm destroyed the crops;-hailstones of an enormous size were falling.	To byla hromová rá-na; — uhodilo z čista jasna. Padají kroupy. — To je silné krupobití. Potluče; — kroupy všecko zničí. — Po-tlouklo; — padaly kroupy ohromné ve-likosti.	tŏ bilă hromŏvá rănă; —ŭhoďilŏ schistă yă-snă. păddyee kroŭpy.— tŏ yĕ silné krŭpobiťee. potlŭchĕ;-kroŭpy fshĕt-sko zñichee. — potloŭ-klŏ; — păddăly kroŭpy ohromné vĕlikosťi.
It is foggy;— this morn-ing there was a thick fog. Dew is falling; — there is a heavy dew. There is a hoary frost, —a gray frost. It is cold;—it is chilly; — it is frosty. I feel cold;—I am freez-ing; —a cold wind is blowing. I want to warm my-self. — Are you cold? Warm yourself. — It is warm here, — al-most too warm.	Jest mlhavo;-ráno by-la hustá mlha. Padá rosa; — je silná rosa. Je jinovatka, — šedý mráz. Je zima;-je sichravo; — je mrazivo. Je mi zima; — mrazí mě; — fouká stude-ný vítr. Chci se ohřáti. — Je vám zima?— Ohřejte se. — Zde je teplo, — až moc teplo.	yest melhăvŏ;-ránŏ bil-lă hŭsstá melhă. pădá rossă; — yĕ silná rossă. yĕ yinovătkă, — shĕdee mráz. yĕ zimă;— yĕ sikhrăvŏ; yĕ mrăzivŏ. yĕ mi zimă; — mrăzee myĕ;—foŭká stŭdĕnee veeter. khtsi sĕ ohrshăt. — yĕ vám zimă? ohrshĕytĕ sĕ.—zdĕ yĕ teplŏ,—ăsh mots teplŏ.

14

It is going to snow; — it snows;—it is snowing.	Bude padati sníh; — padá sníh;—sněží.	*bŭdĕ pădăt sñeeh;— pádá sñeeh;—sñežee.*
What a snow-storm! — a great snow-storm.	To je vánice! — velká metelice.	*tŏ yĕ váñitsĕ! — velká metellitsĕ.*
A great deal of snow fell;—there are snowdrifts.	Napadlo mnoho sněhu; —jsou závěje.	*năpădlo mnohŏ sñehŭ; — soŭ závyĕyĕ.*
How many degrees is it?—It is twenty below zero; — a severe cold.	Kolik je stupňů? — Je dvacet pod nulou; — krutá zima.	*kolík yĕ stŭpñoo? — yĕ dwătset pod nŭlloŭ;— krŭtá zimă.*
The ice is thick; we can skate.	Led je silný; můžeme se klouzati.	*led yĕ silnee; moožemĕ sĕ kloŭzăt.*
It will grow warmer;—it is growing warmer; —the wind is shifting; — it blows from the South.	Ono se oteplí;—oteplu-je se; — vítr se obra-cí; — vane od jihu.	*ŏnŏ sĕ oteplee;— oteplŭ-yĕ sĕ; — veeter sĕ o-brătsee; — vănĕ od yeehŭ.*
The ice breaks; — the snow thaws and the ice melts;— there is a big thaw.	Led puká; — sníh taje a led se rozpouští;— je hodná obleva.	*led pŭká; — sñeeh tăyĕ ă led sĕ rospoŭshťee; yĕ hŏdná oblĕvă.*
In the spring the weather is mild; — in the summer it is usually hot; — in the fall it is cool; — in the winter it is cold and it freezes.	Z jara je mírné poča-sí; — v letě bývá horko; — na podzim je chladno; — v zimě je zima a mrzne.	*zyără yĕ meerné pochă-see; — vleťe beevá horkŏ; — nă podzim yĕ khlădnŏ;— vzimyĕ yĕ zimă ă merznĕ.*
Wisconsin has a hard winter; — Louisiana has a mild winter. — In Texas the winter is short and the summer long.	Wisconsin má tuhou zimu; — Louisiana má mírnou zimu. — V Texasu je krátká zima a dlouhé leto.	*wisconsin má tŭhoŭ zi-mŭ; — louisiana má meernoŭ zimă. — fte-rasŭ yĕ krátká zimă ă dloŭhé letŏ.*

The summer season is warm, — the winter season is cold.	Letní počasí je teplé, — zimní počasí je studené.	*letňee pochásee yě teplé, — zimňee pochásee yě stůděné.*
In the winter days are short and nights are long.	V zimě jsou krátké dni a dlouhé noci.	*vzimyě soů krátké dňi ů dlouhé notsi.*
The day shortens;—the day lengthens.	Den se krátí; — dne přibývá.	*den sě kráťee; — dně prshibeevá.*
The night shortens.	Noc se krátí; (noci u-bývá).	*nots sě kráťee; (notsi ů-beevá).*

VOCABULARY.

Počasí, n. *pochásee* povětrnost, f. *povyět^crnost* } the weather	východ, m. *veekhŏd*, the east západ, m. *zápǎd*, the west
počasí, n. doba, f. *dŏbǎ* } the season;	jih, m. *yeeh* poledne, n. *poledně* } the south
nebe, n. *něbě*, the heaven	sever, *sěcer* půlnoc, *poolnots* } the north
obloha, f. *oblŏhǎ*, the sky	
stín, m. *sťeen*, the shade, the shadow	jiho-východ, m. the south-east
chládek, m. *khlǎdek*, the shady place	severovýchod, m. the north-east
prach, m. *prǎkh*, the dust	jihozápad, m. the south-west
blato, n *blǎtŏ*, the mud	severozápad, m. the north-west
list, m. *list*, the leaf	východní, *veekhodňee*, eastern
velikost, f. *velikost*, the greatness	západní, *zápǎdňee*, western
kéž by, I would that...; would to heaven that...; I wish it would...;	jižní, *yeežňee* polední, *poledňee* } southern
	severní, *severňee*, půlnoční, *poolnochňee* } northern

Vítr, m. *veet^er*, the wind	bouře, f. *boůrshě*, the storm
vichřice, f. *vikh-rshitsě*, the gale, the hurricane;	kouřka, f. *boůrshkǎ*, the thunder-storm;
foukati, *foůkǎt* vanouti, *vǎnoůt* } to blow	hřímati, *hrsheemǎt*, to thunder hřímání, n. *hrsheemáňee*, the thundering

hrom, m. *hrŏm,* the thunder

hromová rána, a peal or crash of thunder;

hromobití, n. *hrŏmobiťee,* peals of thunder;

buráceti, *bŭrátset,* to roar, to crash

blýskati se, *bleeskăt sĕ,* to lighten

blýskání, n. *bleeskáñee,* the lightning

blesk, the flash or stroke of lightning; the thunderbolt;

zablesklo se, *zăblesklŏ sĕ,* there was a flash of lightning;

uhoditi, *ŭhoďit,* to strike

zapáliti, *zăpálit,* to set fire.

Dešť, m. *deshť,* the rain

liják, m. *liyák* } the rainstorm,

příval, m. *prsheevăl* } the heavy shower;

průtrž mračen, *proot°rsh mrăchĕn,* the cloud-burst;

povodeň, f. *pŏvodeň,* the flood

mrak, m. *mrăk* } the cloud

mračno, n. *mrăchnŏ* }

mračiti se, *mrăchit sĕ,* to grow cloudy;

krápati, *krápăt* } to sprin-

poprchávati, *pŏp°rkhávăt* } kle;

pršeti, *p°rshĕt,* to rain

líti se, *leet sĕ* (colloq. *leyt sĕ*), to pour

přestati, *prshĕstăt,* to stop.

Kroupy, pl. *kroŭpy,* the hail

krupobití, n. *krŭpobiťee,* the hail-storm;

potlouci, *potloŭtsi,* to knock down, to destroy;

zničiti, *zñichit,* to annihilate

mlha, f. *m°lhă,* the fog

mlhavo, *m°lhăvŏ,* foggy

rosa, f. *rossă,* the dew

jinovatka, f. *ye-novătkă,* hoary frost

sníh, m. *sñeeh,* the snow

sněhu, *sñehu,* of the snow;

sněžiti, *sñežit,* to snow

metelice, f. *metĕlitsĕ* } the snow-storm,

vánice, f. *váñitsĕ* } the blizzard;

závěje, pl. f. *závyĕyĕ,* snow-drifts

led, m. *led,* the ice

náledi, n. *náleďee,* glazed frost

mráz, m. *mráz,* the frost

mrznouti, *m°rznoŭt,* to freeze

táti, *táťi,* to thaw

tání, n. *táñee* } a thaw

obleva, *oblĕvă* }

Vybirati se, *vybeerăt sĕ,* to clear up

měniti se, *myĕ-ñit sĕ,* to change

páliti, *pálit,* to burn

přibývati, *prshibeevăt,* to increase, to lengthen;

ubývati, *ŭbeevăt,* to decrease, to shorten;

potiti se, *poťit sĕ,* to sweat.

Černý, á, é *chernee,* black

hustý, á, é *hŭsŧee,* thick, dense;

škaredý, á, é *shkárĕdec*, nasty, ugly; | parno, *parnŏ*, very hot
mírný, á, é *meernee*, mild
ohromný, á, é *ŏhromnee*, enormous, terrible;
strach, m. *strákh*, fear
strašný, á, é *stráshnee*, fearful
hrůza, f. *hroozá*, horror, terror;
hrozný, á, é *hrŏznee*, horrible; shocking.

———

Blativo (adv.)*), *blăťivŏ*, muddy
deštivo, *deshťivŏ*, rainy
mokro, *mokrŏ*, wet
vlhko, *vᵉlhkŏ*, damp
sucho, *sŭkhŏ*, dry
teplo, *teplŏ*, warm
horko, *horkŏ*, hot

parno, *parnŏ*, very hot
dusno, *dŭssnŏ*, close, stifling;
zima, *zimă* ⎫
studeno, *stŭdĕnŏ* ⎬ cold
chladno, *khlădnŏ*, cool
sichravo, *sikhrăvŏ*, chilly
mrazivo, *mrăzivŏ*, frosty, freezing cold.

——

Teploměr, m. *teplŏmyĕr*, the thermometer
stupeň, m. *stŭpeň*, a degree
nula, f. *nŭlă*, zero
nad nulou, *năd nŭloŭ*, above zero
pod nulou, below zero;
stoupati, *stoŭpăt*, to rise;
klesati, *klessăt*, to go down.

———

Health and sickness.
ZDRAVÍ a NEMOC.

I hope you are well.	Doufám že jste zdráv.	*doŭfám že stĕ zdráf.*
Only middling;— I am so so.	Jen tak prostředně; — jen tak tak.	*yen tăk prostrshĕdñe;— yen tăk tăk.*
You do not look so well as (you did) lately.	Nevypadáte tak dobře jako nedávno.	*nĕvypădátĕ tăk dobrshĕ yăkŏ nĕdávnŏ.*
Do you think so? — Well, you are right; — I do not look well.	Myslíte? — Ba máte pravdu;—nevypadám dobře.	*misleetĕ? — bă mátĕ prăvdŭ;—nĕvypădám dŏbrshĕ.*

———

*) The adjectives are : **blativý (á, é)**, **deštivý, mokrý**, etc.

Je tam blativo, it is muddy out of doors; — **blativý chodník** (m.), a muddy sidewalk; **blativá cesta** (f.), a muddy road; **blativé pole** (n.), a muddy field.

Je deštivo, it is rainy; — **deštivý den,** a rainy day.

I think I look bad (bad-ly): — I look worse.	**Myslím že vypadám špatně; — vypadám hůř.**	*misleem že vypădám shpătñe; — vypădám hoorsh.*
O no! you do not look badly.	**O ne! nevypadáte zle.**	*O ně! něvypădátě zlě.*
Don't I?—I guess I do!	**Že ne?—Myslím že ano!**	*že ně?—misleem že ănö!*
Listen to me (i.e. let me tell you): you look better than you did the other day.	**Dejte si říci: vypadáte lépe než onehdy.**	*deytě si rsheetsi : vypădátě lépě nesh öněhdy.*
O, be still! — you flatter me.	**I dejte pokoj! — vy mi pochlebujete!**	*E deytě pökoy! — vy me pöklilěbůyetě.*

You look bad (badly);— I do not like your looks.	**Vyhlížíte špatně;— nelíbíte se mi.**	*vyhleežeetě shpătñe; — něleebeetě sě me.*
What is the matter with you?—is anything the matter with you?	**Co je vám? — chybí vám něco?**	*tsö yě vám? — khibee vám ñetsö ?*
Do you not feel well?— what is the matter?— what ails you?	**Není vám dobře? — co vám chybí? — co vás bolí?**	*neyñi vám döbrshě? — tsö vám khibee? — tsö váss bolee ?*
Nothing ails me;—nothing is the matter with me.	**Nic mi není; — nic mi nechybí.**	*ñits me neyñi; — ñits me někhibee.*
Why do you look so bad (badly)? — That's nothing!	**Proč vypadáte tak špatně? — To nic není!**	*proch vypădátě tăk shpătñe? — tö ñits neyñi !*
You deny it (i. e. conceal it).—Don't deny it !	**Vy zapíráte. — Nezapírejte!**	*vy zăpeerátě.— nězăpeereytě.*
I deny nothing; — why should I deny?	**Nic nezapírám;— proč bych zapíral?**	*ñits nězăpeerám;—proch bikh zăpeerăl ?*
If anything is the matter with you, tell me!	**Je-li vám něco, řekněte!**	*yělli vám ñetsö, rshěkñetě !*

Tell me what is the matter with you? – does anything ail you? – tell me if anything ails you.	Povězte co je vám? – bolí vás něco? – povězte chybí-li vám něco.	*pŏvyĕztĕ tsŏ yĕ vám? – bolee váss ñetsŏ?–pŏvyĕztĕ khibeeli vám ñetsŏ?*
If anything were the matter with me, I should say so.	Kdyby mi něco bylo, řekl bych to.	*gdyby me ñetsŏ billŏ, rshĕkᵉl bikh tŏ.*

There is something the matter with you!	Vám něco je! – Vám něco chybí!	*vám ñetsŏ yĕ! – vám ñetsŏ khibee!*
You don't feel well; – I see it by your looks!	Vám není dobře; – vidím to na vás!	*vám neyñi dŏbrshĕ; – vidᵉeem tŏ nŏ váss!*
You are right; I am not well.	Máte pravdu; není mi dobře.	*mátĕ prăvdŭ; neyñi me dŏbrshĕ.*
What is the matter with you?–I do not know what ails me ; – I do not feel quite well.	Co je vám? — Nevím co mi je; – necítím se docela dobře.	*tsŏ yĕ vám?–nĕveem tsŏ me yĕ; – nĕtseeťeem sĕ dotsellă dŏbrshĕ.*
I am not so well as usual.– A little time ago I felt better.	Nejsem tak zdráv jak obyčejně. –Ještě nedávno bylo mi líp.	*neysem tăk zdráf yăk obicheyñe. — Yeshťe nĕdávnŏ billŏ me leep.*
To-day I feel bad (badly);–I was taken sick.	Dnes je mi špatně; — přišlo mi nanic.	*dness yĕ me shpătñe; — prshishlo me năñits.*
I feel badly.	Je mi nanic. — Je mi zle.	*yĕ me năñits. — yĕ me zlĕ.*
Are you sick?	Jste nemocen?	*stĕ nĕmotsĕn?*
Yes, I am sick; I do not feel well;– I feel bad (badly).	Ano, jsem nemocen;– není mi dobře; — je mi zle.	*ănŏ, sem nĕmotsĕn; — neyñi me dŏbrshĕ; — yĕ me zlĕ.*
I hear that Edward is sick.	Slyším, že Edward je nemocen.	*slisheem že Edward yĕ nĕmotsĕn.*
He has been taken sick; – he has fallen sick; –he is very sick;–he	Roznemohl se;—upadl do nemoci; — je silně nemocen; — je	*roznĕmŏhᵉl sĕ; — ŭpădᵉl dŏ nĕmotsi; — yĕ silñe nĕmotsĕn; — yĕ*

has been sick a long time.	dlouho nemocen.	*dloŭhŏ němotsĕn.*
What is the matter with him?— what happened to him?	Co mu je? — co se mu stalo?	*tsŏ mŭ yĕ? — tsŏ sĕ mŭ stălŏ?*
He caught a cold; — he has a bad cold.	Nastudil se; — má silné nastuzení.	*năstŭďil sĕ; — má silné năstŭzĕñi.*
Anthony is also sickly: — but to-day he already feels better.	Anton je také churavý; — ale dnes už je mu lépe.	*ănton yĕ tăke khŭrăvee; — ălĕ dness ŭsh yĕ mŭ lépĕ.* (102)
I was long in poor health;— I was ailing seriously.	Já dlouho churavěl;— povážlivě jsem churavěl.	*yá dloŭhŏ khŭrăvyell; pŏvážlivyĕ sem khŭrăvyell.*
What was the matter with you?— Indeed I do not know what ailed me.	Co vám bylo? — Ani nevím co mi bylo.	*tsŏ vám billŏ?— ăñi nĕveem tsŏ me billŏ.*
I had no appetite. — I had no sleep,— I had a feeling of weariness. — But it all passed away.	Neměl jsem chuť k jídlu, — neměl jsem spaní, — cítil jsem unavenost. — Ale minulo to.	*nemyell sem khŭť k-yeedlŭ, — nemyell sem spăñi, — tseeťil sem ŭnăvĕnost. — ălĕ minŭlŏ tŏ.*
Take care of yourself: — be careful of your health!	Dejte na sebe pozor; — buďte opatrný na zdraví!	*deytĕ nă sĕbĕ pŏzor; — bŭďtĕ ŏpătᵉrnee nă zdrăvee.*
Health is above everything; it is the greatest treasure.	Zdraví je nade všecko; je to největší poklad.	*zdrăvee yĕ nădĕ fshĕtskŏ; yĕ tŏ neyvyĕtshee pŏklăd.*
An unhealthy man is unhappy.	Člověk nezdravý je nešťastný.	*chlovyĕk nĕzdrăvee yĕ neshťăssnee.*
What is the matter with you? are you sick? — you are not sick, are you?	Co je vám? stůněte? — snad nestůněte?	*tsŏ yĕ vám? stooñetĕ? — snăd nĕstooñetĕ?*
Only a little; it is not	Jen tak trochu; není	*yen tăk trŏkhŭ; neyñi*

bad. — I have a pain in the bowels.

to zlé. — Mám bole- ní.

tŏ zlé.—mám boleñi.

That will pass away; — it will stop of itself. — I hope so.

To zase přejde; — to přestane samo. - Doufám.

tŏ zása prsheydě; — tŏ prshěstáně sámŏ. — doŭfám.

Do you have it often?— Quite often; — it comes upon me from time to time.

Mívate to často? — Dost často; — přichází to na mě ob čas.

meeváte tŏ chássto? — dost chássto;—prshikházee tŏ ná myě ob chás.

What do you do against it? — Nothing; I lie down and remain quiet.

Co děláte proti tomu! — Nic; lehnu si a jsem tiše.

tsŏ d'eláte proťi tŏmŭ? — ñits; lehnŭ si á sem ťishě.

That is the best medicine. — I think so. — That helps.

To je nejlepší lék. — Já myslím. — To pomáhá.

tŏ yě neylepshec lék. — yá misleem. -- tŏ pomáhá.

It always helps me; — nothing else helps me.

To mi vždycky pomůže; nic jiného mi nepomáhá.

tŏ mi vžditsky (ditske) pomoožc; —ñits yiného me něpomáhá.

At least it gives relief. — Yes, I feel instant relief.

Aspoň to ulehčí. — Ano, hned se mi ulehčí.

ásspoñ tŏ ŭlěh-chee. — ánŏ, hned sě me ŭlěh-chee.

It relieves instantly; — it is good for relief.

Hned se uleví; — je to dobré pro úlevu, (pro ulehčení).

hned sě ŭlěvee; — yě tŏ dŏbré pro oolévŭ (pro ŭlěh-cheñi).

VOCABULARY.

Nastuditi se, *năstŭd'it sě,* to catch a cold;

nastuzení, n. *năstŭzěñi,* a cold;

churavěti, *khŭrăvyět,* to sicken, to be sickly;

churavý á, é *khŭrăvee,* sickly, indisposed;

churavost, f. *khŭrăvost,* sickliness, indisposition;

pomahati, *pomáhát,* to help;

pomahá, *pomáhá* ⎫ it helps
pomůže, *pomoožě* ⎭

nepomahá ⎫ it does not help;
nepomůže ⎭

pochlebovati, *pokhlěbovát,* to flatter

zapírati, *zăpeerát,* to deny

cítiti, *tseeť'it,* to feel

cítím, *tseeť'eem,* I feel

mívati (reit. form of **míti**, to have; see page 168;) *meevát'i*, to use to have;

přicházeti, *prshikházet*, to use to come;

přestati, *prshěstát*, to stop;

ulehčiti, *ůlěh-chit* }
uleviti, *ůlěvit* } to relieve

ulehčení, n. *ůleh-cheñi* }
úleva, f. *oolěvá* } relief

necítím, *nětseet'eem*, I do not feel;

boleti, *bǒlet*, to ache, to ail;

bolení, n. *bolěñi*, pain (especially in the bowels, belly-ache);

je mi nanic, *yě me nǎñits*, I feel sick

něco mi chybí, *ñetsǒ me khibee*, something ails me; there is something the matter with me.

Chuť, f. *khůť*, the taste, the appetite;*)

chuť k jídlu, *khůť k-yeedlů*, appetite for food;

spaní, n. *spǎñee*, the sleep;

lék, m. *lék,* }
medicína, f. *meditsinǎ* } the medicine

poklad, m. *poklǎd*, the treasure;

pokoj, m. *pǒkoy*, peace, rest;

dejte pokoj! *deytě pǒkoy!* give me a rest! keep still!

ob čas, *ǒb chǎss*, from time to time;

zdravý, á, é *zdrǎvee*, healthy, well, sound;

nezdravý, á, é *nězdrǎvee*, unhealthy, unwell, unsound;

opatrný, á, é *ǒpǎtᵉrnee*, careful

obyčejný, á, é *ǒbicheynee*, usual, common;

obyčejně, *ǒbicheyñe*, usually, commonly;

povážlivě, *pǒvážlivyě*, seriously

prostředně, *prostrshěd ñe*, middling

ticho, n. *t'ikhǒ*, silence, quiet, calm;

tiše, *t'ishě*, quietly, calmly.

The human being.
LIDSKÝ TVOR.

Tělo, n. *t'elǒ*, the body;

tělesný, á, é *t'elessnee*, bodily;

úd, m. *ood*, the member, the limb;

kost, f. the bone;

kostra, f. *kostrǎ*, the skeleton;

kostnatý, á, é *kostnǎtee*, bony;

morek, m. }
špik, m. *shpik,* } the marrow;

---

*) **Chuť** means also "a desire or inclination": **mám chuť jíti tam,** I have a mind to go there; — **mám chuť vyhnati ho,** I have a mind to chase him (or: to turn him out); — **mám chuť říci mu to,** I have a mind to tell him so; — **mám chuť do práce,** I have a desire to work, or a taste for work; I feel like working; — **pracuju s chutí,** I work with a will; etc.

kůže, f. *koožĕ,* } the skin
pleť, f. *plĕť,* }
pokožka, f. *pŏkožkă,* the cuticle
blána, f. *blánă,* the membrane
maso, n. *mássŏ,* the flesh
masitý, á, é *massitee,* fleshy
tlustý, á, é *tlŭstee,* fat
hubený, á, é *hŭbĕnee,* lean, thin;
sval, m. *svăl,* the muscle
svalnatý, á, é *svălnătee,* muscular
šlachy, pl. *shlăkhy,* the sinews
žláza, f. *žláză,* the gland
tuk, m. *tŭk,* } the fat
sádlo, m. *sádlŏ,* }
nerv, m. *nerf,* } the nerve
čiva, f. *chivă,* }
nervový, á, é *nervŏvee,* } nervous
čivní, *chivňee,* }
ceva, f. *tsĕvă,* the vessel
žíla, *žeelă,* the vein

Hlava, f. *hlăvă,* the head
lebka, f. *lebkă,* the skull
temeno, n. *temĕnŏ,* the crown or
top of the head;
týlo, n. *teelŏ,* the back of the head;
kůže na hlavě, *koože nă hlăvĕ*} the
skalp, m. *skălp* } scalp
mozek, m. *mŏzek,* the brain
spánek, m. *spánek,* the temple
spánky, pl. *spánky* } the temples
skráně, pl. *skráňe* }

Oko, n. *ŏko,* the eye
oči, pl. *ŏchi,* the eyes
oční důlek, *ochňee doolek,* the socket

hlavní žíla, *hlăvňee ž.* } the
srdeční žíla, *s*ᵉ*rdechňee ž.* } artery
tepna, f. *tĕpnă,* the pulse
žilka, f. *žilkă,* a small vein;
žilnatý, á, é *žilnătee,* sinewy
krev, f. *krĕf,* the blood
krevnatý, á, é *krĕvnătee,* full blooded
chudokrevný, á, é *khŭdokrĕvnee,*
bloodless, anaemic
krvavý, á, é *k*ᵉ*rvăvee,* bloody
vlas, *vlăss* } the hair on the head
vlasy, pl. }
chlup, *khlŭp* } the hair on the body
chlupy, pl. }
vlasatý, á, é *vlăsătee* } hairy
chlupatý, á, é *khlŭpătee* }
vnitřnosti, *vňitrsh-nosťi,* viscera;
uvnitř, *ŭvňitrsh* } inside, inwardly;
vně, *vňe* }
zevnitř, *zevňitrsh* } outside, outwardly.
zevně, *zevňe* }

čelo, n. *chellŏ,* the forehead
tvář, f. *tvársh* } the cheek
líce, n. *leetsĕ* }
tvář, f. *tvársh* } the face
obličej, m. *oblichey* }
lícní kost, *leetsňee kost,* the cheek-
bone
čelist, f. *chellist,* the jaw-bone
brada, f. *brădă,* the chin
laloch, m. *lălokh,* double chin
důlek, m. *doolek,* the dimple
vrásky, pl. m. *vrăssky,* the wrinkles.

oční jablko, *ochňee yăb*ᵉ*lkŏ,* the eye-
ball
koutek, m. *koŭtek,* the corner

rohovka, f. *rohofkă*, the cornea
duhovka, f. *dŭhofkă*, the iris
zřítelnice, f. *zrsheetelñitsĕ*, the pupil
klapka, f. *klăpkă*, the eyelid

řasy, pl. *rshăssy*, the eyelashes
brvy, pl. *b^ervy* } the eyebrows
obočí, n. *obŏchee* }

Ucho, n. *ŭkhŏ*, the ear
uši, pl. *ŭshi*, the ears

konec ucha, *kŏnets ŭkhă*, the tip of
　　the ear;
laloček, m. *lălŏchek*, the lobe

Nos, n. *nŏss*, the nose
špička nosu, *shpichkă nossŭ*, the tip
　　of the nose.

chřípě, pl. *khrshee-pyĕ* } the
nosové dírky, pl. *nosso-* } nostrils
　　vé ď'eerky }

Ústa, pl. *oostă*, the mouth
pysk, m. *pisk* } the lip
ret, m. *ret* }

pysky, pl. } the lips
rty, pl. }

Zub, m. zuby, pl. *zŭb, zŭby*, the
　　tooth, the teeth
přední zuby, *prshed-ñee zŭby*, the
　　fore-teeth
zadní zuby, *zădñee zŭby*, the back-
　　teeth
špičák, m. *shpicháky*, the canines

stolička, f. *stolichkă*, the molar
kořen zubu, *korshĕn zŭbŭ*, the root
　　of the tooth;
dáseň, f. *dásseñ*, the gum
dásně, pl. *dássñe*, the gums
patro, n. *pătrŏ*, the roof of the mouth
jazyk, m. *yăzyk*, the tongue.

Vousy, pl. *foŭsy*, the beard
licousy, pl. *litsoŭsy*, the whiskers
Hrdlo, n. *h^erdlŏ*, the throat
krk, m. *k^erk*, the neck
hrtán, m. *h^ertán* } the larynx
chřtán, m. *hrshtán* }
hrdelnice, f. *h^erdell-ñitsĕ*, the jugu-
　　lar vein;

kníry, pl. *kñeery*, the moustaches
plnovous, m. *p^elnŏfoŭs*, the full beard
průdušnice, f. *proodŭshnitsĕ*, the
　　windpipe
mandle, pl. *măndlĕ*, the tonsils, the
　　almonds;
ohryzek, m. *ŏhryzĕk*, Adam's apple.

Trup, m. *trŭp*, the trunk
hrud', f. *hrŭď*, the chest
prsa, pl. *persă*, the breast
žebro, n. *žebrŏ*, the rib

klíční kost, f. *kleechñee kost*, the
　　collar-bone
prsní kost, f. *persñee kost*, the
　　breast-bone

záda, pl. *zádă*, the back

zadek, m. *zádek*, the back part, the backside;

předek, m. *prshědek*, the fore-part, the front;

hřbet, m. *hrshbet*) the backbone,
páteř, f. *pátersh*) the spine;

Život, m. *život*, the abdomen

břicho, n. *br×hikhŏ*, the belly

pupek, m. *păpek*, the navel

bok, m. *bŏk*, the hip

slabina, f. *slăbină*, the side

kříž, *krsheež*, the small of the back;

zadnice, f. *zădñilsě*, the seat, the bottom;

půlky, pl. f. *poolky*,) the
zadní tváře, pl. f. *zădñee* (buttocks
tvárshě

Ruka, f. *răkă*, the hand

ruce, pl. *rătsě*, the hands; v rukou, *vrăkoŭ*, in the hands; na rukou, *năr.*, on the hands

rámě, n. *rámyě*) the arm
paže, n. *păže*)

dolní část paže, *dolñee chăst păže*, the fore-arm

horní část paže, *horñee chăst p.*, the upper arm

rameno, n. *rămenŏ*) the shoulder or
paždí, n. *păžďee*) top of the arm;

podpaždí, n. *podpăžďi*, the armpit

loket, m. *lŏket*, the elbow

přehyb, m. *prshěhib*, the wrist

pěst, f. *pyěst*, the fist

zlatá žíla, f. *zlătá žeelă*, the spinal cord;

plece, sing. & pl. *pletsě*, the shoulder

lopatka, f. *lopătkă*, the shoulder-blade

obratel, m. *obrătel*, vertebra

obratle, pl. *obrătlě*, vertebrae.

řiť, f. *rshiť*, the anus

pohlaví, n. *pohlăvee*, the sex

pohlavní úd, m. *pohlăvñee ood*, the sexual parts

mužský úd, m. *măskee ood*, the penis

zálupa, f. *zălăpă*, the fore-skin

varle, (pl. varlata), *varlě*, the testicle

rodidla, pl. *roďidlă*, the genitals.

kloub, m. *kloŭb*, the joint

dlaň, f. *dlăñ*, the palm

prst, m. *p erst*, the finger

palec, m. *pălets*, the thumb

malík, m. *măleek*, the little finger

ukazovák, *ŭkăzovák*, the forefinger

prostřední prst, *prostrshedñee p erst*, the middle finger

článek prstu, m. *chlánek p erstŭ*, the phalange

špička prstu, f. *shpichkă p erstŭ*, the tip of the finger;

nehet, m. *něhet*, the nail

nehty, pl. *něhty*, the nails

kotník, m. *kotñeek*, the knuckle

kloub, m. *kloŭb*, the joint.

Noha, f. *nŏhă*, the leg, the foot;
nohy, pl. *nŏhy*, the legs, the feet;
chodidlo, n. *khŏḍidlŏ*, the foot
tlapa, f. *tlăpă*, the sole of the foot:
stehno, n. *stĕhnŏ*, the thigh
stehenní kost, f. *stĕhĕñee kost*, the thigh-bone
hnát, m. *hnát*, the shin
lýtko, n. *leetkŏ*, the calf of the leg;
koleno, n. *kolĕnŏ*, the knee
přehyb kolena, m. *prshĕhyb kolĕnă*, the knee-joint

Srdce, n. *s^erdsĕ*, the heart
osrdí, n. *oss^erḍee*, the pericardium
komora, f. *kŏmoră*, the ventricle
plíce, pl. *pleetsĕ*, the lungs
játra, pl. *yátra*, the liver
slezina, f. *slezină*, the spleen
ledvina, f. *ledviná*, the kidney
měchýř, m. *myĕkheersh*, the bladder
žluč, f. *žlŭch*, the gall, the bile;

pata, f. *pătă*, the heel
prsty u nohy, pl. *p^ersty ŭ nŏhy*, the toes
palec u nohy, m. *pălets ŭ nŏhy*, the big toe;
malík u nohy, m. *măleek ŭ nŏhy*, the little toe;
kotník, m. *kotñeek*, the ankle
plosko-nohý, *ploskŏ-nŏhee*, flat-footed;
kolo-nohý, *kolŏ-nŏhee*, bow-legged.

žlučni měchýř, m. *žlŭchñee m.*, the gall-bladder
žaludek, m. *žălŭdek*, the stomach
střevo, n. *strshĕvŏ*, the intestine, the gut;
střeva, pl. *strshĕvă*, the bowels
tenká střeva, the lesser intestines
tlustá střeva, *tlŭstá s.* the larger intestines;
konečník, m. *konechñeek*, the rectum.

Ústrojí, n. *oostroyee*, organism, constitution;
dýchati, *deekhăt*, to breathe
dýchání, n. *deekháñi*, breathing, respiration;
dýchací ústrojí, *deekhătsee oostroyee*, respiratory organs;
dech, m. *dĕkh*, the breath;
lehký dech, *lĕhkee dĕkh*, easy breathing;
těžký dech, *ťeshkee dĕkh*, heavy breathing;
dechnutí, n. *dĕkhnŭťee*, one breath

vydechnouti, *vydĕkhnoŭt*, to draw breath;
vydechnouti ze sebe, *v. zĕ sĕbĕ*, to exhale, to force out the breath;
vdechnouti do sebe, *vdĕkhnoŭt dŏ sĕbĕ*, to inhale;
oddechnouti si, *odĕkhnoŭt si*, to breathe easily, to feel relief;
tráviti, *trávit*) to digest, to con-
ztráviti, *strávit* ∫   sume;
zažívati, *zăžeevăt*, to digest

trávení, n. *trávení* ⎫
zažívání, n. *zăžeeváni* ⎭ digestion

zažívací ústrojí, *zăžeeválsee oostro-yee*, digestive apparatus;

moč, m. *mŏch*, the urine

močení, n. *mŏchĕňí*, urination

močiti, *mŏchit*, to urinate

stolice, f. *stolitsĕ*, stool, evacuation;

míti stolici, *meet stolitsi*, to go to stool; to have open bowels;

výkal, *reekăl*, the excrement, the discharge;

lejno, n. *leynŏ* ⎫
trus, m. *trŭss* ⎭ the dung

oběh krve, m. *obyĕh k°rvĕ*, circulation of the blood;

krváceti, *k°rvátset*, to bleed

krvácení, n. *k°rvátseňí*, the bleeding

měsíčné, n. *myĕsеechné*, the menstruation

plod, m. *plŏd*, the fruit

ploditi, *plŏďit*, to bear (fruit etc.); to beget;

Duch, m. *dŭkh*, the spirit; the mind or intellect;

duše, f. *dŭshĕ*, the soul

duchovní, *dŭkhovňee* ⎫ spiritual,
duševní, *dŭshĕvňee* ⎭ intellectual;

mysl, f. *missl*, the mind

důmysl, m. *doomissl* ⎫ the intellect
schop, m. *skhŏp* ⎭

rozum, m. *rozŭm*, the reason, the understanding;

zdravý rozum, *zdrăvee rozŭm*, common sense;

soudnost, f. *soŭdnost*, the judgment

plození, n. *plŏzeňí*, the bearing, the begetting;

porod, m. the childbirth

poroditi, *porŏďit*, to be delivered;

pracovati ku porodu, *prătsovăt kŭ porŏdŭ*, to be in labor;

šestinedělí, n. *shĕsťineďeľe*, lying-in

šestinedělka, f. *shĕsťineďelkă*, a woman in childbed;

je těhotná, *yĕ ťehŏtná*, she is with child;

čeká se do kouta, *cheká sĕ dŏ koŭtă*, she expects to be confined;

je v koutě, *yĕ fkoŭťe* ⎫ she is confined,
slehla, *slĕhlă* ⎭ (in childbed);

po koutě, *pŏ koŭťe*, after childbirth, after confinement;

obcování, n. *obtsŏváňí*, the intercourse

obcovati, *obtsŏvăt*, to have intercourse;

pohlavní obcování, *pohlăvňee o.*
tělesné obcování, *ťelessné o.* sexual intercourse.

smysl, *smissl*, the sense

zrak, m. *zrăk*, the sight

sluch, m. *slŭkh*, the hearing

chuť, f. *khŭť*, the taste

čich, cit, m. *chikh, tsit*, the smell, the feeling;

hmat, m. *hmăt*, the touch

paměť, f. *pămyĕť*, the memory

smyslný, á, é *smisslnee*, sensual

smyslnost, f. *smisslnost*, sensuality

nesmysl, m. *nĕsmissl*, nonsense

nesmyslný, á, é *nĕsmisslnee*, senseless, nonsensical.

A sound body, — a sound mind.	Zdravé tělo, — zdravý duch.	zdrăvé ťelŏ, — zdrăvee dŭkh.
A sound mind in a sound body.	Zdravý duch ve zdravém těle.	zdrăvee dŭkh vě zdrăvém ťelě.
I have sound limbs, — and that is a great gift.	Mám zdravé údy, — a to jest veliký dar.	mám zdrăvé oody, — ă tŏ yest vělikee dar.
The bone is hollow and contains marrow.	Kost je dutá a obsahuje morek.	kost yě dŭtá ă obsăhŭyě morek.
That man is lean but muscular.	Ten člověk je hubený, ale svalnatý.	ten chlovyěk yě hŭběnee, ălě svălnătee.
That lady has excitable nerves.	Ta dáma má popudlivé nervy.	tă dámă má popŭdlivé nervy.
Young blood — hot blood.	Mladá krev — horká krev.	mlădá kref — horká kref.
The pulse beats slowly, —beats fast.	Tepna bije pomalu, — bije prudce.	tepnă biyě pomălŭ, — biyě prŭdsě.
The pulse is normal, — regular, — irregular.	Tepna je normální, — pravidelná, — nepravidelná.	tepnă yě normălñee, — prăvidelná, — něprăvidelná.
The beating of the heart and the beating of the pulse agree.	Tlukot srdce a bití tepny se shodujou (or shodují).	tlŭkot serdsě ă biťee tepny sě s-hodŭyoŭ.
Every little vein in the body contains blood.	Každá žilka v těle obsahuje krev.	kăždá žilkă fťelě obsăhŭyě kref.
Fair hair and blue eyes prevail in the north, — dark hair and black eyes in the south.	Plavý vlas a modré oči panují (or panujou) na severu, — tmavý vlas a černé oči na jihu.	plăvee vlăs ă modré ŏchi pănŭyee nă sěvěrŭ,— tmăvee vlăss ă cherné ŏchi nă yeehŭ.
Long hair, short wit,— says an old proverb.	Dlouhé vlasy, krátký rozum, praví staré přísloví.	dloŭhé vlăsy, krátkee rozŭm, — pravee stăré prsheeslŏvee.
The European race has a white skin, the Af-	Plemeno evropské má bílou pleť, plemeno	plěmenŏ ěvropské má beeloŭ pleť, plěmenŏ

rican race a black skin.	**africké černou.**	*áfritské černoŭ.*
Youth has a smooth face,—old age makes wrinkles.	**Mládí má hladké líce, — stáří dělá vrásky.**	*mláďee má hlădké leetsĕ, —stárshee ďelá vrássky.*
A high forehead, a keen eye, long moustaches, — such was the young man.	**Vysoké čelo, bystré o- ko, dlouhé kníry, — takový byl mladík.**	*visŏké chellŏ, bistré ŏkŏ, dloŭhé kñeery,—tăkovee bill mlăďeek.*
The eyes are the organ of sight, the ears (are the organ of) hearing;—the nose is the organ of smell.	**Oči jsou orgán zraku, uši sluchu; — nos je nástroj čichu.**	*ŏchi soŭ orgán zrăkŭ, ŭshi slŭkhŭ; — noss yĕ nástroy chikhŭ.*
Young girls usually have coral lips.	**Mladé dívky mívají ko- ralové rty.**	*mlădé ďeefky meevăyee korălŏvé rti.*
Babies have chubby cheeks.	**Děcka mají boubelaté tváře.**	*ďetskă măyee boŭbellăté tvárshĕ.*
You still have a full set of teeth (literally: "all the teeth").	**Vy ještě máte všechny zuby.**	*vy yeshťe mátĕ fshĕkhny zŭby.*
I have all (my) front teeth, but a few molars are wanting;— I had them pulled.	**Mám všechny přední zuby, ale pár stoli- ček mi chybí; — dal jsem je vytrhnouti.**	*mám fshĕkhny prshĕdñee zŭby; ălĕ pár stolichek me khibee; — dăl sem yĕvyt*rhnoŭt*
Why did you have them pulled? — Because they ached me; they were decayed.	**Proč jste je dal trhati? — Proto že mě bo- lely; byly vyžrané.**	*proch stĕ yĕ dăl t*rhăt? — proto že myĕ bolĕly; billi vižrăné.*
A decayed tooth always aches; — it is best to pull it out.	**Vyžraný zub vždycky bolí; nejlíp ho vytr- hnouti.**	*vyžranee zŭb ditsky bolee; — neyleep hŏ vy- t*rhnoŭt.*
The pulling of teeth is a painful operation,	**Trhání zubů je bolest- ná operace, — ob-**	*t*rháñee zŭboo yĕ bolest- ná ŏperătsĕ,—obzláshť*

– especially when the tooth has a big root.	zvlášť má-li zub velký kořen.	*má-li zŭb velkee koršĕn.*
Children lose the milk-teeth;— they fall out of themselves.	Děti ztrácí mléčné zuby; — vypadají samy.	*ďeťi strátsee mléchné zŭby; — vypădăyee sămy.*
With the teeth we bite; hence they are of a very hard substance.	Zuby kousáme; proto jsou z velmi tvrdé látky.	*zŭby koŭsámĕ; protŏ soŭ zvellmi tvᵉrdé látky.*
The teeth are set (liter. "sit")in the jaw-bone	Zuby sedí v čelisti.	*zŭby sĕďee fchĕlisťi.*
The windpipe carries the air into the lungs, where the blood is oxydized.	**Průdušnice** vede vzduch do plic, kde krev se okysličí.	*proodŭshñitsĕ vĕdĕ vzdŭkh dŏ plits, gdĕ kref sĕ okyslichee.*
The ribs inclose the thoracic cavity.— There are true ribs and false ribs.	Žebra zavírají hrudní dutinu. — Jsou pravá žebra a falešná žebra.	*žebră zăveerăyee hrŭdñee dŭťinŭ. — soŭ prăvá žebră ă făleshná žebră.*
The spinal column is composed of links; which we call vertebrae.	Páteř skládá se ze článků, které nazýváme obratle.	*pátersh skládá sĕ zĕ chlánkoo, které năzeevámĕ obrătlĕ.*
Burdens are most easily carried (i. e. "we carry") on shoulders.	Břemena nosíme nejsnáze na plecích.	*brshĕmenă noseemĕ neysnázĕ nă pletseekh.*
The hand is an exceedingly important member. — The hand has five fingers.	Ruka jest úd nesmírně důležitý. — Ruka má pět prstů.	*rŭkă yest ood nĕsmeernĕ doolĕžitee. — rŭkă má pyĕt pᵉrstoo.*
The negroes usually have strong arms.	Negrové mívají silné paže.	*nĕgrové meevăyee silné păžĕ.*
Whoever walks a great deal, must have sound legs.	Kdo chodí mnoho pěšky, musí míti zdravé nohy.	*gdŏ khoďee mnŏhŏ pyĕshky, mŭsee meet zdrăvé nŏhy.*
The stubbing of the big toe causes pain.	Zakopnutí palce u nohy dělá bolest.	*zăkopnuťee păltsĕ ŭ nŏhy ďelá bŏlest.*

The digestive apparatus is a vital organ. Food is digested in the stomach and in the bowels.	Zažívací ústrojí jest životní orgán. Pokrm ztráví se v žaludku a ve střevách.	*zăžeevătsee oostroyee yest životňee orgán. pok^erm strávee sě v žălůdkŭ ă vě strshěvákh.*

VOCABULARY.

Dar, m. *dăr,* the gift
tlukot, m. *tlŭkot,* the beating
kyslík, m. *kissleek,* oxygen
okysličiti, *okisslichit,* to oxygenate
dusík, m. *dŭsseek,* nitrogen
vzduch, m. *vzdŭkh,* the air
pokrm, m. *pok^erm,* the food
orgán, m. ⎰ the organ
nástroj, m. *nástroy* ⎱
článek, m. *chlánek,* the link
neger, m. *neg^er,* the negro
mládí, n. *mlăďee,* youth
mladík, m. *mlăďeek,* the young man
dívka, f. *ďeefka,* the girl
látka, f. *látkă,* the material, the stuff;
žilka, f. *žilka,* a small vein;
pleť, f. the skin
přísloví, n. *prsheeslovee,* the proverb
plemeno, n. *plěměnŏ* ⎱ the race
plémě, n. *plémyě* ⎰
břemeno, n. *brshěmenŏ,* the burden
dutý, á, é *dŭtee,* hollow
prudký, á, é *prŭdkee,* fast
prudce, adv. *prŭdsě,* fast, rapidly;
popudlivý, á, é *pŏpŭdlivee,* excitable
normální, *normálňee,* normal
pravidelný, *prăvidelnee,* regular
pravý, á, é *prăvee,* true, right;
falešný, á, é *fălěshnee,* false

plavý, á, é *plăvee,* fair, blonde;
koralový, á, é *korălovee,* coral (adj.)
boubelatý, á, é *boŭbělătee,* chubby
bolestný, á, é *bolestnee,* painful
vyžraný, á, é *vyžrănee,* decayed
důležitý, á, é *doolěžitee,* important
takový, á, é *tăkovee,* such
nesmírně, *něksmeerňe,* exceedingly
pěšky, *pyěshky,* on foot
obsahovati, *obsăhŏvăt,* to contain
panovati, *pănovăt,* to reign, to prevail;
shodovati se, *shodŏvăt sě,* to agree
chyběti, *khibyět,* to be wanting;
trhati, *t^erhăt,* to pull, to tear;
trhání, n. *t^erhăňee,* the pulling
vytrhnout, *vyt^erhnoŭt,* to pull out;
padati, *pădăt,* to fall
vypadati, *vypădăt* ⎱ to fall out;
vypadnouti, *vypădnoŭt* ⎰
kousati, *koŭsăt,* to bite
nazývati, *názeevăt,* to call (by a name)
skládati se (ze), *sklădăt sě,* to be composed (of);
zavírati, *zăveerăt,* to inclose (also "to shut");
zakopnouti, *zăkopnoŭt,* to stub;
zakopnutí, n. *zăkopnŭťee,* the stubbing.

Disease and cure.
NEMOC a LÉČENÍ.

Nemoc, *němots,* sickness, illness, disease;

lehká nemoc, *lĕhká n.* light disease;

těžká nemoc, *ťežká n.* acute or dangerous disease;

nemocen, cna, cno *němotsen* ⎫ sick,
nemocný, á, é*) *nemotsnee* ⎬ ill, diseased

těžce nemocen, *ťeshtsĕ n.* very sick, dangerously sick;

býti nemocen, *beet němotsĕn* ⎫ to be
stonati,   *stonát* ⎬ sick;

roznemocise, *róznĕmótsi sĕ* ⎫ to fall sick; to
rozstonati se, *róstonát sĕ,* ⎬ betaken sick:

choroba, f. *khŏrobá,* ailment, affection;

chorobný, á, é *khŏrobnee,* ailing, affected;

marod, (coloq.) *márod,* ailing, sickly;

maroditi, *márod'it,* to be ailing;

neduh, m. *nĕdŭh* ⎫ ailment, affec-
neduživost, f. *nĕdŭživost,* ⎬ tion, infirmity, disorder;

neduživý, á, é *nĕdŭživee,* ailing, infirm;

neduživec, m. *nĕdŭživets,* ⎫ sickly or
maroda, m. *márodá* ⎬ infirm person;

mrzák, m. *merzák,* cripple

zmrzačiti, *zmerzáchit,* to cripple

zmrzačen, a, o**) *zmerzáchĕn* ⎫ crip-
zmrzačený, á, é *zmerzáchĕnee* ⎬ pled

zmrzačenost, f. *zmerzáchĕnost,* the crippled condition;

rána, f. *ráná,* the wound

raniti, *ráñit* ⎫ to wound
poraniti, *poráñit* ⎬

raněný, á, é *ráñenee,* wounded

poranění, n. *poráñeñee* ⎫ the wound-
úraz, m. *oráz* ⎬ ing, a hurt or injury;

ublížiti, *ŭbleežit* ⎫ to hurt,
uškoditi, *ŭshkod'it* ⎬ to injure;

uhoditi, *ŭhod'it,* to strike, to hurt by striking;

pohmožditi, *pŏhmožd'it,* to bruise;

pohmoždění, n. *pŏhmožd'eñee,* the bruising, a bruise;

uskřípnouti, *ŭskrsheepnoŭt,* to jam, to squeeze;

uskřípnutí, n. *ŭskrsheepnŭťee,* a contusion by squeezing;

říznouti, *rsheeznoŭt,* to cut

říznutí, n. *rsheeznuťee* ⎫ a cut;
řez, m.   *rshĕz* ⎬

píchnouti, *peekhnoŭt* ⎫ to stab, to
bodnouti, *bodnoŭt* ⎬ pierce, to prick;

kousnouti, *koŭsnoŭt,* to bite

kousnutí, n. *koŭsnŭťee,* a bite.

---

*) **Nemocný** is the definite, **nemocen** the indefinite adjective. See Note 2 on page 103.

) **Zmrzačen is the passive participle (see Lesson **XXXVII**), from which the adjective **zmrzačený** is derived.

Lekař, m. *lékarsh,* the physician

doktor, m. *doktŏr,* the doctor

lékařství, n. *lékarsh-stwee,* the medical profession;

lékařský, *lékarshskee,* medical

porodní lékař, *pŏrodñee lékarsh,* the accoucheur

porodní bába, *p. bábă* ⎫
babička, *bábichka* ⎬ the midwife

ranhojič, m. *ránhŏyich,* the surgeon

zubní lékař, *zŭbñee lékarsh,* the dentist

vyléčiti, *vyléchit,* ⎫
vyhojiti, *vyhŏyit* ⎬ to cure, to heal
uzdraviti, *ŭzdrăvit* ⎭

vyléčení, vyhojení, uzdravení, the cure

uzdraviti se, *ŭzdrăvit sĕ* ⎫
pozdraviti se, *pozdrăvit sĕ* ⎬ to get well, to recover;
vystonati se, *vystŏnăt sĕ* ⎭

umříti, *ŭmrsheet,* ⎫
zemříti, *zemrsheet* ⎬ to die
skonati, *skonăt* ⎭

umírati, *ŭmeerăt,* to be dying;

vypustiti ducha, *vypŭsťit dŭkhă,* to breathe one's last;

smrt, f. *smᵉrt,* the death

náhlá smrt, *náhlă s.,* sudden death

prohlédnouti, *prohlédnout* ⎫ to exam-
proskoumati, *proskoŭmat* ⎬ ine, to
vyšetřiti, *vyshĕtrshit* ⎭ probe;

raditi se, *răďit sĕ,* to consult

předepsati, *prshĕdĕpsăt,* to prescribe

dieta, *de-ată* ⎫
mírnost v jídle, ⎬ the diet
meernost v-yeedlĕ ⎭

scházeti, *skházet* ⎫ to be
chřadnouti, *khrshădnoŭt* ⎬ sinking;

sbírati se, *sbeerăt sĕ,* to be recovering;

hubnouti, *hŭbnoŭt,* to lose flesh;

tloustnouti, *tloŭstnoŭt,* to gain flesh;

slábnouti, *slábnoŭt,* to grow weak;

síliti, *seelit,* to gain strength;

slabost, f. *slăbost,* weakness

síla, f. *seelă,* strength.

Bolest, f. *bolest* ⎫ the pain,
bolení, n. *bolĕñi* ⎬ the ache;

bolení břicha, *b. brshikhă,* belly-ache

kolika, f. *kolikă,* the colic

mám bolení, I have a pain in the bowels or stomach;

bolení hlavy, *b. hlăvy,* head-ache

,, **zubů,** *b. zŭbŭ,* tooth-ache

bolest v životě, *b. vživoťe,* pain in the abdomen;

,, **v kříži,** *b. fkrshee-ži,* pain in the small of the back;

bolest v zádech, *b. vzádĕkh,* pain in the back;

,, **v noze (v nohou),** *b. vnŏzĕ (vnŏhoŭ),* pain in the leg, or foot (in the legs, or feet);

,, **v ruce (v rukou),** *b. vrŭtsĕ (vrŭkoŭ),* pain in the hand, or arm (in the hands, or arms);

bolest u srdce, *b. ŭsᵉrdsĕ,* pain in the heart-region;

,, **uvnitř,** *b. ŭvñitrsh,* pain inside

bolestný, á, é *bolestnee*, painful
bolavý, á, é *bolávee*, sore
bolák, m. the sore
boule, f. *boŭlĕ*, a boil, a bump;
vřed, m. *vrshĕd*, ulcer
krtice, pl. *kertĭtsĕ*, scrofula
rak, m. *răk*, cancer
otok, m. *ŏtŏk*, a swelling;
oteklý, á, é *ŏtĕklee*, swelled, swollen
oteci, *otĕtsi*, to swell
horký, á, é *horkee*, hot
horkost, f. } the heat, the fe-
rozpálenost, f. } ver, the feverishness

Zápal, m. *zápăl* } inflammation
zánět, m. *zánet* }
zapálený, á, é *zăpálĕnee* } inflamed
zanícený, á, é *zăneetsĕnee* }
zápal plic, *zápăl plits*, inflammation
of the lungs;
zápal mozku, z. *mŏzkŭ*, inflammation of the brain;
,, mozkové blány, z. *mŏzkŏvé
blány*, meningitis;
zápal střev, z. *strshĕf*, inflammation of the bowels;
zápal pobřišnice, z. *pobrshishñitsĕ*,
peritonitis;
,, pohrudnice, z. *pohrŭdñitsĕ*,
pleurisy;
souchotě, pl. *soŭkhoťe*
úbytě, pl. *oobyťe* } the con-
tuberkule, pl. *tŭberkŭlĕ* } sumption;
ochroma, *ŏkhromă* } paralysis
ochrnutí, *ŏkhᵉrnŭťee* }
mrtvice, f. *mᵉrtvitsĕ*, apoplexy
záškrt, m. *záshkᵉrt*, diphtheria

rozpálen, a, o *rospálĕn*, feverish;
horečka, f. *horĕchkă* } the ty-
horká nemoc, *horká nĕmots* } phus
hlavnička, f. *hlăvñichkă* } fever;
zimnice, f. *zimñitsĕ*, the ague
žlutá zimnice, *žlŭtá z.* the yellow-
fever;
mraziti, *mrăzit*, to chill
mrazení, n. *mrăzĕñi*, a chill, a shiver
mrazí mě, *mrăzee myĕ*, I feel a chill;
třásti se zimou, *trshăst sĕ zimoŭ*, to
shiver with cold.

krup, m. *krŭp*, the croup
psotník, m. *psottñeek*, the fits
spála, m. *spálă* } the measles
šarlát, m. *shărlát* }
osutiny, pl. *ossŭťiny*, the chicken-
pox
neštovice, pl. *neshtŏvitsĕ*, the small-
pox
očkovati, *ŏchkovăt*, to vaccinate
očkování, *ŏchkováñi*, vaccination
očkovaný, á, é *ŏchkovănee*, vacci-
nated
výraz, m. *veerăz*, eruption
vyražený, á, é *vyrăženee*, full of
eruption;
kožní nemoc, f. *kožñee nĕmots*, skin-
desease;
lišej, m. *lishey*, the lichen
mol, m. the ringworm
svrab, m. the itch
svrběti, *svᵉrbyĕt*, to itch
strup, m. *strŭp*, the scab, the scurf;
strupovitý, á, é *strŭpŏvitee*, scabby

hostec, m. *hostěts* } rheumatism
revma, n. *revmǎ* }

hostečný, *hostěchnee* } rheu-
revrmatický, *revmǎtitskee* } matic

srdeční vada, f. *sᵉrděchñee vǎdǎ*,
heart-desease;

vodnatelnost, f. *vŏdnǎtellnost*, drop-
sy;

vodnatelný, á, é *vŏdnǎtellnee*, drop-
sical

záduch, m. *zǎdǔkh*, asthma

záduslivý,á,é *zǎdǔshlivee*, asthmatic
kašel, m. *kǎ*hell*, the cough

modrý kašel, *modreek., the whoop-
ing cough

kašlati, *kǎshlǐt*, to cough

vyhazovati, *vyhǎzŏvǎt*, to throw up;

dáviti, *dǎvit* } to vomit
blíti, *bleet* }

dávení, n. *dǎveñi* } the vomiting;
blití, n. *blǐťee* }

Zlomiti, *zlomit* } to break
zlámati, *zlǎmǎt* }

zlomený, á, é *zloměnee*, broken

zlámanina, f. *zlǎmǎñinǎ* } a broken
bone, a
zlomenina, f. *zlŏm......* } fracture:

puklá kost, f. *pǔklǎ kost*, a cracked
bone;

vymknouti, *vymknŏňt*, to dislocate;

vymknouti kloub, *v. kloǔb*, to sprain
a joint;

vymknutí, n. *vymknǔťee*, a disloca-
tion, a sprain;

srovnati kost, *srŏvnǎt kost*, to set a
bone;

křeče, pl. *krshěᵹhě*, cramps

mdloba, f. faintness, fainting fit;

mdlý, á, é *mdlee*, faint;

omdleti, *ŏmdlět*, to faint, to swoon;

omdlévání, n. *ŏmdlěvǎñi*, fainting
fits, swooning.

nezáživnost, f. *nězǎživnost* } indi-
špatné trávení, n. *shpǎtné* } gestion
trǎveñi }

záživný, á, é *zǎživnee*, digestible

nezáživný, *nězǎživnee*, indigestible

větry, pl. *vyětry* } wind, flatu-
nadouvání,n.*nǎdouvǎñi* } lence:
nadýmání,n.*nǎdeemǎñi* }

nadmutý, á, é *nǎdmǔtee*, flatulent

běhavka, f. *byěhǎfka* } the
průjem, m. *prooyem* } diarrhea

zástava, f. *zǎstǎvǎ* } stoppage in
the bowels,
těžká stolice, *ťeshkǎ* } constipation,
stolitsě, } costivene-s;

úplavice, f. *ooplǎvitsě*, dysentery.

dáti do desek, *dǎt dŏ děssek*, to splint

obvázati ránu, *ŏbvǎzǎt rǎnǔ*, to dress
a wound;

obvazek, m. *ŏbvǎzek*, a dressing, a
bandage;

průtrž, m. *prootᵉrsh*, the rupture

průtržní pás, m. the truss

hrb, m. *hᵉrb*, a hump, a hunch;

hrbáč, *hᵉrbǎch*, a humpback;

hrbatý, á, é *hᵉrbᵌtee*, humpbacked;

kulhati, *kǔlhǎt*, to walk lamely;

kulhavý, á, é *kǔlhǎvee* } lame
chromý, á, é *khromee* }

dopadati, *dŏpǎdǎt*, to halt.

It is said that Mr. Hanush is sick. | Pan Hanuš je prý nemocen. | *păn hănŭsh yĕ prey nĕmotsĕn.*

Is he laid up?—Yes, he took to his bed. | Leží ?—Ano, ulehnul. | *ležee? — ănŏ, ŭlĕhnŭl.*

Is he very sick? — I think it is serious. | Je mu tuze zle? — Myslím že je to povážlivé. | *yĕ mŭ toozĕ zlĕ? — misleem že yĕ tŏ pŏvážlivé.*

Call a physician.—Send for a doctor. | Zavolejte lékaře.—Pošlete pro doktora. | *zăvoleytĕ lékărshĕ.—pŏshlĕtĕ prŏ dŏktorŭ.*

We have sent for him. — The doctor has been here already. | Poslali jsme pro něj. — Doktor už tu byl. | *pŏslăli smĕ prŏ ñey.—dŏktor ŭsh tŭ biŭ.*

When was Mr. Hanush taken sick?—Yesterday morning; all at once he felt a chill, then he felt feverish. | Kdy se pan Hanuš rozstonal? — Včera ráno; z nenadání dostal mrazení, pak horkost. | *gdy sĕ păn h. rostŏnăl? — fcherŭ ránŏ; znĕnădáñi dostăl mrăzĕñi, păk horkost.*

What is the trouble?—What disease has he? | Co je mu?—Nač se rozstonal? | *tsŏ yĕ mŭ? — năch sĕ rostŏnăl?*

I think it is inflammation of the lungs. | Myslím že na zánět plic. | *misleem že nă záñet plits.*

That would be dangerous.—What does the physician say? | To by bylo nebezpečné. — Co povídá lékař ? | *tŏ bi billŏ nĕbespĕchné. — tsŏ poveedá lékarsh ?*

The doctor thinks that he has inflammation of the lungs. | Doktor myslí že má zápal plic. | *dŏktor mislee že má zápăl plits.*

Then I pity him. | To ho lituju. | *tŏ hŏ litŭyŭ.*

How is Mr. Swoboda to-day? is he better? | Jak je panu Svobodovi dnes? Je mu líp? | *yăk yĕ pănŭ swŏbŏdŏvi dness? yĕ mŭ leep?*

Always the same thing; — no better,. no worse; — there is no change. | Pořád stejně; — ani líp, ani hůř; — nic se to nemění. | *porshád steyñe; — ăñi leep, ăñi hoorsh; — ñits sĕ tŏ nemyĕñee.*

It does not grow worse, — it doesn't grow better.	Nehorší se to, — nelepší se to.	něhorshee sě tŏ — nelepshee sě tŏ.
What disease has he?— What is his disease? —What ails him?	Co má za nemoc?—Jakou má nemoc! — Nač stůně?	tsŏ má zá němots? — yákoŭ má němots? — nách stooñe?
The physician himself doesn't know yet; — until it develops.*)— It is not known what will come of it.	Lékař sám neví ještě; — až jak se to ukáže. — Neví se co z toho bude.	lékarsh sám něvee yeshťe; — ásh yák sě tŏ ŭkáže. — něvee sě tsŏ stŏhŏ bŭdě.
I hope it will not be so bad.	Doufám že nebude to tak zlé.	doŭfám že něbŭdě tŏ ták zlé.
I hope he will recover. — Perhaps he will soon get well.	Doufám že z toho vyjde. — Snad se brzo uzdraví.	doŭfám že stŏhŏ veedě. — snád sě berzŏ ŭzdrávee.
I don't know if he will get over it. — Who knows if he will get well.	Nevím vyjde-li z toho. — Kdož ví jestli z toho vyjde.	něveem veedělli stŏhŏ. — gdŏž vee yestli stŏhŏ veedě.
He is well along in years already.	Už je v letech.	ŭsh yě vletěkh.
Well, he needs good nursing. — Give him the best care possible.	Inu, potřebuje dobré ošetření.—Dejte mu všemožnou péči.	inŭ, potrshěbŭyě dŏbré oshětrshěñi.-deytě mŭ fshěmožnoŭ péchi.
We nurse him faithfully.—We tend him as best we can.	Ošetřujeme ho pilně. — Sloužíme mu co nejlíp můžeme.	ŏshětrshŭyěmě hŏ pilñe.—sloŭžeemě mŭ tsŏ neyleep moožemě.
Yes, tend him as well	Ano, služte mu co	áno, slŭshtě mŭ tsŏ

---

*) **Až jak se to ukáže,** — until it shows itself or develops, — is in fact an elliptical sentence, meaning: "*We must wait,* until it develops". Sentences of this character are frequently used; for instance:

Až jak bude, "until (we see) how it will be;" — "(it depends upon) how it will be".

Až jak to dopadne, "until (we see) how it will come out"; — (it depends upon) how it will come out".

as you can. — Nurse him in every possible manner.	možná. — Obslužte ho se vším.	možná.—obslŭshtĕ hŏ sĕ fsheem.
We are with him day and night.	Jsme u něj ve dne v noci.	smĕ ŭ ñey vĕ dnĕ vnotsi.
Has the doctor prescribed for him? — Yes, he wrote a prescription.	Předepsal mu doktor? — Ano, napsal recept.	prshĕdĕpsăl mŭ dŏktor? — ănŏ, năpsăl rĕtsept.
Have you sent to the drug-store?—We sent there right away. — The druggist prepared it immediately.	Poslali jste do lékárny? — Poslali jsme tam hned. — Lékárník to připravil okamžitě.	pŏslăli stĕ dŏ lékárny? — pŏslăli smĕ tăm hněd. — lékárñik tŏ prshiprăvil ŏkămži-t'e.
The patient takes his medicine regularly.	Pacient užívá pravidelně.	pătsient ŭžeevá prăvidelñe.
I hope to God that he will get well.	Dá bůh že se pozdraví.	dá booh že sĕ pozdrăvee.
I hope that he will soon be on his legs.	Doufám že bude brzo na nohou.	doŭfám že bŭdĕ bᵉrzŏ nă nŏhoŭ.
I fear that he will soon be "on the board" (i. e. dead).	Bojím se že bude brzo na prkně.	boyeem sĕ že bŭdĕ bᵉrzŏ nă pᵉrkñe.
I am afraid that nothing will help him.	Bojím se že nic mu nepomůže*).	boyeem sĕ že ñits mŭ nĕpŏmoože.
I fear that he will die.	Obávám se že umře.	ŏbávám se že ŭmrshĕ.
Is it true that Mr. Aleš died?	Je to pravda, že pan Aleš umřel?	yĕ tŏ prăvdă že păn Alesh ŭmrshell?
I am sorry to say it is true.	Bohužel, je to pravda.	bŏhŭžel, yĕ tŏ prăvdă!
When did he die? – He died at midnight. — He died toward morning.	Kdy zemřel? — Skonal o půlnoci. — Skonal k ránu.	gdy zemrshell?? — skonăl ŏ poolnotsi. — skonăl kránŭ.

---

*) See Note 1 on page 36, about double negation.

English	Czech	Pronunciation
What did he die of? — Of inflammation of the lungs.	Nač umřel?—Na zapálení plic.	*nách ümrshell? — ná zápáleñi plíls.*
Very few get over that, — at his age.	Z toho málo kdo vyjde,—v jeho věku.	*stǒhǒ málǒ gdǒ veedě, — vyěhǒ vyěkü.*
Indeed very few! — There was no help for him. — The doctor said so right off.	Ba málo kdo!—Nebylo mu žádné pomoci.— Doktor povídal to hned.	*Bă málǒ gdǒ! — nebillǒ mŭ žádné pomotsi. — dǒctor pǒveedál tǒ hněd.*
He said: There is no help for him; — the desease has been neglected.	Pravil: Není mu pomoci;—nemoc je zanedbána.	*právil: neyñi mŭ pomotsi; — němots yě zánedbáná.*
He neglected it. — He sent for the doctor too late.	Zanedbal to. — Poslal pro doktora pozdě.	*zánedbál tǒ. — pǒslál pro doctǒrá pozďe.*
He should have sent for the doctor sooner. — When the doctor came, it was too late.	Měl poslati pro doktora dříve.—Když doktor přišel, bylo pozdě.	*myěll pǒslál pro doctǒrá drsheecě. — gdyž doctǒr prshishell, billǒ pozďe.*
A desease must not be neglected.	Nemoc nesmí se zanedbati.	*němo!s něsmee sě zánedbát.*
Old Mrs. Hoshek died this morning.	Stará paní Hošková skonala dnes ráno.	*stárá páñi hoshkǒvá skonálá dness ránǒ.*
She died suddenly, — of heart desease.	Zemřela náhle, — na srdeční vadu.	*zemrshellá náhlě, — ná srdechñee vádŭ.*
She was taken sick and in half an hour it was all over with her.	Přišlo jí zle a za půl hodiny bylo po ní.	*prshishlǒ yee zlě ă zä pool hoďiny billo pǒ ñi.*
That was a sudden death.	To byla náhlá smrt.	*tǒ billá náhlá smert.*
It is better than to suffer long.	Je to lepší než trápiti se dlouho.	*yě tǒ lepshee nesh trápit sě dloůhǒ.*
Preserve us from long suffering!	Jen ne dlouhé trápení!	*yen ně dloůhé trápěñi.*

Chronic consumption is a slow disease; — acute consumption has a quick run.	Chronické souchotiny jsou zdlouhavá ne-moc;-akutní soucho-tě mají rychlý běh.	*khronitské soŭkhoťiny soŭ zdloŭhăvă nĕmots; — ăkŭtñee soŭkhoťe măyee rykhlee byĕh.*
Drowning is a cruel death:— so is strang-ling.— Hanging is an easy death, if the neck is broken.	Utopení je těžká smrt; udušení taky. — O-běšení je lehká smrt, zlomí-li se vaz.	*ŭtŏpeñi yĕ ťeshká smᵉrt; — ŭdŭshĕñi tăke. — obyĕshĕñi yĕ lĕhká smᵉrt, zlomee-li sĕ văz.*
A. took his own life;— he committed suicide	A. vzal si život;—spá-chal samovraždu.	*A. vzăl si život; — spá-khăl sămŏvrăždŭ.*
He drowned himself;— he hanged himself.— he poisoned himself; — he shot himself; — he cut his throat; — he thrust a knife into his breast.	Utopil se; — oběsil se; otrávil se; — zastře-lil se; — podřezal si krk; — vrazil si nůž do prsou.	*ŭtopil sĕ; — ŏbyĕsil sĕ; — otrăvil sĕ; — ză-strshĕlil sĕ; — pod-rshĕzăl si kᵉrk; — vrăzil si noož dŏ pᵉr-soŭ.*
And why did he do it? — Most likely he was insane.	A proč to udělal? — Nejspíš byl šílený.	*ă proch tŏ ŭďelăl? — neyspeesh bill sheelĕ-nee.*

VOCABULARY.

Nemocný, m. *nĕmotsnee* } the male
pacient, m. *pătsiĕnt* } patient;
nemocná, f. *nĕmotsná* } the female
pacientka, f. *pătsiĕntkă* } patient;
lékárna, f. *lékárná* } the drug store,
apatyka, f. *ăpătiká* } the pharmacy;
lékárník, m. *lékárñik* } the druggist,
apatykář, m. *ăpătikărsh* } the apothecary;
horkost, f. *horkost*, the fever heat;
mrazení, n. *mrăzĕñi*, the chill;
předpis, m. *prshĕdpis* } the prescrip-
recept, m. *retsept* } tion, receipt, the recipe.
předepsati, *prshĕdĕpsăt*, to prescribe

připraviti, *prshiprăvit*, to prepare;
péče, f. *péchĕ*, the care
pečovati (o), *pĕchovăt*, to care (for);
ošetření, n. *oshĕtrshĕñi*, the nursing
ošetřovati, *oshĕtrshŏvăt*, to nurse, to tend;
sloužiti, *sloŭžit* } to serve, to wait
obsloužiti, *obsloŭžŭ* } on, to tend;
potřebovati, *potrshĕbŏvăt*, to want, to need;
báti se, *bát sĕ*, to fear
obávati se, *obăvăt sĕ*, to apprehend
trápiti se, *trăpit sĕ*, to suffer

trápení, n. *trápĕňi*, the suffering
zanedbati, *zănedbăt*, to neglect
zanedbán, a, o, neglected
měniti se, *myĕňit sĕ*, to change
neměuí se, *nemyĕňee sĕ*, it does not change;
horšiti se, *horshit sĕ*, to grow worse
nehorší se, *nehorshee sĕ*, it does not grow worse;
ukázati, *ŭkázăt*, to show
ukáže se, *ŭkáżĕ sĕ*, it will show itself;

vyjíti z toho, *ve-yeet stŏhŏ*, to come out of it;
nebezpečí, n. *nĕbespĕchee*, the danger
nebezpečný, á, é *nĕbespĕchnee*, dangerous
okamžik, m. *okămżik*, the moment
málo kdo, *mălŏ gdŏ*, very few people
bohužel, *bŏhŭżell*, alas; I am sorry to say;
vaz, m. *văz*, the back of the head; the neck.

Drugs and medicines.
LÉČIVA a LÉKY.

Míra, f. *meeră*, the measure
váha, f. *váhă*, the weight
měřiti, *myĕrshit*, to measure
vážiti, *vážit*, to weigh
míchati, *meekhăt*, to mix
prositi, *proseet* } to garble
přebrati, *prshĕbrăt* }
libra, f. *libră*, a pound
unce, f. *ŭntsĕ*. an ounce
lot, m. (about half an ounce);
kvintlík, m. *quintleek*, (about ⅛ of an ounce);
grán, m. a grain
lžíce, f. *lżeetsĕ* or *żeetsĕ*, a spoon, a spoonful;

Prášek, m. *práshek*, a powder
 ,, na zuby, *p. nă zŭby*, tooth-p.;
 ,, šumivý, *p. shŭmivee*, Seidlitz-powder;
 ,, perský, Persian powder;

lžička, f. *lżeechkă* or *żeechkă*, a small spoon; a small spoonful;
kávová lžička, f. a coffee or tea spoonful;
čajový šálek, m. *chayovee shálek*, a tea-cup;
sklenice, f. *skleňitsĕ*, a glass
vinná sklenice, f. wine-glass
hrstka, f. *herstkă* } a hand
přehoušle, f. *prshĕhoŭshlĕ* } ful
špetka, f. *shpetkă*, a pinch
kapka, f. *kăpkă*, a drop
kapky, pl. *kăpky*, drops
pět kapek, *pyĕt kăpek*, five drops; etc
dávka, f. *dáfkă*, a dose.

prášky, pl. *práshky*, powders
pilulka, f. *pillŭlkă*, a pill
pilulky, pl. pills
kašička, f. *kăshichkă*, a poultice
těstíčko, n. *ťesťichkŏ*, a paste

mazání, n. *mázáňi*, an ointment
masť, f. *mâsť*, salve
lektvar, m. confection
tinktura, f. *tinctoorā*, tincture
flastr, m. *flâster* } plaster
náplast, m. *náplăst* } plaster
fizikátor, m. vesicatory
olej, m. *olĕy*, oil
extrakt, m. extract
výstřelek, m. *ceestrshĕlek*, spirit
semeno, n. *semĕnŏ* } seed
semínko, n. *semeenkŏ* } seed
list, m. *list*, leaf
listí, n. *lisťee*, leaves
kořen, m. *korshĕn*, root
kořínek, m. *korsheenĕk*, little root
bobule, f. *bobŭlĕ*, bulb
kůra, f. *koorā*, bark, peel
šťáva, f. *shťávā*, juice
bylina, f. *billinā*, herb
lékařská bylina, *lékarshská b.*, medicinal herb;
odvar, m. decoction
nálev, m. *nálef* } infusion
výmok, m. *veemok* } infusion

Aloe, n. *ăloĕ*, aloes
anjelika, f. *ănyellică*, angelica
anýz, m. *ăneez*, anise
arabská guma, f. gum arabic
arnika, prha, f. arnica

Baldrian (odolen, kozlík), m. water-avens;
balšám, balzám, m. *bălshám, bălzám*, balsam
bavlna, f. *băv^elnā*, cotton

roztok, m. *rostŏk*, solution
dávidlo, n. emetic
počisťovadlo, n. *pochisťovădlŏ*, purgative
lehký, á, é *lĕhkee*, light, soft, easy
prudký, á, é *prŭdkee*, drastic
projímavý, á, é *proyeemăvee*, laxative
silící, *seelitsee*, tonic
silivka, f. *silifkā*, a tonic
pro spaní, *pro spâňi*, soporific
narkotický, *narkotiskee* } narcotic
omamující, *omâmŭyeetsee* } narcotic
močohnavý, *mochŏhnăvee*, diuretic
pijavka, f. *piyăfkā*, a leech
pijavky, pl. *piyăfky*, leeches
baňka, f. cupping-glass
příjemný, á, é *prshee-yemnee*, agreeable, pleasant;
odporný, á, é *odpornee* } nauseating
ošklivý, á, é *oshklivee* } nauseating
ošklivost, f. *oshklivost*, nausea
kyselina, *kissellină*, acid
kysličník, *kisslichňeek*, oxide
síran, m. *seerăn*, sulphate.

bedrník, m. *bed^erňík*, pimpernel
bezový květ, m. *bĕzovee kvyĕt*, elder flowers;
běloba, f. *byĕlobă*, white lead;
bílkovina, f. *beelkŏvină*, albumen
blín, m. *bleen*, henbane
bobko-třešně, f. cherry-laurel
bolehlav, m *bolĕhlăv*, hemlock
boží tráva (řecké seno), fenugreek seed

brambořík (svinský chleba, svinský ořech), sow-bread;
broskvové listí, n. peach-leaves;
brutnák obecný, m. borage
bříza, f. *brsheezä*, birch,(bitula alba);

Celík, m. *tsellik*, golden-rod
cesmina (lesní kopřiva), f. holly
cink, m. *tsink*, zink
citron, m. *tsitron*, lemon
citronová kůra, f. lemon peel
citronová šťáva, f. lemon juice
cukr, m. *tsŭker*, sugar
cukr hroznový, glucose
cukr mléčný, *ts. mléchnee*, sugar of milk;
cukr olověný, *ts. olovyĕnee*, sugar of lead.

Dávičný kámen, m. *dávichnee kámen*, tartar emetic;
dehet, m. *dĕhĕt*, tar
divizna, f. *ďiviznä*, mullein
dobrá mysl, f. see marjánka;
dračí krev, f. *dráchee krĕf*, dragon's blood;
draslík, m. (kalium, n.), *drässléek*, potassium
draslo, n. see salajka;
dřevo myší, n. *drshĕvŏ mishee*, bitter-sweet
dřevo sladké, liquorice
dřín, m. *drsheen*, dogwood
dřistal, m. barberry
drnavec,m. *dernávets*, wall-pellitory
droždí, see kvasnice;
dubinky, pl. nutgall, galls;

durman, m. (panenské jablko pichlavé), stramonium seed;
dusík, m. *dŭsseek*, nitrogen
dusičnan olovnatý, nitrate of lead.

Ether, m. *éter*, ether
euforbium, *eŭforbiŭm*, euforbia.

Fenikl, m. fennel
fialka, f. *fiálkä*, violet
fík, m. *feek*, fig
fosfor, m. phosporus.

Gdoulové semeno, m. quince seed;
granátové jablko, n. pomegranate
guma arabská, f. gum arabic
    " elastická, f. gum elastic

Heřmánek, m. *hershmánek*, chamomile
hořčice, f. *horchitsĕ*, mustard
hořec, m. *horshets*, gentian
houba, f. *hoŭbä*, sponge
houby, pl. mushrooms,
hřebíček, m. *rshĕbeechek*, cloves
hulevník, m. hedge-mustard

Chinin, m. *khinin*, quinine
china, f.   } cinchona, Pechinník pravý, m. } ruvian bark;
chlorové vápno, n. *khlorŏvé vápnŏ*, chloride of lime;
chmel, m. *khmell*, hops.

Ibiš (proskurník), m. *ibish*, marshmellow

Jalovec, m. *yállovĕts*, juniper
jaterník, m. *yäterñik*, liverwort

jed, *yĕd,*
utrejch, *ŭtreykh* } poison

jelení roh, *yelleñee rŏh,* hartshorn
 " lůj, *y. looy,* hart's tallow
jeřáb, m. *yersháb,* mountain ash;
jetelice, f. (janovec, m.) broom tops
jód, m. *yód,* iodine.

Kafr, m *kăf^er,* camphor
kalamín, m. calamine
kalanka, f. pinkroot
kamenec, m. *kămenĕts,* alum
kampeška, f. *kămpeshkă,* logwood
kastoreum, n. castor
kaštan, m. *kăshtăn,* horse-chestnut;
kaučuk, m. India rubber;
klejt, (kysličník olovnatý) m. *kleyt,*
 oxide of lead;
klejicha bulvatá, butterfly-weed
kmín, m. *kmeen,* caraway seed;
kmín vodní, *k. vodñee,* water-hem-
 lock (fine-leaved);
konítrud, m. hedge-hyssop
konopí, n. *kŏnopee,* hemp
konopí indické, *k. inditské,* Indian
 hemp;
konopný extract, m. extract of hemp
kopytník tupolistý, m. asarum Eu-
 ropaeum;
kopr, m. *kop^er,* dill
kořalka, f. see pálenka;
korek, m. cork
kořen hadí, m. *korshĕn hăďee,* bistort
 " maliny, blackberry root;
 " omanu, elicampane
 " omějový, aconite root;

kosatec, m. *kossătets,* blue flag, iris
 versicolor;
kozinec, m. *kozinets,* tragacanth
kozlík odolen, m. valerian
kožokvět, m. queen's root;
křen, m. *krshĕn,* horse-radish
krevnice, f. *krĕcñitsĕ,* bloodroot
křída, f. *krsheedă,* chalk
kroupy, pl. *kroŭpy,* pearl barley;
krtičník, m. *k^erťichñeek,* figwort
krušinka, *krŭshinkă,* dyer's weed,
 genista;
krusíček, (pampalík), m. marigold
kůra dubová, f. *kooră dŭbŏvá,* black-
 oak bark;
 " divoké třešně, wild cherry bark
 " vrbová, *k. v^erbŏvá,* willow bark;
 " jilmová, *k. yilmŏvá,* elm bark;
 " červené jilmy, slippery elm bark
kvasnice, pl. *kwăssñitsĕ,* yeast
květ, m. *kwyĕt,* flowers
květel, f. *kwyĕtell,* common toad flax
kyprej, m. *kiprey,* loosestrife
kyslík, m. *kissleek,* oxygen
kyselina, f. *kisselină,* acid
 " citronová, citric acid
 " karbolová, carbolic acid;
 " sanytrová, nitric acid;
 " solná, muriatic acid;
 " vínová, tartaric acid.

Lep na ptáky, m. bird-lime
lentyšek, m. mastic
levandule, f. lavender
líh, m. *leeh,* alcohol
lílek červený, see dřevo myší;
limonka, f. marsh rosemary;

listí bobkové, n. laurel leaves;
lomikmát, m. common groundsel;
lopuch, (hořký lupen) m. burdock
lůj, m. *looy*, tallow;
,, jelení, hart's tallow;
,, skopový, mutton suet
lžičník, m. *lžichňik*, common scurvy-grass;
lék proti hlistám, vermifuge.

Mák, m. poppy-seed
mandle hořké, pl. *mǎndlě horshké*,
bitter almonds;
,, sladké, sweet almonds;
mařena, f. *mǎrshěnǎ*, madder
marjánka, f. *mǎryánkǎ*, common
marjoram;
máta, (marulka) f. catnep
máta peprná, f. peppermint
máta kadeřavá, pennyroyal
med, m. honey
měď, f. *myěď*, copper
medokvět, m. *mědǒkwyět*, marsh
trefoil, buckbean;
medvědice obecná, *medvyěďitsě o-
betsná*, bearberry leaves;
mejlí, n. (mišpule, f.) *meylee*, mistletoe
melasa, f. molasses
mléko, n. milk
mlékový punč, milk-punch, toddy;
morušová šťáva, mulberry juice;
mouka bílá, f. *moŭkǎ beelá*, wheat
flour;
,, černá, *m. chernǎ*, rye flour;
,, ovesná, *m. ověssná*, oatmeal;

mrkev, f. *merkef*, carrot seed;
mýdlo, n. *meedlǒ*. soap
,, mazavé, soft soap
,, amygdalinové, amygdaline
soap;
,, mandlové, almond oil soap;
myrha, f. myrrh

Naháč, m. see ocún;
námel, m. ergot
náprstník červený, m. foxglove
narcis kadeřavý, m. daffodil
nátržník, m. tormentil
netík, m. see ženský vlas;
netýkalka, f. touch-me-not
nové koření, n. *nové korshěňi*, allspice;
nickaminek, see skalice;
nátrium, see sodík.

Ocet, m. *otset*, vinegar
ocún, m. *otsoon*, colchicum seed;
odolen, m. valerian
olej, m. *ǒley*, oil
,, bavlněný, cotton-seed oil
,, z bergamotek, oil of bergamot
,, citronový, lemon oil
,, dymianový, oil of thyme, oil of
origanum;
,, hořčičný, oil of mustard
,, heřmánkový, chamomile oil
,, jantarový, oil of amber
,, kafrový, camphor oil
,, kokosový, cocoa-nut oil
,, koprový, oil of dill
,, krotonový, croton oil
,, lněný, flaxseed oil

16

olej mandlový, almond oil
„ olivový,   ⎫
„ dřevěný   ⎬ olive oil
„ brabancový   ⎭
„ ricinový, castor oil
„ růžový, oil of roses
„ sesamový, benne oil
„ skořicový, cinnamon oil
„ terpentinový, oil of turpentine
„ z volské nohy, neats-foot oil
olovo, n. *olŏvŏ*, lead
ořech, m. *orshěkh*, nut
„ muškátový, nutmeg
orlíček, m. *orleechek*, columbine
osládič, m. *osláďich*, male fern
ožanka, f. (gamandr), germander.

Pálenka obyčejná, f. whisky
„ vinná (francouská), brandy
pampeliška (smetanka), f. dandelion
paprika, f. red pepper, cayenne p.
pekelný kamínek, m. lapis infernalis;
pelynek, m. wormwood
peltrám, m. pellitory
pepř, m. *pěprsh*, black pepper
petružel, f. parsley root
pijavky, pl. f. *piyăfky*, leeches
pížmo, n. *peežmŏ*, musk
plavuň, f. lycopodium
plicník, m. *plitsňik*, Iceland moss;
ploštičník, m. black snakeroot, cimicifuga;
pomoranč, m. *pomoránch*, orange
pomorančový květ, orange flowers;
pomorančová kůra, orange peel;

popel z kostí, m. *popell skosťi*, bone ash;
posed, m. white bryony
potaš (draslo), see salajka;
potměchuť, f.   ⎫
psí víno červené, n.   ⎬ bittersweet
protěž, f. cudweed, life-everlasting;
pryskyřice, f. *pryskirshitsě*, resin, rosin;
pryskyrky, see španělské mouchy;
psí rmen, m. mayweed
pukavec (vlčí mák), m. *pŭkăvets*, red-poppy petals;
puškvorec, m. *pŭshkworets*, sweet flag;

Rauta, f. *răŭtă*, rue
rebarbora, f. *rebarbŏră*, rhubarb
rozinky, pl. f. raisins
rozmarina, f. rosemary
rozrazil, m. speedwell
rtuť, f. *rtŭť*, mercury
rulík zlomocný, m. deadly nightshade, belladonna root;
rum myrtový, m. bay-rum
rumělka, f. cinnabar
růže stolistá, f. hundred-leaved rose.

Sadec, m. *sădets*, eupatorium, thoroughwort;
sádlo, n. lard
salajka, f. *sălăykă*, potash
salmiak, m. sal ammoniac
sanytr, m. *sănyt°r*, saltpeter
semeno lněné, n. flaxseed, linseed;
„ tykvové, pumpkin seed;

semínko citvárové, European worm-
seed;
senes, m. purging cassia;
senesové listí, n. senna leaves;
seno řecké, n. *senŏ rshĕtské*, fenugreek;
sesamové listí, n. benne leaf;
síra, f. *seerá*, sulphur, brimstone;
síran, m. *seerán*, sulphate
síran draselnatý, sulphate of potash
síran měďnatý, sulphate of copper;
sirob, m. sirup
skalice bílá, f. *skállitsĕ beelí*, white
vitriol;
skila, f. squile
skořice, f. *skorshítsĕ*, cinnamon
 " bílá, canella
sladká vrbka, f. bittersweet
slíz, m. *sleez*, common mallow
smola, f. pitch
sodík, m. (natrium), n. sodium
soda suchá, f. (suchý nátron, kysličník sodnatý), dry soda,
protoxide of sodium;
soda žiravá, (nátron žíravý, hydrát
sodnatý), caustic soda, hy-
drate of soda;
sporýš, m. see železník;
starček, m. see lomihnát;
sůl kuchynská, f. *sool k.*, common
salt;
 " hořká, (Glauberova), Glauber's
salt, Epsom salt;
 " morská, bay salt;
 " křištálová, nitrate salt;
suřík, m. red oxide of lead;
svlačec, m. *svláchets*, scammony.

Šafrán, m. *sháfrán*, saffron
šalvěj, m. *shálvyĕy*, sage
šípek, m. *sheepek*, dog-rose, hip;
šišák, m. *shishák*, scullcap
škrob, m. *shkrob*, starch
škrobovina americká, f arrow-root
škumpa jedovatá, f. poison-oak
španělské mouchy, pl. f. Spanish
flies, cantharides;
špargl, m. *shpargl*, asparagus
šťovík, m. *shťovik*, sorrel
švestky, pl. f. *shwĕstky*, prunes.

Tabák, m. *tábák*, tobacco
tavola, f hardback
terpentýn, m. *terpenteen*, turpentine
tinktura arniková, f. tincture of
arnica;
tis, m. common European yew tree;
tojest, f. dog's-bane
tolije, f. *tolliyĕ*, parnassia palustris;
tomel virginský, persimmon
trán jaterní, m. cod-liver oil;
trnka, f. *ternká*, wild plumtree;
trojpecka, f. *troypetská*, fever root
třemdava, f. dictamnus, bastard
dittany;
třezalka, f. St. John's wort;
tuk velrybí, m. spermaceti
turan, m. fleabane, erigeron.

Uhel dřevěný, m. charcoal
uhel zvířecí, animal charcoal; bone-
black;
uhlík, m. *úhleek*, carbon
uhličitan hořečnatý, m. carbonate
of magnesia;

uhličitan sodnatý, carbonate of soda
užanka, f. hound's tongue.

Vanilka, f. vanilla
vápno, n. lime; quicklime;
vápno chlorové, chloride of lime;
vápno karbolové, carbolate of lime;
vavřín, m. laurel tree;
vejce, n. *veytsĕ.* egg
bílek, m. *beelek,* the white
žloutek, m. *žloŭtek,* the yelk
vinný kámen, m. cream of tartar;
víno bílé, n. *veenŏ beelé,* white wine
" červené, *v. chervĕné,* red wine,
virginská hadovka, f. Virginia
   snakeroot
vítod, m. *veetod,* bitter polygala;
vlašťovičník, m. *vlăshťovichñik,* ce-
   landine
voda čistá, f. *vŏdă chisstá,* pure water
voda minerální, mineral water
koupel, f. *koŭpell* } bath
lázeň, f. *lázeñ*
vodička, f. *vočichkă,* wash, lotion;
vodička na oči, *v. nă ochi,* eye-wash
vosk bílý, m. white wax
vosk žlutý, yellow wax

vraní oko, n. *vrăñee okŏ,* paris quad-
   rifolia;
vrátič, m. *vráťich,* tansy
výstřelek, m. *veestrshĕllek,* spirit
" pižmový, spirit of musk;
" terpentinový, spirit of
   turpentine;
vyzí klí, n. *vizee klee,* isinglass.

Zázvor, m. ginger
zázvor divoký, wild ginger
zeměžluč, f. *zemyĕžlŭch,* common
   centaury;
zerav, m. *zerăf,* arbor vitae;
zimostráz, m. box plant;
zmíjovec, m. *zmeeyŏvets,* skunk cab-
   bage;

žábník, m. *žábñik,* water-plantain
žebříček, m. *žebrsheechek,* yarrow
železnice lysá, s. snake-head, turtle-
   head;
železník, m. *železñik,* vervain
ženský vlas, m. maidenhair
žluč volská, f. *žlŭch volská,* ox-gall
žlutidlo, n. turmeric
žtutodřev, m. prickly-ash.

At home.
DOMA.

I like domestic com- fort.	Miluju domácí poho- dlí.	*millŭyŭ domátsee po- hodlee.*
We have a comfortable home on tenth street.	Máme pohodlný domov na desáté ulici.	*mámĕ pohodelnee dŏ- mof nă děsáté ŭlitsi.*
We have a hall, five rooms and a kitchen	Máme síň, pět pokojů a kuchyň dole, a	*mámĕ seeñ, pyĕt pokŏ- yoo ă kŭkhiñ dŏlĕ,*

down stairs, and four bedrooms upstairs.	čtyry ložnice nahoře.	ǎ shtiriložňitsě něhorshě.
The stairs have a railing.	Schody mají zábradlí.	skhŏdy mǎyee zábradlee.
We have new furniture,—tables, chairs, sofas and beds.	Máme nový nábytek,— stoly, židle, pohovky a postele.	mámě novee nábytěk, — stolly, židlě, pohofky ǎ postellě.
The writing-desk and library stand in the front room.	Psací stůl a knihovna stojí v přední světnici.	psátsee stool ǎ kňihovnǎ stoyee f p r s h ě d ň e e swoyětňitsi.
The windows have both shutters and curtains.	Okna mají okenice i záslony.	oknǎ mǎyee okěňitsě e záslony.
On the walls there are pictures in frames.	Na stěnách jsou obrazy v rámech.	nǎ sťenǎkh soǔ obrǎzy vrámekh.
Our clothes-press is very handy.	Naše šatnice je tuze příručná.	nǎshě shǎtňitsě yě tuuzě prsheerǔchnǎ.
The fuel we keep down cellar. — Hard and soft water is in the house.	Palivo máme ve sklepě. — Tvrdá i měkká voda je v domě.	pǎlivŏ mámě vě sklepyě. — tveerdá e myěká vodǎ yě vdŏmyě.
We have a good stove and the chimney does not smoke.	Máme dobré kamna a komín nekouří.	mámě dobré kǎmnǎ ǎ komeen někoǔrshee.
It is time to eat. — The meal is ready.	Je čas k jídlu. — Jídlo je hotovo.	yě chǎss k-yeedlǔ. — yeedlŏ yě hotŏvŏ.
The table is spread; — everything is on the table: dishes, plates, forks, knives.	Je prostřeno; – všecko je na stole: mísy, talíře, vidličky, nože.	yě prostrshěnŏ. — fshětsko yě nǎ stollě: meesy, tǎleershě, vidlich ky, nože.
Come and eat; — sit down by the table.	Pojďte jísti; — sedněte ke stolu.	poďtě yeest; — sedňetě kě stollǔ.
Hand (thou) me that chair. — Hand (you) me the soup; I shall deal it out.	Podej mi tu sesli. — Podejte mi polívku; já rozdám.	poděy me tǔ sessli. poděytě me poleefkǔ; yǎ rŏzdám.

Is it not salt enough? — Here is the salt; take some more salt.	Není dost slaná?— Zde je sůl; přisolte si.	*neyňi dost slǎná?—zdě yě sool; prshisollě si.*
The meat is cut; — I shall cut up the roast into pieces.	Maso je nakrájeno;— rozdělím pečeni na porce.	*mǎssǒ yě nǎkráyěnǒ;— rozď'eleem pěcheňi nǎ portsě.*
Help yourself; — here is roast goose,—here is fried chicken.	Poslužte si; — zde je pečená husa, — zde smažené kuře.	*poslůshtě si; — zdě yě pěchěná hůssǎ, — zdě smǎžené kůrshě.*
Take a piece of bread.	Vemte si kousek chleba.	*vemtě si koŭsek khlěbǎ.*
Do you eat pastry? — Sometimes.	Jíte pečivo? — Někdy.	*yeetě pěchivo? ňeydy.*
Do you want a cup of coffee? — or a cup of tea?	Chcete šálek kávy? — anebo šálek čaje?	*khtsětě shálek kávy? — ǎnebǒ shálek chǎyě?*
Is the coffee sweet enough?— Here is sugar.	Je káva dost sladká?— Zde je cukr.	*yě kávǎ dost slǎdká? — zdě yě tsůk⁽e⁾r.*
After a meal a cigar tastes well.	Po jídle chutná doutník.	*pǒ yeedlě khŭtná doŭtňik.*
Will you smoke?—Here are cigars; light one.	Budete kouřiti? — Tu jsou cigara; zapalte si.	*bŭdětě koŭrshit? — tŭ soŭ tsigarǎ; zǎpǎltě si.*
Hand me the matches. — There in the corner is a spittoon.	Podejte mi sirky. — Tam v koutě je plivátko.	*poděytě me seerky. — tǎm fkoŭťe yě plivátkǒ.*

It is growing dark. — It is dark. — Make a light.	Stmívá se.—Je tma.— Udělejte světlo.	*stmeevá sě.— yě tmǎ.— ŭď'elěytě swyětlo.*
Here is a candle-stick and a candle.—Light the lamp;— light the gas.	Zde je svícen a svíčka. — Rozžete lampu;— rozžete plyn.	*zdě yě sweetsěn ǎ sweechkǎ. — rožetě lǎmpŭ; — rožetě plyn.*

It is growing chilly, isn't it? — Make a fire.	Dělá se chladno, je-li pravda! – Zatopte.	*ďelá sě khlădno, yelli prăvdă? — zătoplě.*
There is a fire already in the stove.	Už je oheň v kamnech.	*ŭsh yě ohěň fkămněkh.*
It is late; – let us go to sleep.	Je pozdě; — pojďme spat.	*yě pozďe; — poďmě spăt.*
It is time to go to bed.	Je čas jíti do postele.	*yě chăss yeet dŏ postellě.*
Is the bed made?—The beds are made for all.	Je ustláno?— Je ustláno pro všechny.	*yě ŭstlánŏ? — yě ŭstlánŏ pro fshěkhny.*
I shall lie down on the sofa. — Do as you please.	Já si lehnu na sofa. — Jak chcete.	*yá si lehnŭ nă sofă. — yăk khtsětě.*
Undress; — take off your clothes; — pull off your boots; here is the boot-jack.	Odstrojte se; — svlékněte se; — zujte se, — tu je zouvák.	*odstroytě sě; — svlékňetě sě; — zŭytě sě; — tŭ yě zoŭvák.*
Sleep well. — Good night!	Spěte dobře.—Dobrou noc!	*spyětě dŏbrshě.—dŏbroŭ nots.*
It is time to get up. — Our folks are up.	Je čas vstáti. — Naši jsou zhůru.	*yě chăss fstát. — năshi soŭ zhoorŭ.*
Wencel is still sleeping; — wake him up, or he will oversleep.	Václav posud spí; — zbuďte ho, sice zaspí.	*vátslăv posŭd spee; — zbŭďtě ho, sitsě zăspee.*
How did you sleep? — I slept well.	Jak jste spal? — Spal jsem dobře.	*yăk stě spăl? — spăl sem dŏbrshě.*
Didn't that noise wake you up? — I slept fast; nothing disturbed me.	Nebudil vás ten hluk? — Spal jsem tvrdě; — nic mě nebudilo.	*nebŭďil váss ten hlŭk? — spăl sem tverďe; ňits myě něbŭďilo.*
I had a bad night; — I could not fall asleep very long; — I only fell asleep towards morning.	Já měl zlou noc; — nemohl jsem usnouti dlouho; — usnul jsem teprvé k ránu.	*yá myěll zloŭ nots; — němohel sem ŭsnoŭt dloŭhŏ; — ŭsnŭl sem tepervé kránŭ.*

Henry says he never shut his eyes (i.e. had no sleep at all).	**Jindřich povídá že ani oka nezamhouřil.**	*yindrshikh poveedá že áñi oká nězămŏŭrshil.*

VOCABULARY.

Síň, f. *seeň*, the hall
schody, pl. m. *skhody*, the stairs
zábradlí, n. the railing
stěna, f. *sťená*, the wall
šatnice, f. *shătňitsě*, the clothes press;
kumbál, m. *kŭmbál*, the closet
kout, m. *koŭt*, the corner
okenice, f. *okěňitsě*, the blind
záslona, f. *zásloná*, the curtain
domácí, *dŏmátsee*, domestic
nábytek, m. the furniture
stoly, m. *stŏly* ⎱ tables
tabule, f. *tăbŭlě* ⎰
psací stůl, *psătsee stool*, the writing-desk
židle, f. *židlě* ⎱ the chair or chairs;
sesle, f. *sesslě* ⎰

pohovka, f. *pŏhofká* ⎱ the lounge
sofa, n. *sofá* ⎰
obraz, m. *obráz*, the picture
rám, m. the frame
Palivo, n. *pállivŏ*, the fuel
kamna, pl. *kămná*, the stove
komín, m. *komeen*, the chimney
kouřiti, *koŭrshit*, to smoke
oheň, m. *ŏheň*, the fire;
svícen, m. *sweetsěn*, the candlestick
svíčka, f. *sweechká*, the candle
plyn, m. the gas
rozžíti, *rožeet*, to make a light;
zapáliti, *zăpálit*, to light
sirka, f. *seerká*, a match
cigaro, n. *tsigăro* ⎱ a cigar
doutník, m. *doŭtňik* ⎰
plivátko, n. *plivátko* ⎱ spittoon.
plivnik, m. *plivňik* ⎰

Prostříti, *prostrsheet*, to set the table;
mísa, f. *meesá*, the dish
talíř, m. *tăleersh*, the plate
šálek, m. *shálek*, the cup
sůl, *sool*, the salt
slaný, á, é *slănee*, salt, salted;
přisoliti, *prshi-solit*, to put in some more salt;
sladký, á, é *slădkee*, sweet

nakrájeti, *năkráyet*, to cut in pieces;
rozděliti, *rozď elit*, to divide
rozdati, *rozdăt*, to deal out;
pečivo, n. *pěchivo*, the pastry
pečený, á, é *pěchenee*, roasted
smažený, á, é *smăženee*, fried
husa, f. *hŭssá*, goose
kuře, n. *kŭrshě*, chicken.

Stmívati se, *stmeevát sě,* to grow
   dark;
odstrojiti se, *odstroyit sě,* to undress
zouti se, *zŏŭt sě,* to pull off one's
   boots;
zouvák, m *zoŭvák,* the boot-jack
ustlati, *ŭstlát,* to make the bed;
usnouti, *ŭsnoŭt,* to fall asleep;
zaspati, *záspál,* to oversleep
buditi, *bŭďit,* to wake, to disturb;

zbuditi, *zbŭďit,* to wake up, to call;
vstáti, *fstát,* to get up;
zhůru, *zhoorŭ,* up;
nahoře, *nähorshě,* up stairs;
dole, *dŏlě,* down stairs;
tvrdě, *tvrdʼe* } fast
pevně, *pevňe* }
hluk, m. *hlŭk,* noise
je-li pravda? *yelli právdá?* isn't it so?

Buying and selling.
KOUPĚ A PRODEJ.

English	Czech	Pronunciation
How much is this? — What is the price of it?— How much does it cost?	Zač je to? — Co to stojí? — Co to koštuje?	zách yě tŏ? — tsŏ tŏ stoyee? — tsŏ tŏ koshtŭyě?
What do you sell it for? What do you want for it?—What do you ask for it? — How much shall I give you for it?	Po čem to prodáváte? Co za to chcete? — Co za to žádáte? — Co vám za to dám?	pŏ chem tŏ prodáváte? tsŏ zá tŏ khtsětě? — tsŏ zá tŏ žádátě? — tsŏ vám zá tŏ dám?
What is the price?	Jaká je cena?	yáká yě tsená?
A dollar and ten cents. — A dollar and a quarter.	Dollar deset centů. — Dollar a čtvrt.	dollär desset sentoo. — dollär a shtwᵉrt.
Two dollars and a half. — Two and a half dollars.	Dva dollary a půl. — Půl třetího dollaru.	dvá dolláry ä pool. — pool trshěťćehŏ dolláŭ.
Five dollars sixty cents	Pět dollarů šedesát centů.	pyět dollároo shědessát sentoo.
It costs a little over six dollars.	Stojí to něco přes šest dollarů.	stoyee tŏ ňetsŏ prshěs shest dollároo.
Is it worth that much?	Stojí to za to?	stoyee tŏ zá tŏ?

I think it is; — why should it not be?	Myslím že stojí;—proč by nestálo?	*misleem že stoyee; — proch be nestálŏ?*
It seems to me too much. — I think it is dear.	Mně se to zdá moc. — Myslím že je to drahé.	*myě sě tŏ zdá mots. — misleem že yě tŏ drá-hé.*

That is too much. — That is too dear.— I won't give so much.	To je moc. — To je drahé. — Tolik ne-dám.	*tŏ yě mots. — tŏ yě drá hé. — tŏlik nědám.*
That is too much;—will you take off some-thing?	To je tuze mnoho; — slevíte něco?	*tŏ yě toozě mnohŏ; — slěveelě ňetsŏ?*
You must take off something.	Něco musíte sleviti.	*ňetsŏ mŭseelě slevit.*
I shall not take off any-thing.—I cannot take off anything.	Neslevím nic. — Ne-mohu sleviti nic.	*něslěveem ňits.— němŏ-hŭ slevit ňits.*
We have a fixed price. — We sell at a fixed price.	Máme pevnou cenu. — Prodáváme za pev-nou cenu.	*mámě pevnoŭ tsenŭ. — prodávámě zá pevnoŭ tsenŭ.*
It is cheap.— It is low-priced.	Je to laciné. — Je to levné.	*yě tŏ lătsiné. — yě tŏ levné.*
I shall get it cheaper elsewhere.	Dostanu to levněji jin-de.	*dostănŭ tŏ levňey yindě.*
You will not get it cheaper anywhere.	Nedostanete to levněji nikde.	*nedŏstănetě tŏ levňey ňigdě.*
I will try it. — I don't want to haggle. — I don't like to haggle over the price.	Zkusím to. — Nechci smlouvati. — Nerad smlouvám.	*skŭseem tŏ. — někhtsi smloŭvăt. — nerăd smloŭvám.*
That is the lowest price; — it cannot be any cheaper.	To je nejnižší cena; — nemůže býti laciněj-ší.	*tŏ yě neyňishee tsenă; — němoože beet lătsi-ňeyshee.*

What do you wish? — What is your pleasure?	Co si přejete! — Co račte!	tsŏ si prshĕyetĕ? — tsŏ rāchtĕ!
What can I do for you?	Čím mohu sloužiti?	cheem mohŭ sloŭžit?
Have you satchels for sale?— I want to buy a satchel.	Máte tašky na prodej! —Chci koupit tašku.	mātĕ tāshky nŭ prodey? — khtsi koŭpit tāshkŭ.
I would like to get a nice traveling bag.	Rád bych nějakou pěknou kabelu.	rād bikh ñākoŭ pyĕknoŭ kābellŭ.
We have a stock of them. — We have a large choice.	Máme je na skladě. — Máme velký výběr.	māmĕ yĕ nŭ sklād'e. — māmĕ velkee veebyĕr.
Show me some. — I wish to see them.	Ukažte mi některé. — Podívám se na ně.	ŭkāshtĕ me ñekteré.-pod'eevām sĕ nŭ ñe.
This is the best kind we have. — They are good.	Tohle je nejlepší druh co máme. — Ty jsou dobré.	tŏhlĕ yĕ neylepshee drŭh tsŏ māmĕ. — ty soŭ dŏbré.
This one is nice.— This will suit you.	Tahle je pěkná. — Ta se vám hodí.	tāhlĕ yĕ pyĕkná. — tā sĕ vām hod'ee.
How much is it? — What is the price?	Zač je! — Co stojí!	zāch yĕ? — tsŏ stoyee?
Four dollars and a half. — That is the regular price.	Čtyry dollary a půl.— To je pravidelná cena.	shtiry dollāry ŭ pool.— tŏ yĕ prāvidelná tsĕnā.
That is a little too much. —don't you think so?	To je trochu moc; — nemyslíte!	tŏ yĕ trokhŭ mots; — nĕmisleetĕ?
I do not think so.	Nemyslím.	nemisleem.
I will give four dollars for it.— Will you sell it for that?	Dám za ni čtyry dollary. — Dáte ji za to!	dām zā ñi shtiry dollāry — dātĕ ye zā tŏ?
I cannot. — I cannot take off anything.	Nemohu. — Nemohu nic sleviti.	nemohŭ. — nemohŭ ñits slĕvit.
The price is fixed.	Cena je pevná.	tsenā yĕ pĕvná.
Then I will not buy it. — Do as you please;	Teda ji nekoupím. — Jak vám libo. — Ne-	tĕdā ye nĕkoŭpeem. — yāk vām leebŏ.-- ney-

—it is not dear at that price.	ní drahá za tu cenu.	ñi dráhá zá tŭ tsenŭ
You will not get it elsewhere. — They have not got them elsewhere.	Jinde ji nedostanete.— Jinde je nemají.	yindě ye nědostănětě.— yindě yě nemáyee.
They are not to be had elsewhere. — Only I alone have them for sale.	Nejsou jinde k dostání. — Jenom já je mám na prodej.	neysoŭ yindě gdostáñi. — yenom yá yě mám ná prodey.
They have not got these goods on hand anywhere.	Nemají to zboží na skladě nikde.	nemáyee tŏ zbŏžee ná skládě ñiydě.
I keep honest goods on hand.	Já držím poctivé zboží.	yá děržeem potsťivé zbožee.
Small profits, quick sales — that is my motto.	Malý zisk, rychlý prodej,—to je mé heslo.	málee zisk, rykhlee prodey,— tŏ yě mé hesslŏ.
Small but frequent profits.	Malý výdělek, ale častý.	málee veeďelek álě chástee.

Have you some pocket-books?	Máte nějaké tobolky?	mátě ñáké tŏbolky?
We have a large stock. — What kind do you wish,—expensive?—cheap?	Máme velkou zásobu. — Jaké chcete, — drahé? — laciné?	mámě velkoŭ zásobŭ. — yáké khtsětě, — drahé? — látsiné?
What is the price of these? — How much are they? — How do you sell them?	Zač jsou tyhle? — Po čem jsou? — Po čem je prodáváte?	zách soŭ tyhlě? — pŏ chem soŭ? — pŏ chem yě prodáváte?
A dollar a piece. -They are good and lasting.	Po dollaru kus.— Jsou dobré a trvanlivé.	pŏ dollárŭ kŭss. — soŭ dobré á tervánlivé.
Those are dearer; a dollar and a half.	Tam ty jsou dražší; po dollaru a půl.	tăm ty soŭ drăshee; pŏ dollárŭ á pool.

They are somewhat better.	Jsou trochu lepší.	*soŭ trokhŭ lepshee*
I will take one:— wrap it up for me.	Vezmu si jednu;— zabalte mi ji.	*vezmŭ si yednŭ; — zĭbŭltě me ye.*
Here is the money; give me back.	Tu jsou peníze; dejte mi zpátky.	*tŭ soŭ peňeezě; deytě me spátky.*
There is fifty cents coming to you.— Here is half a dollar back.	Přijde vám padesát centů. — Zde je půl dollaru zpátky.	*prsheedě vám pădessát sentoo. — zdě yě pool dollărŭ spátky.*

I should like to buy a few tons of coal: but I have no money.	Rád bych koupil pár tun uhlí; ale nemám peníze.	*rád bikh koŭpil pár tŭn ŭhlee; ălě němám peňeezě.*
I will take it on credit: — will you trust me?	Vezmu ho na dluh; — počkáte mi?	*vezmŭ hŏ nă dlooh; — pochkátě me?*
I do not trust anybody; —I sell only for cash.	Nečekám žádnému; — prodávám jen za hotové.	*něchekám žádnémŭ; — prodăvám yen ză hotŏvé.*
I give no credit. — I want cash.	Nedávám kredit.- Chci hotové.	*nědăvám credit.—khtsi hotŏvé.*
I want to have no bad debts.	Nechci míti žádné špatné dluhy.	*nekhtsi meet žádné shpătné dloohy.*
I need money. — I am raking up money to buy goods;—I do not want to borrow.	Potřebuju peníze. — Sháním peníze na zboží; nechci se dlužiti.	*potrshěbŭyŭ peňeezě. — shăňeem pěňeezě nă zbožee; — někhtsi sě dlŭžit.*
For cash one buys cheap.	Za hotové koupí se lacino.	*ză hotŏvé koŭpee sě lătsino.*

| How is business? — So so;— tolerably good. | Jak jde obehod?— Tak tak; — projde to. | *yăk dě obkhŏd? — tăk tăk;—proydě tŏ.* |
| Have the goods a ready sale?—I have a good sale, but a small profit. | Jde zboží na odbyt? — Mám dobrý odbyt, ale malý zisk. | *dě zbožee nă odbyt? — mám dŏbree odbyt, ălě mălee zisk.* |

I often sell at a loss.— I have a loss on my sales.	Prodávám často se ško- dou. — Mám na tom ztrátu.	*prodávám chǎsstǒ sě shkodoǔ. — mám nǎ tom strátǔ.*
That is bad. — Have you a large stock?	To je zlé. — Máte vel- kou zásobu ?	*tǒ yě zlé. — mátě velkoǔ zásobǔ?
I have still many goods on hand; — I expect again fresh goods; — they are on the way.	Mám ještě hodně zbo- ží; — čekám zase čerstvé zboží;—je už na cestě.	*mám yeshťe hodňe zbo- žee; — chekám zǎss cherstvé zbožee; — yě ǔsh nǎ tsesťe.*
I was in New York to make purchases.	Byl jsem v New Yorku nakupovat.	*bill sem vnew-yorkǔ nǎ kǔpovǎt.*
Did you make a good bargain?—I am satis- fied.	Koupil jste dobře! — Jsem spokojen.	*koǔpil stě dǒbrshě? — sem spokoyěn.*

VOCABULARY.

Na skladě, *nǎ sklǎďe,* on hand;

odbyt, m. sale (of goods);

zisk, m. profit

škoda, f. *shkodǎ* ⎫ loss
ztráta, f. *strátǎ* ⎭

tašku, f. *tǎshkǎ* ⎱ satchel,
kabela, f. *kǎbellǎ* ⎰ traveling bag;

tobolka, f. *tǒbolkǎ,* pocket book;

heslo, n. *hesslǒ,* motto

pevný, á, é *pevnee,* fast, fixed;

trvati, *tervǎt,* to last

trvanlivý, á, é *tervǎnlivee,* lasting.

Stojí to, *stoyee tǒ,* it costs, it is worth;

koštuje, *koshtǔyě,* it costs

dostati, *dostǎt,* to get

dostanu, *dostǎnǔ,* I shall get;

dostanete, *dǒstǎnětě,* you will get;

je k dostání, *yě gdǒstáňi,* is to be got; is to be had;

držeti, *děržet,* to keep

hoditi se, *hoďit sě,* to suit; to fit;

sleviti, *slěvit,* to take off;

smlouvati, *smloǔvǎt,* to haggle; to bargain;

sloužiti, *sloǔžit,* to serve

dlužiti se, *dlǔžit sě* ⎫ to borrow
vydlužiti se, *vydlǔžit sě* ⎭

počkati, *pochkǎt,* to wait, to trust;

nečekám, *něchekám,* I do not wait; I do not trust;

nakupovati, *nǎkǔpovǎt,* to make purchases;

zabaliti, *zǎbǎlit,* to wrap up.

In a grocery store.
U GROCERISTY.

I want some groceries.	Chci nějaké grocerie.	*khtsi ňáké grocerič.*
Please, command;—we have fresh goods of all kinds.	Poroučejte; — máme čerstvé zboží všeho druhu.	*poroúcheytě; — mámě cherstcé zbožee fšhěhŏ druhů.*
Give me a pound of coffee, two pounds of sugar and a package of chicory.	Dejte mi libru kávy, dvě libry cukru a paklíček cikorie.	*deytě me librŭ kávy, dvyě libry tsŭkrŭ á pŭkleechek tsikorič.*
Anything else?	Ještě něco?	*yeshťe ňetsŏ?*
Five pounds of rice, half a dozen of lemons and some spices.	Pět liber rýže, půl tuctu citronů a nějaké koření.	*pyět liber reyže, pool tŭtstŭ tsitrónoo á ňáké korshěňi.*
How do you sell eggs?	Zač prodáváte vejce?	*zách prodávátě veytsě?*
Twenty cents a dozen.	Dvacet centů tucet.	*dvŭtset sentoo tŭtset.*
Give me two dozen of eggs, three quarts of kerosene and a pint of sirup.	Dejte mi dva tucty vajec, tři kvarty petroleje a pint sirobu.	*deytě me dvŭ tŭtsty vŭyets, trshi quŭrty pětroleyě á pint sirobŭ.*
How do you sell kerosene by the gallon?	Zač prodáváte petrolej na gallony?	*zách prodávátě petroley nŭ gŭllony?*
I will take a bottle of mustard, a pound of raisins, a pound and a half of dried apples.	Vezmu si lahev horčice, libru rozinek, půldruhé libry křížal.	*vezmŭ si lŭhev horchitsě, librŭ rŏzinek, pooldrŭhé libry krsheežŭl.*
Besides, I want four ounces of pepper.	Ještě chci čtyry unce pepře.	*yeshťe khtsi shtiry ŭntsě pěprshě.*
Send me a sack of flour and five pounds of barley.	Pošlete mi pytel mouky a pět liber krup.	*poshlětě mi pytel moŭky á pyět liber krŭp.*
I want the best kind of flour, —patent flour.	Chci nejlepší druh mouky, — patentní mouku.	*khtsi neylepshee drŭh moŭky, — pŭtentňee moŭkŭ.*

| A bushel of potatoes and a peck of onions. | Bušl bramborů a pek cibule. | *bŭshel brămboroo ă peck tsibŭlě.* |
| Give me five cents worth of cinnamon, five cents worth of mace and ten cents worth of ginger. | Dejte mi za pět centů skořice, za pět centů květu a za deset centů zázvoru. | *deytě me zŭ pyět sentoo skorshitsě, zŭ pyět sentoo kwyětŭ ă zŭ desset sentoo zázvorŭ.* |

VOCABULARY.

Note. Many articles sold in groceries are to be found under the heading "Drugs and medicines".

Cukr kouskový, *tsŭker koŭskovee,* crushed sugar;

,, zrnkový, *ts. zernkovee,* granulated sugar;

,, utlučený, *ts. ŭtlŭchenee,* pulverized sugar;

,, hnědý, *ts. hňedee,* brown sugar;

káva pražená, *kávă prăženă,* roasted coffee;

,, mletá, *k. mlětă,* ground coffee

koření, n. *korshěňi,* spice

nové koření, allspice

květ, m. *kwyět,* mace

dymián, m. thyme

šafrán, m. *shăfrăn,* Spanish saffron

rozinky, pl. f. raisins

drobné rozinky, currants

křížaly, pl. f. *krsheežăly,* dried apples;

sušené švestky, pl. f. *sŭshěné shwestky,* prunes

cibule, f. *tsibŭlě,* onions

česnek, m. *chessnek,* garlic

zázvor loupaný, bleached ginger-root;

zázvor neloupaný, unbleached ginger-root;

prášek na pečení, *prăshek nă pěcheňi,* baking powder;

kvasnice, pl. *kwassňitsě*
droždí, n. *drožďee* } yeast;

suché kvasnice, dry yeast;

lisované kv., compressed yeast;

salajka, f. *sălăykă,* saleratus

prací soda, f. *prătsee sodă,* washing soda;

kornout, m. *kornoŭt,* paper cornet;

paklík, m. *păkleek,* package;

paklíček, m. *păkleechek,* small package;

balik, m. *băleek,* bundle, parcel;

zabaliti, *zăbălit*
zapakovati, *zăpăkovăt* } to pack up

zavázati, *zăvăzăt,* to tie up;

svázati, *svăzăt,* to bind or tie together.

Garments.
ODĚV.

English	Czech	Pronunciation
Dry goods have a ready sale.	Loketní zboží jde rychle na odbyt.	*loketñee zbožee dě rikhlě ná odbyt.*
I intend to start a dry goods store.	Hodlám založiti střižní krám.	*hodlám založit strshižñee krám.*
My brother has a clothing store.	Můj bratr má oděvní krám.	*můy brátʳr má oďevñee krám.*
He employs many tailors.	Zaměstnává mnoho krejčích.	*záměstnává mnohǒ kreycheekh.*
The tailor makes (*liter.* sews) clothes.	Krejčí šije šaty.	*kreychee she-yě sháty.*
Thread and needle, scissors and shears, a thimble, a sad-iron and a press-board are his tools.	Nit a jehla, nůžky a velké nůžky, náprstek, cihlička a koza jsou jeho nástroje.	*ñit á yěhlá, nooshky á ˈ velké nooshky, nápʳrstek, tsihlichkǎ á kózǎ soǔ yěhǒ nástroyě.*
Nowadays much sewing is done on the machine.	Dnes mnoho šije se na stroji.	*dness mnohǒ she-yě sě ná stroyí.*
The sewing machine is a useful invention.	Šicí stroj jest užitečný vynález.	*shitsee stroy yest ǔžitechnee vynález.*
It is an American invention.	Jest to americký vynález.	*yest tǒ ǎmeritskeeˈrynález.*
I need a suit of clothes. — I want a new suit.	Potřebuju oblek. — Chci nový oblek.	*potrshěbǔyǔ oblek. — khtsi novee oblek.*
Take my measure.	Vemte mi míru.	*vemtě me meerǔ.*
The cutter takes measure and cuts the cloth	Kraječ bere míru a nakrájí sukno.	*kráyěch běrě meerǔ á nǎkráyee sǔkno.*
What sort of stuff do you want?	Jakou látku chcete!	*yǎkoǔ látkǔ khtsetě?*
Show me your patterns	Ukažte mi své vzory.	*ǔkǎshtě me své czory*
This wears well.	Tohle se dobře nese.	*tǒhlě sě dǒbrshě nessě.*

17

How will you have your coat made(i.e.sewed)?	Jak chcete míti kabát ušitý?	*yăk khtsetĕ meet kăbát ăshitee?*
After the present fashion.	Dle nynější mody.	*dlĕ nyñeyshee mody.*
Try your coat on.	Zkuste váš kabát.	*skŭstĕ vásh kăbát.*
It pinches me under the arms — It is too tight.	Svírá pod pažema. — Je tuze těsný.	*sweerá pod păžemă. — yĕ toozĕ ťessnee.*
It is too wide round the waist. — It makes folds.	Je tuze volný v půli. — dělá faldy.	*yĕ toozĕ volnee fpooli. — ďelá făldy.*
The skirts are long enough.—It has pockets behind and breast-pockets.	Šosy jsou dost dlouhé. — Má kapsy v zadu a kapsy na prsou.	*shŏssy soŭ dost dloŭhé. — má kăpsy vzădŭ ă kăpsy nă p^ersoŭ.*
Make me a pair of pants	Udělejte mi pár kalhot	*ŭďeleytĕ me pár kălhot.*
Get it done pretty soon; — take a good stuff.	Zhotovte je hezky brzo; — vemte dobrou látku.	*zhotoftĕ yĕ hesskee b^erzŏ; — vemtĕ dŏbroŭ látkŭ.*
Do you want lining in your pants?	Chcete podšivku do kalhot?	*khtsetĕ podshifkŭ dŏ kălhot?*
I do not want any lining. — Without lining.	Nechci žádnou podšivku. — Bez podšivky.	*nekhtsi žádnoŭ podshifkŭ. — bĕs podshifky.*

VOCABULARY.

Kabát, m. *kăbát*, the coat
frak, m. *frăk*, a dress-coat
svrchník, m. *sverkhñik*, an overcoat
zimník, m. *zimñik*, a greatcoat
plášť, m. *plăshť*, a cloak
kalhoty, pl. spodky, pl. } pants, trousers;
nohavice, f. *nohăvitsĕ*, leg of the pants;
vesta, f. *vestă*, the vest

kazajka, f. *kăzăykă*, the jacket
bunda, f. *băndă*, the sack-coat
límec, m. *leemets*, the collar
laple, f. *lăplĕ*, the lapel
rukáv, m. *rŭkáf*, the sleeve
šos, m. *shŏss*, the skirt
šev, m. *shĕf*, the seam
štych, m. *shtikh* steh, m. *stĕh* } a stitch
podšivka, f. *podshifkă*, the lining
záplata, f. *záplătă*, the patch

kapsa, f. *kápsă,* the pocket
knoflík, m. *knofleek,* the button
knoflíková dírka, the button-hole.

Prádlo, n. linen, underclothing;
košile, f. *koshillě,* the shirt
spodní košile, *spodňeek.,* the undershirt
podvlečky, pl. } the drawers
spodní kalhoty
punčochy, pl. f. *pănchokhy,* the stockings, the socks;
podvazky, pl. *podvăsky,* the garters
šandy, pl. f. *shăndy* } the
šle, pl. f. *shlě* } suspenders
šátek, m. *shătek,* kerchief
š. na krk, *sh. nă kerk,* neckerchief
š. do kapsy, *sh. dŏ kăpsy,* pocket handkerchief;
mašle na krk, *măshlě nă kerk,* a necktie.

Sukno, n. *săknŏ,* cloth, broadcloth;
samet, m. *sămmet,* velvet
pliš, m. *plish,* plush
atlas, m. *ătlăss,* satin
hedvábí, n. *hedvăbee,* silk
plátno, n. linen
kartoun, m. *kartoŭn,* cotton, print;
šňůra, f. *shňooră,* cord
civka, f. *tsifkă,* a spool
klubko, n. *klŭbko,* a ball
přadýnko, n. *prshădeenko,* a skein
hrubá nit, f. *hrŭbá ňit,* a coarse thread;
tenká nit, a fine thread;

hrubá jehla, f. *h. yěhlă.* a coarse needle;
tenká jehla, a fine needle;
štepovací jehla, *shtepovătsee yěhlă,* darning needle;
drát (na pletení), m. knitting needle;
stříhati, *strshihăt,* to cut with a pair of scissors;
žehliti, *žehlit,* to iron.

Klobouk, m. *kloboŭk,* the hat
ženský klobouk, a bonnet, a lady's hat;
čepec, m. *chěpets,* the hood
čepice, f. *chěpitsě,* the cap
cilindr, m. *tsilindr,* a beaver, a silk hat;
nízký klobouk, *ňeeskee kloboŭk,* a low hat.

Švadlena, f. *shvădlenă,* a needlewoman
šička, f. *shichkă,* a sewing-girl
modistka, f. a milliner
modní zboží, *modňee zbožee,* millinery
šaty, pl. *shăty,* a dress
život, m. *život,* the waist, the bust;
šňerovačka, f. *shňerovăchkă,* the corset, the bodice;
spodnička, f. *spodňichkă,* the petticoat
košile (ženská), *koshillě,* the chemise
karnýr, m. *karneer,* a flounce
karnýrek, m. a ruffle
pentle, f. *pentlě,* a ribbon
mašle, f. *măshlě,* a sash

mašlička, f. *măshlichkă*, a bow
klička, f. *klichkă*, a loop
krajky, pl. *krăyky*, lace
obruba, f. *obrŭbă*, hem, border;
pinta, f. *pintă*, belt
závoj, m. *závoy* ⎫
flór, m. *floor,* ⎬ the veil
rouška, f. *roŭshkă,* ⎭
černý flór, *chernee floor*, crape

týl, m. *teel*, mosquito bar;
pera na klobouk, pl. plumes
perka, pl. tips
rukavičky, pl. f. *rŭkăvich-* ⎫
ky, ⎬ gloves
rukavice, pl .f. *rŭkăvitsĕ,*
pár rukavic, *pár rŭkăvits*, a pair of
gloves;
štucel, m. *shtŭtsell,* a muff.

Shoemaking.
OBUVNICTVÍ.

Obuv, f. *obŭv*, footgear
obuvník, *obŭvñik* ⎫ shoemaker
švec, *shwets* ⎭
obuvnický krám, *obŭv-*
ñitskee krám ⎫ boot and
Ševcovský krám, *shef* ⎬ shoe store;
tsofskee k.
bota, (pl. boty), f. *bottă*, boot
střevíc, (pl. střevice), m. *shtrshĕ-*
veets, shoe
pár bot, a pair of boots;
pár střevíců, a pair of shoes;
botky (ženské), pl. gaiters
pantofle, pl. *păntoflĕ*, slippers
svrchní střevíce, *swerkhñee strshĕ-*
vitsĕ, overshoes.

Holínka, f. *holeenkă*, leg of a boot;
podešev, m. *podĕshef*, the sole

kramflek, m. ⎫ the heel
podpatek, m. ⎭
nárt, m. the vamp
přaska, f. *prshăsskă*, the buckle
kanice, f. *kăñitsĕ*, shoe-lace, shoe-
string;
floky, pl. pegs
nejtky, pl. *neytky*, brass nails
šroubek, m. *shroŭbek*, a screw
lastyng, m. serge
dratev, f. *drătef*, waxed thread;
poteh, m. *pŏťeh*, strap
knejp, m. *knĕyp*, knife
kladivo, n. *klăďivŏ*, hammer
kopyto, n. *kopytŏ*, last
štipce, *shťiptsĕ*, a pair of pincers;
nádobí ševcovské, n. *nădŏbee shef-*
tsofské, findings
kůže, f. *koožĕ*, leather.

Diverse trades.
ROZLIČNÁ ŘEMESLA.

Barvíř, *barveersh*, dyer
barvíř domů, house painter
bednář, *bednársh*, cooper
cihlář, *tsihlársh*, brickmaker
cukrář, *tsŭkrársh*, confectioner
čaloumík, *chăloŭñik*, upholsterer
doutníkář, *doŭtñikársh*, cigar-maker
dlaždič, *dlăžďich*, paver
formář, *formársh*, moulder
hodinář, *hoďinársh*, watchmaker
havíř, *hăveersh*, miner
kameník, *kămeñik*, stone-cutter
klempíř, *klempeersh*, tinner
knihař, *kñihărsh*, bookbinder
kloboučník, *kloboŭchñik*, hatter
kolář, *kolársh*, wagon-maker
kotlář, *kotlársh*, boiler-maker
kovář, *kovársh*, blacksmith
koželuh, *koželŭh*, tanner
kožešník, *koželshñik*, furrier
krejčí, *kreychee*, tailor
kufrář, *kŭfrársh*, trunk-maker
lakýrník, *lăkeerñik*, laquerer
litec, *litets*, founder
malíř, *măleersh*, painter
mydlář, *mydlársh*, soap-maker
mlynář, *mlynársh*, miller
natěrač, *năťerăch*, painter
obuvník, (švec), *obŭvñik, (shvets)*, shoemaker
pekař, *pekarsh*, baker
plynovodník, gas-fitter
puškař, *pushkarsh*, gunsmith
řezník, *rshězñik*, butcher

rybář, *rybársh*, fisherman
rytec, *rytets*, engraver
sazeč, *sázech*, typesetter
sedlář, *sedlársh*, saddler
sekerník, *sekerñik*, millwright
sládek, brewer
sochař, *sokharsh*, sculptor
stavitel, builder
strojník, *stroyñik*, machinist
tesař, *tessarsh*, carpenter
tiskař, *ťisskarsh*, printer
tkadlec, *kădlets*, weaver
truhlář, (stolař), *trŭhlársh*, cabinet-maker
zahradník, *zăhrădñik*, gardner
zámečník, *zámechñik*, locksmith
zedník, *zedñik*, stone-mason, brick-layer;
zlatník, *zlătñik*, goldsmith.

———

Barvířství, n. *barveershstvee*, the dyer's trade;
bednářství, n. *bednárshstvee*, the cooper's trade;
doutníkářství, *doŭtñikárstvee*, cigar-making;
krejčovství, *kreychofstvee* } the tailor's trade, tai-
krejčovina, *kreychovină* } loring:
ševcovství, *shĕftsof-stvee*, } the shoemak-er's trade,
ševcovina, *shĕftsovină* } shoemaking;
sazečství, *sázechstvee*, type-setting; etc.

On the farm.
NA FARMĚ.

I want to go on a farm.	Chci na farmu.	*khtsi nă farmŭ.*
Do you want to be a farmer?	Chcete býti farmerem?	*khtsětě beet farmerem?*
Yes; I want to buy land.	Ano; chci koupiti pozemek.	*ănŏ; khtsi koŭpit pŏzěmek.*
What is land worth in this neighborhood?	Co stojí pozemky v tomto okolí?	*tsŏ stoyee pozemky ftomtŏ okolee?*
What are improved farms worth?	Co stojí vzdělané farmy?	*tsŏ stoyee vzďelăné farmy?*
Fifty to sixty dollars an acre, and over.	Padesát až šedesát dollarů akr, i více.	*pădessát ăsh shědessát dollăroo ăkᵉr, e veetsě.*
How is the soil?— The soil is good, fertile.	Jaká je půda? — Půda je dobrá, úrodná.	*yăká yě poodă?— poodă yě dŏbrá, oorodná.*
Good land all over.	Samá dobrá zem.	*sămá dŏbrá zem.*
What is the character (or "lay")of the land?	Jaká je poloha?	*yăkă yě polohă?*
The land is level, (flat, broken, hilly).	Půda je rovná, (plochá. lomená, kopčitá).	*poodă yě rovná,(plokhá, loměná, kopchitá).*
The land is loamy, — sandy.	Zem je hlinitá, — pís-čitá.	*zem yě hliñitá, — peeschitá.*
Black loam, — mixed with sand.	Černá hlína,—smíchaná s pískem.	*cherná hleenă, — smeekhănă speeskem.*
Gravel at the bottom,— in some places clay.	Štěrk vespod,— někde jíl (mazník).	*shťerk vespod, — ñegdě yeel (măzñik).*
Rich land;--poor land.	Bohatá půda; — chudá půda.	*bohătá poodă;— khŭdá poodă.*
That land is bad — swampy; — it has no drainage.	Ten pozemek je špatný, — bahnitý; — nemá odpad.	*ten pŏzemek yě shpătnee — băhñitee,; — němá odpăd.*
That land looks poor. --Everything grows here; — but it wants manuring.	Ta půda vypadá hubená. -- Všechno zde roste; — ale musí se hnojiti.	*tă pooda vypădá hŭbená. — fshěkhnŏ zdě rostě; — ălě măsee sě hnoyit.*

How will the harvest be? — good? — bad?	Jaká bude úroda?—dobrá? — špatná?	yăká bŭdĕ oorodă?—dŏbrá? — shpátná?
How does grain look?— Grain shows a good stand.—Wheat stools out thickly.	Jak stojí obilí?— Obilí stojí dobře. — Pšenice nasazuje hustě.	yăk stoyce obilee? — o- bilee stoyee dŏbrshĕ. — pshĕñitsĕ năssăzŭ- yĕ hŭssťe.
Rye is in bloom.—Barley is heading.	Žito je ve květu.—Ječmen vymetá.	žitŏ yĕ vĕ kwyĕtŭ. — yĕchmen vymĕtá.
Wheat has lodged;-the rainstorm laid it flat.	Pšenice lehla; — ten liják ji položil.	pshĕñitsĕ lehlă;— ten li- yák ye položil.
It has a good ear;—the berries are plump.	Má dobrý klas;— zrno je jadrné.	má dŏbree klăss;— zᵉr- nŏ yĕ yădᵉrné.
Corn is poor; — early corn looks better than late corn.	Kukuřice je špatná; — ranná korna je lepší než pozdní.	kŭkŭrshitsĕ yĕshpătná; — rănná kornă yĕ lep- shee nesh pozdñee.
Have you a great deal of corn? — We have twenty acres of it.	Máte mnoho korny? — Máme jí dvacet a krů.	mátĕ mnohŏ korny? — mámĕ ye dwătset ă- kroo.
We planted it towards the end of May. — I think it will pick up.	Sázeli jsme ji ke konci máje. — Já myslím že se sebere.	sázelli smĕ ye kĕ kontsi máyĕ. — yá misleem že sĕ sĕberĕ.
Our neighbor planted corn in the sod. — How does it grow?— Poorly.	Soused sázel kornu do drnu. — Jak roste? — Mizerně.	soŭsed sázel kornŭ dŏ dᵉrnŭ. — yăk roste? — mizerñe.
How is the pasture? — Poor.	Jaká je pastva? — Hubená.	yăká yĕ păstvă? — hŭ- bĕná.
Everything is parched up. — Hay will be short.	Všecko je vyprahlé. — Sena bude málo.	fshĕtsko yĕ vyprăhlé.— sennă bŭdĕ málŏ.
Do you raise a great deal of stock?	Chováte mnoho dobytka?	khovátĕ mnohŏ dŏbyt- kă?
About fifty head.	Asi padesát kusů.	ăssi pădessát kŭssoo.
What do you feed (to your stock)?	Čím krmíte?	cheem kᵉrmeetĕ?

What do you feed your stock upon?	Co dáváte dobytku žráti?	*tsŏ dáváté dŏbytkŭ žrát?*
What do you feed to your horses.	Čím krmíte koně?	*cheem k^ermeetě koňe?*
Do you fatten your stock for the butcher (*liter.* "for meat")?	Krmíte dobytek na maso?	*k^ermeetě dŏbytek na mássŏ?*
Last year I fattened fifteen head of beefsteers.	Loni vykrmil jsem patnáct volů na maso.	*lŏňi vyk^ermil sem pátnáist voloo ná mássŏ.*
I feed many hogs for the market.	Krmím mnoho prasat pro trh.	*k^ermeem mnohŏ prássát pro t^erh.*
I have a stock farm not far from here.	Mám dobytčí farmu nedaleko odtud.	*mám dŏbitchee farmŭ nedălekŏ otŭd.*
There is a creek on it; — but now it is almost dry.	Je na ní potok; — ale teď je skoro suchý.	*yě ná ňee pŏtok; — ălě teď yě skorŏ sŭkhee.*
This is a dry year (a dry season);—there is no moisture (no rain).	Je suchý rok; — není vláhy.	*yě sŭkhee rok; — neyňi vláhy.*
A wet year (wet season) is better.	Mokrý rok je lepší.	*mokree rok yě lepshee.*
There is a great deal of insects this year.	Je síla hmyzu letos.	*yě seelá hmizŭ letoss.*
Grasshoppers we never had;— neither did we have chinch bugs.	Kobylky nikdy jsme neměli; — polní štěnice také ne.	*kobylky ňigdy smě němyělli;—polňee shťěňitsě tăké ně.*
Farming implements cost a great deal.	Rolnické nářadí stojí mnoho.	*rolňitské nárshăď ee stoyee mnohŏ.*
At present we have machines for everything	Teď máme stroje na všecko.	*teď mámě stroyě ná fshětskŏ.*
Farming is improving.	Rolnictví se zvelebuje.	*rolňitstvee sě zvelěbŭyě.*

VOCABULARY.

Note. From the preceding lessons the student is familiar with a great many words and phrases relating to agriculture. To repeat the same in the following vocabulary would be a waste of space.

LAND and HARVEST.
Půda a žeň.

Dolina, f. *dollinā* } bottomland
úpad, m. *oopād* }
výšina, f. *veeshinā*, upland
svah, m. *svāh*, slope
stráň, f. *strāň*, bluff
rokle, f. *rocklě*, ravine, gully;
mez, f. *měz*, boundary, line;
pěšina, f. *pyěshinā* } path
stezka, f. *steskā* }
lávka, f. *lāfkā*, footbridge
mostek, m. *mŏstek* } little bridge
můstek, m. *moostek* }
kanál, m. *kānál*, culvert
strouha, f. *strouhā*, ditch
břeh, m. *brshěh*, bank
hráz (hráze), f. *hráz*, dam.

Orati, *orāt*, to plow
vláčeti, *vlāchet*, to harrow
přeorati, *prshěorāt*, to backset
přivláčeti, *prshi-vlāchet*, to scour
oráč, m. *orách*, plowman
brázda, f *brāzdā*, furrow
kolej, f. *kolley*, rut
hnojiti, *hnoyit*, to manure

hnojivo, n. *hnoyivŏ*, } manure,
hnůj, m. *hnooy* } dung;
mrva, f. *mervā* }
zaseti, *zāsset*, to sow, to seed (with);
zaseto, *zāssetŏ*, sown, seeded;
sázeti, *sāzet*, } to plant
zasázeti, *zāssāzet*, }
zasázeno, planted
žíti, *žeet*, } to reap, to mow;
požíti, *požeet* }
sekati, *sekāt* } to cut
posekati, *pŏsekāt* }
skliditi, *sklidľit*, to harvest
sláma, f. *slāmā*, straw
snop, m. *snŏp*, sheaf
vázati, *vāzāt*, to bind
stoh, m. *stŏh*, stack
stohovati, *stŏhovāt*, to stack
kupa sena, *kūpā sennā*, hay-stack
kupka sena, *kūpkā s.*, hay-rick
voziti, *vozit* } to haul,
s,sážeti, *svážet* } to carry;
droliti se, *drolit sě*, to shed, to shell;
zralý, á, é *zrālee*, ripe
přezralý, á, é *prshězrālee*, over-ripe.

PLANTS.
Rostliny.

Tráva, f. *trāvā*, grass
plevel, m. *plěvell*, weeds
pleti, *plet*, to weed
koukol, *koŭkol*, cockle
jetel, m. *yetell*, clover
pohanka, f. *pohānkā*, buckwheat
proso, n. *prossŏ*, millet

hrách, m. *hrákh*, pease
boby, *bŏby* } beans
fazole, *fāzolě* }
čočka, f. *chochkā*, lentils
řepa, f. *rshěpā* } beets
řípa, f. *rsheepā*, }
řepa pro dobytek, rutabaga

voduatka, f. turnips
keř, m. *kersh*, shrub
živý plot, *živee plot*, hedge
háj, m. *háy*, grove
houština, f. *hoŭshťiná*, thicket, copse;
chrastí, n. *khrăsťi*, brushwood, undergrowth;

pařez, m. *părshěs*, stump
klada, f. *klădă*, trunk
větev, f. *vyětef*, branch, bough;
větvička, f. *vyětvichkă*, twig
ratolest, f. spring
káceti stromy, *kátset*⎫ to fell (trees)⁻
poráželi ,, *porăžet*⎭

Teams and domestic animals.
Potah a domácí zvířata.

Potah, m. *pŏtăh*, a team
pár koní, *pár koňee*, a pair of horses
pár volů, *pár voloo*, a yoke of oxen
pár mladých volů, a pair of steers;
na koni, *nă koňi*, on horseback;
jeti na koni, *yet nă koňi*, to ride a horse;
jeti s koňma, *yet skoňmă*, to drive horses;
zapřahnouti, *zăprshăhnoŭt*, to harness;
uvázati, *ŭvázăt*, to hitch
náklad, m. *năklăd*, the load
nakládati, *năklădăt*, to load
skládati, *sklădăt*, to unload
uváznouti, *ŭváznoŭt*, to get fast, to stick fast;
splašiti se, *splăshit sě*, to run away
lekati se, *lekăt sě*, to shy
zarážlivý kůň, *zarăžlivee kooň*, a balky horse;
zlý kůň, *zlee kooň*, a vicious horse;
klus, m. *klŭss*, trot
krok, m. pace
krmiti, *krmit*, to feed
napojiti, *năpoyit*, to water.

Klisna, f. *klissnă*⎫ brood mare;
hřebice, f. *hrshěbitsě*⎭
hřebná, *hrshěbná*, with foal;
hříbě, n. *hrsheebyě*, foal
hřebeček, m. *hrshěběchek*, colt
hřebička, f. *hrshěbichkă*, fill
cucati, *tsŭtsăt*, to suckle
cucák, m. *tsŭtsák*, a suckling
hřebec, m. *hrshěbets*,⎫ stallion
hengst, m. *hengst*⎭

Kráva, f. *krávă*, cow
dojnice, f. *doyňitsě*, milch cow;
jalovice, f. *yăllovitsě*, heifer
tele, n. *tellě*, calf
bulík, m. *bulleek*, bull calf;
jalovička, f. *yăllovichkă*, heifer calf
roční, *rochňee*, yearling
stelná, *stellná*, with calf;
jalová, *yăllová*, farrow
pometati, *pŏmetăt*, to slink, to slip the calf;
běhati se, *byěhăt sě*, to be bulling; to want the bull;
býk, m. *beek*⎫ bull
bejk, *běyk*⎭

Ovce, f. *oftsĕ,* sheep
bahnice, f. *băhñitsĕ,* ewe
beran, m. *berăn,* ram, buck;
jehně, n. *yĕhñe,* lamb
bahněni, n. *băhñeñi,* lambing season
vlna, f. *velnă,* wool
stříhání, n. *strsheehăñi,* shearing.

Prase, n. *prăssĕ*
vepř, m. *veprsh* } pig, hog;
kanec, m. *kănets,* boar
svině, f. *sveeñe,* sow
sele, n. *selĕ* } sucking
podsvínče, n. *podsveinchĕ* } pig.

Mezek, m. *mĕzek,* mule
osel, m. *ŏsell,* donkey
koza, f. *kŏză,* goat, she-goat;
kozel, m. *kŏzell,* he-goat
kůzle, n. *koozlĕ,* kid
pes, m. *pess,* dog
čuba, f. *chŭbă,* bitch
štěně, n. *shťeñe,* whelp

kočka, f. *kŏchkă,* cat
kocour, m. *kotsoŭr,* tom-cat.

Drůbež, f. *droobĕsh,* poultry
slepice, f. *slepitsĕ,* hen, chicken;
kvočna, f. *kvŏchnă,* clucking hen;
kuře, n. *koorshĕ,* chick, young chicken;
kohout, m. *kohoŭt,* rooster
kachna, f. *kăkhnă* } duck
kačena, *kăchenă,* }
kačer, m. *kăcher,* drake
husa, f. *hŭssă,* goose
houser, m. *hoŭsser,* gander
housata, pl. *hoŭssătă,* goslings
krocan, m. *krotsău,* turkey-cock
krůta, f. *kroota,* turkey-hen
páv, m. *páf,* peacock
pávice, f. *păvitsĕ,* peahen
hnízdo, n. *hñeezdă,* nest
nesti vejce, *nest veytsĕ,* to lay eggs;
líhnouti se, *leehnoŭt sĕ,* to hatch.

TOOLS and MACHINES.
Nástroje a stroje.

Vůz, m. *vooz,* wagon
kolo, *kollŏ,* wheel
kolečko, n. *kollechkŏ,* wheelbarrow
ráf, m. tire
náboj, m. *năboy,* hub
náprava, f. *năprăvă,* axletree
špice, f. *shpitsĕ,* spokes
voj, f. *voy,* pole
vojky, *voyky,* shafts
hamovák, m. *hămovák,* brake
pera, pl. n. *peră,* springs
sedadlo, n. *sedădlŏ,* seat

kšír, m. *ksheer,* harness
oprať, f. *oprăť,* line
sedlo, n. *sedlŏ,* saddle
uzda, f *vozdă,* bridle
ohlávka, f. *ohlăfkă,* halter
popruh, m. *poprŭh,* girt
čabraka, f. *chăbrăkă,* horse-cloth
třemen, m. *trshĕmen,* stirrup
hřebílce, *hrshĕ-beeltsĕ,* curry-comb
bič, m. *bitch,* whip
bičiště, n. *bitchishťe,* whip-stick.

Saně, pl. *săñe*, sleigh

sanice, f. *săñitsĕ*, runner, (also: sleighing);

korba, f. *korbă*, cutter

řezačka, f. *rshĕzăchkă*, straw-cutter, feed-cutter;

řezanka, f. *rshĕzănkă*, chopped straw;

brány, pl. harrow, drag;

válec, m. *válets*, roller

pluh, m. *plooh*, plow

radlice, f. *rădlitsĕ*, plowshare

kleče, pl. *klĕchĕ*, handles

krajadlo, n. *krăyădlŏ*, coulter

řetěz, m. *rshĕťez*, chain

pospěchy, pl. *pospyĕkhy*) culty-
podrývač, m. *podreevăch*) vator

kosa, f. *kossă*, scythe

motyka, f. hoe

špičatá motyka, *shpichătá m.*, pick-
axe

rýč, f. *reech*, spade

lopata, f. *lopătă*, shovel

hrábě, pl. *hrábyĕ*, rake

hrabati, *hrăbăt*, to rake

podávky, pl. *podáfky*, hayfork

vidle, pl. *vidlĕ*, pitchfork

sekyra, f. *sekyră*, axe

sekyrka, f. hatchet

pila, f. *pillă*) saw
pilka, *pillkă*)

ruční pilka, *răchñee pillkă*, hand saw

nebozez, m. bore, auger;

Mlatidlo, *mlăťidlŏ*) threshing
mlatička, *mlăťichkă*) machine

mlátiti, *mlăťit*, to thresh

mlácení, n. *mlátseñi*, threshing

mlatič, m. *mlăťich*, thresher

fofr, m. *fŏf^er*, fanning mill;

sečka, f. *sechkă*, grain-drill

žací stroj, m. *žătsee stroy*, mower

sekací stroj, *sekătsee stroy*, reaper

samovazač, m. *sămovăzăch*, self-
binder

rám, m. frame

sýto, n. *seetŏ*, sieve

řešeto, n. *rshĕshĕtŏ*, screen

řemen, m. *rshĕmen*) belt
pruh, m. *prooh*)

tyč, f. *tich*, rod

panty, pl. m. *pănty*, hinges

zuby, pl. m. *zuby*) cogs
palce, *păltsĕ*)

žlábek, m. *žlábek*, spout

mlýnek, m. *mleynek*, mill

loupač (na kukuřici), m. *lŏŭpăch*,
corn-sheller;

loupati, *lŏŭpăt*, to shell.

PART IV.

Bohemian grammar.

1. ORTHOGRAPHY.

SECTION 1. — The full Bohemian alphabet, as given in the first Part, contains the following vowels : **a, á, — e, é, ě, — i, í, y, ý, — o, ó, — u, ú, ů.**

The other letters are consonants. There is only one diphthong: **ou,** *oŭ.* When **ou** occurs in a compound word, ending one and beginning the next syllable, it is not a diphthong and must be divided : **použiti (po-užiti),** *pŏ-ŭžit,* to use, to make use off; **samouk (samo-uk),** *sămo-ŭk,* a self-educated man.

An accute accent (or comma) over a vowel marks a long sound: **kam,** *kăm,* where to; **kámen,** *kámen,* a stone.

A ring over the vowel **u (ů)** is also a prolongation mark : **sup,** *sŭp,* a hawk; **sůl,** *sool,* the salt.

When a word begins with a long **u,** the accute accent is used: **úrok,** *oorok,* the interest. In such cases the vowel **ú** may be and frequently is changed into the diphthong **ou: ourok,** *oŭrok.*

The accented vowel **ě** has always the short sound of *yě:* **svět,** *swyět,* the world.

The vowels **a, o, u, y,** are called *hard;* the vowels **e, ě, i,** are called *soft.*

SECTION 2. — The consonants are divided into three classes :

hard consonants. — **h, ch, k, r, d, n, t;**
soft consonants, — **c, č, ď, j, ñ, ř, š, ť, ž;**
neutral consonants, — **b, f, l, m, p, s, v, z.**

After the hard consonants the hard vowel **y** is always used :

hynu, *hinnŭ,* I am perishing;
chyba, f. *khibŭ,* a mistake, a fault;
kyt, m. *kit,* putty
ryba, f. *ribŭ,* a fish

vždyť, dyť, *diť,* but, to be sure;
nynčko (nyní), *ninchkŏ,* now, at present;
tykev, f. *tikef,* a pumpkin.

When the sound is long, an accented **ý** is used : **hýbati,** *heebŭt,* to move; **tichý (á, é),** *ťikhee,* quiet; **rýti,** *reet,* to spade, to dig, to root; **dým,** m. *deem,* smoke; **týrati,** *teerŭt,* to misuse, to torment.

In such cases the vowel **ý** is usually changed into **ej** (*ěy*), in common pronunciation : **hejbati,** *hěybŭt;* **tichej,** *ťikhey;* **rejti,** *rěyt;* **dejm,** *děym;* **tejrati,** *těyrŭt.*

Words derived from foreign languages, also foreign names, make an exception, their original spelling being retained : **historie,** *historiě,* history; **Amerika, Riga,** etc.

The soft consonants are always followed by the soft vowel **i** (or **í,** when the sound is long) :

cit, m. *tsit,* the feeling
čin, m. *chin,* the deed
divoký*), *ďivokee,* wild
jistý, *yistee,* certain
nic, *ňits,* nothing
římsa, f. *rshimsŭ,* a cornice
šikovný, *shikŏvnee,* smart, clever;
tisk, m. *ťisk,* the printing
život, m. *život,* the life

cíl, m. *tseel,* the goal
číslo, n. *cheesslo,* the number
díl, m. *ďeel,* a part
jísti, *yeest,* to eat
hníti, *hňeet,* to rot
říci, *rsheetsi,* to say
šíti, *sheet,* to sew
tíže, f. *ťeežě,* the weight
žíla, f. *žeelŭ,* the vein.

The neutral vowels are followed by the soft **i** or **í,** with the following exceptions :

b : **aby, by,** that; **bych, bys,** etc, that I, that thou, etc.; **bylina,** f. the plant; **bystrý,** quick, sharp; **býti,** to be; **kobyla,** the mare; **obyčej,** m. the custom.

l : **lysý,** bald; **lysina,** f. bald spot, or white spot; **lýko,** n. the bast; **lyska,** f. the coot; **mlýn,** m. the mill; **oplývati,** to abound; **pely-**

---

*) The soft consonants **ď, ň, ť** lose their accent, when followed by **i, í** or **ě,** and are written simply **d, n, t.** See Part I, section 2.

něk, m. the wormwood; **plyn,** m. the gas; **plynouti,** to glide;
plýtvati, to waste; **polykati,** to swallow; **slyšeti,** to hear; **vzly-
kati,** to sob.

m : **hmyz,** m. the insects; **my,** we; **mýdlo,** n. the soap; **mýliti,** to mis-
lead, to confuse; **mýliti se,** to mistake; **omyl,** m. a mistake; **mysl,**
f. the mind; **mysliti,** to think; **myš,** f. the mouse; **mýti,** to wash;
smyčec, m. the fiddle-stick; **smykati,** to drag; **zamykati,** to lock up.

n : **nyní,** now.

p : **kopyto,** n. the hoof; **netopýr,** m. the bat; **pýcha,** f. the pride; **py-
kati,** to regret; **pyl,** m. the pollen; **pýr,** m. the quick-grass; **pysk,**
the lip; **pytel,** the sack; **třpytiti,** to glitter; **zpytovati,** to search,
to inquire.

s : **osyka,** f. the aspen; **osypky,** pl. the measles; **posýlati,** to send; **sy-
četi,** to hiss; **sychravý,** chilly; **syn,** m. the son; **sypati,** to pour;
sýpka, f. the granary, the bin; **sýr,** m. the cheese; **syrový,** raw;
syrup, the syrup; **sysel,** m. the gopher; **syt, nasycen,** full, satiated.

v : **povyk,** m. the noise; **vy,** you; **vydra,** f. the otter; **výheň,** f. the forge;
vykýř, m. the dormer-window; **výr,** m. the horn-owl; **vysoký,** high;
výti, to howl; **vyza,** the sturgeon; **zvyk,** the habit; **žvýkati,** to chew.

z : **brzy,** soon; **jazyk,** the tongue; **nazývati,** to call, to name.

SECTION 3. — As in English, the spelling makes sometimes a great
difference of meaning, though the pronunciation may be identical. For
instance :

býti, *beet'i* or *beet* (colloquially *běyt*), to be	**bíti,** *beet'i* or *beet,* to beat
mýti, *meet'i* or *meet* (colloq. *měyt*), to wash	**míti,** *meet'i* or *meet,* to have
my, *me,* we	**mi,** *me,* to me
vy, *ve,* you	**ví,** *vee,* he knows
výr, *veer,* (colloq. *věyr*), the horn-owl	**vír,** *veer,* the whirl-wind
výti, *veet'i* or *veet* (colloq. *věyt*), to howl	**víti,** *reet'i* or *reet,* to wind.

SECTION 4. — The Bohemian verb shows a distinction of gender in
the past tense*). In the plural, there is only an orthographical distinction

---

*) See Note 2, Lesson IX.

between the masculine and *feminine* gender, the latter always terminating in **y.** For instance :

masculine	*feminine*
byli jsme, we were .	byly jsme, we were
byli, they were	byly, they were
měli jsme, we had	měly jsme, we had
měli, they had	měly, they had
muži měli, the men had;	ženy měly, the women had
hoši viděli, the boys saw;	holky viděly, the girls saw.

The same is true of verbs relating to *inanimate* nouns of the masculine gender, or names of lifeless things : **stromy vyrostly,** the trees grew up; **domy shořely,** the houses burned down.

SECTION 5. — The general rule of Bohemian spelling is: A sound for every letter and a letter for every sound, and no silent letters*). From this rule there are but few exceptions. In some words the initial letter **j** is silent :

jdu, *dŭ*, I go	jmeno, n. *menŏ*, the name
jsem, *sem*, I am	jmenovati, *menŏvát*, to name
jsme, *smě*, we are	jmění, n. *myěňi*, the property.

The letter **d** is also silent in a few cases: **dcera,** *tserá*, the daughter, **srdce,** n. *sertsě*, the heart.

In some cases the letters **k, s, t, v, z, ž** modify their sound in order to facilitate pronunciation:

kdo, who, — *gdŏ*	v peci, in the oven, — *fpetsi;*
kdy, when, — *gdy*	bez peněz, without money, — *běs*
s bohem, farewell, — *zbŏhem*	*pĕňez;*
kletba, f. the curse, — *kledbá*	zpívati, to sing, — *speevát.*

SECTION 6. — The prepositions **s** and **z** (**se, ze**) are governed by the following rule :

When the tendency is *from above downwards* **s** or **se** is used: **spadl s okna, s nebe, se stromu,** *spádl sokná, snebě, sě stromá,* — he fell from the window, from heaven, from the tree.

---

*) See Part III, Note 1.

When the tendency is from below upwards, or from the inside to the outside, z or ze is employed : **vylezu ze studně,** I shall crawl up from the well; **vyndal jsem peníze z kapsy,** (*skápsy*), I took the money from my pocket, *or* out of my pocket; **vyskočím z okna ven,** I shall jump out of the window.

SECTION 7. — It is a vulgar English custom to place the sound of *h* before initial vowels : *heye* (eye), *Henglund* (England). In Bohemian a similar vulgar custom obtains, namely that of placing the letter **v** before an initial **o.** We hear, for instance :

von, instead of **on** (he)	**vokno,** instead of **okno** (window)
vona, " " **ona** (she)	**voko,** " " **oko,** (eye)
vono, " " **ono** (it)	**vosel,** " " **osel,** (ass).

This vulgarity must be carefully avoided in writing as well as speaking. On the other hand, when the letter **v** belongs to the root of the word, care must be taken not to omit the same :

voda, water; **voják,** soldier; **vosk,** wax; **voskovati,** to wax.

SECTION 8. — In writing, words have often to be divided in syllables. The principal rules to be observed are the following :

a) A consonant standing between two vowels belongs to the next syllable : **o-ba,** both; **o-ko,** the eye; **kla-da,** the log.

b) A consonant succeeding the letter **l** or **r** also belongs to the next syllable : **vl-na,** *velná,* the wool; **hr-dlo,** *h^erdlŏ,* the throat.

c) Two vowels, if they do not form the diphthong **ou,** are always divided : **Ma-ri-e,** *márié.*

d) Compound words are divided according to their component parts: **bez-hlavý (bez-hla-vý),** headless; **roz-ličný (roz-lič-ný),** different; **oka-mžik,** the twinkling of an eye; a moment.

Other rules are less important and are sometimes sinned against even by the best writers.

SECTION 9. — The use of capital letters follows the same rules as in English, excepting that adjectives derived from the names of countries or nations do not, in Bohemian, commence with a capital letter (**anglický,** English; **český,** Bohemian; etc.); neither does the personal pronoun **já** (I) use a capital letter.

18

2. ETYMOLOGY.

SECTION 1. — The Bohemian language has seven cases, the nature of which is sufficiently explained in Note 5, on page 82.

SECTION 2. — The declension of Bohemian nouns differs in regard to *gender*, and also in regard to *termination*.

Nouns of the masculine gender, moreover, form two classes : (*a*) names of living creatures, or *animate* nouns; (*b*) names of lifeless beings, or *inanimate* nouns.

According to this division there is also a slight difference in their declension.

DECLENSION OF MASCULINE NOUNS.

SECTION 3. — The first declension of nouns of the masculine gender is fully shown by the following examples*):

	Animate	*Inanimate*
	Singular number.	
nominative	syn, the son	strom, the tree
genitive	syn-a, of the son;	strom-u, of the tree;
dative	syn-u, -ovi, to the son	strom-u, to the tree;
accusative	syn-a, the son	strom, the tree
vocative	syn-e**), son !	strom-e, tree !
locative	syn-u, -ovi, (in) the son	strom-u, (in) the tree;
instrumental	syn-em, with the son;	strom-em, with the tree.
	Plural number.	
nom.	syn-i, -ové, the sons	strom-y***), the trees
gen.	syn-ů, -ův, of the sons;	strom-ů, -ův, of the trees;
dat.	syn-ům, to the sons;	strom-ům, to the trees;
acc.	syn-y, the sons	strom-y, the trees
voc.	syn-i, -ové, sons !	strom-y***), trees !
loc.	syn-ech, (in) the sons;	strom-ech, (in) the trees;
inst.	syn-y, with the sons;	strom-y, with the trees.

---

*) Compare Note 3, on page 55; also Note 1, on page 69.
) In this particular case the common usage is **synu ! o son ! **Sy-nu můj,** o my son !
***) It has also the long termination **ové,** when used as an *animate* noun, especially in poetic language: **stromové se klonili,** the trees bowed.
— **O stromové, promluvte !** o trees, speak out !

The first masculine declension (*ten* **syn,** *ten* **strom**) comprises nouns ending in hard or neutral consonants.

SECTION 4. — The **second** declension of nouns of the masculine gender is presented in full by the following examples:

Animate	*Inanimate*

Singular.

nom.	**muž,** the man	**meč,** the sword
gen.	**muž-e,** of the man;	**meč-e,** of the sword;
dat.	**muž-i, -ovi,** to the man;	**meč-i,** to the sword;
acc.	**muž-e,** the man	**meč,** the sword
voc.	**muž-i,** man!	**meč-i,** sword!
loc.	**muž-i,** (in) the man;	**meč-i,** (in) the sword;
inst.	**muž-em,** with the man;	**meč-em,** with the sword.

Plural.

nom.	**muž-i, -ové,** the men	**meč-e*),** the swords
gen.	**muž-ů, -ův,** of the men;	**meč-ů, -ův,** of the swords;
dat.	**muž-ům,** to the men;	**meč-ům,** to the swords;
acc.	**muž-e,** the men	**meč-e,** the swords
voc.	**muž-i, -ové,** men!	**meč-e*),** swords!
loc.	**muž-ích,** (in) the men;	**meč-ích,** (in) the swords;
inst.	**muž-i,** with the men;	**meč-i,** with the swords.

The second masculine declension (*ten* **muž,** *ten* **meč**) comprises nouns ending in soft consonants or in **el** (for inst. **učitel,** the teacher).

SECTION 5. — Nouns of the first declension, terminating in **h, ch, k, r,** change these hard consonants into **z, š, c, ř,** in the *nominative* case of the plural number, as explained in Note 3 on page 70, to which we refer.

SECTION 6. — Nouns of the first declension ending in **ek** eliminate the vowel e in the inflected cases, as stated in Note 2 on page 80. For instance:

svědek, *swyědek,* the witness; **svědka,** *swyědka* (not **svědeka**), of the witness; **svědku** or **svědkovi,** to the witness; etc. — (Plural:) **svědci** or **svědkové,** the witnesses; **svědků,** of the witnesses; **svědkům,** to the witnesses; etc.

---

*) It may also have the long termination (**mečové**), when used as an animate noun, especially in solemn or poetical language.

The same is true of nouns ending **et** and **en.** The nouns **loket** (the yard, *or* the elbow) and **den** (the day) follow in their declension the example of **meč:**

loket, the yard; **lokte,** of the yard; **lokti,** to the yard; etc.

den, the day; **dne,** of the day; **dni,** to the day; etc.

In the plural, **den** is quite irregular: **dni** or **dnové,** the days; **dní** or **dnův,** of the days; **dnům,** to the days; **dni** or **dny** (accus.), the days; **dnech,** (in) the days; **dněmi** or **dny,** with the days.

SECTION 7. — The vowel **ů,** when it occurs in the nominative, changes into **o** in the inflected cases : **kůň,** the horse; **koně,** of the horse; **koni (or koňovi),** to the horse; etc. — See Note 4 on page 56.

SECTION 8. — Nouns ending in **el** are mostly declined like **muž** or **meč;** for instance : **učitel,** the teacher; **učitele,** of the teacher; **učiteli, (-ovi),** to the teacher; etc.

Přítel (the friend) has in the nominative plural **přátelé** (the friends); in the genitive **přátel,** of the friends. —

The word **peníze** (the money) is a plural noun: **peněz,** of the money; **penězům,** to the money; **v penězích,** in the money; **penězi,** with the money.

DECLENSION OF FEMININE NOUNS.

SECTION 9. — The **first** declension of nouns of the feminine gender (*ta* **žena**) is shown by the following example*) :

	Singular		Plural	
nom.	žen-a,	the woman	žen-y,	the women
gen.	žen-y,	of the woman	žen,	of the women
dat.	žen-ě,	to the woman	žen-ám,	to the women
acc.	žen-u,	the woman	žen-y,	the women
voc.	žen-o,	woman!	žen-y,	women!
loc.	žen-ě,	(in) the woman	žen-ách,	(in) the women
inst.	žen-ou,	with the woman	žen-ami,	with the women.

All nouns of the feminine gender ending in **a** belong to this declension.

SECTION 10. — There are some masculine nouns terminating in **a,** which follow this declension in the singular, excepting the dative and locative cases, which have the long masculine form. For instance: **vévod-a,** the duke; **vévod-y,** of the duke; **vévod-ovi,** to the duke; etc.

---

*) Compare Note 3 on page 60.

In the plural number, such nouns follow the first masculine declension: **vévod-ové,** the dukes; **vévod-ŭv,** of the dukes; **vévod-ŭm,** to the dukes; etc. (See "plural" of first declension of masculine nouns.) — Some masculines ending in **a** take in the nominative plural always the short form **i** or **é**; for instance: **basista,** the basso; **basisti** (or **basisté**), the bassoes.

SECTION 11. — Nouns of the feminine gender ending in **ĕ**, belong to the **second** declension (*ta* **zemĕ**), which is as follows*) :

	Singular			Plural	
nom.	**zem-ĕ,**	the earth	**zem-ĕ,**	the earths
gen.	**zem-ĕ,**	of the earth	**zem-i,**	of the earths
dat.	**zem-i,**	to the earth	**zem-ím,**	to the earths
acc.	**zem-i,**	the earth	**zem-ĕ,**	the earths
voc.	**zem-ĕ,**	earth!	**zem-ĕ,**	earths !
loc.	**zem-i,**	in the earth	**zem-ích,**	(in) the earths
inst.	**zem-í,**	with the earth	**zem-ĕmi,**	with the earths.

SECTION 12· — Nouns of the feminine gender ending in a *consonant* (*ta* **daň**), belong to the **third** declension, which has two branches showing a slight divergence at least in the written language, if not always in common discourse; hence we subjoin two examples :

Singular

nom.	**kosť,**	the bone	**daň,**	the tax
gen.	**kost-i.**	of the bone	**dan-ĕ,**	of the tax
dat.	**kost-i,**	to the bone	**dan-i,**	to the tax
acc.	**kost,**	the bone	**daň,**	the tax
voc.	**kost-i,**	bone !	**dan-i,**	tax !
loc.	**kost-i,**	(in) the bone	**dan-i,**	(in) the tax
inst.	**kost-í,**	with the bone	**dan-í,**	with the tax.

Plural

nom.	**kost-i,**	the bones	**dan-ĕ,**	the taxes
gen.	**kost-í,**	of the bones	**dan-í,**	of the taxes
dat.	**kost-em,**	to the bones	**dan-ím,**	to the taxes
acc.	**kost-i,**	the bones	**dan-ĕ,**	the taxes
voc.	**kost-i,**	bones !	**dan-ĕ,**	taxes !
loc.	**kost-ech,**	(in) the bones	**dan-ích,**	(in) the taxes
inst.	**kost-mi,**	with the bones	**dan-ĕmi,**	with the taxes.

*) Compare Note 3 on page 60.

Nouns terminating in eñ drop the vowel e in the inflected cases; for instance: **lázeñ,** the bath; **lázuě,** of the bath; **lázni,** to the bath; etc.

DECLENSION OF NEUTRAL NOUNS.

SECTION 13. — The **first** declension comprises nouns of the neutral gender ending in **o** (*to* **slovo**). They are declined as follows*):

	Singular		Plural	
nom.	slov-o,	the word	slov-a,	the words
gen.	slov-a,	of the word	slov,	of the words
dat.	slov-u,	to the word	slov-ům,	to the words
acc.	slov-o,	the word	slov-a,	the words
voc.	slov-o,	word!	slov-a,	words!
loc.	slov-ě, (-u)	(in) the word	slov-ech, (-ích),	(in) the words
inst.	slov-em,	with the word	slov-y,	with the words

SECTION 14. — The **second** neutral declension embraces nouns ending in e and ě (*to* **pole,** *to* **poupě**). It has two branches, differing somewhat in their inflected endings, as will be seen from the subjoined two examples**).

Singular.

nom.	pol-e,	the field	poup-ě,	the bud
gen.	pol-e,	of the field	poup-ěte,	of the bud
dat.	pol-i,	to the field	poup-ěti,	to the bud
acc.	pol-e,	the field	poup-ě,	the bud
voc.	pol-e,	field!	poup-ě,	bud!
loc.	pol-i,	(in) the field	poup-ěti,	(in) the bud
inst.	pol-em,	with the field	poup-ětem,	with the bud.

Plural.

nom.	pol-e,	the fields	poup-ata,	the buds
gen.	pol-í,	of the fields	poup-at,	of the buds
dat.	pol-ím,	to the fields	poup-atům,	to the buds
acc.	pol-e,	fields	poup-ata,	the buds
voc.	pol-e,	fields!	poup-ata,	buds!
loc.	pol-ích,	(in) the fields	poup-atech,	(in) the buds
inst.	pol-i,	with the fields	poup-aty,	with the buds.

*) Compare Note 2 on page 65.
**) Compare Note 2 on page 65.

The following nouns are declined like poupě: hrabě, the count, (hrab-ěte, of the count; hrabata, the counts); kníže, the prince; pachole, the little boy; děvče, the girl; vnouče, the grandchild; — zvíře, the animal; dobytče, the beast; hříbě, the foal; jehně, the lamb; kotě, the kitten; kůzle, the kid; káče, the duckling; kuře, the chick; háďe, the young snake; house, the gosling; tele, the calf; — doupě, the den; koště, the broom; vole, the crop (the craw).

The nouns břemeno, the burden; rameno, the arm or upper arm; semeno, the seed; temeno, the crown of the head, — and some others, have also a short form: břímě, rámě, símě, témě. The declension of these shortened nouns deviates somewhat from the above examples of the second neutral declension, for which reason a full paradigm is subjoined:

	Singular	Plural
nom.	sím-ě, the seed	sem-ena, the seeds
gen.	sem-ene, of the seed	sem-en, of the seeds
dat.	sem-eni, to the seed	sem-enům, to the seeds
acc.	sím-ě, the seed	sem-ena, the seeds
voc.	sím-ě, seed !	sem-ena, seeds !
loc.	sem-eni, (in) the seed	sem-enech, (in) the seeds
inst.	sem-enem, with the seed	sem-eny, with the seeds.

SECTION 15. — The **third** declension of neutral nouns is characterized by the terminal í:

	Singular	Plural
nom.	znamen-í, the sign	znamen-í, the signs
gen.	znamen-í, to the sign	znamen-í, of the signs
dat.	znamen-í, to the sign	znamen-ím, to the signs
acc.	znamen-í, the sign	znamen-í, the signs
voc.	znamen-í, sign !	znamen-í, signs !
loc.	znamen-í, (in) the sign	znamen-ích, (in) the signs
inst.	znamen-ím, with the sign	znamen-ími, with the signs.

This declension embraces also: 1. *Feminine* nouns terminating in í, like: paní, the mistress or lady; biblí, (also bible), the bible; but these nouns retain the terminal í in the instrumental of the singular number: s paní, with the lady. — 2. Some *masculine* nouns ending in í: rukojmí, the surety.

Section 16. — There is a *dual* number in Bohemian, limited in the modern language to the names of parts of the human body, which appear in pairs : **oči,** the eyes; **uši,** the ears; **ruce,** the hands; **nohy,** the feet; **prsa,** the breasts; **ramena,** the arms; **kolena,** the knees. They are declined in the dual number as follows :

nom.	**oč-i,** the eyes	**uš-i,**	**ruc-e,**	**noh-y**	**prs-a,**
gen.	**oč-í,** of the eyes	**uš-í,**	**ruk-ou,**	**noh-ou**	**prs-ou**
dat.	**oč-ím,** to the eyes	**uš-ím,**	**ruk-ám,**	**noh-ám**	**prs-ům**
acc.	**oč-i,** the eyes	**uš-i,**	**ruc-e,**	**noh-y**	**prs-a**
voc.	**oč-i,** eyes !	**uš-i,**	**ruc-e,**	**noh-y**	**prs-a**
loc.	**oč-ích,** (in) the eyes	**uš-ích,**	**ruk-ou,**	**noh-ou**	**prs-ou**
inst.	**oč-ima,** with the eyes	**uš-ima,**	**ruk-ama,**	**noh-ama**	**prs-oma.**

DECLENSION OF ADJECTIVES.

Section 17. — There are two leading classes of adjectives : definite and indefinite.

Definite adjectives present two subdivisions : 1. adjectives with a changing termination, according to gender : **dobr-ý (muž), dobr-á (žena), dobr-é (dítě),** — the good man, the good woman, the good child; 2. adjectives with the same termination in all three genders : **dnešn-í (vítr) dnešní (zima), dnešní (parno),** — to-day's wind, to-day's cold, to-day's heat.*)

Indefinite adjectives are either derived from definite adjectives, being only a different form of the same ; for instance : **zdravý, zdravá, zdravé,** healthy or well (definite); **zdráv, zdráva, zdrávo** (indefinite)**) ;

Or they are so-called possessive adjectives, derived from nouns :

(otec, the father) **otc-ův, otc-ova, otc-ovo,** the father's; **(matka,** the mother) **matč-in, matč-ina, matč-ino,** the mother's***).

Section 18. — Definite adjectives with a changing termination are declined in the following manner****) :

---

*) Compare Note 1 on page 85, and Note 1 on page 94.
**) Compare Note 2 on page 103.
***) Compare Notes 2 and 3, on pp. 94, 95.
****) Compare Note 1, on page 85.

Singular.

masculine	*feminine*	*neutre*
nom. dobr-ý muž, a good man;	dobr-á žena;	dobr-é dítko
gen. dobr-ého muže, of a good man	dobr-é ženy;	dobr-ého dítka
dat. dobr-ému muži, to a good man	dobr-é ženě;	dobr-ému dítku
acc. dobr-ého muže, a good man;	dobr-ou ženu,	dobr-é dítko
voc. dobr-ý muži, good man !	dobr-á ženo!	dobr-é dítko!
loc. dobr-ém muži, (in) a good man	dobr-é ženě;	dobr-ém dítku
inst. dobr-ým mužem, with a good man	dobr-ou ženou;	dobr-ým dítkem.

Plural.

nom. dobř-í muži, good men	dobr-é ženy	dobr-á dítka
gen. dobr-ých mužů, of good men	dobr-ých žen	dobr-ých dítek
dat. dobr-ým mužům, to good men	dobr-ým ženám	dobr-ým dítkám
acc. dobr-é muže, good men	dobr-é ženy	dobr-á dítka
voc. dobř-í muži, good men!	dobr-é ženy	dobr-á dítka
loc. dobr-ých mužích, (in) good m.	dobr-ých ženách	dobr-ých dítkách
inst. dobr-ými muži, with good men	dobr-ými ženami	dobr-ými dítkami.

Note 1. The hard consonants **h, ch, k, r,** are changed in the nominative plural of the *masculine* gender into the soft consonants **z, š, c, ř,** when the adjective qualifies an *animate* noun : **dobrý muž, — dobří muži; velký hoch, — velcí hoši.** The terminations **cký** and **ský** change into **čtí** and **ští: německý** (sing.) — **němečtí** (plur.); **český** (sing.) — **čeští** (plur.).

In common discourse, however, this rule is neglected.

Note 2. When the adjective qualifies a masculine *inanimate* noun, it agrees in the nominative and accusative plural with the feminine gender: **dobré stromy,** good trees; and the accusative singular is like the nominative: **dobrý strom.**

Section 19. — Definite adjectives, having the same termination (**í**) in all genders and both numbers, are declined in the following manner*):

---

* Compare Note 1, page 94.

	Singular			Plural
	masculine	*feminine*	*neutre*	*all three genders*
nom.	dnešn-í	dnešn-í	dnešn-í	dnešn-i
gen.	dnešn-ího	dnešn-í	dnešn-ího	dnešn-ích
dat.	dnešn-ímu	dnešn-í	dnešn-ímu	dnešn-ím
acc.	dnešn-ího	dnešn-í	dnešn-í	dnešn-í
voc.	dnešn-í	dnešn-í	dnešn-í	dnešn-í
loc.	dnešn-ím	dnešn-í	dnešn-ím	dnešn-ích
inst.	dnešn-ím	dnešn-í	dnešn-ím	dnešn-ími

Note. When the adjective qualifies a masculine *inanimate* noun, the accusative singular is like the nominative. We say: **čekám dnešního hosta**, I wait for to-day's guest; but: **"čekám dnešní list"**, I wait for to-day's paper.

SECTION 20. — Indefinite adjectives like **zdráv** (from **zdravý**), **vesel** (from **veselý**), etc. *) are now used only in the nominative and accusative cases. *Possessive* adjectives have the following declension:

Singular

	masculine	*feminine*	*neutre*
nom.	bratr-ův, my brother's	bratr-ova	bratr-ovo
gen.	bratr-ova, of my brother's	bratr-ovy	bratr-ova
dat.	bratr-ovu, to my brother's	bratr-ově	bratr-ovu
acc.	bratr-ova, my brother's	bratr-ovu	bratr-ovo
voc.	bratr-ův! brother's!	bratr-ova!	bratr-ovo!
loc.	bratr-ovu (-ově) in my brother's	bratr-ově	bratr-ovu
inst.	bratr-ovým, with my brother's	bratr-ovou	bratr-ovým.

Plural

(Only three cases differ, the other four being identical. In conversation there is no difference at all.)

nom.	bratr-ovi, my brother's	bratr-ovy	bratr-ova
gen.		bratr-ových	
dat.		bratr-ovým	
acc.	bratr-ovy	bratr-ovy	bratr-ova
voc.	bratr-ovi!	bratr-ovy!	bratr-ova!
loc.		bratr-ových	
inst.		bratr-ovými	

---

*) See Note 2, page 103.

Note 1. — When the possessive adjective qualifies a masculine *inanimate* noun, the accusative singular is like the nominative: *vidím* **bratrův** *dům*, "I see my brother's house"; and the nominative and vocative plural have a final **y**, like the feminine gender : **bratrovy** *domy*, "my brother's houses".

Note 2. — The adjective **páně** is not inflected : **leta Páně 1890,** in the year of our Lord 1890; — **chrám Páně,** the Lord's house; — **večeře Páně,** the Lord's supper: ·– **dům páně Hodanův,** Mr. Hodan's house.·

Note 3. — Possessive adjectives formed from feminine nouns and having the termination **in** (fem. **ina,** neut. **ino**)*), are declined like those formed from masculine nouns : **bratrův, bratrova, bratrovo.**

In their formation hard consonants are softened down in the usual manner : **mat-ka,** the mother; **mat-čin (matčina, matčino),** the mother's.

COMPARISON OF ADJECTIVES.

SECTION 21. — The comparison of adjectives is fully explained in Notes 1 and 2, Lesson XXII. The termination **ký** changes into **čí,** in the second and third degree : **hezký,** nice; **hezčí,** nicer; **nejhezčí,** nicest.

DECLENSION OF PRONOUNS.

SECTION 22. — *Personal pronouns.**)

Singular.

nom.	**já,** I	**ty,** thou	**on,** he; **ono,** it	**ona,** she
gen.	**mě (mne)** of me	**tě (tebe)**	**jeho (ho)**	**jí**
dat.	**mi (mně)** to me	**ti (tobě)**	**jemu (mu)**	**jí**
acc.	**mě (mne)** me	**tě (tebe)**	**jeho (ho, jej); je,** it	**ji**
loc.	**mně,** in me	**tobě**	**něm**	**ní**
inst.	**mnou,** with me	**tebou**	**ním (jim)**	**ní (jí)**

Plural.

nom.	**my,** we	**vy,** you	**oni,** (fem. **ony;** neut. **ona**) they
gen.	**nás,** of us	**vás**	**jich**
dat.	**nám,** to us	**vám**	**jim**
acc.	**nás,** us	**vás**	**je**
loc.	**nás,** (in) us	**vás**	**nich**
inst.	**námi** (with) us	**vámi**	**nimi (jimi)**

*) See Note 3, page 95.

*) Compare Note 1 on page 102, and Note on page 106.

Section 23.—*Possessive pronouns.**)

Singular.

	masculine	*feminine*	*neutre*	*masc.*	*fem.*	*neut.*
nom.	můj	má (moje)	mé (moje)	náš	naše	naše
gen.	mého	mé (mojí)	mého	našeho	naší	našeho
dat.	mému	mé (mojí)	mému	našemu	naší	našemu
acc.	mého (inan. **můj**)	mou (moji)	mé (moje)	našeho (inan. **náš**)	naši	naše
voc.	můj	má (moje)	mé (moje)	náš	naše	naše
loc.	mém	mé (mojí)	mém	našem	naší	našem
inst.	mým	mou (mojí)	mým	naším	naší	naším.

Plural.

(Cases showing no difference of gender are left in blank.)

nom.	moji (moje)	mé (moje)	má (moje)	naši (naše)	naše	naše
gen.	mých			našich		
dat.	mým			našim		
acc.	mé (moje)	mé (moje)	má (moje)	naše		
voc.	moji (moje)	mé (moje)	má (moje)	naši (naše)	naše	naše
loc.	mých			našich		
inst.	mými			našimi		

Section 24. — *Indicative pronouns.***)

	Singular			*Plural*					
	masc.	*fem.*	*neut.*	*masc.*	*fem.*	*neut.*			
nom.	ten	ta	to	ti	ty	ta	kdo		co
gen.	toho	té	toho	těch			koho		čeho
dat.	tomu	té	tomu	těm			komu		čemu
acc.	toho (ten)	tu	to	ty	ty	ta	koho		co
loc.	tom	té	tom	těch			kom		čem
inst.	tím	tou	tím	těmi			kým		čím

Section 25. — The relative pronouns **který** (fem. **která**, neut. **které**) and **jenž** (fem. & neut. **jež**), are translated by *which* or *that*.

The pronoun **který, á, é** is declined like the definite adjective **dobrý, á, é**; the pronoun **jenž** is declined as follows:

---

*) Compare Lessons XXV and XXVI.
**) Compare Note 1 on page 115, and Note 5 on page 82.

	Singular			Plural
	masc.	*fem.*	*neut.*	*of all three genders.*
nom.	jenž	jež	jež	již (masc.), jež (f. & n.)
gen.	jehož	jíž	jehož	jichž
dat.	jemuž	jíž	jemuž	jimž
acc.	jehož (jejž)	jíž	jež	jež
loc.	(v) němž	(v) níž	(v) němž	(v) nichž
inst.	jímž	jíž	jímž	jimiž

NUMERALS.

SECTION 26. — The *cardinal* numeral **jeden** (fem. **jedna**, neut. **jedno**) is declined like **ten (ta, to)** :*)

	Singular			Plural
	masc.	*fem.*	*neut.*	*of all three genders.*
nom.	jeden	jedn-a	jedn-o	jedn-i, -y, -a
gen.	jedn-oho	jedn-é	jedn-oho	jedn-ěch
dat.	jedn-omu	jedn-é	jedn-omu	jedn-ěm
acc.	jedn-oho (inan. jeden)	jedn-u	jedn-o	jedn-y, -y, -a
loc.	jedn-om	jedn-é	jedn-om	jedn-ěch
inst.	jedn-ím	jedn-ou	jedn-ím	jedn-ěmi

The declension of **dva** (fem. & neut. **dvě**), **tři, čtyři** (fem. & neut. **čtyry**) is sufficiently explained in Note 1, page 122.

The numerals **pět, šest, sedm** until **devadesát devět** (*five till ninety nine*) take in all cases an **i**, except the accusative and vocative, which are like the nominative. For instance : **pět mužů,** five men; **pěti mužů,** of five men (or "of the five men"); **pěti mužům,** to five men; **v pěti mužích,** in five men; **s pěti muži,** with five men.

In the nominative and accusative they are *always* followed by the *genitive case* of the noun: *pět* **mužů** (or **mužův**), five men; *šest* **holek,** six girls; *sedm* **dětí,** seven children.

---

*) See Note 2 on page 116.

Numerals like *twenty one, twenty two, twenty three,* and so forth, may be rendered in Bohemian in two ways : 1. — **dvacet jeden, dvacet dva, dvacet tři,** etc.,*) in which case both parts are inflected : **dvaceti dvou,** of twenty two; **dvaceti dvěma,** to twenty two; etc.

2. — **jeden-a-dvacet, dva-a-dvacet, tři-a-dvacet,** etc., *one and twenty, two and twenty, three and twenty;* etc., but usually written together: **jedenadvacet, dvaadvacet.** In this case only the second part is inflected : **jedenadvaceti,** of twenty one, to twenty one; **s jedenadvaceti,** with twenty one.

Sto (one hundred) is declined like the neutre noun **slovo,** excepting that in connection with **dvě** (two) it retains the *dual* number in the nominative and accusative : **sto, sta, stu,** etc. (a hundred, of a hundred, to a hundred); **dvě stě,** two hundred; **dvou set,** of two hundred; **dvěma stům,** to two hundred; **o dvou stech,** about two hundred; **s dvěma sty,** with two hundred.

Tisíc (one thousand) is declined like the masc. noun **meč : tisíce,** of a thousand; **tisíci,** to a thousand; **s tisícem,** with a thousand.

SECTION 27. — *Ordinal* numerals, **první** or **prvý, druhý, třetí,** etc; (first, second, third,) are declined like adjectives of a corresponding termination, i. e. like **dobrý, á, é** or **dnešní.****)

The same rule obtains in relation to the *special* and *multiplicative* numerals : **dvojí, trojí,** etc. (twofold, threefold); **dvojnásabný, trojnásobný,** etc. (double, treble).

The neutral form of special numerals : **čtvero, patero, desatero,** etc., is declined like the neutre noun **slovo;** for instance : **desatero přikázání,** the ten commandments; **desatera přikázání,** of the ten commandments; **v desateru přikázání,** in the ten commandments; etc.

The *names* of numbers : **jednotka** (the figure one), **dvojka** (the figure two), **trojka** (the figure three), etc., are declined like the fem. nouns ending in **a : žena.**

SECTION 28. — The indefinite numeral **všechen** (also **všecek** or **všecken)***),** *all,* has the following declension :

---

*) See page 120.
**) See Note 3 on page 124.
***) See Note 1 on page 127.

Singular.

	masculine	*feminine*	*neutre*
nom. & voc.	všechen	všechna	všechno
gen.	všeho	vší	všeho
dat.	všemu	vší	všemu
acc.	všeho	všechnu	všechno
	(inan. všechen)		
loc.	všem	vší	všem
inst.	vším	vší	vším

Plural.

nom. & voc.	*masc.*	všichni	*gen.*	všech	}	in all
	(*masc. inan.*)	všechny	*dat.*	všem		
	fem.	všechny	*loc.* (*ve*)	všech	}	three
	neut.	všechna	*inst.*	všemi	}	genders.
acc., masc. & fem..		všechny	*acc. neut.*	všechna		

The indefinite numeral **veškerý, á, é** has the same meaning as **vše-chen, na, no** (*all*), and is declined like adjectives of the same termination (**dobrý, á, é**).

VERBS.

SECTION 29. — 1. The verb is said to be s u b j e c t i v e, when the action or condition is strictly confined to the subject : **sedím,** I am sitting; **běhám,** I am running; *růže* **kvete,** the rose is blooming.

2. It is called o b j e c t i v e, when the action relates to another person or thing : *slunce* **zahřívá** *zemi,* the sun is warming the earth; *učitel* **chválil** *žáka,* the teacher praised the scholar; **důvěřuj** *v Boha!* trust in God!

The objective verb is *transitive* or *intransitive.*

The transitive verb is accompanied by the accusative case without any preposition : *učitel chválí* **žáka,** the teacher is praising the scholar; *matka vede* **dceru,** the mother is leading her daughter.

The intransitive verb is accompanied by the accusative case with a preposition : *důvěřuj* **v Boha;** or by some other case with or without a preposition : *lakomec baží* **po bohatství,** the miser craves for riches; *žák po-slouchá* **učitele,** the scholar obeys his teacher.

3. A verb is called r e f l e x i v e, when the action reverts to the subject. Such verbs are accompanied by the reflexive pronoun **se: Modli se!**

pray! *Chlapec* **se strojí,** the boy is dressing (himself). **Radujeme** se *z toho,* we are rejoicing over it.

But sometimes the pronoun se expresses the *passive* mood, and not a reflected action : *maso* se jí, the flesh is eaten; **jablka se česají,** the apples are being picked; **pole se orá,** the field is being plowed.

4. I m p e r s o n a l verbs express an action or condition regardless of the person or thing, from which it proceeds : **prší,** it rains, it is raining; **rozednívá se,** it dawns, (the day is breaking).

Section 30. —The classification of the Bohemian verbs in regard in to the character of the action is fully explained in Lesson XXXIX.

Tense–inflection shows a difference in the *time* of the action or condition. There are three tenses :

1. *The present tense* **(přítomný čas): píšu,** I write, I am writing; **pes štěká,** the dog barks, the dog is barking.

2. *The past tense* **(minulý čas): psal jsem,** I wrote, I was writing; **pes štěkal,** the dog barked, the dog was barking.

The past tense may be *continuous,* when a continued past action is expressed: **šel jsem,** I went, I was going; or f i n i t e, when a finished action is expressed : **přišel jsem,** I came.

3. *The future tense* **(budoucí čas): budu psáti,** I shall write, I shall be writing; **pes bude štěkati,** the dog will bark, the dog will be barking.

The future tense may also be either *continuous:* **budu psáti;** or *finite,* when a completed future action is to be expressed: **napíšu,** I shall write out.

The Bohemian verb, like the English, has an indicative mood: **mluvím,** *I speak;* a subjunctive or conditional mood : **mluvil bych,** *I should speak;* and an imperative mood: **mluv!** *speak!*

Section 31. — There is only one auxiliary verb in Bohemian: **býti,** to be. — But certain verbs are used in connection with other verbs, to make a complete assertion or declaration; for instance : **musiti,** must; **smíti,** may, dare; **moci,** can; **ráčiti,** please; etc. We say : **musím jíti,** I must go; **smím mluviti?** may I speak? **račte vejíti!** please to come in!

Section 32. — The Bohemian verb has *six conjugations,* fully illustrated in Lessons XXXI — XXXV incl.

The auxiliary verb **býti,** aiding in the formation of the past and future tenses, is conjugated thus :

Present: **jsem, jsi, jest; jsme, jste, jsou.**
Imperative: **buď, buďme, buďte.**
Past participle: **byl, byla, bylo; byli, byly, byla.**
Subjunctive: **bych, bys, by; bychom (bysme), byste, by.**
Future: **budu, budeš, bude; budeme, budete, budou.**
Present transgressive*): **jsa, jsouc, jsouc; jsouce;** (being).
Past transg.: **byv, byvši, byvši; byvše;** (having been).
Future transg.: **buda, budouc, budouc; budouce;** (to be, expecting to be).

---

*) This participial construction occurs only in the written language; it is explained in Note 4, page 164.

SECTION 33. — Table of the six conjugations.

		Person	I. Termination ti directly attached to the root.				II Term. -outi	III Termin.
			nés-ti to carry	**pí-ti** to drink	**tří-ti** to rub	**péc-i*)** to bake	**min-outi** to pass	**hled-ěti** to look, to look after
Indicative mood	Singular	1	nes-u	pij-u (-i)	tr-u	pek-u	min-u	hled-ím
		2	nes-eš	pij-eš	tř-eš	peč-eš	min-eš	hled-íš
		3	nes-e	pij-e	tř-e	peč-e	min-e	hled-í
	Plural	1	nes-eme	pij-eme	tř-eme	peč-eme	min-eme	hled-íme
		2	nes-ete	pij-ete	tř-ete	peč-ete	min-ete	hled-íte
		3	nes-ou	pij-ou (í)	tr-ou	pek-ou	min-ou	hled-í
Imperative	Sing.	2	nes	pij	tři	peč	miň	hleď
	Plur.	1	nes-me	pij-me	tř-eme	peč-me	miň-me	hleď me
		2	nes-te	pij-te	tř-ete	peč-te	miň-te	hleď-te
Active participle	Sing.	*masc.*	nes-l	pi-l	tře-l	pek-l	minu-l	hled-ěl
		fem.	nes-la	pi-la	tře-la	pek-la	minu-la	hled-ěla
		neut.	nes-lo	pi-lo	tře-lo	pek-lo	minu-lo	hled-ělo
	Plur.	*masc.*	nes-li	pi-li	tře-li	pek-li	minu-li	hled-ěli
		fem.	nes-ly	pi ly	tře-ly	pek-ly	minu-ly	hled-ěly
		neut.	nes-la	pi-la	tře-la	pek-la	minu-la	hled-ěla
Passive participle	Sing.	*masc.*	nes-en	pi-t	tře-n	peč-en	minu-t	hledě-n
		fem.	nes-ena	pi-ta	tře-na	peč-ena	minu-ta	hledě-na
		neut.	nes-eno	pi-to	tře-no	peč-eno	minu-to	hledě-no
	Plur.	*masc.*	nes-eni	pi-ti	tře-ni	peč-eni	minu-ti	hledě-ni
		fem.	nes-eny	pi-ty	tře-ny	peč-eny	minu-ty	hledě-ny
		neut.	nes-ena	pi-ta	tře-na	peč-ena	minu-ta	hledě-na
Present transgressive	Sing.	*masc.*	nes-a	pij-e	tr-a	pek-a	min-a	hled ě
		fem.	nes-ouc	pij-íc	tr-ouc	pek-ouc	min-ouc	hled-íc
		neut.	nes-ouc	pij-íc	tr-ouc	pek-ouc	min-ouc	hled-íc
	Plur.	m. f. n.	nes-ouce	pij-íce	tr-ou	pek-ouce	min-ouce	hled-íce
Past transgressive	Sing.	*masc.*	nes	pi-v	tře v	pek	min-uv	hledě-v
		fem.	nes-ši	pi-vši	tře-vši	pek-ši	min-uvši	hledě-vši
		neut.	nes-ši	pi-vši	tře-vši	pek-ši	min-uvši	hledě-vši
	Plur.	m. f. n.	nes-še	pi-vše	tře-vše	pek-še	min uvše	hledě-vše

*) Popularly **pecti**, originally **pékti**.

III -ěti or -eti	IV. Termin. -iti	V. Termin. -ati			VI Termin. -ovati
ház-eti to throw	**čin-iti** to do	**vo-ati** to call	**maz-ati** to rub	**hn-áti** to drive	**mil-ovati** to love
ház-ím	čin-ím	vol-ám	maž-u (-i)	žen-u	miluj-u (-i)
ház-íš	čin-íš	vol-áš	maž-eš	žen-eš	miluj-eš
ház-í	čin-í	vol-á	maž-e	žen-e	miluj-e
ház-íme	čin-íme	vol-áme	maž-eme	žen-eme	miluj-eme
ház-íte	čin-íte	vol-áte	maž-ete	žen-ete	miluj-ete
ház-ejí	čin-í	vol-ají	maž-ou (-í)	žen-ou	miluj-ou (-í)
házej	čiň	volej	maž	žeň	miluj
házej-me	čiň-me	volej-me	maž-me	žeň-me	miluj-me
házej-te	čiň-te	volej-te	maž-te	žeň-te	miluj-te
háze-l	čini-l	vola-l	maza-l	hna-l	milova-l
háze-la	čini-la	vola-la	maza-la	hna-la	milova-la
háze-lo	čini-lo	vola-lo	maza-lo	hna-lo	milova-lo
háze-li	čini-li	vola-li	maza-li	hna-li	milova-li
háze-ly	čini-ly	vola-ly	maza-ly	hna-ly	milova-ly
háze-la	čini-la	vola-la	maza-la	hna-la	milova-la
háze-n	čině-n	volá-n	mazá-n	hná-n	milová-n
háze-na	čině-na	volá-na	mazá-na	hná-na	milová-na
háze-no	čině-no	volá-no	mazá-no	hná-no	milová-no
háze-ni	čině-ni	volá-ni	mazá-ni	hná-ni	milová-ni
háze-ny	čině-ny	volá-ny	mazá-ny	hná-ny	milová-ny
háze-na	čině-na	volá-na	mazá-na	hná-na	milová-na
háze-je	čin-ě	vola-je	maž-e	žen-a	miluj-e
háze-jíc	čin-íc	vola-jíc	maž-íc	žen-ouc	miluj-íc
háze-jíc	čin-íc	vola-jíc	maž-íc	žen-ouc	miluj-íc
háze-jíce	čin-íce	vola-jíce	maž-íce	žen-ouce	miluj-íce
háze-v	čini-v	vola-v	maza-v	hna-v	milova-v
háze-vši	čini-vši	vola-vši	maza-vši	hna-vši	milova-vši
háze-vši	čini-vši	vola-vši	maza-vši	hna-vši	milova-vši
háze-vše	čini-vše	vola-vše	maza-vše	hna-vše	milova-vše.

SECTION 34. — Irregular verbs.

Jeti, to ride, to drive;—*present,* **jedu, jedeš, jede, jedeme, jedete, jedou;** *imper.* **jeď, -me, -te;** *active partic.* **jel, -a, -o;** *passive partic.* **jet, -a, -o;** *pres. transg.* **jed-a, -ouc, -ouce;** *supine,* **jet** (to ride);

jíti, to go;— *pres.* **jdu, jdeš, jde, jdeme, jdete, jdou;** *imper.* **jdi, jdě-me, jdě-te;** *act. part.* **šel, šla, šlo;** *pres. transg.* **jda, jdouc, -ce;** *sup.* **jit** (to go);

chtíti, to want; — *pres.* **chci, chceš, chce, chceme, chcete, chtějí;** *imper.* **chtěj, chtěj-me, -te;** *ac'. part.* **chtěl, -a, -o;** *pres. transg.* **chtěj-e, -íc, -íce;** *past. transg.* **chtěv, -ši, -še;** *sup.* **chtět** (to want);

míti, to have; — *pres.* **mám, máš, má, máme, máte, mají;** *imper.* **měj, měj-me, měj-te;** *act. part.* **měl, -a, -o;** *pres. transg.* **maj-e, -íc, -íce;** *past. transg.* **měv, -ši, -še;**

spáti, to sleep; — *pres.* **spím, spíš, spí, spíme, spíte, spí;** *imper.* **spi, spě-me, -te;** *act. part.* **spal, -a, -o;** *pres. transg.* **spě, spíc, spíce;** *past. transg.* **spav, -ši, -še;** *sup.* **spat** (to sleep);

státi se, to happen, to become; — **stanu se, staneš se, stane se, stan-eme, -ete, -ou se;** *imper.* **staň se, -me, -te se;** *act. part.* **stal, -a, -o se;** *pres. transg.* **stav, -ši, -še se;** (**stává se,** *it happens,* is impersonal);

viděti, to see; — **vidím, vidíš, vidí, vidíme, vidíte, vidí;** *imper.* **viz, -me, -te;** *act. part.* **viděl, -a, -o;** *passive part.* **viděn, -a, -o;** *present transg.* **vid-a, -ouc, -ouce.**

SECTION 35. — The derivation and comparison of a d v e r b s is ex plained in Notes 2 and 3, on page 128.

P r e p o s i t i o n s govern or require particular cases.

The *genitive* case, responding to the question **čí? koho? čeho?***), is governed by the following prepositions, and adverbs used as prepositions:

bez,	without	**do,**	to, till, until;	**krom** ⎫	aside from,
dle ⎫	according to;	**od,**	from	**kromě** ⎭	except;
podle ⎭	next to;	**u,**	at, by;	**kolem** ⎫	round,
vedle,	next to, along-	**z, ze,**	from, out of;	**okolo** ⎬	around;
	side of;			**vůkol** ⎭	

---

*) See Note 5, page 82. In the genitive case the question **koho?** *whose?* was inadvertently omitted.

vně, outside of;	daleko, far	výše, higher
vnitř, inside of;	stranu, about	prostřed, amidst
blízko, near	níže, lower	místo, instead of.

The *dative* case (responding to the question komu? čemu?) is governed by the following:

k ⎫	proti, against	naproti, towards, a-
ke ⎬ to, for;	k vůli for the sake of;	gainst, opposite;
ku ⎭		vstříc, towards.

The *accusative* case (responding to the question koho? co?) is governed by the following:

| mimo, besides, past; | pro, for | skrze, through. |
| ob, over | přes, over, across; | |

The *locative* case (responding to the question v kom? v čem? o kom? o čem? etc.) is always governed by the preposition při, *by, at;* and in most instances by the following prepositions:

| v ⎫ in | o, about, on; | po, after, by, during. |
| ve ⎭ | na, on, upon, for; | |

The preposition v or ve, when it occurs before a word beginning with the letter v, is often changed into u; for instance : u velikém počtu (instead of ve velikém počtu), *in a large number,* or "in large numbers."

The above five prepositions often require the *accusative* case; for example : na potupu, *for disgrace,* i. e. "in order to disgrace or dishonor"; bojí se o život, he fears for his life.

The prepositions mezi, between, among; nad, over, above; pod, under, below; před, before, — govern either the *accusative* or the *instrumental* case : půjdu mezi lidi, I shall go among people; byl jsem mezi lidmi, I was among people.

The preposition s, se governs the *genitive* case, when it means *from, off:* spadl s vozu, se stromu, he fell from the wagon, from the tree; and it governs the *instrumental* case, when it means *with:* pojď se mnou, come with me; šli jsme za nim, we went after him, we followed him.

Za governs the *genitive* case, when it means *during, in:* **za času Washingtona,** in the time of Washington; — it governs the *accusative* case, when it means *for:* **koupil jsem to za dollar,** I bought it for a dollar; — and it governs the *instrumental* case, when translated by *behind, after:* **pojď za mnou,** come behind me; **přijdu za tebou,** I will come after thee.

In rare instances it requires the accusative case : **nejsem s to poslou-žiti vám,** I cannot (I am not able to) accommodate you.

CONTENTS.

SLAVIE a RODINA.

Slavie, časopis národní a politický. Nejstarší, nejoblíbenější a nejrozšířenější časopis český v Americe. List ryze národní, v politice rovný a nezávislý, fedrující vždy zásady jedině té strany politické, kteráž zemi a veškerému obyvatelstvu, najmě pak všemu lidu pracovnému bez výminky, na ten čas jest nejprospěšnější.

Rodina, zábavník "Slavie", přináší výbor nejlepších románů cizojazyčných i českých a povídky i romány do roka v Rodině vyšlé mají samy o sobě mnohonásobnou cenu předplatného. Romány v Rodině vycházejí jsou veskrz dobré, mravně ušlechťující. Hledíme, aby se české mládeži pomocí zábavy dostalo toho, čeho se jí nedostatkem českého školství nedostalo.

Tlumač. Nový Tlumač Americký od Karla Jonáše. Žádná publikace česká v této zemi nebyla přijata od obecenstva s takovým vděkem a uznáním a žádné se nedostalo rozšíření tak rychlého a velikého, jako Tlumači, knize ku snadnému a rychlému přiučení se jazyku anglickému, bez jehož znalosti nikdo se zde valného pokroku nedodělá. Cena $1.50 i se zásylkou a prodává se jedině za hotové.

Slovník česko-anglický, od Karla Jonáše. Druhé rozmnožené a opravené vydání. Postupná kniha učebná po Tlumači a nezbytná pro každého ku zdokonalení se v jazyku anglickém. Pro počátečníka ku rychlému seznámeni se s nejobecnější, každodenní mluvou postačí Tlumač; povrchní znalec angličiny musí pak k ruce míti Slovník, aby se v jazyku zdokonalil. Cena $1.50. Jenom za hotové. — Slovník anglicko-český vyjde u Slavie tiskem později.

Americké právo od Karla Jonáše. Sbírka zákonů a výkladů právních, pro osadníky česko-americké zvláště užitečných. Alespoň povrchní znalost zdejších zákonů nutna jest každému občanu americkému, anať neznalost zákonů nikoho před škodou neuchrání. Sbírka tato obsahuje toliko zákony nejnutnější, ve všech státech stejně platné a zvláště důležitý zákon homstední se všemi doplňky. "Právo farmerské" a smlouva rakousko-americká jsou spisu přidány. Cena 75c. Jen za hotové.

Zlatá kniha pro farmera. Dle rozličných pramenů sestavil Karel Jonáš. Kniha tato pojednává o vnitřních i zevnitřních nemocech koni a rozbytka hospodářského. Obsahuje návod o koupi koní, dodatek o domácích pomůckách pro všeliké nehody, a recepty na rozličné léky v jazyku českém i anglickém. Prospěla již stům českých farmerů a na žádné farmě neměla by chyběti. Cena 65c. Jen za hotové.

Politické zřízení americké. Napsal Charles Nordhoff. Se svolením spisovatele a nakladatelů přeložil Gustav B. Reišl. Znáti politické zařízení země v níž žijeme a prospívati chceme, jest jednou z nejpřednějších povinností každého přistěhovalce. Až do nedávna nebylo spisu, z něhož by nově příchozí takové známosti mohl nabýti. Nedostatku tomu odpomohl pan Reišl překladem tohoto výtečného díla Nordhoffova, jež se u Amerikánů cení co nejvýše. Cena pouze 50c. i se zásylkou. Jen za hotové.

Přihlášky poštou a zásylky peněz buďtež adresovány prostě: «Slavie», Racine, Wis.